MÉTRO BOULOT DODO

BY
GN HETHERINGTON

First Published in 2022 by GNH Publishing.

The right of Gary Hetherington to be identified as the author of this work has been asserted by him in accordance with the Copyright, Designs and Patents Act 1988.

Copyright © Gary Hetherington

All rights reserved. No part of this book may be reproduced, stored in a retrieval system or transmitted in any form or by any means, electronic, mechanical, photocopying, recording or otherwise, without the prior permission of the publisher.

www.gnhbooks.co.uk

The story, the places and characters are a work of fiction.

grâce à :

my beaux parents, Bill & Chris Bailey, and my amazing friends Jackie Waite, June Russell, Sandra Scott, Pam Pletts, Suse Telford, Kathleen Pope, Joy Edwards and Jennifer Trieb. Much love to you all. I'm also incredibly grateful to Katy Anna Harris for her amazing work on turning Coco into an audiobook, it's everything I hoped it would be and so much more.

Special thanks to Francesca Tibo for introducing me to Italy, and to Julien Doré and Sheena Easton for constantly inspiring me.

Merci beaucoup, Bastien Greve for all his hard work teaching me. He not only works diligently to improve my French (ha!) he is always on hand to answer my questions. The title for this book (Métro Boulot Dodo) came from him in one of our lessons. I was so taken with the title that as soon as the lesson was over the idea was formed and I was off! Métro Boulot Dodo is really the equivalent of English expressions such as 'the rat race' or 'the daily grind.' The three sections of the book span a period of three days in Coco's hectic life (Métro = her daily commute, Boulot = work and Dodo = sleep) and how they are all affected by what happens on that daily commute. I'm still amazed that an entire story came from that one phrase, but I'm thrilled that it did and I hope you will be as well!

For Dan, Hugo and Noah. Mon Dieu - you are *everything*.

Charlie, Seth and Dawn. Jusqu'à ce que nous nous revoyions.

Notes:

The story and characters are a work of fiction.

For further information, exclusive content and to join the mailing list, head over to:

www.gnhbooks.co.uk

We are also on Facebook, Twitter and Instagram. Join us there!

The artwork on the cover, website and social media accounts were created in conjunction with the incredible talent of Maria Almeida and I'm indebted to her for bringing my characters to life.

For Charlie, Seth and Dawn. Tu me manques.

Also available:

Hugo Duchamp Investigates:

Un Homme Qui Attend (2015)
Les Fantômes du Chateau (2016)
Les Noms Sur Les Tombes (2016)
L'ombre de l'île (2017)
L'assassiner de Sebastian Dubois (2017)
L'impondérable (2018)
Le Cri du Cœur (2019)
La Famille Lacroix (2019)
Les Mauvais Garçons (2020)
Prisonnier Dix (2021)
Le Bateau au fond de l'océan (2022)
Chemin de Compostelle (2022)
Hotel Beaupain (2023)

The Coco Brunhild Mysteries:

Sept Jours (2021)
Métro Boulot Dodo (2022)
Cercueils en Spirale (2022)
Quatre Semaines (2023)

Also available:

Hugo & Josef (2021)
Club Vidéo (2022)
Hugo & Madeline (2023)
Josef (2023)

MÉTRO

LUNDI
08H00

Charlotte "Coco" Brunhild caught her reflection in the window and instantly recoiled. Her first thought was to look over her shoulder and demand why the hell her aged mother had suddenly appeared on Métro Line 8 at the Strasbourg–Saint-Denis station, but then she remembered one of the distinct differences between the two of them. Coco's mother, an Orthodox Jew, always wore a wig and had it cut and styled bi-weekly, whilst Coco, who had never worn a wig (well, apart from that *one* time) and probably not had it cut or styled in more than a year. More importantly, her mother would be appalled to be seen in public with dyed blue locks which no matter what Coco tried, more often than not frizzed like she had stuck her finger in a socket. *I'm turning into my mother.* The thought terrified Coco as she shuffled along the carriage, eyes darting from side to side as she tried to find a seat which was not adjacent to someone who looked like a serial killer, or was high on drugs, or still drunk, or basking in an odour which would offend even the hardiest of noses like hers.

Ultimately, Coco knew wherever she sat, she would most likely end up sitting next to someone who was a combination of all those disparate factors. And to top it all, he would most likely sit with his legs spread, pushing a squidgy thigh against her as if he was instigating some archaic mating ritual. Then he would almost certainly turn his head to her, flash her a wink, conveying a simple message. *Yeah babe, you could have a piece of this if you play your cards right.*

Coco sighed. It had been a long night, in a rotten bed filled with lumps and sheets which seemed to delight in sticking to her pyjamas. She could also still smell the faint aroma of urine, not hers she was fairly sure, rather that of her four-year-old daughter, Esther, who had taken to bed wetting again, only months after having seemingly grown out of it. Coco shared her bed with Esther and her second youngest child, Cedric, who at almost twelve, had started with the tell-tale signs of puberty and all its relevant pitfalls, mainly, she envisaged, manifesting in an intense hatred for his mother and the fact he was still having to share a bed with her.

Coco flopped heavily onto a seat, a cloud of musty dust covering her. She wrinkled her nose, nostrils flaring at the dirt cloud as it landed on the trusty blue-green-checked wool coat she wore. It was dirty enough as it was, without absorbing dead skin cells, or worse, from Métro seats.

She closed her eyes. It was Monday morning, and she had spent two whole days at home intending to clean the cramped two-bedroom apartment she shared with her four children and the nanny, Helga, a mature German woman who slept at the foot of Coco's bed on a rollout bed. Helga was prone to night terrors, which usually resulted in her shouting what sounded like expletives in German. When they had first begun, Coco had tried to wake her and had received a black eye as a thank you. Neither Coco nor her kids had tried to drag Helga from her slumber since then.

The apartment, on the tenth floor of a block which might have once been considered chic, but was now bordering on being condemned, was accessed by a rickety lift which barely worked, and following an unwelcome encounter in it the previous year, Coco faced a daily dilemma - risk an asthma attack tackling the narrow winding staircase, or to face her demons in the lift. Most days, the lift won, but it always broke her day, and she spent it with flashbacks of what had transpired. *Find out who made me do this.* The words still haunted her. If she could move to a different apartment, she would, but the fact remained she could barely afford the apartment she had, let alone afford to find one better.

'Hey, mama. You like this?'

Coco's eyes snapped open. She had not noticed the morbidly obese pig who had squeezed into the seat next to her. He was gesturing at his groin, pointing at what appeared to be an erection in his pants. Her eyes widened. At least she assumed it was an erection, though she could not exactly be sure. She pushed herself up from the seat with a weary sigh.

'When my son was born, he had a bigger penis than you, you useless waste of semen,' she spat in the man's direction. He snorted, giving her a two-finger gesture.

Coco shuffled away. She spotted an elderly man sitting on the other side of the carriage. The only available seat was next to him. She took a moment to assess him. He was sleeping, his head resting on his chest. As far as she could tell, he appeared respectable enough. The raincoat he was wearing appeared clean and expensive, and his shoes seemed new and highly polished. His hair was white and neat. She dropped her body heavily into the seat next to him, hopeful that she could squeeze in a quick nap before arriving at her final destination. *Work*. The place she spent more time than anywhere else in return for a pay cheque which barely covered her living expenses.

She accidentally nudged the man with her elbow. 'Oh, désolé, Monsieur,' she sighed, pulling her arms together into her lap.

The man slumped towards her. She tutted and pushed him away from her, hoping it would not be another one of those sorts of mornings on Line 8. His head fell backwards, his face pivoted in her direction. His eyes were wide open, staring straight at her, a trickle of blood escaping down his chin. She sighed again. She did not need a doctor to tell her what she was looking at.

'Goddamnit, this can't be how my week begins!' she exhaled, her body crumbling.

LUNDI
09H00

Lieutenant Cedric Degarmo stepped onto the platform, resting his hand on the wall. He recoiled, realising he had just pressed his palm onto a wad of used chewing gum. He hissed a curse and moved away, wiping his hands on a tissue.

'Stop, you stupid idiot!' a harsh, heavily accented voice called out.

Cedric spun around, already knowing who was accosting him. Ebba Blom, pint-sized Swedish forensic expert, with hair as coarse as her tone. Cedric kept his own hair to a buzz cut, and he still had more hair than she did. He fixed her with a cold stare from ice-blue eyes. 'Whaddya yelling at?' he snapped.

She gestured from his head to his feet. 'Where's your forensic suit?'

Cedric pointed at his jean pockets and his t-shirt. 'Do I look like a carry one around with me?'

Ebba tutted, mouthing something in Swedish, before tossing him a forensic suit. 'Not a step further until you put this on,' she warned.

Cedric grabbed the suit and pulled it over his left foot, his boot immediately ripping through the bottom.

'Oh, you great oaf!' Ebba hissed, stamping angrily towards him. She threw another suit at him. 'Be careful with this one, or you can damn well pay for it yourself.' Her nose wrinkled. 'Why do you always smell like you've taken a bath in tar?' she demanded.

Cedric shrugged. 'Why do you always smell like you've just crawled out a skip?'

'Enfants! Enfants!' Coco appeared from the carriage

doorway, clapping her hands. 'When you've done waving your things around, perhaps we can get on with the matter at hand.' She pointed at her watch. 'It's 09H00 and I need to get to the commissariat. I have a pot of rotten café and stale croissants to get to.'

'I'm still waiting for Dr. Bernstein,' Ebba retorted.

'Non, you're not.' Dr. Shlomo "Sonny" Bernstein called out from the shadows of the tunnel. He stopped, pushing thick, wavy jet black hair into a cap. He was small with a rugged, worn complexion, but kind eyes which twinkled with mischievousness. He stopped in front of Coco, shaking his head. 'It seems when you call a halt to the entire Line 8, it rather slows down one's progress in navigating the Parisian streets.'

Coco shrugged nonchalantly. 'I don't see why it should just be my day ruined.'

'What do you want me to do, Captain Brunhild?' Cedric asked.

She appraised him, a smirk hovering on her face. 'Well, in no particular order. I'd like you to get a personality transplant, to find me a man who is both a millionaire and not too fussy…'

'And blind,' Ebba mumbled under her breath.

Coco shrugged again. 'Whatever. As I said, I'm not fussy.' She turned back to Cedric. 'Then, I'd like…'

'Related to actually solving a crime,' Cedric interjected wearily. 'You know, the thing we're actually paid to do.'

'Spoilsport,' she pouted. She pointed over his shoulder. 'I had the station guards round everyone up, grab some help and start taking statements.'

He nodded and turned around.

'And pay particular attention to a man in a raincoat,' she called after him.

He stopped. 'Why? Is he a suspect?' he asked.

'Dunno,' Coco retorted. 'But he claims to have a penis in his pants. I'm not so sure, so you'd better take down his particulars, just in case,' she answered with utmost seriousness. 'You may be able to sympathise with his lack of endowment.'

'I hate you,' Cedric sighed, trudging in the direction of the other travellers.

Coco noticed the smile on Ebba's face. It disappeared quickly when she noticed Coco looking. 'Ah, c'mon kid,' Coco laughed. 'You've got to admit you're starting to like me.'

Ebba pushed past her. 'I admit nothing.'

Dr. Bernstein cleared his throat. 'Well, shall we get on with the job at hand?'

LUNDI
09H05

Dr. Bernstein stepped carefully into the métro carriage. Ebba had already placed stepping blocks. He nodded, seemingly satisfied, and moved across them, Coco following close behind him. She was tugging irritably at the transparent forensic suit she was wearing.

'Since when did they start making these damn things in one size only?' she complained.

Ebba pushed past her again. 'They don't. You're in the biggest size - an <u>extra</u>-large.'

Coco's mouth twisted into a snarl.

'Any-way,' Sonny drawled, pointing toward the dead man.

Coco turned away from Ebba huffily. 'You're dead to me,' she quipped.

'Non, he's dead,' Sonny declared, pointing at the corpse.

Coco snorted. 'No shit, Sherlock! The question is, for how long, and how did he go?'

The doctor moved towards the deceased and pulled open his jacket, revealing a large circle of blood in the middle of a crisp white shirt. 'That might have something to do with it.'

Coco bent down, narrowing her eyes to stare at the wound. She noticed Sonny's nose was twitching in her direction. She placed her hand in front of her mouth and blew, sniffing the air she emitted. Her nose wrinkled. 'Désolé,' she said softly, 'garlic prawns.'

Sonny gave her a concerned look. 'How old were they?'

She shrugged. 'Can't be sure. I found them in the back of the fridge. Waste not, want not.' She turned her head. 'Anything else?'

Sonny moved around the body, moving quickly but carefully. 'I can't feel or see any other injuries,' he stated. 'And he's still warm. He's not been dead long, certainly no more than an hour, I'd say, I'll know…'

'… more when you get him back to the morgue, yeah, I know the drill,' Coco completed his sentence. 'But in the meantime, is there anything you can tell me? Like for starters - did he die here?'

Ebba shone a torch around the body. 'There's no sign of blood around him.'

Sonny pointed at the man's thick woollen overcoat. 'His coat appears to have absorbed most of the blood, which might explain why there isn't blood around him.'

'Then he was killed in his seat?' Coco pressed.

'Peut être,' Sonny replied. 'Mais, until I understand the extent of his injuries, we can't rule out him being stabbed elsewhere.'

'And then somebody moved him here?' Coco asked doubtfully. 'How would that work? It was rush hour, somebody would have seen him.'

'He could have been stabbed elsewhere,' Sonny reasoned, 'and walked here under his own steam. He may not have known how bad his wound was. Hell, he may not have even known he was stabbed at all. He might have thought someone bumped into him, and that it hurt. I've seen cases where victims walk on, oblivious to the fact they're bleeding out and often by the time they realise it's too late.'

Coco sighed. 'Well, that doesn't help me very much.'

Cedric appeared in the doorway. 'The stationmaster is getting tetchy. He wants to know when he can get the trains running again. Apparently, there's a tailback five miles long and a lot of pissed off people complaining about being late for work.'

'Tough,' Coco sniffed. 'Tell him we'll be done when we're done. Might give him a taste of his own medicine. I had to wait twenty minutes to get a damn métro this morning.'

'Good job you did,' Sonny said, tipping his head towards the dead man. 'Or we may have missed this.'

'And it would have been someone else's problem,' Coco mused. She looked at the man again. 'White men in fancy suits tend not to die on the métro for any good reason.' She took a long, deep breath. 'D'accord. Let's first assume our friend here met his untimely demise in this very carriage, then it needs to be examined from top to bottom.'

Ebba raised an eyebrow. 'With the thousands of samples on this carriage, that's going to take me a long time, maybe all day.'

Coco smiled. 'Exactly.'

'Coco,' Sonny laughed. 'Don't be mean. People have to get to work.'

She sighed. 'Okay. Cedric, have a word with the station master and tell him we'll open the station as long as he can get this train somewhere off the line where we can examine it properly and in our own time.'

Cedric nodded. 'I'm on it.'

Coco turned back to Sonny. 'Can you check his body for ID?'

Sonny moved back to the dead man and began rummaging through his pockets. 'Nothing,' he said.

'Then a robbery?' Coco mused.

'Oh, wait, there is something in the back pocket of his trousers,' Sonny added, extracting a small square paper card. He dropped it into an evidence bag and handed it to Coco. She lifted it to the light.

Coco's eyes flicked over the card. There appeared nothing special about it. It was a dull peach colour and one side had perforated edges, as if it had been separated from something else. 'It looks like a receipt of some kind,' she said with a frown. 'But there's no name, only a letter and a number. B4.'

'B4?' Sonny related with a frown. 'A ticket stub, maybe for a coat check in a restaurant or something like that?'

Coco shrugged. 'It could be a number for waiting in line for something, like a cheese counter, or a doctor's surgery, or something like that. It could be bloody anything, so it's not really a lot of help to us, is it?' She sighed. 'D'accord, get him to the morgue and see if you can rush through his teeth and fingerprints for me, so at least I can put a name to the expensive suit.' She stared wearily at the dead man. 'I'm sorry for whatever happened to you. I'll do what I can to help.'

LUNDI
10H00

Commander Imane Demissy raised a cup to her mouth and took a sip from it. Her eyes were closed and her smooth face was passive and pale, accented only by the purple hijab and coordinated lipstick she chose to wear. She was a striking woman of Syrian descent, though she had lived in Paris for almost twenty years, and in that time had risen through the ranks of the Police Nationale with lightning speed. A result which had left her wondering how much it had to do with her natural talent, as opposed to the colour of her skin and the need to fulfil quotas, or rather more, as she suspected, because she was married to a world-famous violinist, who was the toast of Paris and friend to several high-ranking politicians. The fact that she had been chosen to command the failing Commissariat de Police du 7e arrondissement, was a clear indication to her that the "powers-that-be" were expecting her to fail in her remit. Demissy was determined to prove otherwise. She opened her eyes slowly, recoiling at the staring face of Coco inches from her.

'Are you alright, Commander?' Coco asked. 'You looked a little spaced out. Busy weekend with your fiddle player?'

Demissy suppressed a sigh as if she was used to the Captain's behaviour and had resigned herself to the fact that chastising her only seemed to encourage the bad behaviour. Instead, she glanced at her watch. Unlike Coco's, which was plastic and held together with tape, Demissy's was encased in diamonds. 'Alors, it is barely 10H00 on a Monday morning, and even before you make it into the office, late I might add, you bring with you a dead body.'

Coco gurned. 'Well, it's not like I murdered him myself, or

anything.'

Demissy twisted her head in the direction of Cedric. 'Lieutenant Degarmo. Tell me, what do we have so far?'

He gulped. 'Not a lot. I took statements from everyone in the carriage at the time, and,' he stole a sideways look at Coco, 'apart from the usual oddball, they all seem to be genuinely shocked and surprised. I've got someone checking them for criminal records now, so we'll soon see if there's anything there.'

'And nobody saw anything?' Demissy asked with incredulity.

Coco snorted. 'When was the last time you were in the métro, rather than a limousine?' she asked with more bite than she intended. She lowered her head demurely. 'What I mean is - on the métro, you get on, you keep your head down and you try to find a seat that isn't *too* soiled, next to someone who also hopefully isn't *too* soiled and doesn't look likely to want to stick his hand up your skirt or crack open your skull and nibble on your brain.'

Demissy rolled her eyes. 'And that's how you discovered the deceased? You sat next to him?'

'He was my second choice, actually,' Coco responded. 'The first wanted to introduce me to his gherkin.'

Demissy frowned. 'Gherkin?'

Coco extended her pinky finger and wiggled it downwards.

The Commander shook her head. 'Why do I ask? I never learn!' she muttered to herself. 'What about the cause of death and identification?'

'Almost certainly a knife wound,' Coco replied. 'But the doc didn't want to commit to anything until he gets the old man on the slab later. There was nothing on the body other than some weird ticket stub. Sonny's going to run the prints and teeth and get back to me as soon as he finds anything.'

Demissy nodded. 'Then we have a dead man on a busy métro line. He must have boarded somewhere. Lieutenant Degarmo, while Captain Brunhild is attending the autopsy, I want you to go through the CCTV footage at the métro HQ. Find out where our deceased got on. Maybe then we try to understand where he came from. Do they have cameras on the trains?'

'Some of them,' Cedric answered. 'I'll check.'

'The working theory is he may not even have been attacked on the train,' Coco interrupted. 'There was very little blood around him. Which suggests it could have happened elsewhere.'

Demissy tutted, picking angrily at a fingernail. 'Well, that makes it even more important we discover when he got on, I...' Before she could finish, she was interrupted by Coco's cell phone ringing.

'Oui, Allô,' Coco answered. 'Oh, hey, Sonny. How's it going? You do, already? D'accord, let me get some paper.' She reached across for a notepad and pen. 'Go for it. Spell that for me. R-I-C-H-A-R-D S-E-V-E-R-I-N. Merci, Sonny,' she stopped upon noticing the change in expression on Demissy's face. 'How did you find him so quickly? Oh, he is,' she laughed, 'well, that might explain why Commander Demissy looks as if she's about to have a heart attack. I'll call you back, Sonny.' She disconnected the call and moved to Demissy. 'What is it, Commander? Who is Richard Severin?'

'You haven't heard of him?' Cedric countered. 'Richard Severin is one of the richest property developers in Paris, hell, probably the whole of France.'

'*Was* one of the richest,' Coco corrected. 'Sonny said his prints came up instantly.'

'There's no doubt it's him?' Demissy interrupted.

Coco shrugged. 'I can't see how it could be someone else. Sonny doesn't tend to get things wrong.' She stared at Demissy's anxious face. 'I don't get it - why are you so freaked out?'

'This is bad news,' Demissy mumbled to herself. 'This is *really* bad news.'

Coco ran a hand through frizzy blue hair. 'Pourquoi? Some

rich dude gets offed. It wouldn't be the first time, and it certainly won't be the last.'

Demissy glared at her. 'You don't do things by half, do you, Captain Brunhild?'

'Why is it always my fault?' Coco cried with incredulity. 'Everyone seems to think I always go looking for trouble…'

'Well…' Cedric interrupted, before stopping, noticing Coco's hateful glare.

'What's the problem?' Coco questioned again. 'So, he's rich?'

'Richard Severin is not… was not just rich,' Cedric replied. 'He may not quite have been Bill Gates kinda rich, but he can't have been far off.'

'He gave half of his fortune away,' Demissy added. 'To charitable causes.'

Coco laughed. 'I bet that made his family happy!' She paused, an eyebrow raising as several different scenarios presented themselves to her. 'Ah-ha…'

Demissy fixed her with a steely glare. 'Don't get carried away, Captain,' she scolded. 'Not until we are in receipt of all the facts. Do I make myself clear?'

'Crystal,' Coco replied demurely. 'Hey, wait. Now you mention it, I think I do remember the name. I think I read his autobiography once.'

Cedric regarded her with surprise. 'You read?'

'Bien sûr,' she retorted. 'Well, I say I read it, what I mean is that I found an old copy of the book on the métro once and I was bored so I picked it up.' She shrugged. 'Mind you, I think I only read a chapter or two before I nodded off.'

'It's actually a remarkable book,' Demissy added, 'about a remarkable man. Do you know he grew up in a slum in Marseille? He said it was his motivation for building decent, affordable housing for those who couldn't afford it. I met him once. He was as charming as he was modest.'

Coco snorted again. 'That's not how he came across in his book,' she replied. 'It read like an audition for a Nobel Prize. After the twelfth anecdote citing how much of a saint he was, it was enough for me.'

Demissy shrugged. 'What's wrong with that? He achieved a lot.' She flicked her eyes appraisingly over Coco. 'We should all strive to such aspirations.'

'Well,' Coco replied tartly. 'If you have to say it yourself, or pay others to say it, then it's worth bupkis as far as I can tell.' She paused. 'And besides, and more to the point, if he was really a zillionaire, what the hell was he doing in the métro during rush hour?'

'I told you, he was a humble man,' Demissy answered.

'Bulls…' Coco began, before stopping and flattering her eyelashes demurely. 'Désolé. My point is, humble man or not, it is my experience that men like that don't travel incognito in their thousand euro suits for the sake of it.'

'Then why do they?' Demissy questioned.

Coco smiled wickedly. 'For no good reason, that's why.'

Demissy narrowed her eyes. 'Now listen to me, and listen to me well, Captain Brunhild. I want you to go and break the news to his family, but I want you to do so carefully and with immense sensitivity.' She glanced at her watch. 'I would do it myself, but I'm due at court in half an hour.' She turned to Cedric. 'I'm sure I can count on you, Lieutenant. Oui?'

Coco stood. 'You can count on me, too. This isn't my first rodeo, y'know. You can be sure, I know exactly how to interact with the hoi polloi. I can do sensitive when it's called for.'

Demissy looked at her as if she was sure of no such thing. 'And get changed before you go, Captain Brunhild. You have blood on your blouse.'

Coco glanced down at her crinkled blouse. She touched it with her finger before raising it to her lips. Demissy's hand flew to her mouth and she appeared to be about to retch.

'That's not blood,' Coco said, smacking her lips. 'It's jam.'

Demissy waved her hand dismissively. 'Get changed, Captain and just get… get gone.'

LUNDI
10H30

With her usual dexterity, Coco wove the police vehicle in and out of the Parisian traffic, the sirens blazing and terrifying passers-by. Cedric was next to her, gripping tightly on the armrest, his eyes wide with fear and panic.

'You know, you're not supposed to use the sirens unless it's an emergency. We could get into trouble,' he yelled above the din.

Coco gawped at him. 'We could get in trouble,' she repeated mockingly. 'What are we in kindergarten?' She shrugged, narrowly avoiding an elderly man who had stepped onto the road to pass a woman and a pushchair. He jumped back in shock and stumbled back onto the pavement and into the pushchair. 'Désolé!' Coco cried, waving her arm out of the window. She turned back to an even more anxious-looking Cedric. 'Besides, what are you talking about? We're about to go and break the awful news of Saint Richard Severin's demise to his family. Now, if that isn't an emergency…'

They continued in silence for a minute or two.

'What's eating your ass, anyhow?' Coco asked finally. 'Or is it because *no one* is eating your ass? You've had a stinking attitude for weeks now.'

'It's nothing,' he spat.

'It doesn't sound like nothing.'

'It's nothing,' he repeated. 'So, just leave it, okay?'

She watched him, her eyes flicking over him as if assessing what was wrong with him. Finally, she sighed. 'Fine. Don't tell me, see if I care,' she stated huffily. A few moments passed. 'Oh, why won't you tell me?' she wailed. 'I tell you everything. I mean, goddamnit, you've seen parts of my body only a few men or medical professionals have seen.' She smiled wickedly. 'You've seen clean inside of me, so you KNOW I have no secrets.'

Cedric moaned and buried his head in his hands. 'Why do you have to always bring that up?' he cried.

Coco extended her hand in front of her, twisting and moving it around. 'Because it's a beautiful thing we share, you and I. You extended your hand like this and placed it right inside of me.'

'And pulled out a baby!' Cedric shouted, slamming his fist on the dashboard. 'Why do you always leave that bit out! It's just to torture me, isn't it? You live to torture me, don't you?'

'Chill baby, chill,' Coco said passively. It was true that on his first day working at the Commissariat de Police du 7e arrondissement almost twelve years earlier, Cedric had accompanied a very pregnant Coco on what was supposed to be a routine drug bust. However, a chase had resulted in Coco going into labour and giving birth to her second son on the ground of a filthy warehouse with only the support of Cedric while they waited for the Pompiers. By the time they had arrived, Cedric was elbow deep in her blood and clutching a screaming baby, who Coco had later decided to call Cedric in honour, a fact which had only resulted in everyone assuming that the elder Cedric was actually the child's real father. A fact Coco had found both amusing and fodder for baiting the young lieutenant.

They lapsed into silence again.

'You don't have to tell me if you don't want to,' Coco tried again.

Cedric looked away. 'Bon. Because I'm not going to.'

Coco opened her mouth to speak, but before she could, the electronic voice on the dashboard announced:

YOU HAVE REACHED YOUR FINAL DESTINATION.

Coco laughed sadly. 'Story of my life.' She pushed open the door and climbed out of the car.

The first thing which struck Coco about Richard Severin's four-story house in the heart of Paris was that it was less austere than she had imagined it would be. It was tall and foreboding. The windows were covered with shutters, and she imagined she could see bars behind them. There were no plants, rather a row of impeccably pruned shrubs, and nor was there any sign of who lived there. She supposed he was not the sort of man who wished to announce his presence.

'Where's the damn knocker?' Coco grumbled, pulling back her head and looking around the doorway.

Cedric snorted. 'Houses like these don't have them.' He passed her and pressed his finger across a tiny button on the side of the door.

'Oui,' came a lightening fast response.

Coco's brow creased as she tried to work out where the voice was coming from.

Cedric stepped forward, lifting his head towards a small box in the corner of the wall. 'Bonjour. Je m'appelle Lieutenant Cedric Degarmo, and this is Captain Brunhild. We're from Commissariat de Police du 7e arrondissement. Would it be possible to speak to someone?'

'Pourquoi?'

'Because we asked nicely,' Coco interrupted, 'and it's rather important.'

'Your identifications?'

Coco grimaced. There was something about the voice which irritated her. It sounded like a snooty British woman with an affected French accent which she spoke in a way as if was beneath her to do so. Coco pulled out her ID and held it up. Cedric tutted and moved her hand toward the tiny security camera and then displayed his own ID.

A loud sigh. 'Wait there, I'll be down in a moment.'

'No hurry, m'lady,' Coco replied in a broad Cockney accent.

Coco shuffled uncomfortably on the wide sofa in the centre of the vast living room. The entire room appeared as if no one spent any time in it, she thought, and as if it was in a constant state of being ready for being photographed for some high-brow magazine. The surly British woman had shown them to the room, pointed to the sofa and left without saying another word, all the time shooting Coco with a disparaging look that told Coco she had most likely heard her mocking her. The woman looked exactly as Coco expected. Tall and thin, with an air of pomp and promptness, most likely in her forties, but she dressed and acted older. She walked as if she had a broom stuck down her calf-length black skirt and she constantly patted the back of a neat pile of shiny black hair as if she was ensuring not a single strand was out of place.

'Do you think she's coming back?' Coco whispered.

'Why are you whispering?' Cedric asked.

Coco shrugged. 'I'm frightened she'll put me in detention.'

The tall entrance doors swung open, and the Brit swept into the room, closely followed by an older woman. The elder of the two women was the polar opposite of the Brit, as small as she was tall and as wide as she was thin. She was dressed in a misshapen floral frock dress, stubby hands stuffed in two front pockets. Her hair was curly and dark and bounced as she moved. She fixed Coco and Cedric with a pair of watery, tired eyes laced with concern.

'What do the police want with us?' she demanded. Her voice was deep, but it was not hard, and clearly betrayed that she was fearful, Coco thought.

Coco rose to her feet. 'My name is Captain Charlotte Brunhild. And you are?'

'Mona Gagnon.'

Coco nodded. 'And you Madame?'

'Mademoiselle,' the British woman corrected. 'My name is

Emma Fitzgerald. I am Monsieur Severin's housekeeper.'

'And Richard was married to my sister,' Mona Gagnon stated with what appeared to be irritation. 'I'll ask you again, what do the police what with us? Richard isn't here if it's him you're looking for. He keeps his own hours,' she added with evident distaste.

'Do you know where he is?' Cedric interjected.

Mona snorted, exchanging a knowing look with Emma. 'I do not know,' she retorted. 'We share a house, but little else.'

The housekeeper took a step forward. Although she was not much taller than Coco, she felt small next to her and took a step backwards, until she bumped into the sofa.

'Why are you here?' Emma questioned. 'Is this about Caroline?'

Coco frowned. 'Caroline?'

'Monsieur Severin's daughter,' Emma answered.

'Is she here?' Coco asked, looking around. She tried to remember what she had read about Severin in her brief scanning of his autobiography, but she could remember little, other than she seemed to recall reading he had children and his wife was dead.

'My niece hasn't lived here for many years,' Mona stated. 'Nor has my nephew.'

Cedric extracted his notepad. 'Could you give me their addresses? We really need to speak with them.'

Mona's lips tightened. 'I don't have their addresses. Caroline is…' she stopped, tilting her head, 'not the sort of woman who likes to live in one place,' she said, rubbing her temples as if she had a headache.

'Emile, Monsieur Severin's son, works at an outreach in Seine-Saint-Denis,' Emma spoke softly, before adding with veiled pride. 'He helps poor people - people just out of prison, to get their life back on track, that sort of thing.'

'Do you have the address?' Cedric asked.

Emma shook her head quickly. 'Non, but it's called

communautés, and is in Drancy. That's all I know I'm afraid.'

Cedric nodded. 'Merci. I'll sure we can find it.'

Coco took a step forward, moving past Emma directly towards Mona. 'Isn't it strange that you don't see your niece and nephew, or even know where they live, Madame?'

Mona turned her head. 'I am also a mademoiselle. After my sister… after my sister.' She stopped as if she could not bear to finish the sentence. 'I helped raise Caroline and Emile. They needed me… until they didn't.' She finally answered. 'What is this about?' she demanded again.

Coco took a deep breath. 'I'm afraid I have some terrible news to give you.'

Mona moved to a chair and sat. She did not speak, but gestured for Coco to continue.

'I have to inform you that earlier this morning we discovered the body of a man we have since identified as Monsieur Richard Severin. Obviously, we still need formal identification to take place to be sure, but I can tell you we have used his fingerprints to identify him, so you should prepare yourself for the shock.'

Emma moved across the room and closed the doors. Coco frowned, unsure who else in the house she might be attempting to keep the news from. She approached Coco. 'What happened to him?'

'We'll know more in an hour or two,' Coco replied. 'However, at this stage, we are treating his death as suspicious.'

Emma nodded. 'Where did it happen?'

'We believe it happened in the métro,' Coco answered. 'Mais, it's early days. We're still trying to figure it all out. When was the last time you saw him?'

Mona cleared her throat. 'This morning at breakfast.'

'And what time was that?' Cedric asked.

'At 07H00 on the dot,' Emma answered. 'Monsieur Severin is…' she lowered her head, '*was* a man who liked his routine. Every morning at 07H00, not a second earlier, not a moment later. And then he would leave at 07H30 to take Laure to school.'

'Laure?' Coco asked sharply.

Emma nodded. 'His granddaughter. Since Monsieur Severin retired, he takes Laure to school every morning and then picks her up each afternoon. He dotes on her,' she added with a sad smile.

'And Laure is whose child?'

'Caroline's,' Mona sniffed haughtily, before adding under her breath, 'though perhaps she might need reminding of that fact, from time to time.'

Coco continued. 'And where is this school?'

'About a ten-minute walk from here,' Emma replied.

Coco pursed her lips. 'Then, can you tell me why Monsieur Severin may have been on the métro?'

Mona moved her shoulders slowly. 'He would have had his reasons, reasons no doubt known only to him,' she answered tartly.

Coco frowned. There was something about the elder woman which bothered her. It was not that she seemed to be displaying no emotions regarding Richard Severin's death, rather she appeared to be displaying a complete lack of interest one way or another. 'And what might they be?' Coco pushed.

Mona moved her shoulders slowly as though such a movement troubled her. 'As I already told you, Richard kept his own hours and his own… *interests.*'

Emma coughed. 'Since he retired,' she took over, 'I believe Monsieur Severin had grown tired of only ever seeing Paris from the back of a limousine, his nose buried in various reports. So, the first thing he did was fire his driver, and since then he walks, or uses the métro whenever he can.' She smiled. 'Despite his many successes, he was a very simple man.'

'Beluga caviar for breakfast is hardly simple, dear,' Mona laughed, 'and neither is Dom Pérignon with lunch.'

Emma raised her head, tipping her nose towards the elder

woman. 'Monsieur Severin worked very hard. He should enjoy the finer things in life.'

Mona snorted.

Coco watched the interaction between the two women and it intrigued her because she could not pinpoint what it meant. She had never really understood the dynamics of the upper-class and the way in which they treat their staff, but in this instance, it appeared almost as if Emma, the British snoot, had the upper hand. There could, Coco reasoned, be several reasons for that, some of which might involve another kind of service the Brit provided for the master of the house, Coco assumed.

'After he left,' Coco said softly, conscious not to put the two of them on the defensive, 'what did the two of you do?'

The two women exchanged a look Coco could only describe as anxious.

'I cleared up after breakfast,' Emma replied, 'and continued with my usual morning chores around the house.'

'And I retired to my room,' Mona added. 'I like to read the newspapers on my balcony.'

'Neither of us has left the house this morning,' Emma concluded matter-of-factly.

Mona stood and moved slowly to Coco. She walked with a slight limp. 'I will identify Richard for you.'

'Well, it really should be his next of kin,' Coco replied.

Mona laughed. 'Richard was an only child, and he has no living relatives. And as for his children, well, good luck finding Caroline, and I feel confident in informing you that Emile will have as much interest in seeing his father dead as he did alive. Whereas I, a woman who has known that man for almost fifty years, would be delighted to see him in his present state. In fact, you might say it would make my day.'

Coco desperately tried to suppress the inappropriate smile that was threatening to appear on her face. Instead, she nodded.

'D'accord. I'll call you in an hour or two and let you know where to come.'

Mona smiled sweetly. 'I'll be waiting for your call.'

Coco gestured for Cedric to move towards the doors. He opened them, Coco following close behind him.

'We'll inform your nephew,' she said. 'Is there anything you'd like me to say to him?'

Mona stared at her as if she was unsure what she meant. She considered. 'Tell him, he can come home whenever he wants now.'

Coco nodded and stepped out of the room.

LUNDI
11H30

Coco pulled the car to a halt and jumped out. She leaned against the bonnet and lit a cigarette. Cedric stepped around the car and moved next to her, carefully keeping a distance from her while eyeing the cigarette in her hand.

'I thought you were quitting,' he stated. 'You said you couldn't afford it.'

Coco stared at the cigarette. It was one of her ten-a-day rations and she believed it was one of the few remaining things in her life which kept her sane. She had long since resigned herself to her life being a disaster. Four children varying in ages from twenty-one to three, and not a single one of their fathers on the scene. At least she knew where one of them was, she reasoned. It was just a shame that he was serving a life stretch in prison for a multitude of crimes, including murder. She had no money. She had no genuine prospects. Her apartment was a cramped disaster. Her eldest daughter was dating a drug dealer and was threatening to move in with him, her elder son was obviously gay but had seemingly taken it as his life mission to hide as far in the closet as he could, despite Coco's many rainbow-tinted hints to ease him out. The two younger children would grow in the confused knowledge they would likely never see their father outside of a prison, even if Coco were to allow them to see him in the first place.

Despite all that. Despite everything that was against her, Coco would not let herself be dragged down, because that would, she felt, be the ultimate insult. *I won't be beaten.* She tugged her oversized antique Chanel bag and dropped it at her feet. It was the only thing she had of value, though it had likely ceased being of any value to anyone else a long time since. But to her, it contained everything. Photographs. Hair cuttings from her children and their beloved dog, who had died years earlier. She dragged it with her wherever she went because it was something tangible she could hold on to. *This is mine. This is my life.* She looked at the cigarette. The ten cigarettes a day were hers, and that was that. Something only for her. She did not go to the hairdresser's or buy clothes. Anything she had, anything she made, was for her children. For her, it was her antique Chanel bag filled with nonsense and ten cigarettes a day. And it was enough.

'What did you make of that, back there?' Cedric asked, breaking the silence.

Coco turned her head in surprise, flashing a rare smile at the young lieutenant. They had been through so much together, and she had come to rely on him in ways she knew she should not. She hoped that whatever was wrong with him; it was not what she suspected, that he was finally going to leave her. She knew he should. To move on to a bigger department, to further his career, was the only sensible course of action for him. If Coco was aware of anything, it was that her career was toxic for her, and most likely those around her. Cedric had chosen to stand by her, and for that, she would always be grateful, but she knew if he asked, she was going to have to let him go, and she would do so willingly, no doubt making a sarcastic joke to hide the fact she was heartbroken to be losing one of the few men in her life she knew she could count on.

'Those two made Cruella de Ville and Lily Munster look like normal women,' Coco answered with as much bravado as she could muster.

Cedric chuckled. 'You could say that,' he replied. 'There certainly didn't seem to be much grieving going on.'

'Or shock that he was dead,' Coco mused. 'Mind you, I think there's little doubt snotty-nosed Ms Downton Abbey was most certainly schlepping her boss.'

Cedric's eyes widened. 'What makes you think that?'

'Oh, I have a few million reasons to think that,' Coco shot back, 'and although she was pretty good at hiding it, a woman knows when another woman has just lost her paramour.'

'A woman knows,' Cedric mouthed sarcastically.

'I saw that!' Coco scolded. 'Mais, it's true. She was softer when she spoke about him. You must have noticed that.'

Cedric shrugged. 'Yeah, but that's just sucking up to the man who pays the wages, non?'

'Peut être,' Coco conceded, her voice laden with doubt. 'Anyway, we'll talk about that later. We have to get to the matter at hand.' She stepped away from the car and stubbed out the cigarette. She looked around, her face clouding. They were on the corner of a busy street in downtown Drancy. She did not know the area of Seine-Saint-Denis well, though she had been warned not to travel there alone at night. During the day, however, it did not seem so dangerous to her, but she did not doubt it could change when darkness descended. Even then, at barely midday, there were prostitutes and drug dealers going about their daily business. She narrowed her eyes, scanning the busy street for the outreach centre where Emile Severin worked. After a while, she found it, a nondescript building with shuttered windows and doors.

She took a deep breath. 'Let's get this over with..' She pointed towards the rundown building. 'What's the story with the son? This place is a shithole. I can't imagine there were too many hookers and dealers lining the fancy pants street he grew up on.'

Cedric smiled at a buxom prostitute. 'Maybe, this is his thing.'

Coco scoffed. 'With that kind of money, he could be in some kind of cosy office somewhere, far away from here and the common people.'

'You of all people should understand what it's like to rebel,' Cedric pointed out. 'Haven't you made it your life mandate to do just that?'

She waved her hand. 'Exactly! That's how I know there is something off with this.'

Cedric frowned. 'What are you talking about? Rich spoilt kids often rebel against wealthy parents, especially when the parents try to get tough. Whatever was going on between father and son, this is probably the kid's way of making his father stand up and take notice.'

Coco gave him a doubtful look. 'This seems different to me. You're right, I understand rebelling against parents. And while we were never rich, I've seen plenty of rich kids and most of them like to think they're rebelling, but they don't tend to wander too far from the trust fund.'

'You know nothing about this family.'

'Not yet,' she agreed. 'What I'm getting at is there's no doubt the kid is here to either piss off his father, or because he wanted to make a difference. This kind of rebelling is about something else. It's about not wanting to play ball. I've no doubt if he toed the line, his father would have let him lead pet projects that didn't involve getting his hands dirty. He's here because he hated something about his old life, that's all I'm saying. And then there's his sister. There's something off there. I could tell by the way those two women spoke about her. Let's hope he at least has an idea where she might be.' She cleared her throat. 'Let's go before we get mugged, or worse, propositioned!' She looked over her shoulder. An old man was watching her from a car. 'I don't like the way that decrepit pervert is eyeing my ass.'

Cedric looked at the man and shook his head. 'I'll never understand weird fetishes.'

Coco watched dumbfounded as Cedric passed her, her mouth opening and closing in rapid succession as she struggled to find a suitable retort. 'You'll pay for that later,' she grumbled, stomping towards the building.

LUNDI
11H45

'I'm very sorry, Monsieur Severin, but I have to inform you that your father died this morning.'

'Et?'

Coco took a step back in surprise. She was not sure what sort of reaction to expect from Richard Severin's only son, but it had not been that. Emile Severin was staring at her, his tone challenging and mocking. She looked into his eyes. They were clear blue, and he was unable to hold her gaze for more than a few seconds. He turned away, running his hand through wavy blond hair. She supposed he was handsome, in a sort-of GQ way, with a lithe body with a square jaw and cheekbones which looked as if they could cut glass. He was dressed in jeans (too tight, not that it offended her) and a plain white t-shirt (also tight, and also something which did not offend her).

'*Et?*' Coco repeated. 'You don't sound...' she trailed off.

Emile Severin pulled back his shoulders. 'Bothered?' he finished for her. His voice was light, but it was also masculine. He shook his head. 'Non, I'm not bothered. Nor am I surprised, if that is going to be your next question.'

Coco's eyes widened. 'And why wouldn't you be surprised?'

Emile stepped away, moving quickly around the cramped office. It reminded Coco of her own. Organised chaos known only to the person who inhabited the space on a daily basis. She recognised it. It was the office of a person who had too little time but cared about what they were doing. She knew if she asked him for a particular file concerning a particular person, he would have it in his hand in less than ten seconds. She liked him. She did not know him, but she liked him, she was sure of that.

Emile pointed at a cracked café pot. 'I'd offer you a drink, mais…'

'You don't hate us,' Coco replied with a smile, moving her eyelashes quickly. 'Don't worry, the café's as bad at the station.' She pushed her arms together, elevating her bosom.

Emile studied her and finally returned the smile. Behind her, Cedric tutted.

Coco cleared her throat. 'Why wouldn't you be surprised?' she pressed.

Emile moved muscular shoulders. 'I guess, I'm just surprised it's taken this long.'

'For someone to murder your father?' Cedric interrupted with a surprised frown.

Emile raised an eyebrow in Cedric's direction. He tipped his head, a warm smile appearing on his face. This time it was Coco's turn to tut.

'Then he was murdered?' Emile asked.

'We can't confirm that at the moment,' Coco replied. 'Your aunt has offered to identify him, but we would prefer…'

'Good,' he snapped. 'Because I certainly have no intention of seeing him again. Mais, I would like confirmation that the old bastard is finally gone.'

Cedric moved across the cramped office. 'Do you have any idea who might have wanted to hurt your father?'

Emile threw back his head and laughed. 'Have you got a few hours?' he asked.

Coco frowned. 'Rumour has it your father was a beloved man, saviour of the underclass…'

'A rumour most certainly started by him,' Emile interrupted.

'You really hated him, didn't you?' Cedric stated, pulling back his shoulders.

'Yeah, I did,' Emile confirmed. 'What's your point?'

Cedric locked eyes with him. 'My point is, where were you this morning between 07H00 and 08H00?'

Emile smiled. 'On the métro, with about two hundred other poor commuters who can most assuredly confirm I wasn't off murdering my father if you care to check.'

Coco and Cedric exchanged a look. They had not mentioned where Richard Severin had been murdered, and nor did it appear his son was aware of it.

Emile scratched at the perfect square jaw. 'Listen. What is this about? You think I'm involved?'

Coco was not sure what she thought at that point. She shook her head. 'It's just you're his son,' Coco said. 'It is our duty to inform his next of kin.'

He nodded. 'Then you've done your job, Captain Brunhild. Merci et au revoir.'

'What about your sister?' Coco diverted.

He stared at her. It only lasted a second, but she saw the softness appear on his face. A moment later, it was replaced by sadness. He said nothing.

'Your aunt doesn't seem to know how to contact her,' Coco added.

Emile still did not speak.

Cedric stood in front of him. 'Do you know where she is?'

Emile turned away. 'Non. I don't know where Caroline is,' he whispered. 'And even if I did, she'd be even less interested in the news than I am.'

Coco laughed. 'Yeah, I'm sure she'd hate to hear the fact she's about to come into a shitload of money.'

Emile shook his head irritably. 'Six years ago, our father gave her two choices. She either quit drugs forever, or he would disown her. She chose drugs because she thought it was the lesser of two evils.'

Coco nodded. 'And her kid?'

Emile flopped heavily onto the chair opposite his crowded desk. He picked up a photograph of a dark-haired woman, who Coco assumed was his sister. 'Caroline didn't even know she was pregnant. They found her in a squat after an overdose. Laure was born three months early, barely alive and addicted to drugs.' He smiled. 'She defied the odds. She was in hospital for six months, but she made it.'

'And that's when your father gave Caroline the ultimatum?'

'Yeah,' Emile answered. 'He said he would take her and Laure in, but only if Caroline got clean. He paid for her rehab, probably the hundredth time they'd both done that particular useless dance, but by the time he left her, she'd snuck out.'

'And she left her daughter with your father?' Cedric asked.

He nodded. 'Oui.'

'Then he can't have been all that bad,' Cedric retorted.

'Or my sister is so fucked up, she's past caring. How about that?' Emile snapped back.

The door to his office was thrown open with such force it reverberated against the wall. A teenager burst into the room, dressed in shorts and an oversized t-shirt, a cap thrown across hair that hung over his face. 'Oh, hey, you've got company,' he said, his voice croaking in the unmistakable way of a young adolescent.

'Ah, Timo,' Emile said, clearly flustered.

The youth stepped into the office, dropping his skateboard. He moved in front of Coco and Cedric. He was so close Coco could smell the pot on his breath. He nodded, smiling. 'Not bad for a grandma,' he said cheerfully.

'Timo!' Emile wailed.

Coco turned to Cedric and pointed at herself. *Not bad,* she mouthed.

Grandma, Cedric mouthed.

'May I present my son. This is Timo.'

Coco raised an eyebrow, clearly surprised.

'Timo, this is Captain Brunhild and Lieutenant Degarmo.'

Timo raised his hands. 'I'm innocent, I swear I am! I wasn't where anyone may have said I was…' he laughed.

'Timo, your grandfather is dead,' Emile interjected.

Timo studied his face. 'Dead? As in, we're now fucking rich, dead?'

Coco raised her hand to cover the smile on her face.

Emile exhaled. 'Timo,' he sighed.

'Anyway, we should go,' Coco moved towards the exit. She placed a card on the table. 'Here is my card. If you think of anything that could help, please call me, or even if you just want to talk, or to ask questions, then please don't hesitate.'

Timo grinned. 'Does that go for me too?' he asked.

'Au revoir,' Coco smiled.

Emile moved quickly after them. 'Captain Brunhild. Come back later today. I can't promise you anything, but I can take you to some of the places Caroline used to hang out. There were a few squats she used to hang out in the evenings.' He closed his eyes. 'I'd hate for the first time she finds out about our father is waking up in some drug den, her face stuck to a newspaper with his face on it.'

Coco nodded. 'D'accord. I'll see you later.'

Coco and Cedric moved in silence out of the building towards the car. Coco stopped and lit a cigarette.

'Stop smiling,' Cedric huffed. 'The kid's barely legal.'

Coco flicked her hair over her shoulders. 'A girl can never get too many compliments. If you understood that, you wouldn't always complain about having a sore left wrist.'

Cedric stared at his left hand. He shook his head irritably. 'And while we're on the subject. We were there to impart bad news, and all you seemed concerned about is flashing your cleavage at the bereaved.'

Coco sniffed. 'For all the good it did me. He's obviously gay.'

Cedric threw back his head and laughed. 'Because he didn't come on to you?'

Coco glanced down at her chest. 'He never looked at my rack once, or my ass.'

'That just means he's got taste,' Cedric retorted.

She shot him a disparaging look. 'I'll treat that with the contempt it deserves,' she snapped. 'Well, I may be in denial, but then so are you.'

'What do you mean?'

She laughed. 'Well, he may not have been checking out me, but that's because he was checking out your very own pert rack and ass.'

'Don't be ridiculous!' Cedric interrupted.

'In fact,' Coco continued. 'I'd go so far as to say he was looking at you as if you were the appetiser, main course and dessert, if y'know what I'm saying,' she added with a giggle.

'He has a kid.'

'No shit, Sherlock,' Coco retorted. 'I'd better call the newspapers. They're going to want to know about this. I can see the headline now. *Gay man has a child!*'

Cedric moved quickly around the car and pushed her out of the way, jumping into the driver's seat. He glared at her. 'I hate you.'

Coco smiled and moved to the passenger door. 'I don't know what you're being so huffy about. It shows that despite everything you do to deter paramours, your natural sex appeal is still bubbling beneath the surface and the stench of carbolic soap.'

'Get in the car, or I swear I'm leaving you here,' he growled.

Coco looked at the old man who was still sitting in the car. He smiled at her. She shrugged. 'I have other choices, you know.' She jumped in the car. She winked at the old man staring at her from his own car. 'You're just lucky I have a lot on today,' she added cheerfully.

LUNDI
12H30

Commander Demissy ran a finger across the corner of Coco's desk, her face crinkling in distaste as it stuck to an unknown substance. *I never learn,* she mouthed. She turned abruptly to Coco, who was reclining on her chair, one foot over her knee, where she was liberally applying sticking tape to a hole in one of her socks.

'What on earth are you doing?' Demissy snapped.

'Who can afford new socks?' Coco answered. 'And besides, these have a bit of life left in them yet.'

Demissy turned again, facing Cedric. He smiled, giving a shrug of his broad shoulders. 'What do we have so far?' Demissy asked.

'The CCTV footage has arrived,' Cedric confirmed. 'I have Fitz going through it right now. I'll go and join him in a minute. We believe we know where Richard Severin got on the métro, but it's just a matter of tracing his journey there and while he was on Line 8 until the Captain found him dead.'

Demissy turned back to Coco. 'And what about the family?'

Coco grimaced. 'Well, let's just say there doesn't seem to be any love lost between them.'

'Your email mentioned a daughter that you could not locate?'

'She's got a record as long as my arm,' Cedric replied. 'Mainly drug busts, a couple of public intoxications and even a few for soliciting.'

Demissy raised an eyebrow. 'Richard Severin's daughter?'

He nodded. 'Well, sort of. The first arrest was as part of a protest against capitalism, or communism, something like that, and that arrest was under the name Caroline Severin. But all the other arrests are under the name Caroline Gagnon, which I think was her mother's maiden name. It's linked in our database by her date of birth and fingerprints.'

'But never ended up in the press,' Coco added. 'Rather convenient, non? Daddy dearest pulled a few strings to keep it out of the courts and the newspapers?'

Demissy shot her a warning look. 'When was the last arrest? She could have only been released if she had a valid address to go to.'

'Four months ago,' Cedric responded. 'And yeah, she gave the address of a hostel she was staying in. I rang them and they said they haven't seen her for at least six months and have no idea where she could be.'

Coco flashed a smile. 'Emile Severin, the son, has offered to escort me around some of her old haunts tonight. He says he doesn't know where she is, but I suppose it's worth a try.'

Demissy tapped her chin. 'So, both children hated their father?'

'<u>Really</u> hated him, if you ask me,' Coco agreed.

Demissy frowned. 'Then what are we looking at? Abuse?'

Coco considered. 'Caroline Severin gave up her daughter to her father's care. Emile said it could be just because she didn't care, but I can't imagine a woman, no matter how messed up she is, would give birth and then hand a kid over to an abuser.'

Demissy sighed. 'We're all aware that in some circumstances, abused children can grow up to be abusers themselves. Do any of them have records apart from the daughter?'

Cedric shook his head. 'Non, clean as a whistle.'

'It's a strange set-up,' Coco mused. 'And it's bothering me. Mona Gagnon obviously hated Richard Severin, so why the hell did she stay with him all this time?'

Cedric rubbed his thumb and forefinger together. 'Money talks more than pride.'

'While you were out, I downloaded his autobiography,' Demissy said. 'I wanted to familiarise myself with his story. His wife, whose name was Lauren, was kidnapped in 1990. There was a ransom demanded, with the instruction no police were to be involved. Richard Severin talks about it movingly in his book. Against his instincts, he listened to advice and brought in the police. A drop-off was arranged and a police operation mounted, mais the money was never collected and Lauren Severin was never returned.'

'Never?' Coco gasped. 'The kidnappers didn't come back and ask for more money?'

Demissy shook her head. 'Non. I accessed our own files, and it appears there was an extensive investigation, which continued well into the nineties, and not only was there no trace of the kidnappers, there was never any trace of Madame Severin. No body. No clues.' She shrugged. 'And after a while, no investigation.'

'Hmm,' Coco murmured. 'How odd.'

'Why odd?' Cedric asked. 'Kidnappings go wrong all the time. The creeps didn't get their money, so they offed the victim and made a run for it. We all know if you get lucky and dump a body in the right place, like landfill or a back garden where no one is likely to look, then a corpse can lay undetected forever.'

'I suppose,' Coco replied. '1990. Emile and Caroline would have been kids. It can't have been much fun, though I suppose it might explain why Mona Gagnon stuck around. She probably wanted to look after her niece and nephew while she waited for her sister to come home. Poor woman.' She paused. 'Still, it might also explain why she hated Richard Severin so much.'

'And how is that?' Demissy asked.

'Oh, I don't know,' Coco mused. 'It may just be my suspicious mind, but if I was a zillionaire, and I wanted to get rid of a nagging spouse without giving them bupkis, well, I might just be tempted to come up with some alternative way of getting them out of my life.'

Demissy laughed. 'You've been doing this job for too long. It's made you cynical and prone to always seeing the bad in people.'

'Ain't that the truth, sista,' Coco retorted.

Demissy glanced at her watch. 'Anyway, I have a few calls to make. I've arranged a press conference for this afternoon, once formal identification has been made, therefore I would like something to give them. Get on with the CCTV and we'll meet back here in an hour. D'accord?'

Coco saluted. Demissy shot her a withering look and hurried out of the office.

LUNDI
13H30

'So, we know Richard Severin joined Line 8 at Bastille station,' Coco began. 'It's a fifteen-minute walk from his house, to the school and then to the station.'

'And you have him walking into the station?' Commander Demissy questioned.

Cedric nodded. 'Oui.' He pressed a button on the laptop. Moments later, the screen was filled with a distinguished man hurrying along a street and heading, without hesitating or turning around, into Bastille Station. Cedric pressed another button. 'Here we have him using a pre-paid card and entering the station and making his way to the platform. He walks down the escalator, and he doesn't look or talk to anyone.'

Demissy pursed her lips. 'He is walking briskly, which suggests he may have been in a hurry.'

'Or his shoes are too tight,' Coco quipped.

Demissy ignored her and continued. 'My point is that he doesn't seem to be in any kind of distress.'

Coco stared at the screen. The image was blurry, and it was difficult to see anything specific. 'I don't know how you conclude that, you can barely see his face.'

'Well, he's hardly walking like he's just been stabbed, is he?'

Coco's mouth contorted, but she said nothing, instead, she turned to Cedric. 'What about the platform?'

Cedric clicked another button. The screen was filled with an overcrowded platform.

'Damn,' Coco cried. 'You can't even see him, or anyone next to him.'

'Yet he got on the train and a few stops later, you found him dead,' Cedric added.

'There must be a hundred people on that platform,' Demissy sighed. 'We're never going to be able to identify them.'

'The station should have a record of who swiped in and out,' Cedric suggested.

Coco shook her head. 'Mais, that doesn't include anyone who paid by cash. Hell, we don't even know if Severin was murdered while sitting in his seat.'

'What about the cameras on the trains?' Demissy asked.

Cedric snorted. 'There are cameras, but they weren't working.'

'They weren't working?' Demissy snapped.

'Oui,' Cedric replied. 'They had stickers over the lenses. But, I wouldn't get too excited, most of the cameras in the others carriages have them as well. Some people take great offence at being watched, and take action to protect their privacy.'

Demissy smacked her teeth. 'Then all we know is that Richard Severin walked into Bastille station under his own steam and seemingly under no duress, made his way to the platform, got on a train and a short time later was dead.'

Coco nodded. 'That's about it.'

'And that's what you want me to tell the press and our superiors? That's what you want me to tell them? That between us, it's all we've managed to come up with?'

Coco turned to Cedric. 'What about Severin's journey from home to the school?'

'There aren't many cameras in those streets,' he answered. 'Rich folks also don't like their privacy infringed upon. I've sent some uniforms to canvass the neighbourhood to see if anyone spotted anything, but so far nothing.'

'What about the ticket stub you found on him?' Demissy asked.

'According to Ebba, it's impossible to pull any prints from it. There are lots of smudges, mais not a single perfect one to pull,' Coco responded. 'Apart from that, I don't know where to begin. B4. It doesn't tell us anything, or give us an idea where to start.'

Demissy considered. 'Ask the family,' she said. 'Just because it means nothing to us, it might mean something to them. They may take one look at it and say, *oui, that's our dry cleaners.* The chances are it may mean nothing, but either way, rule the damn thing out and then move on.'

Coco's cell phone beeped. She picked it up and sighed as she read the message. 'Sonny is ready for us,' she said. 'I'll call Mona Gagnon and arrange the identification.'

Demissy uncrossed her legs and stood. 'Keep me updated.'

LUNDI
14H00

Dr. Bernstein pulled back a curtain and took a discreet step backwards. He lowered his head, a mound of curls falling over his face. Coco took a deep breath, suddenly overwhelmed with emotion. He had taken care of his presentation, obviously pushing a forked comb through his unruly mop because he wanted to look as tidy as possible in front of the strangers entering his domain. She knew what he was trying to say. *I am not the man who has just invaded the body of your loved one.* He was kind in ways she knew she never could be, but in the decade or so they had known each other, she had learnt so much from him. He was also the kind of man she wished she could have fallen in love with. Her life would have been different with him, she was sure, but she was also sure they would have torn each other apart.

The door opened and Mona Gagnon entered the room, shortly followed by the British housekeeper, Emma Fitzgerald. It surprised Coco to see her there, but then again, if her suspicions were right, it would probably make perfect sense. Emma had dressed in a simple black dress, while the elder lady had not changed her clothes since that morning.

'Are you ready?' Sonny asked gently.

Mona cocked her head in his direction as if she was not sure what he was asking her. In the end, she waved her hand irritably.

Sonny stepped forward and gently folded the white sheet away from Richard Severin's face. A sob escaped Emma, and she exited the room, slamming the door behind her. Mona, on the other hand, took a tentative step forward, her hand moving slowly around the shadow cast on the floor. She moved to the head of the table and stopped, her head pivoting downwards.

Coco stepped forwards. 'Madame Gagnon, could you tell me, is this man, Richard Severin?'

Mona pulled back her head, sucked her throat and released a mouthful of spittle on Richard Severin's face. Coco gasped and pulled her away. Sonny rushed forward, clearly unsure what to do. He ran to a table and pulled open a drawer. He extracted a cloth and quickly used it to wipe Severin's face.

'Have I destroyed evidence?' Mona asked simply.

Sonny regarded her in confusion. 'Non, the body has been cleaned, ready for autopsy.'

She shrugged her shoulders. 'That's good, I suppose.'

Coco stared dumbfounded at Sonny. She did not know what to do or how to proceed. One thing was obvious to her. The hatred Mona Gagnon felt for Richard Severin was real, and it was very raw, which, as far as she was concerned, was most likely an excellent motive for murder. 'Don't you want to know what happened to Richard?' she asked.

Mona turned, studying Coco with a burning intensity. 'What is the answer you want to that question, Captain Brunhild?'

Coco smiled. 'The real one. I always want the real one. Bullshit is boring.'

Mona folded her hands in front of her chest. 'I spoke to our avocat this morning, and he told me not to speak to you at all.'

Coco nodded. 'And what did you say?'

Mona smiled. 'I told him Richard was dead, and that he worked for the family now, not <u>him</u>.' She paused, stabbing a stubby finger towards Richard Severin. 'Mais, that doesn't mean I'm going to give you what you want.'

'And what is it you think I want?' Coco questioned.

Mona did not answer. She was staring at the door. The sound of nearing voices had caught her attention. 'Emile?' she whispered. Moments later, the door to the suite swung open and Emile Severin and his son Timo burst in.

Emile stopped dead in his tracks. 'Tante Mona?' he asked, almost as if he was unsure.

Mona took a deep breath and held it for a long time. Finally, she released it and ran towards him, pulling him into her embrace. She buried her face in his hair, kissing and whispering soft words. After a few moments, he pulled away, stepping across the room. He stared at his father's body. 'Then he really is dead,' he stated. 'I imagined I'd dreamt it.'

Timo moved behind him. He stood behind Emile, peering over his shoulder. 'Is that him?' he asked.

Emile nodded.

Emma suddenly appeared in the doorway. 'You shouldn't be here,' she stated matter-of-factly.

Timo pulled back in surprise. 'And who the fuck are you, Princess Di, to tell me where the hell I should or shouldn't be?' he snapped.

'I am…' she paused, lowering her head and stamping backwards. Her cheeks were flushed, and it appeared she could not make eye contact with him. 'I was Monsieur Severin's housekeeper,' she stuttered.

Timo stepped in front of her, widening his legs and placing his hands on his hips. A cocky smile appeared on his face. 'Then I guess it means you work for me now.'

'How have you been, Emile?' Mona asked.

'I've been better,' he replied. 'Better for a long time, over fifteen years to be exact.'

Coco watched the interaction between them, and she assumed it meant he had been out of his father's house for that long. She moved her attention to Timo. There was something off about him. It was not the usual brattiness of adolescence. She was used to that and was sure it was not the case with him. It was something else. Something she could not quite put her finger on.

There was an arrogance and entitlement to his tone and his demeanour. She had seen it before with children of the wealthy, but she had assumed Timo, like his father, had no involvement with Richard Severin.

'Have you spoken to Caroline?'

Emile turned his head to Coco for a moment, before turning back to his aunt. 'Non.'

Mona sighed. 'I've spoken with Horst Lavigne.'

'Horst Lavigne?' Coco questioned.

Mona nodded. 'Oui. He was Richard's avocat, or rather, his business partner. He's briefing the board of directors now, and they were trying to keep it out of the press until everyone in the family could be informed.' She shot Coco a dirty look. 'However, it appears the police are holding a press conference soon. I just hate the fact Caroline will find out on the news.'

Emile snorted. 'If it's any consolation, I imagine wherever Caroline is right now, there likely won't be a television or even electricity for that matter.'

'Still, we need to find her.' Mona turned her head towards Timo, but Coco noticed she could not look at him for long. 'There are certain matters we need to discuss as a family,' Mona added.

'Je sais, je sais,' Emile said wearily. 'That's why I've agreed to show Captain Brunhild some of her old haunts this evening.'

Mona nodded. 'Can I come?'

Emile laughed heartedly. His eyes flicked over her outfit. 'I don't think you have the wardrobe for it, tante Mona.'

She waved her hand dismissively. 'Don't be cheeky. I do have normal clothes, you know.' There was no malice in her tone, only the hint of playfulness, but it sounded like an echo of a memory of a woman talking to a child.

Emile turned away from her. If he had been softening towards her, it seemed to have passed. 'If she is there, I don't want to scare her off.' He gestured to Timo. 'Come on, Timo, we're going.'

Timo grinned. He waved at Mona. 'See you, *tante* Mona.' He nodded at Emma and nodded curtly. 'Princess Di,' he said cheerfully as he followed Emile out of the door.

Mona faced Richard. 'What happens next?' she asked no one in particular.

Coco moved next to her. 'Shortly, Dr. Bernstein will begin his examination.'

'And then?'

Coco frowned. 'I'm not sure what you mean?'

'Once you know what happened to Richard, does that mean we can have him for burial?'

'I can't say for certain,' Coco responded. 'It depends on what we find and a lot of other things, but I will call you and let you know.'

Mona pursed her lips. She hastened towards the exit. 'Come along, Emma. We have to prepare the house. Once this goes public, we're going to be inundated with people bothering us,' she added with a weary sigh.

LUNDI
14H30

Sonny began the careful dissection of Richard Severin with a swift slice of the scalpel. As usual, Coco held her breath as if she was always ready for the expected. She put it down to watching too many late-night horror films on the small portable television at the bottom of her bed. Helga, like her, was an aficionado of such movies - the more low-budget the better. And because of that, a part of Coco always expected an autopsy to begin with something horrendous escaping the chest cavity. She breathed a sigh of relief when Severin's apparently normal chest cavity was exposed.

'There's no way we're not looking at murder, is there?' Cedric asked.

The doctor shrugged. 'You know I say nothing until I'm certain…'

'But the bloody big hole in his chest is probably a bit of a clue,' Coco chimed in.

Sonny moved around the body. 'I once performed an autopsy on a woman who had been shot in the head.'

'Well, that was a waste of time,' Cedric suggested.

Sonny shook his head. 'Not at all. The poor woman died of a heart attack in her sleep after a particularly nasty argument with her ex. It seems he'd had enough of her dating other people, so he snuck into her house and shot her.' He paused. 'Trouble was, she was already dead.'

'He still shot her,' Cedric replied. 'And he deserved to be punished for it.'

'That's always for a court to decide,' Sonny continued. 'But, if I hadn't performed an autopsy, he'd likely be spending the rest of his life in prison for a crime he only *wanted* to commit, rather than the one he did.' He clapped his hands together. 'Well, let's get on with this, shall we?'

Forty minutes later, Sonny removed his gloves and cap and placed them in the hazardous waste bin. He moved across the autopsy suite and extracted a water cup from the fountain and filled it. He took a sip.

'Richard Severin most certainly died as a result of a knife wound,' he stated.

Cedric extracted his notepad. 'What kind of knife are we looking for?'

Sonny moved across to the computer and clicked some buttons. Moments later, the screens above him filled with images. 'I'm afraid I can't be helpful regarding that. I imagine we're looking at a pretty common sort of knife, six inches or so, with a single cutting edge.' He pointed at a photograph. 'This is an amplification of the knife wound itself. The right side of the wound is caused by the cutting side of the blade, and if you look here, you can see what looks like a ragged square, or what we generally call a fishtail end. That comes from the non-cutting side of the knife.' He shrugged. 'Bring me a weapon, and I may be able to confirm it as the murder weapon.'

Coco nodded. 'Can you tell us where he was stabbed?'

'The knife penetrated the fourth intercostal space,' Sonny replied.

'Non-geek, if you don't mind,' Coco sighed.

Sonny pointed to his chest. 'Just below the nipple. The knife perforated the large intestine. It would have been quick and relatively painless. He may not have even noticed it had happened at first.'

'How could he not know he'd just been stabbed?' Coco

frowned. 'I still don't get that.'

'It would have happened quickly,' Sonny reasoned. 'And it may have just felt like a sharp scratch. Like I said earlier, someone may have bumped into him. It might have hurt and because of the crowd he stumbled onto the train, a little dazed, possibly confused, but he could have managed it under his own steam.'

'Are you saying he could have been stabbed on the platform and walked onto the métro and died in his seat without knowing what happened to him?' Cedric proposed.

Sonny nodded. 'It's certainly possible. However, under circumstances such as these, it is difficult to say with any degree of certainty one way or another.'

Coco scratched her head. 'Are you sure, Sonny?'

'It's possible,' he repeated. 'He could have well walked the short distance to the carriage and taken his seat.'

Coco sighed. 'Why didn't he get help? There were so many people around. He could have just called out.'

Sonny shrugged. 'I can't answer that, other than to say, under circumstances such as these, adrenaline often kicks in. As I said, he likely would have been confused and dazed and with this type of wound, he would have died quickly.'

'And not one single person even noticed?' Coco asked sadly. She shook her head. 'What am I talking about? Of course, no one noticed. No one notices anything on the métro.'

'Apart from you,' Cedric interrupted.

Coco looked at her arms. 'Only because my fat arms got in the way.' She took a deep breath and then exhaled slowly. 'Anything else, Sonny?'

Sonny looked at the covered remains of Richard Severin. 'Not really. For a man of his age, he was remarkably healthy. His heart was strong, his liver a little fatty, but that's not so unusual. I've taken all the usual blood tests. When they come back, we may get a clearer picture, but I wouldn't hold your breath.' He pursed his lips in contemplation. 'His lungs are a little tar lined, so I imagine he was a smoker for most of his life, but I wouldn't say a heavy one.' He paused. 'Oh, and he's had extensive cosmetic surgery over the years.'

Coco raised an eyebrow. 'Really?'

He smiled. 'Not so much of a surprise for a person of his stature and wealth.'

'What kind of surgery?' she asked.

'He's had at least one facelift,' Sonny began, 'as well as eye work, nose augmentation and cheek transplants. He's also had extensive hair transplants and what I would imagine was a tummy tuck at some point. Some recent, some old.'

Coco whistled. 'That's rather a lot.'

Sonny shrugged again. 'Oh, I don't know. If money wasn't a problem, wouldn't you get work done?'

Coco extended her hands in front of her. 'Moi? Are you kidding? How could you possibly improve on perfection?'

Cedric giggled. Coco rounded on him. 'Something to say, lieutenant?'

'Not at all,' he conceded. 'You're right, you're perfect.'

She nodded contentedly. 'That's what I thought.' She smiled at Sonny. 'What about forensics?'

Sonny picked up the telephone. 'Ebba, can you come into the morgue, if you have a moment?'

A minute passed before the surly forensic technician stomped into the room, her face instantly clouding when she saw Coco and Cedric.

'What you got for us, sweetie?' Coco asked.

Ebba shot her a disparaging look. When she spoke, she addressed Sonny. 'Whoever they pay to clean the métro carriages is having a laugh at all of our expenses. Do you want to guess what I found on the seats?'

Coco shuddered and looked down at her woollen overcoat,

reminding herself once again that whenever she had a spare few euros, she really should get it dry cleaned. 'I can imagine.'

Ebba shook her head. 'No, you can't. Not really. More faeces than you'll find in a public toilet, more semen than you'd find in a whore's trash bin, more…'

Coco held up her hands. 'Okay, okay. We get it,' she said in English. 'What about the area around Richard Severin's seat?'

'Nothing,' Ebba replied. 'There were traces of blood, but none of it was his, and it wasn't recent. His fancy suit and overcoat soaked most of the blood up.'

'There was nothing around him?'

Ebba stared at Coco's coat with distaste. 'I suppose I should check your coat to rule it out.'

Coco's eyes widened with delight. 'Well, anything to help. Mais, if you're going to mess about with my coat, I want it dry-cleaned before it's given back. And take very good care of it, it's one of a kind.'

Ebba looked to Sonny. He smiled and nodded.

Coco smiled. 'Bon. Pick it up later at the **Commissariat** when I've found something else to wear.'

'Sure,' Ebba muttered, 'because apparently I'm running a dry-cleaning service now, too.'

Cedric laughed. He stood, his face creasing. 'It seems to me we have nothing to go on in this damn investigation.'

They all remained silent. 'We have the platform and the people who used cards to enter the station,' Coco said finally.

'You mean the needle in the haystack?' he retorted.

She flicked her eyes over him. 'What else do you have to do with your evening? A night at the gym and then falling asleep in front of the porn on your laptop?'

Ebba laughed and then turned her head as if embarrassed to be laughing with Coco.

Sonny pointed to the clock on the wall. 'As much fun as this is, Coco, but aren't you supposed to be at the commissariat for the press conference?'

'Oh, shit!' Coco gasped. 'Demissy is going to kill me… *again*!' She ran towards the door. 'Salut, Sonny, et merci!'

LUNDI
16H00

'Is it true that there is a serial killer loose on the streets of Paris?'

Coco spun her head toward the pimply faced reporter in the second row. She had seen him before and had wanted to slap the silly from his face then. She opened her mouth to respond, but before she could, Commander Demissy poked her sharply in the leg with a pen, glaring at her. The look was one Coco was becoming accustomed to and mightily fed up with. *Behave.* It was the same look Coco used on her children and it did not work on them either. But it had to work on Coco. She could not afford to lose her job, and Demissy was most likely capable of making sure she did.

Coco took a deep breath before pulling her face into a stoic state. She shook her head. 'There is no reason to assume any such thing, and it is dangerous to suggest otherwise.'

The cocky reporter smirked so widely, Coco worried that his lips would burst the spots on his cheeks. 'And yet, one of the most prominent Parisians was murdered on the métro in broad daylight, in plain sight, and if I am to understand it correctly, the police have *absolutely* no idea what happened, or who is responsible.'

Coco stole a look at Demissy. *He's got a point.* She shrugged. 'Who said that?' she quipped. 'Because as far as I can tell,' she smiled sweetly, 'and I realise, someone as young and…' she trailed off for a moment, 'inexperienced as you, might not understand the logistics of a police investigation. What I can tell you is this. We are appealing for witnesses to come forward regarding the sudden death of Richard Severin.'

The reporter snorted. 'What about the rumours concerning a Russian conspiracy?'

Demissy stepped forward. 'I think that is about it for now. And as Captain Brunhild said, we would ask for the press to step back on speculation and concentrate instead on assisting us in understanding what happened to Monsieur Severin this morning.'

'Then the truth is, you have no idea how one of Paris's most prominent citizens died?' the reporter interrupted, sarcasm clear in his voice.

Demissy stepped from the podium and moved towards him. 'Do you know what irritates me, Monsieur?' she posed. 'It is when the members of the press think that it is appropriate to work *against* the police, not with them as if they are two distinct entities which have to work against one another.' She pulled her body straight. 'I am here as commander because I am entrusted to investigate heinous crimes, and that is what I intend to do.' She paused again. 'And what I am not prepared to do is to answer and respond to questions which are both irrelevant and unhelpful. It has always been my intention to encompass all the resources which are available to us because I feel that it is the only way to truly fight against those who have no interest in adhering to law and order. And because of that, I would assume that the press would be more interested in joining us, rather than concerning themselves in looking for something more scandalous to sell their newspapers, or blogs, or apps, or whatever else nonsense they deem appropriate.'

Coco smiled, flashing Demissy with an impressed look. 'What she said,' she added. 'Listen. As you all must know, we are dealing with a suspicious death on the Paris Métro, which in itself is a logistical nightmare, but it is one we are taking with the utmost seriousness. Whatever happened to Richard Severin, there is no reason to believe it is part of a grand conspiracy or a wider problem.' She stopped and nodded, seemingly impressed with herself.

A female reporter held up her hand. 'What was Richard Severin even doing in the métro? I mean, doesn't he have a chauffeur?'

'I'm afraid that's a question we can't answer at this moment,' Demissy responded.

'What about his family? Don't they know what he was doing?' the reporter countered.

'The family are asking for privacy right now,' Demissy gave as an answer. 'And I hope you would all honour that.' She cleared her throat. 'Now, I think it is time to bring this press conference to a halt. As you can understand, we are in the middle of a very sensitive investigation, and for that reason, there will be no further comment until an arrest has been made.' She pointed to a screen behind her. 'Please print the email address and telephone number shown behind me. We really need the assistance of the public, and in particular, anyone who used line 8 this morning between 07h00 and 08h00. Merci for your time. Bon Soir.'

Demissy moved swiftly from the platform without looking back and strode purposefully from the room. Coco stared at the crowd and stepped away, moving swiftly towards the exit. Cedric ran to her side, pulling her head next to his mouth. 'We've got a problem,' he whispered.

Coco's eyes widened. 'Just the one?'

LUNDI
16H30

Commander Demissy pressed her body back into her chair. She reached for her hijab, her hands smoothing it as if it soothed her to do so. Coco noticed it was a tic of hers, a way to calm herself perhaps before dealing with whatever problem was in front of her. Coco only knew that because it appeared most times she was in front of the commander, and no doubt Demissy thought she was looking at the cause of all of her problems.

'I don't believe this,' Demissy murmured through gritted teeth. 'I just don't believe this.'

'Well...' Coco began.

Demissy raised her hand. 'I don't want to hear from you right now, Captain Brunhild.' She turned her head swiftly to Cedric. 'Lieutenant Degarmo. Tell me everything we know so far.'

Cedric lifted his head and nodded. He looked at his watch. 'Approximately forty-five minutes ago, Richard Severin's housekeeper, Mlle. Emma Fitzgerald went to the school attended by Laure Severin to collect her. The child was not at the gates and Mlle. Fitzgerald went into the school and tracked down a teacher who told her that Laure Severin had not attended school that day, and her grandfather, Richard Severin, had informed them that the child was sick and was not likely to be back at school for some time. Mlle. Fitzgerald knew that not to be true, so she rushed home to check with Mlle. Gagnon, the child's aunt, in case there was something she was not aware of. Mlle. Gagnon was naturally shocked, it seems. Then, before they could do anything,' he glanced at his watch again, 'about thirty minutes ago, they received a telegram.' He pulled out his cell phone and held it up in front of

Demissy and Coco.

We have the child. Do not call the police, or she will die. We will be in touch soon with further details.

Coco scratched her head. 'That's strange.'

Demissy frowned at her. She smiled at Cedric. 'Merci, Lieutenant Degarmo, for that. It was very succinct and well explained.' She tilted her head in Coco's direction. 'Just what I want from my officers.'

Coco smiled at him and mouthed one word. *Swot.* Cedric stuck out his tongue.

Demissy rolled her eyes. 'I'm working with children. I might as well be in a kindergarten.' She stared at the picture on the cell phone. 'And yet they called us, right away and with little consideration for the child's safety, nor the kidnappers' instructions, it seems.'

'Don't you think they should have?' Coco asked with a frown.

Demissy raised an eyebrow. 'What would you do if you received a similar message regarding one of your…' she trailed off, searching for a word, '*brood?*'

A smirk appeared on Coco's face. 'Well, for a start, anyone who was crazy enough to kidnap one of my kids ought to know I haven't got a pot to…' she flattered her eyelashes demurely, before adding, 'I mean, I have no money to spare.'

'That's not what I meant,' Demissy countered. 'Would you call the police?'

Coco snorted. 'Are you kidding? I'm not fucking stupid.'

'Captain Brunhild, your language,' Demissy sighed. She took a deep breath. 'Mais, you have a point.'

Cedric shook his head. 'Well, I don't think she does. If it was my kid, I'd call the cops right away.'

Coco shrugged. 'I suppose.' She frowned again. 'Wait. Aren't telegrams an old thing?'

'What do you mean?' Demissy asked.

'I dunno. But why a telegram, rather than an email, or a telephone call?'

'Peut être, they're more easily traceable,' Demissy reasoned. 'What are we doing about the telegram?'

'I have Ebba on it,' Cedric replied. 'Apparently, you can send a telegram online, or you can go into a store and do it. We should know shortly where and how it was sent. If it was from a store, Ebba's going to look for CCTV footage.'

Coco grabbed Cedric's phone and looked at the message again. 'The child,' she read. '*The child?* Don't you think that's an odd way of describing her?'

'Maybe they didn't know her name,' Cedric interjected.

'Then that would make them pretty crappy kidnappers, wouldn't it?' Coco replied.

Demissy sighed. 'What is your point, Captain?'

'I don't know if I have one,' Coco stated, 'other than it seems odd to me. Why not use her name. *Laure*. There's only one reason I can think of.'

'And what's that?' Demissy asked. 'And why does it matter?'

Coco stroked her chin. 'It matters because if they're not using her name, it suggests something else, something which terrifies me because I think it means they're dehumanising her. They don't want to think of her as a person because that will make it easier to do what they need to do.'

Demissy shook her head. 'You're making no sense.'

'They're going to kill her,' Coco said flatly.

'You can't know that,' Demissy snapped.

Coco nodded. 'Je sais, and believe me, I hope I'm wrong, mais…'

'As do I,' Demissy said quickly. 'In fact, I've never hoped you be more wrong than I do now.'

Cedric interrupted. 'But why? It makes little sense? Why the hell would they kidnap the kid just to kill her? They have to know the Severin's are loaded.'

'I agree,' Coco replied, 'and as I said, I hope I'm wrong. Mais, the fact is, this has happened before, hasn't it? Richard Severin's wife, Laure Severin's grandmother, was kidnapped, and no ransom was collected and she was never heard of again.'

'That was a bungled drop off,' Demissy stated. 'And they killed her because of it and so that they could escape. As far as I can see, that was a whole different thing. The ransom was requested, but it was bungled. It was awful, and it was tragic, but in the end, it makes sense, non?' She buried her head in her hands. 'Mon Dieu, the press is going to have a field day over this. We're going to look stupid, and negligent.'

'Pourquoi?' Coco questioned.

The commander glared at her. 'Because they're going to ask why we didn't check on the girl this morning after what happened to her grandfather.'

'Why would we?' Coco interjected. 'According to Mona and Emma, it was perfectly normal for Severin to drop off the kid and then go do whatever it was he did. There was no reason to think otherwise. The school didn't raise the alarm, so why should we?' She took a breath. 'Right now, I'm more concerned with the fact that Richard Severin told the school that Laure was sick, which she obviously wasn't. So, that can only mean he knew she'd been taken.'

'And that was why he was in the métro,' Cedric continued with the theory. 'He was going to meet the kidnappers, or drop off the ransom, peut être?'

'That would be one explanation,' Coco conceded. Her phone beeped. She lifted it up. 'Damn, it's a message from Emile Severin. He wants me to meet him in an hour to go look for his sister. I'll call him and cancel.'

Demissy raised her hand. 'Wait. I need to think about this for a moment.'

'What's there to think about?' Coco quipped. 'We have more pressing issues at hand than looking for a junkie who most likely doesn't want to be found and isn't very likely to care about her father's death in the first place.'

'But it is her daughter,' Demissy murmured pensively. 'And that raises a few questions of its own.'

'What do you mean?' Cedric asked.

The commander looked at Coco. She nodded. 'It occurred to me too,' Coco agreed.

Cedric leaned forward. 'Quoi?'

Coco picked a piece of fluff from the shirt she had changed into for the press conference. She frowned angrily upon seeing the stain which had already appeared around her breasts. *I haven't even eaten anything. How am I dirty already?* she asked herself in dismay. 'Well, Caroline Severin, or the black sheep of the Severin family, as she is probably known, is AWOL. Nobody "apparently" knows where she is, or where she has been for Dieu knows how long. And we also know she is a drug addict with an extensive criminal record. She is also the mother of Laure.'

Cedric nodded. 'You think she murdered her father and kidnapped her own daughter?'

Coco shrugged. 'We can't rule it out. We don't know how Richard Severin ended up with custody of his granddaughter, or whether Caroline even agreed to it. I doubt even there's an official custody agreement in place. Rich folks like to handle their issues internally, far away from prying eyes and ears. Richard Severin could have taken his granddaughter away from her mother and refused her access. What would a drug addict with not a lot of choices do?' She shrugged again. 'She could try selling her story to the press, I suppose, but who's to say Papa didn't have them in his back pocket? Non, peut être, Caroline Severin finally took the opportunity to rid herself of a father she hated, for whatever reason, we can't be sure, and then she took her daughter back.'

'I have to say,' Demissy said with apparent reluctance, 'that whilst I concur your theory is… *possible*, there are several gaping holes.'

'Such as?'

'Well, for starters - why would Caroline Severin murder her father and at the same time kidnap her daughter?' Demissy posed. 'There would be no need. Surely she must know she was likely to come into a rather large inheritance and that with him gone, she would get access to her daughter if that was what she wanted?'

Coco nodded. 'You're probably right. Mais, she may not have the smarts you and I do. You're right though, we need to find Caroline Severin, not just because she might somehow be involved.'

'What other reason?' Cedric asked.

Coco turned to him. 'Because the fact she is missing could mean something else altogether. She could have been kidnapped as well. None of it makes a lot of sense, but until we find Caroline, we won't know whether we're dealing with a spoilt rich kid who offed her father and took back her daughter, or a rich kid who is in actual real danger herself.'

'Either scenario is giving me a headache,' Demissy said with a deep sigh. She pulled herself up in her chair. 'D'accord. Captain Brunhild. Meet with Emile Severin and do what you can to find his sister.' She turned to Cedric. 'Lieutenant Degarmo. I need you to take Ebba and get over to the Severin home. We need to make sure the telephone lines are all tapped. But do it discreetly. Don't burst in there like you're the police just in case the house is being watched.' She raised herself to her feet. 'Let's keep in touch for the next few hours.' She headed towards the door. 'I'll brief the procurer and the minister. They've been waiting for an update.

Richard Severin was a well-known member of Parisian high society, so whatever we do, people will be watching, and more importantly, they will be judging.'

Coco sniffed. 'Story of my life. One of these days, I won't be judged and it will come as a complete surprise.'

Demissy locked eyes with her. 'I doubt that will ever happen, Captain Brunhild.' She gesticulated towards the door. 'Go, the pair of you, and whatever else happens. Don't make any of this worse!'

Coco headed towards the door. She smiled. 'I'll try my best,' she responded demurely.

Demissy raised her hands to her head. 'S'il vous plaît, don't say that! Just be less...' she trailed off, searching for the word but seemingly could not come to it. She sighed, finally adding. 'Just be less.'

Coco nodded. 'Sure. I can do that,' she shot a look at Cedric. He smiled. He shook his head and mouthed. *Non, you cannot.*

LUNDI
17H30

Coco stepped into Emile Severin's office for the second time and found him slouched over his desk, his head resting amongst a pile of papers. She stopped, concerned that he had been attacked before taking a tentative step towards him. The floorboards creaked beneath her, causing him to jerk upright. He stared at her wild-eyed, and though she could not be certain, he appeared to have been crying at some point. His eyes were red and appeared raw, as if he had been rubbing them. His cheeks flushed when he noticed Coco staring at him. He turned his head.

'I saw the press conference,' he said. 'You made a good stab at making him actually sound like a decent human being.'

Coco flopped onto a chair opposite him. 'I'm afraid something else has happened.'

He faced her. 'Quoi?'

'Your niece has disappeared,' Coco blurted. 'And I'm afraid to say it appears she was kidnapped.'

Emile took a sharp breath. 'Like my mother,' he said in a whisper.

'I know this must be a terrible shock,' Coco said in the most reassuring tone she could muster. 'But you can't think like that. We are doing everything we can to find Laure.'

He nodded. 'Is it connected to what happened to my father?'

Coco hunched her shoulders. 'All we know so far is that your father told the school she was sick when it appears she wasn't.'

Emile frowned. 'Why would he say that if it wasn't true?'

'Peut être, that's why he was in the métro,' Coco answered. 'He may have been instructed to do so.' She sighed. 'Je suis désolé,

I don't have more for you. Would you like me to take you so you can be with your aunt?'

He flashed her a puzzled look. 'Pourquoi?'

'Well, I'm sure you would like to be together at a time like this,' Coco replied.

Emile coughed. 'I'm sorry about Laure, truly I am, but the fact remains I never even met the kid.'

Coco's eyes widened in surprise. She knew the Severin family was fractured, but she was not aware of the extent of it.

'And as for my aunt,' Emile continued. 'She hated my father, she hated his house, but she insisted on being there, and she never once did a thing to stop the hate or make it a better place for any of us. In that respect, she was as bad as him.'

'But they took in your niece.'

He snorted. 'They dragged her from her mother to save face. That's all they did. And as fucked up as Caroline is, even raising her kid in a squat would be better than leaving her in that house.'

'Then why didn't she fight for her?' Coco asked. She bit her lip. 'Désolé, it's not my business.'

Emile shrugged. 'It doesn't matter. It's all ancient history. Caroline was a smackhead and father gave her a chunk of money in exchange for the kid. Of course, she snapped his hand off. That money allowed her to be high for months, probably even longer.' He stopped, staring at a photograph on the corner of his desk. Coco could not see who was in it. 'When I found out what happened, I tried to see the baby, mais...' he swallowed, 'father wouldn't even let me through the front door. It was just like the last time I was there, only then he was throwing me out of the front door. He found me with a boy, you see, and for my father, being gay equated to being a paedophile. He said he would never let someone "like me" near the baby.'

Emile closed his eyes for a moment. 'I should have tried harder to see her, I suppose, but I knew there was no point. He would never let me, no matter how hard I tried. And you ask why I don't want to go and be with my aunt? Why would I console a woman who never consoled me? She was standing behind my father both of those times, and she said nothing, she did nothing, and for that, I hate her as much as I hated him.' He rose to his feet. 'I don't want to talk about this anymore. I've spent a long time trying to forget about those people. Shall we go and try to find Caroline?'

Coco nodded and stood. She followed Emile towards the door. Emile stopped. His son, Timo, was standing in the doorway, his skateboard in his hands.

'How long have you been there, Timo?' Emile asked.

Timo shrugged but said nothing.

'Go home, Timo,' Emile said, moving past him. 'I'll be back later.'

Timo grabbed his father's arm. 'I'm coming with you.'

Emile shook himself free. 'Non, you're not. These are dangerous places, and I don't want you anywhere near them.'

Timo guffawed. 'If you only knew half of the places I hang out at…'

Emile waved his hand dismissively. 'I don't care about that now. Go home, I don't want you there,' he added, his voice cold and harsh. He gestured to Coco. 'Let's go before I change my mind.'

LUNDI
19H00

After each den of iniquity, Coco found herself becoming more and more depressed. The vacant and resigned look on each face was the same, and their eyes were all hungry, but not for food or help. They were hungry only for their next hit and they did not seem to care what they had to do for it. Coco had not said it to Emile, but the thought was foremost on her mind - what had led Caroline Severin to choose that kind of life over the comfortable one she could have had? There was one reason Coco could think of, but she hoped it was not true.

Emile pressed his body against the hood of his car and pulled out a packet of cigarettes. He offered one to Coco.

'Merci,' she accepted. He lit them both.

'I'm sorry we haven't found her,' Emile said softly. 'There is one more place we could look if you have time.'

Coco nodded. 'Sure, but we've done five of her old haunts and no one seems willing or able to help.'

'This last place might.'

'Then it's worth a try,' Coco responded. 'We have to try our best to give her the news. But if she wants to hide, I have a feeling there's probably not a lot we can do about it.'

Emile smiled. 'She always managed to hide when it suited her. She ran away from home the first time when she was thirteen, and even though father dragged her back, she never really came home, if you know what I mean.'

Coco nodded, shaking away a sense memory from her own childhood. She had loved her father until it became clear it was only reciprocated when she behaved. Being well behaved was not something she wore well, especially when she was told it was a requirement for anything.

'There could be another reason we can't find your sister,' she stated.

Emile took a long drag on the cigarette. 'You think she's taken Laure, don't you?'

'We can't rule it out,' Coco replied. 'That's why it has become even more important to find her. If someone else took Laure, they could have also taken her mother.'

Emile snorted. 'For what purpose? My father might pay to get Laure back, but I'm fairly sure he wouldn't pay a cent to get Caroline back.'

Coco nodded slowly. 'What about Laure's father?'

Emile pivoted his head away from Coco. 'I don't know who he is. I'm not even sure Caroline knew who it was,' he continued. 'He was certainly never on the scene, as far as I could tell.'

'Caroline could have known, and she could have gone along with his plan to get money from your father,' Coco stated. 'I understand I don't know your sister, but I know how drug addicts react when they need money. And I've seen her rap sheet. She seems keen on doing whatever she needs to for her next hit.'

'You're probably right,' Emile retorted. 'I used to know my sister, but even I couldn't say whether she is capable of doing something like what you're describing. And as far as I know, she's had no connection with her daughter.'

Coco sucked on her cigarette, taking a moment to enjoy it. 'I'm sorry to say this, but I am going to have to ask you to level with me.'

He stared at her. 'What do you mean?'

'I know this is difficult. But I also know you must be aware of how strange your family dynamics were,' Coco replied. 'And believe me, I'm not looking for gossip, and I will treat whatever you tell me with discretion, but I have to know everything if I am to understand what connection it might have with what happened to your father and your niece.'

Emile nodded. 'I know, I know.' He took a deep breath. 'And I will tell you what you need to know, but I have to do something else first.'

'What's that?' Coco asked.

'I need to speak to Timo,' he breathed. 'I need to tell him first. I owe him that. He can't find out second-hand.'

Coco nodded. 'Does it have something to do with your father's murder?'

Emile shrugged. 'I doubt it. At least I don't think so.' He smiled sadly at her. 'I just have to have a conversation with him. A conversation I never wanted to have, but I knew I would have to one day.'

'It's about your father?' Coco asked. 'Or his will?'

Emile stared at her. 'I don't doubt it's all written down in legal terms. He wouldn't have done it any other way. You see, I think it was his only way of controlling the situation and what was going to happen after he died. He was terrified of the truth coming out, and he knew that I, or my sister, would probably tell everyone the truth after he was dead, and he didn't want that. So, he put this in place to try and prevent that.'

'What is "this"?' Coco asked.

'Money,' Emile replied. 'It's always about money. *Here, I'll give you a fortune if you keep up the lie,* that sort of thing.'

Coco nodded. 'You don't seem the sort of person who is prone to bribes.'

'You're right,' he answered. 'Mais, this isn't about me. This is about something I didn't really have a choice in. Something I've spent half of my life trying to ignore. Now, I don't have a choice.'

Coco scratched her head. 'You don't have to go along with anything you don't want to.'

'That's not true,' Emile responded. 'I knew I would have to

one day when my father died, but I suppose I always assumed the old bastard would live forever,' he added with a sad laugh.

Coco reached over and touched his shoulder. 'It's okay to be conflicted.'

'I'm not conflicted,' he shot back. 'Maybe that's the trouble. I'm not sad my father's dead. I hated him and I wished he had died sooner. I'm just sad for the mess he made of all of our lives.' He stopped, a wry smile appearing on his face. 'I realise I shouldn't be using words like hate, rather makes me look guilty, doesn't it?'

Coco laughed. 'Non, it makes you normal. I think we all hate our families at some point. I can't say I'm particularly fond of my own father, despite the fact he's not done anything particularly bad to me.' She paused. 'So, this is about his will?'

Emile nodded. 'I don't know what's in it, and that's the truth. Well, not as far as I'm concerned at least.'

Coco frowned and stubbed out her cigarette. 'Then it's about your son?'

'*My son,*' Emile repeated distantly, in a way that troubled Coco. 'Shall we keep looking?'

Coco considered. 'Do you think we'll find her?'

He shook his head. 'Who knows? I love my sister and believe me, it gives me no pleasure to say that I don't know if she's even alive or dead. I hate myself for that. And I hate that I've never been able to reach her, but the truth is, I barely survived my childhood myself. I have nothing to offer her, or myself.'

'That's not true,' Coco interrupted. 'You've devoted your life to helping people, haven't you?'

Emile moved away, staring back towards the squat they had just left. 'When my father threw me out of his house, I promised myself I would do whatever I could to negate the terrible things he had done in his life.'

Coco frowned. 'See, all I've heard about your father is that he was a saint.' She smiled. 'And a fucking humongous saint at that.

But then he winds up dead, and all I see, all I hear from his family is that he was a…'

'Bastard?' Emile interrupted. 'Evil manipulative asshole?' He smiled. 'Should I go on? Do you want more?'

Coco took a deep breath. 'Listen. I don't know a lot, but I know that people in the public eye often project a very different image to the way they are in real life. What I'm wondering is, regarding your father's death, is it relevant? I get the fact his family most likely didn't like him, but does it matter? Am I looking at something irrelevant? I mean, I don't know you at all. I suspect you had good reason to hate your father, but probably not enough to murder him.'

Emile pulled back his head. 'And what exactly are you basing that on?'

She shrugged. 'Rien. Other than if you'd wanted to get rid of your papa, you most likely would have done it sooner.'

Emile laughed. 'Aint that the truth! You're right about one thing. I hated him. I fucking hated him. He was a despicable person. He ruined more than one life. The bastard ruined hundreds in one way or another. And I'm not just talking about his family, though he seemed to take extra pride in destroying us all because he knew it didn't matter. We wouldn't talk and therefore destroy his precious image, but that wasn't enough for him. He wanted our silence, mais he also wanted our devotion. If he didn't have our subservience, then he wanted nothing from us. When I left, or rather when he made me leave, and I decided to serve the community he had so royally fucked over, it never occurred to me that eventually he would take ownership of what I was doing. It was like he was sanctioning it, and everyone saw it as yet another example of how amazing he was. He actually told people he had funded my outreach program.'

'And did he?' Coco asked.

Emile's mouth twisted in contemplation. 'Not a damn cent of

his own, but yeah, he opened doors for us. We were given grants from the government because of what he said. Mais non, he never paid a cent towards what we do here. All he was interested in what the publicity. *Severin Industries* gives back, was the slogan. The truth was, he gave back fuck all. He ran his business in two ways. To secretly make the most money for him, but also to make it look as if all his interest was to make affordable housing. Ask anyone who lives in one of his damn banlieues and they'll tell you the same.'

'I read his book,' Coco said, before stopping and smiling sweetly. 'I say read it. What that really means is I picked it up on the métro once and got through a page or two.'

'I've never read it,' Emile responded. 'Mais I have heard enough about it to know that whoever wrote it for him deserves a best fiction award.'

Coco nodded. 'Despite not reading the book, I have heard enough about your father to believe that…' she trailed off, searching for the words, 'he was beloved and respected.'

Emile laughed. 'That's what I mean, whoever does his PR deserves an award.'

Coco considered for a moment. She did not want to argue with Emile, but she knew it was important to understand the discrepancy between the public and private Richard Severin. 'I've been a flic for a long time,' she began, 'and in that time I've come across many types of people, filthy rich, dirt poor, and more often than not I've found there's very little difference between them when it comes down to it. But when it comes to rich folks, especially those who have skeletons buried everywhere, it's pretty much impossible for them to hide it forever and from everyone. I'm not just talking about gossip, but of course, that helps. What I mean is, I haven't heard a single bad word against your father. And then this happened, and I met his family, and…' she trailed off. 'I'm presented with a very different picture. You, your aunt, presumably your sister all seem to be indifferent about his death, and I have to tell you, that troubles me.'

Emile shrugged but did not respond.

'What do you know about his housekeeper?' Coco asked.

'Emma?'

'Oui,' Coco replied.

Emile shrugged. 'She was devoted to him, I suppose. If you're asking whether he was her mistress, then I couldn't say. My father probably had a lot of mistresses, but I certainly never saw any. He was all about discretion, so he really wouldn't want any of us, or the press or his colleagues to know about what he got up to behind closed doors.'

'And your mother?'

'What about her?' Emile asked sharply.

'What do you remember about her?'

He shrugged again. 'Not a lot. I was very young when she… when she went.' He stopped, his forehead creasing. It was almost as if the description made no sense to him. He continued. 'All I really remember feels like snippets, so much so, I don't know what's real and what isn't. I remember a smell, her perfume probably, but very little else. I have a photograph of her on my dresser at home, and I see it every day, and my only thought is, *who is this woman?* He took a breath. 'After what happened, she was never spoken of again. Not by my father, not by my aunt. At least, not to Caroline and me. It was almost as if she'd just stopped existing.'

Coco nodded. 'And what do you think happened to her?'

Emile gave her a puzzled look. 'What do you mean? She's dead. The alternative is something else altogether.'

'The alternative?' Coco questioned.

'Oui,' he replied. He lit another cigarette. 'Don't you think I've heard this all before? All the gossip in the schoolyard? *There goes the kid whose mother staged her own kidnapping just to get away from him.* There was a particularly mean girl who used to spit on Caroline every day and say, *you're disgusting, no wonder your mother left you.*' He shook his head sadly. 'I barely stood a chance, but Caroline never did. She was different. She never learnt to be strong.'

Coco turned to him. 'There was no ransom paid. Therefore, there was no reason to think your mother had anything to do with it.'

Emile stared at her. 'You should speak to Horst.'

'Horst Lavigne? Your father's avocat and business partner?'

He bit his lip. 'You should talk to him. You should *really* talk to him.'

Coco raised an eyebrow. 'What do you mean by that?'

Emile shrugged. 'It's not for me to say.'

Coco exhaled. 'There are a lot of secrets in your family. If the suggestion was your mother staged her own kidnapping. Why? Why not just divorce your father?'

He continued staring at her. 'You have no idea. Horst once told me my mother wanted a divorce, but of course, divorce was out of the question because it would mean casting aspersions on my father's "good" name. A divorce would make people look at him differently and he couldn't allow that.'

Coco scratched her head. 'These aren't the dark ages. Life has changed for rich people,' she said. 'They can lead separate lives and still be on each other's arms to be seen by the right people. Even if your father didn't want a divorce, he could have given your mother freedom, surely?'

'You would think, wouldn't you?' Emile retorted. 'The theory from Horst was that my father wouldn't tolerate it, so my mother, who had taken about as much from the bastard as she could, came up with the kidnapping scheme, probably with the help of some nameless lover of hers.'

'You don't sound convinced,' Coco stated.

He shrugged. 'All I know is this. She is dead. I never could tow the party line, and that pissed Richard and Horst off. Because the truth was, even though I remember little about her, I remember this - she loved both her children and she wouldn't have done anything to hurt us. There were two theories presented. Either she was dead at the hand of kidnappers, or she had escaped with a ransom to live a new life away. Neither was true.'

Coco stared into his eyes. 'How do you know?'

He turned his head. 'I know. But believe me, Captain. I dream every night that my mother escaped him and is living a wonderful life far away. If she was, I'd forgive her for leaving us in that house, because it would mean at least one of us escaped. I dream she escaped and is living a nice neat life elsewhere.'

'Mais, you don't think she is?'

Emile shook his head. 'She would never have left us.' He exhaled the words as if they were knives in his throat. 'Not by choice.'

Coco closed her eyes. She did not want to disabuse him, and for his sake, she hoped he was correct, but she knew from experience that some men and women were not necessarily designed to be parents. She was reminded of her friend, Hugo Duchamp, a police captain in another region of France, a man she loved and admired very much, but his own childhood had been devoid of the love and emotion of parents who in the end had chosen to leave him. Their reasons were their own, though they undoubtedly rationalised it by believing it was for the benefit of their child. Coco could not ignore the fact that Lauren Severin may have come to the same conclusion.

Emile played with his hair, running his fingers through it. He truly was ridiculously handsome, Coco concluded, but behind the beauty, she could sense the innate sadness in him. It was apparent in the small lines around his eyes, which were at odds with his smooth face. She imagined he was barely into his thirties, and the thought occurred to her that he must have been very young when he had fathered Timo.

Coco cleared her throat. 'This conversation you have to have with Timo…'

He met her gaze, interrupting her. 'I wish there was a different way to do this. You can't imagine how much I do, but I have to speak to Timo first. As I said, believe me, I honestly don't want to have this conversation with him, but I always knew I would have to and now Richard is dead, it will come out.'

Coco nodded. 'Then this is about tarnishing your father's image, somehow?'

He moved away from the car. 'Can't we have this conversation tomorrow?' he asked with his back to her. 'I promise you I will tell you everything, but I must speak to Timo first.'

'Bien sûr,' she replied. Her eyes scanned his face. 'You look worried. Is this because you imagine Timo is going to react badly to what you have to say?'

He moved towards the car. 'Well, let's just say, I'm glad we've still got one last place to look for Caroline before I have to go home and face him, because what I have to tell him is going to destroy all of our lives, in one way or another.'

LUNDI
20H00

Coco lifted her foot over the threshold and instantly regretted it. Whatever she had stepped in was soft, with a pungency that caught the back of her throat. It squelched beneath her, and seconds later she felt it seeping through the holes in the bottom of her boots. She hoped it was not what she thought it was, but she knew instinctively it most certainly was. She rushed across the foyer of the abandoned building searching for something to wipe her feet on and she realised there was probably only worse to see. She reached for her cell phone, her finger poised over the torch button, before thinking better of it. There was just enough moonlight seeping through the gaps in the boarded windows and the open door to illuminate the path in front of her, any more, she reasoned, would just be depressing.

'Are you okay?' Emile Severin asked, his arm outstretched, wrapping around her back.

Instead of recoiling against his touch, Coco found herself leaning into it. It had been a long time since a man had touched her, and it felt good. It felt so good that it annoyed her to her core. She had sworn off men. She did not *need* a man; she had told herself over and over. Men had been nothing but trouble for her. Although she had four children by three different men, not to mention the exaggerated talk of her sex life, it had, in her forty-one years alive, amounted to little more than that. Exaggerated talk. Her dreams had more fun than she did. She realised it was not a question of her own hang-ups, her inherent distrust of men and what they could give her in a relationship, the truth remained - she was not a catch, but then, and this was something she felt strongly about, nor were most men.

She glanced down at the stained blue and green woollen jacket she always wore, the boots which had more holes than she could plug, the ripped socks held together by tape and the misshapen shirts, also speckled with stains nothing seemed to remove. And then there was the fact she had four children which none of the fathers supported. She smiled to herself. *Oui, you're a catch, Charlotte!* In recent years, she had come close to easing her dry spell, once with a bartender who was younger than most of the things in her refrigerator, and the other, an alcoholic cop whose own career was in tatters. She had resisted both men. *So far.* But she knew she was just one drunken night away from a text message booty call.

'Are you okay?' Emile repeated.

Coco turned to him in surprise. It took her a moment to recall where she was. Her face crumpled into a smile. There was something about Richard Severin's son which appealed to her. It was not just because he was gay, and therefore out of bounds for her. She considered herself an excellent judge of character, and she believed there was something about him, something hidden beneath the surface, which was inherently good. He had escaped something; she was sure of that, and it had been bad and marked him. She could sense that, but he had risen above it. It was evident in the way he walked and the way he talked. It bothered her that her profession negated reaching out to him. He had to be a suspect until he was not. Those were the rules and despite everything, she knew not to ignore them.

'I stepped in shit,' she responded finally, with a nonchalant shrug of her shoulders. 'It's not the worst thing to happen to me today, so that's a win-win as far as I'm concerned.' She paused, staring at him. 'Désolé. That must have sounded insensitive. Actually, I'm sure it was, because most of the crap that comes out of my mouth is, but it's not intentional if that matters.'

Emile laughed. 'You are a really interesting woman, Captain Brunhild.'

Coco laughed back at him. 'Well, that's probably true, but you don't need to call me Captain Brunhild,' she replied, before adding, 'unless I'm arresting you, of course.'

His eyes widened. 'Is that a possibility?'

Coco flicked her hair over her shoulders. 'The jury is out on that one, I think,' she responded.

'Pourquoi?'

She sighed. 'Because your father was murdered and as far as I can tell, you don't care a damn, nor have an alibi that's worth shit.'

'I did the same thing I do every fucking day,' Emile snapped. 'I get up at 07H00, spend an hour screaming at Timo to get out of bed, then I take the métro four stops to spend the day in my office helping people who really don't want my help and treat me like I'm the posh kid slumming it.'

'Then why do you do it?' Coco shot back.

'Because,' he replied with a heavy sigh, 'out of the forty people I see in a day, there are generally one or two who genuinely need and appreciate what I do to help them. Those two people allow me to go home and feel good about myself. It makes a pleasant change, and it sustains me.'

Coco nodded. She understood only too well his reasoning. Most days she trudged home, desperately shaking off the stench of another rotten day, but occasionally, just occasionally, something happened during her day which made a difference, making her understand that SHE had made a difference. It was enough to sustain her, too.

'I hope we find your sister,' she said.

Emile cast his gaze around the dank foyer. He scrunched his nose and Coco understood what it meant. The building stunk of every human secretion possible. She did not need to look to know that there were people, probably dozens of them, scattered around, slumped against walls in various stages of stupor. It saddened her in ways she knew she could never articulate, because ultimately she knew there was nothing she could do for them. The only reason she would enter a building like this was to search for someone who had committed a crime. That night she was there for a different reason perhaps, but in the end, it did not cancel out the fact that Richard Severin had been murdered and his drug-addled only daughter was high on the list of suspects.

'What the fuck you doing, bitch?'

The sudden, harsh voice emanating from the darkness startled Coco, causing her to step back, stumbling over what appeared to be a cardboard box and several blankets.

'What the <u>fuck</u> are you doing, you <u>fucking</u> bitch?' the voice repeated with a burning intensity. The venom appeared as poisonous as the tongue of a snake.

Coco struggled to see in which direction it was coming from. She could not see the man, but she imagined it belonged to a young man, probably in his twenties. There was no obvious accent to it, but the lilt told her he was originally from somewhere other than Paris.

'Hey, a little manners here?' Emile spoke in a calm, passive tone. Coco could tell he was used to dealing with people from very different walks of life to his own.

The man finally stepped out of the shadows. He was tall and slender, but his shadow was enough to cover Coco. She was not much smaller than him, she imagined, and she was certainly wider, but she felt encased by him. He took a step closer and she could see him better. He was dark-skinned with matted braids falling to his shoulders, and Coco could see that despite his eyes being light blue, they were cold and filled with darkness. The man's clothes were old and tattered and covered with stains, and his left hand was resting on the pocket of his jeans. Coco reached to her hip, again relieved to feel the coolness of her service weapon. She hated it, but sometimes it comforted her.

The man stared at Coco as if he was weighing her up, but instead of speaking to her, he turned his head sharply towards Emile. 'Are you really lecturing me on manners, princess?' he asked, a sarcastic smile hovering over his face. It was an obvious challenge.

Emile squared up to him. Coco raised an eyebrow, poised for danger. But then something changed. There was something about the way in which Emile had pulled back his shoulders. It appeared that he was not accepting a challenge, rather he was the one making the challenge.

'What's your name?' Emile said. His tone was still passive, but it was also forceful.

'What's it to you?' the man spat back. His tone had changed. The confrontation had been replaced by something altogether less.

'Because I know who you are,' Emile snapped. 'And I know what you do. Where is Caroline?'

'Who?'

Emile grabbed the man by his t-shirt and pulled him closer to him. 'You know damn well who I'm talking about. Caroline Severin. My sister.' Emile's eyes flicked over the other man. 'And you, what's your name? Jeff, isn't it? Something like that, at least.'

'My name is *Jihef*,' the man hissed, carefully annunciating his name.

'Ah, that's right,' Emile laughed. '*Jihef*. AKA - the drug dealer.'

The man called Jihef shook his head quickly, his braids bouncing angrily against his face. 'I'm no more of a drug dealer than your sister is a whore who'd do just about anything for a hit.'

Emile pushed him back. 'Then you remember her? Where is she?'

Jihef shrugged. 'Who knows? And who fucking cares? For all I know, for all I care, she's dead in a ditch. Bitch owes me a fortune, and even her skank ass is no use to me anymore. Not even the winos want to fuck that.'

Coco stepped out of the darkness. 'As the monsieur says, watch your manners.'

Jihef laughed in her face. 'You want to talk to me about manners?' he spat at her through gritted teeth. 'You just walked all over my bed with your shitty shoes, and you don't even have the decency to apologise?'

Coco looked behind her, realising what she had stood on. 'Oh, je suis désolé, truly,' she gushed.

'Sorry means shit to me,' he retorted. He sized her up, tapping his pocket again. 'So, let's solve this the right way. Give me money, or I'll have to fuck you up.'

It was Coco's turn to laugh.

'What you laughing at, bitch?' Jihef shouted.

Coco stabbed her finger towards him. 'Call me bitch one more time, and you'll really give me something to laugh about.'

Jihef studied her, his eyes flicking over her face. He smirked. 'Okay, my apologies, didn't mean to offend you.' He turned. 'Damn. Filthy jews are always so sensitive.'

Coco's eyes widened angrily. 'What did you say?' she hissed.

'You heard me,' Jihef bluffed. 'You're all the same. You destroyed my bed and you don't even see the need to pay for it.' He turned his head away, and mouthed again, *filthy jew*.

Coco threw back her shoulders, staring straight into Jihef's face. With her left hand, she gently touched her nose, while at the same time balling her right hand into a fist. She smiled at Jihef and before he understood what was happening; she threw her fist towards his face, socking him on his chin with such force it spun him around and knocked him to the ground. She shook her hand free, waving it as she moaned in pain.

'This Jew fights back, you fucking prick,' she spat.

Emile ran in between the two of them, pushing Jihef away

with his foot. He gawped at Coco. 'Are you allowed to do that?' he whispered.

Coco shrugged. 'What's he gonna do? Report me?' She stepped around Emile towards Jihef, who was still flailing on the ground. 'Where is Caroline Severin?'

Jihef angrily rubbed his chin. 'I told you, I don't know where the bitch is…' he stopped upon seeing the anger flash on Coco's face again. 'I don't know where she is.'

Coco nodded. 'When was the last time you saw her?' she asked. Jihef did not respond, so she balled her fist again. 'Don't make me go in for a second attempt, I've still got plenty of fight left in me.'

Jihef stared at her hand as if he was assessing the validity of her statement. 'Two, maybe three days ago.'

Emile gasped. 'Are you sure?'

Jihef shrugged noncommittally. 'Yeah, more or less.'

'Are you sure?' Emile repeated with urgency.

Jihef nodded. 'Yeah.'

'And how was she?'

He shrugged again. 'Desperate, as usual. She'd been off drugs for a few days, so she was desperate. She offered to blow me.' He smiled. 'I let her, but that was that. Her breath stunk, so I wasn't really into it. I gave her a hit, just a bit, and off she went to score some more. That was the last I saw of her.'

Emile looked at Coco. The relief was clear on his face. His face displayed the message. *She's alive.*

Coco nodded, though she did not share his happiness. If it was true, Caroline Severin had been actively looking for a way to score only a matter of days before her father was murdered and her daughter kidnapped. Coco did not share his enthusiasm, because whatever else was going on with the Severin family, she could not ignore the fact that Caroline Severin was her prime suspect. She reached inside her pocket and withdrew her card. She stared at

Jihef before tossing the card onto his ramshackle bed.

Jihef cackled. His cockiness seemed to have reappeared. 'Where's my cash?'

Coco pointed towards her card. 'That's my card. Find Caroline within the next twenty-four hours and use it to call me. If you don't, then I'll make sure this place is turned over.'

He cackled again. 'That's supposed to work as a threat?'

She faced him. 'I don't threaten creeps like you. I don't need to because there are far more powerful ways of dealing with you. Sure, I'll have the place turned over,' she pointed towards his bed. 'Every part of this shithole - except your bed. We'll round up some of the deadbeats again, apart from you. Just enough so that everyone thinks it's you who tipped us off. You'll be finished here, and once word spreads, you'll be finished everywhere, and forever known as a police informant.'

Jihef stumbled to his feet. The panic spread quickly across his face. 'You can't do that. It would be my death sentence.'

Coco shrugged. She pulled out her cell phone and used the camera to snap his face. The flash caused him to recoil. 'That's not my problem. Find me Caroline Severin and you and I won't have a problem. Don't find her, and then we will.' She extended her arm over her body. 'Has this particular Jewish princess made herself perfectly clear to you?'

Jihef glared at her but said nothing.

'I said,' Coco hissed, poking her finger in his direction, 'have I made my intentions clear to you?'

He still did not speak, but slowly nodded his head.

'Bon,' Coco said, pulling her coat closed. She gestured to Emile. 'Emile, let's get out of here.'

He fell into step behind her as she moved swiftly towards the exit. She pushed open the door and stamped into the street.

'That was amazing,' Emile called after her. '*You* were amazing.'

Coco did not look back. 'Let's just get out of here before he gets his second wind,' she spoke into the night. 'Because between you and me, it was all a front. I'm crapping myself, really.'

Emile struggled to keep up with her. 'Well, you would never know that. I think he was the one crapping himself.'

Coco moved towards her car. 'Let's just hope it was enough to shake your sister out of whatever hole she's gotten herself into.'

LUNDI
21H00

As she entered Richard Severin's living room for the second time, Coco was surprised by the marked change in the two women, Mona Gagnon and Emma Fitzgerald. They were seated on the opposite side of the room, their bodies pivoted away from each other. Mona Gagnon was staring out of the tall, narrow windows which entirely covered one side of the room, and Emma Fitzgerald was positioned towards the door, her right foot turned at an angle as if she was ready to make a hasty exit from the room. Coco nodded at Cedric, who was perched seemingly uncomfortably on the edge of a chair which looked too old and fragile to contain his muscular frame. The only other person in the room was the forensic technician, Ebba Blom. Her slender frame did not seem at odds with the chair she was sitting on. She was wearing headphones with a box of wires and equipment perched on her knees. The wires extended to the telephone on a side table. Coco nodded in Ebba's direction. It was not reciprocated.

Mona Gagnon turned her head slowly in Coco's direction. 'Do you have any news?'

'Non, désolé,' Coco responded. 'Have the kidnappers made any further contact?'

Ebba shook her head. 'Non, they have not,' she answered irritably.

Mona turned away again. 'This is just like before. I can't bear it.'

'This is nothing like before,' Emma snapped, without looking away from the direction of her door.

Coco followed her gaze. The English woman seemed to be

waiting for something. 'What do you mean?' Coco pressed.

Emma moved her shoulders slowly. 'I mean nothing.'

Mona snorted. 'It wasn't your sister who was murdered,' she stated with venom. 'You never even met her.'

Emma looked towards the mantelpiece, her eyes locked on a photograph. 'I knew her, in one way or another. I *knew* her. Her presence was always here in this house.'

Mona threw back her head and laughed. 'Her presence was *never* here. Not even when she lived here.' She threw up her arms. 'This room, this decor, was never about her. It had <u>nothing</u> to do with her. Like everything else, it was always all about Richard. It was *always* about Richard. Every rug, every painting - they were always as per his explicit instructions. Everything was, from the food we ate to the times we ate it.'

After a few moments, Emma turned to face the elder woman. 'Then why did you stay?'

Mona smiled. 'To make sure he never got away with anything else ever again, and to remind him that at least one person knew what he was, and what he had done.'

Emma covered her mouth. 'Monsieur Severin did not deserve the family he was given.'

'Finally, we agree on something,' Mona scoffed. 'He certainly did not deserve his family. But he deserved…'

'He deserved what?' Emma shot back. 'Because you and I know the actual truth. Not the lies you whispered behind his back.'

Mona folded her hands in front of her and lowered her head. She said nothing.

Coco watched the interaction with interest, but she could not pinpoint what it meant, or whether it had any connection to what had happened. There was evidently no love lost between the two women, and yet they had, without recourse, given each other an alibi. Coco took a moment to study them. Were they such excellent actors that they could mask a conspiracy behind a seemingly mutual loathing? She could not be sure.

'Did you find Caroline?' Mona asked, breaking the silence.

'Not yet,' Coco answered. 'Mais, I am hopeful. We met someone…' she paused, searching for the right words to say, 'we met *someone* who knew her, and if he is to be believed, he saw her only a few days ago, so I am hopeful he will help us track her down.'

On her way over to the Severin townhouse, Coco had called the Commissariat to check on Jihef. Emile had been unable to provide any details, and Coco had known it would be pointless to push Jihef for his full name because he would undoubtedly give a false one. No report attached to that prenom had come to light on the police databases. She wondered whether that was odd, but realised it was probably not. Whether Jihef was his name at all was most likely debatable, but his physical description was not likely to throw up many red flags either. She knew she needed to go through mugshots to see if she could find him, but the fact remained, she was exhausted and it would most likely have to wait until morning.

Mona nodded. 'Bon. She should be here,' she stated with determination. 'Especially for when Laure comes home.' Her lips twisted. 'Her mother should be here for her. Laure would like that, I'm sure.'

'Then let's hope we find her soon,' Coco replied.

Before she could continue, the doors slid open and a man strode purposefully into the room, brushing past Coco and engulfing her in a thick, musky scent. He was dressed in a dark cashmere coat, which Coco guessed probably cost more than she made in a year, if not longer.

'Darling, Mona,' the man swamped Mona, pulling her into an embrace. Coco noticed by her expression, it was not an entirely pleasant experience for her.

'Horst,' Mona said, extracting herself and moving away. She stopped in front of the fireplace, putting a table between them.

Horst Lavigne. Coco had been trying to track him down. The former avocat and current business partner of Richard Severin was a man of mystery as far as she could tell.

'I came as soon as I heard the news,' he gushed. His words were thick and expressed quickly.

Coco observed him. His voice was heady, thick like caramel, and while such a smooth voice on someone else might suit them, on him it seemed somewhat fake. He was small, with grey hair and matching beard impeccably groomed.

'I would have come sooner,' he continued, 'mais, I've been in meetings all day with the board of directors.'

'And the money?' Mona asked. Her tone was cold and direct, and Coco noticed she was not looking in his direction. It was almost as if she had chosen a spot on the wall over his left shoulder and was staring at that instead.

'The money?' Horst asked with an arched eyebrow. Coco also noticed that his forehead barely moved, which was odd for a man she imagined being in his sixties. 'Ah. Don't worry about the money. You'll be fine.'

Mona cackled. 'Easy for you to say.' Her eyes narrowed angrily. 'And I wasn't talking about me. I'm talking about the ransom.'

For the first time, Horst looked toward Emma Fitzgerald. 'Has there been further contact?'

She was still staring out of the window and did not turn to face him. She shook her head.

'Is there money available to pay it?' Mona asked with obvious desperation.

'Bien sûr, there's money,' Horst answered with a smug smile and an expressive stretch of his hands. 'The bank has been informed and we have a team of professionals working on it.'

'Professionals?' Coco interrupted.

He nodded. 'Specialists who are trained to deal with

situations such as these.' He turned in her direction. 'Who are you?'

Coco stepped forward and extended her hand. Horst regarded it with suspicion but did not take it. 'I'm Captain Charlotte Brunhild from the Commissariat de Police du 7e arrondissement.'

He regarded her with distaste. 'I thought Demissy was in charge of this investigation?'

'*Commander* Demissy is in charge of the 7e arrondissement,' Coco quipped. 'But I am directly in charge of this investigation.'

He snorted. 'I wouldn't be so proud to announce that, if I were you,' he replied with a sarcastic sneer.

'We're doing everything we can,' Coco huffed. 'And I would remind you, this is a police matter and you shouldn't be bringing in outsiders.'

'She's right,' Mona implied through gritted teeth. 'We all know what happened last time, with you and your bright ideas.'

Horst opened his mouth to respond, but thought better of it. Instead, he moved closer to Coco. 'Then tell me, where are you in the investigation?'

Coco squared up to him. She was pleased that she towered over him. 'Who are you exactly?' she demanded. 'Monsieur Severin's avocat?'

He shook his head. 'Not anymore. I am a partner in the firm who represented his legal interests, but for some years now, I have operated firstly as Richard's partner, and then when he stepped back, I took over the full-time managing of his company, or rather, *our* company.'

Coco nodded. 'And when was the last time you saw Monsieur Severin?'

Horst took a deep breath. 'This morning,' he replied. He noticed the fleck of interest in Coco's eyes and added. 'Rather, I spoke with him this morning. Richard often called me on his morning walk.'

'Interesting,' Coco mused. 'And what did he say to you?'

'It was private business.'

Coco clapped her hands. 'Oh no, there's nothing private now. Not when the Monsieur ended up dead on Line 8.'

Horst flashed her a scolding look she immediately recognised after having received it so many times. He tutted. 'Regardless of the appalling circumstances and events of this awful day, some things have to remain private and confidential. I have already discussed this with your Commander Demissy and I was under the impression she understood. Perhaps you would like me to call her for you and have her explain it to you?'

Coco noticed the smirk on Ebba's face and had to fight the urge to go over and slap it away. She stared at Horst. She had been dealing with men such as him for most of her life, and the only thing they ever had in common was that they were always lacking something and trying to make up for it in different ways. She moved across the room, standing in front of the window. 'Tell me Monsieur Lavigne. When did you discover Laure Severin had been kidnapped?'

Horst pointed at Mona. 'Mona called me as soon as she received the telegram.'

'I see,' Coco said, tapping her chin. 'I just find that a little odd, considering you claim to have spoken with Richard Severin this morning when it appears he already knew of the kidnapping.'

'We know no such thing,' Horst retorted.

'Then why did he tell the school she was sick?' Coco posed.

Horst said nothing, instead turning back to Emma Fitzgerald, who was still staring out of the window.

Whatever the lie was, Coco realised, Horst was not going to be bullied into revealing it. She would have to think of another way to get to him. 'How did he seem when you spoke to him?'

'What do you mean?'

'I mean,' Coco replied wearily, 'did he appear anxious,

stressed, busy, worried…'

Horst sighed. 'He seemed like Richard,' he answered. 'He could be all of those and more, but it means nothing. It could have resulted from a poor breakfast or his newspaper being late. He was a man who lived by his routines and did not like them being derailed.'

'And yet it most certainly was derailed this morning,' Coco reasoned. 'And yet he didn't seem any different to you?'

He sighed again. 'I don't know what you want from me, Captain Brunhild,' he stated. 'All I can tell you is that it was a normal conversation. We talked briefly about an upcoming merger and a board meeting he wanted to attend in the coming weeks.'

'I thought you said he was retired?' she retorted.

'Essentially, oui,' Horst confirmed. 'But men such as Richard never really retire. He was very much still involved in the business, just to a lesser degree,' he added. There was a snipe of bitterness in his tone, Coco noted.

'And this meeting? Was it something special?' she asked.

Horst ignored her and glanced at his watch. He moved towards the fireplace. Mona Gagnon was still staring into the flames. 'I have to go to a meeting, Mona. There is so much to sort out. Can I come back later?'

She did not turn, but nodded slowly. 'I doubt I'll sleep, so if you must, I can't stop you. This isn't my house, after all.'

Horst moved swiftly towards the door. 'I'd like to speak to you again, Monsieur Lavigne,' Coco called after him.

He did not look around. 'Commander Demissy has my personal cell phone number. I have told her to keep me regularly updated. If you have any further questions for me, ask her to pass them on. Au revoir.'

Coco glanced around the room. The only person looking at her was Cedric, who gave her an irritated look. She gestured to him and nudged Ebba. 'Could I see you in the hallway for a moment?'

Cedric and Ebba rose and followed Coco out of the room.

'What do you think?' Coco whispered.

Cedric shrugged. 'There's a bit of an atmosphere between the two women, and that short creep is a bit of prick,' he added with a sneer.

'I got that too,' Coco laughed. 'But before I got here, the two broads said nothing?'

'Not to me,' Cedric replied. 'The stuck up Brit looks like she wants to say something but keeps stopping herself.'

'They said nothing to me either,' Ebba added. 'And I've been checking their phone records. Apart from a few calls to various people who seem to be their friends and about fifty to the lawyer-slash-business partner, there doesn't seem to be anything out of the ordinary.'

Coco nodded. 'Can you check the last few days also?'

'Sure,' Ebba replied. 'Do you want me to stay all night? I've set up traces on the line, but if it's okay with you, I'd like to stay until morning just in case anything happens. I hate kids, but I hate kids being kidnapped even more.'

Coco regarded her with surprise. Despite the diminutive Swedish young woman's abrasive demeanour, which matched her stubbled head, she was beginning to see that Ebba Blom was serious and dedicated to doing her job. It made Coco happy because she understood how social niceties were unimportant to her, but her job was not. 'If you're okay with that, then it would be very helpful,' Coco replied. She lifted her hand and gasped when she saw the time. It was after nine. She had promised her nanny, Helga, that she would be home before eight so that Helga might finally enjoy what was remaining of the night.

Cedric stepped forward. 'I'm staying too. You should go home and be with your kids.'

'Just because I've got kids doesn't mean I can't do my job,' Coco snapped with more bite than she intended. She flashed him an apology with her eyes that she hoped he understood.

He smiled at her. 'I never said that, but I was just trying to be polite. The truth is, you smell like you've crawled through a sewer, so you should probably have a shower.'

Coco stared at her feet. She had brushed them off on a curb and hoped that had been the end to it. 'Are you sure you're okay to stay?' she asked.

Cedric nodded. Coco resisted the urge to reach out and touch his arm. She cleared her throat. 'D'accord. I'll go home and…' she sniffed. 'Have a rest and I'll come back first thing to relieve you.'

He smiled.

'Oh, wait,' Coco continued. 'I'll go into the Commissariat first. I just want to gallop through the mugshots to see if I can pick out this Jihef character, but once I've done that, I'll be right over.'

Cedric smiled at Ebba. 'No hurry,' he said.

Ebba glared at him. 'Don't even think about it, or I'll taser you before you get within two feet of me.'

Coco raised her hands. 'Enough with the foreplay enfants!' she cried. She nodded. 'Again, Lieutenant, if anything happens here tonight, call me right away. Do you understand?'

Cedric nodded. 'It won't. See you in the morning, Captain.'

Coco moved away. As she did, her attention was caught by creaking floorboards in the living room. She turned her head sharply just in time to see a figure retreating away from the doorway. She frowned, gesturing for Cedric to get back in the room, her brain processing whether she had just said anything untoward. 'À demain,' she exhaled.

LUNDI
22H00

Coco walked as fast as her legs would take her along Rue de Penfeld, the street which lead to her apartment building, but she could feel the steam had left her body. All she wanted was to crawl into bed, pull a blanket over her head, and sleep for eight hours or more. But she knew that would not happen. She knew that once she opened her front door, the problems of her day would just be replaced with the problems of her night. There would be a myriad of complaints to deal with, the refereeing of numerous fights. Meals to make out of nothing, breakfasts to prepare from nothing.

She shook her head and wondered, not for the first time, whether her whole life was pointless. It was certainly exhausting. Her father had once said to her that Dieu never asks for more than a person can bear. She agreed with little her father ever said, but something about her current circumstances had struck a chord with Coco. Her life might seem impossible and exhausting, but it was within her reach to cope with it. Because there were rewards, and although she could not really count them on any given day, she knew with the utmost certainty that her whole life was a reward.

'Hey princess.'

Coco immediately recognised the slow, dragged out drawl of the homeless man who lived in the narrow alleyway which sliced between her apartment building and the one next to it. It was so narrow, Coco could not imagine what it was there for. She knew it was not wide enough for her to walk straight, but somehow the homeless man had made it his home, and she supposed because no one else had a use for the space, everyone had just chosen to ignore his presence. She never had. And she never would. Most days it felt as if she was one pay date away from asking him to scoot up and make a space for her to drop her own cardboard box.

She knew little about him. His body was always covered in layers of filthy clothes, his head shrouded in scarfs and an ill-fitting hat. His face also told her nothing. A beard covered most of his face and snaked down onto his chest. She was sure he was white, but could never be certain because of the pallor and dirt on his face. The only thing she was certain of was that his voice did not lie. He was an optimist, but additionally, he was most evidently younger than she was. It broke her heart to see him that way, but she knew enough to know that the only real help he needed from her was not to judge him. She had told him once. *I judge no one, so long as they don't judge me first.* It had worked, and she had shared with him her cheese and onion baguette. He had taken two bites and handed it back to her. She had wondered if it was a test to see how repulsed she might be. Perhaps it had been a test, and perhaps she was repulsed, but the fact remained she was hungry and could not afford to be picky. She took back the baguette and took her own two bites before handing it back to him. That had been some months earlier, and while their conversations never stretched into anything substantial, she passed a brief amount of time with him twice a day. She knew nothing more of him, other than he claimed his name was Denis.

Denis gestured at a torn cardboard box next to him. 'Take the weight off, princess.'

Coco looked at it for a moment.

Denis pointed around him. 'It's my best box. It's not so bad.' He paused, flashing her with a crooked, stained teeth grin. 'Well, it's not that dirty, at least.'

Coco sighed and looked at her coat. 'I'm not worried about your box,' she stated with a sad laugh. 'I'm more worried about me making it dirtier.'

Denis threw back his head and guffawed. There was

something about his laugh which stabbed at her heart. It was hopeful. It was young. It was everything she was struggling to find in her own life. If Denis could find it, why could she not? 'I think that ship has sailed, princess.'

Coco frowned. 'Why do you never call me by my name?'

He shrugged. 'You told me once not to call you Coco until you told me I could.'

'I don't remember that,' she replied. 'But you can call me Coco now. I think we've passed that point in our relationship.'

Denis took a deep breath. 'Merci,' he whispered. He pointed at the box again. 'Won't you take a seat?'

Coco looked up towards her apartment. 'I've been out since 07H00, I really should at least pretend to be a mother.'

'Barbra is out, so is Julien,' Denis replied. 'I heard Helga talking with the old witch who lives in 3C and it seems bingo was cancelled tonight, so she was having a night in.'

Coco took a deep breath. She knew she should probably be concerned that Denis seemed to know so much about what went on in her apartment building, but she could not bring herself to be.

As if reading her thoughts, he added. 'I sit here most of the day. Everyone sees me, but no one *really* sees me.'

'*I* see you,' she corrected.

'You're different,' Denis replied. 'And so are your kids. Like you, they always take the time to say bonjour to me every day.'

Coco's eyes widened in surprise. 'My kids?' she gasped. 'Are you serious?'

He nodded. 'Don't knock them. They're kids, they're probably a pain in your ass, but living how I live, I know one thing for certain - they're decent human beings. And that is because they are their mother's children. They don't look down on the likes of me, because they've learnt from you not to.'

Coco turned her head. She was not sure of any such thing, but it touched her to think it might somehow be true. 'They've had a hard time,' she breathed. 'And I'm fucked if I can think of a way to make it better for any of them…' she trailed off, 'any of *us*.'

Denis shrugged. 'You will. They've learnt from you not to look down their noses at people the way people look down their noses at you. Believe me, that's a lesson they will carry with them for the rest of their lives, and they will thank you for it.' He smiled. *'Eventually.'*

Coco appraised him. 'Where the hell did you come from?'

He shrugged again. 'Here. There.'

'One day we're going to have a sensible conversation,' Coco replied. She then laughed. 'Well, not so much a sensible conversation. I'm not sure I'm capable of that, but a conversation nonetheless.'

Denis pointed again at the box. 'One day, but for now,' he extended his hand.

Coco flopped onto the box, emitting a heavy, prolonged sigh.

Denis' nose crinkled. He looked her up and down. 'You smell like shit,' he stated.

Coco pulled back her head and gawped at him. 'No offence, but you don't smell so hot yourself.'

Denis gestured around him. 'Oui, but d'oh! My only running water is from the overflow pipe, and I have a sneaky suspicion 1B is putting something extremely freaky down their sink.'

Coco stared at her boots. 'Look at these boots. They're my favourite shoes, but they've got more holes than Swiss cheese.' She laughed. 'Who am I kidding? They're my only shoes!'

Denis pointed at his own feet. 'Think you've got it tough. These shoes aren't even mine and they're four sizes too small!'

Coco shrugged her shoulders. 'What is this, a pissing contest to see who has the most fucked up life? Because believe me, I'm not sure you'd lose.'

Denis slugged her softly on her cheek. 'D'accord, get up to your lovely kids and give them cuddles. You'll feel better after that, you'll see.'

She nodded. She stared at him. 'Are you honestly okay, Denis?'

Denis pointed to the sky. 'Are you kidding? I've got that, I've got your company. I'm a lucky man.'

Coco struggled to her feet. 'Dieu, it gets harder every day to get up.'

'How's your day gone?' he asked.

'Same shit, people dead and no one wants to help.' She opened her bag and pulled out a piece of paper. 'And it seems this is all I have to go on.'

Denis narrowed his eyes, looking at the image on the photocopy. 'B4? What does that mean?'

Coco shrugged. 'As always - beats the hell out of me.'

'But it's important?' Denis asked.

'I don't know,' Coco replied. 'It's one of the few things I have to go on at the moment.'

Denis grabbed the paper and then pointed to the half-empty wine bottle nestled between his legs. 'I'll have a few more sips of this. That normally makes things more clear for me. Maybe I'll solve your problem for you.'

She laughed. 'If it was only that simple.' She moved towards the entrance to her building and turned back to him. 'Seriously though, you and I are going to have a serious chat one day soon. I hate you sleeping out here. There's got to be a better life for you.'

He lowered his head. 'Maybe this is what I deserve.'

Coco shook her head. 'I don't believe that, and that's why you and I are going to have a serious no bullshit talk very soon. D'accord?'

Denis smiled at her. 'I can't wait.'

BOULOT

MARDI
09H00

Coco trudged unhappily along the boulevard leading towards the Commissariat de Police du 7e arrondissement. It had been a particularly trying journey on the métro and one in which she had eyed everyone with suspicion and appraising them in case one sleeping commuter was, in fact, not sleeping at all. Her night had not been much better. She had slept fitfully, often awakened by sharp kicks in the ribs from Esther, but also disturbed by the glaring likelihood that Richard Severin's murder was going to prove very difficult to solve.

Despite Coco having instructed teams of police officers to canvas Severin's neighbourhood, they had found no witnesses, nor any real indication of what might have happened to Severin. The kidnapping of his granddaughter troubled Coco, primarily because it appeared Severin had known of it, and therefore it was feasible to assume wherever he was going on the métro, it had something to do with his granddaughter. Then what had gone so terribly wrong? And why were the kidnappers not stepping up their ransom demand? Coco knew there was something very amiss with the whole situation, but worried that the answer would not be forthcoming. They needed a break in the case, and they needed it quickly. Commander Demissy was already circling, no doubt about to ultimately level all the blame firmly on Coco's shoulders. Coco could just imagine the verbal diatribes heading her way from Demissy.

She stopped walking and pressed her left fingers against her temple and with her right, deftly extracted a cigarette. She dropped her hand, realising whatever cloud was in her head, it would not go away so easily. Moments later, the cigarette, already her fourth of the morning, was alight and soothing her. Her troubled nights were not just about work. Coco understood that. She had always compartmentalised the work part of her life, as troubling as it might be. It was in the dark of night when her other demons came. Her dreams were far ranging, from despair to downright pornographic. The previous night she had spent a few wonderful hours with a certain police Captain she had met the previous year. His name was Tomas Wall, and he was most likely perfect for her. But he was troubled. And the fact was, she had her own troubles, but more importantly, she had dealt with the troubles of enough men to know she could not take on any more. She could not allow herself, or her children's lives to be affected by someone else. In the end, however, it did not matter when she was at her most vulnerable. When she woke from her dreams, breathless and desperate and feeling more alone than ever, it was all she could do to stop herself from picking up her phone and calling him. In the end, she had thrown the phone to Helga, instructing her to keep it from her. The response had been less than kind.

Coco stepped across the road, dodging the cars which speeded past her. She gesticulated at a honking driver, pointing at the speed limit sign above her. 'You're speeding outside a goddamn police station, you moron!' she yelled. She continued ahead, hoping that when she finally made it into her office, the damn cleaner had not tossed away the remains of yesterday's half-eaten baguette. Coco stopped, noticing something on the opposite side of the road, directly opposite the entrance to the commissariat. Emma Fitzgerald, Richard Severin's British housekeeper, was standing stock-still on the sidewalk, staring ahead, her hand resting on her chin in contemplation.

What the hell is she up to? Coco wondered as she contemplated crossing the road and talking to her. Fitzgerald looked as if she was wrestling with something and Coco did not want to scare her away.

She also hated the fact that even so early in the morning Emma Fitzgerald looked as if she was catwalk ready, dressed in a flowing red dress that Coco was sure would have cost more than her monthly salary. *I wonder what she had to do for that,* Coco smirked.

The loud revving of a tinny-sounding engine stopped Coco in her tracks. It seemed to her mopeds overran the streets of Paris, and that most of the people riding them had little consideration of the people around them. She turned, ready to fix whoever was driving with an angry pout. The noise was deafening and annoying. She could not make out where it was coming from, other than it was moving fast. It took her a few moments to locate it. The moped was speeding along the opposite sidewalk, darting in-between people and the signs outside the shops and cafes. A woman screamed, and she jumped back inside the shop she had just come from. Coco yelled out even though she knew it was useless. Instead, she stepped into the street, but the traffic was busy from both sides. She yelled out again, waving her hands wildly hoping one of the cars would stop and allow her to cross the road. They did not, so she screamed into the air. The drivers ignored her, instead flashing an irritated glare as they sped past her.

Coco twisted her head to her right. Emma Fitzgerald was still staring at the commissariat, seemingly unaware of the nuisance moped fast approaching. Coco watched in horror as the scooter moved closer to Emma, hoping that Emma would finally break out of her trance and move out of the way. Even though it only took a matter of seconds, to Coco it all flashed by her in confusing slow motion, but she at least hoped that the maniac on the moped would do what he had done all along the sidewalk and that he would weave his way around her and veer back into the road.

Coco's heart stopped as she realised there was altogether something very different happening. The moped driver steered in Emma Fitzgerald's direction, twisting his body to the left. He let go of one handlebar and extended his arm and with a thrust pushed hard against Emma Fitzgerald's shoulder, projecting her directly onto the road into an oncoming car. Coco's hand flew to her mouth as she watched helplessly as Emma was struck and thrown like a rag-doll into the air, over the bonnet and roof of the car which had just hit her and into the path of the car behind. The second car screeched to a halt, but it was too late. The sound of the brakes and the smell of burning rubber hit Coco and she felt vomit rising into her throat. The second car skidded over Emma's body, throwing her into the air again. She crashed against the steps in front of the commissariat, a red high-heeled shoe falling back into the road, her eyes rolling backwards.

With all her might, Coco lurched forward into the street, her arms flailing widely in every direction as she screamed. She knew she should concentrate on the moped, which was screeching away, but she lowered her head and ran directly toward Emma Fitzgerald. 'Call the fucking pompiers!' she screamed into the air.

MARDI
10H00

Dr. Stella Bertram ran a small hand through short, dark hair and flashed Coco with a warm smile. 'You look well, Charlotte.'

Coco looked down at her dishevelled clothes, her mouth contorting into a grimace. She was, as seemed usual for her, covered in the blood of someone else. 'I look like someone dug me up and threw me into a rubbish tip,' she stated.

Stella shook her head. 'Non, you look the same as you always do.' She stopped, biting her lip, realising what she had said.

Coco guffawed. 'Hey, Stella - you've really got to work on your chatting up technique.'

The doctor blushed, her eyes quickly darting from side to side as if satisfying herself no one had overheard. She cleared her throat. 'I see you've had an eventful morning again.'

Coco flopped into a chair. She did not want to give it more thought. She had spent the journey to the hospital trying her best to recover her composure. She did not want to seem vulnerable, though it was not for the benefit of others. Her mask was to convince herself, not others. 'I have,' she began, before stopping abruptly, 'absolutely nothing constructive to say in response to that. Does your life ever feel like it's out of control, Stella?'

She shrugged. 'Only since I met you and you refused to acknowledge how useless men can be, and how *useful* I can be.'

Coco sighed. 'I have to say, I've tried dreaming about,' she lowered her voice and mouthed, 'women's bits, mais,' she shook her body with a shudder, 'it just feels a bit like I'd be too good at it.'

Stella raised an eyebrow. 'And you base that on what?'

Coco winked at her. 'In the one dream I had, you said you'd

hate every woman who ever touched you again after feeling my touch.' She spread her hands in front of her. 'Don't shoot the messenger, Stella. Your words, not mine.'

The doctor chuckled. 'As you are prone to say, Charlotte - I have seen your vagina.'

Coco frowned. 'What's that supposed to mean, don't you think there's anything special about my sugar walls?'

Stella pulled herself straight. 'Charlotte, your commander is standing behind you.'

Coco laughed. 'Nice try. Don't try to fob me off. You can't leave me hanging on like that when you've seen my goods...'

Commander Demissy cleared her throat. 'Captain Brunhild,' she said, her voice even and calm but with a frostiness which chilled Coco.

Coco remained rigid. She's really behind me, isn't she? she mouthed. 'This isn't just another waking nightmare where I always imagine she's following me around waiting for me to fuck up? She's really there?'

Stella nodded, lowering her head to cover her smile.

Coco turned slowly, forcing her mouth into the sweetest smile she could manage.

Demissy's eyes widened, focusing on Coco's mouth. 'You have something green stuck in your teeth, Captain?'

Coco lifted her finger and used it to wipe her teeth. 'I have eaten nothing green since the nineties,' she mumbled.

Commander Demissy clenched her fists. Coco watched her, wondering whether finally Demissy would leave the comfort of passive-aggressiveness.

'You disappoint me,' Demissy said instead.

Coco fought the urge to blow a raspberry. 'I have so many derogative things designated for my tombstone,' she said, 'but that is most certainly right up there.'

Demissy's eyes flicked over Coco. 'I'm going to have to be

the one to buy you a new coat, aren't I?'

Coco glanced down at it, offended. 'No need. It was already booked in for a deep clean by the forensics lab thanks to Richard Severin, now we've just saved a second go.'

Demissy sighed. 'I'm not able to deal with you right now. I don't have the strength.' She turned to Dr. Bertram. 'What can you tell me about the victim?'

Stella took a long breath. 'I was here when she was brought in,' she began. 'And I have to tell you if it wasn't for Captain Brunhild's quick thinking and ensuring that Mlle. Fitzgerald wasn't moved until the pompiers arrived, then the situation may have been much worse.'

Demissy flashed Coco with an irritated look. She turned back to the doctor. 'And how bad is it?'

Stella shrugged. 'I stabilised her as best I could,' she replied. 'But her injuries are very serious.'

'How serious?' Coco interrupted.

'She's in surgery now,' Stella replied, 'and she's likely to be there for some hours. She has multiple issues, some worse than others, but unless they can control the bleeding in her brain, then...' she trailed off.

'Then?' Demissy snapped.

'Then she's fucked,' Coco added.

Demissy tutted. 'What's the likelihood she'll survive, Dr. Bertram?'

'I can't say,' Stella replied. 'If she makes it through the surgery, she stands a chance, but if I were you, I wouldn't count on it from what I've seen of her scans. At the very least, she's unlikely to walk again, but as I say, the bleed to the brain is the most serious issue. If they don't deal with that, then nothing else matters really.'

'Damn,' Demissy hissed. 'Will she come around?'

Stella considered. 'Hard to say. But if she does, it won't be for at least twenty-four to forty-eight hours.'

The commander took a deep breath. She turned to Coco. 'And what do you have to say about all of this?'

Coco felt her hackles rising, realising she was about to reach her limit of taking the blame for something that was out of her hands. She looked at Demissy and realised that rising to her was something she could only do when her options were limited. In this instance, she reasoned, there was nothing, could have been nothing she could have done to prevent what happened to Emma Fitzgerald. Demissy was going to have to accept, eventually, that blaming Coco for everything was not only too easy, it was something that would ultimately be her own downfall. That was, at least, the reasoning behind the thought which expressed itself into her mouth. 'Well, I was hoping the kid would fall off his moped and I could have nabbed it for my kid's birthday.'

Demissy tutted again. 'And you didn't get a look at the driver?' she asked with irritation.

Coco held her gaze, fighting the urge to retort sarcastically. 'He, or she, was dressed all in black with a black helmet. I'm afraid I left my x-ray specs at home this morning, or I would have been able to tell you more.' She bit her lip upon noticing Stella's alarmed expression. 'What I can tell you is that he, or she, wasn't very tall, or fat, and was wearing white sneakers,' she added.

Demissy raised an eyebrow. 'How do you know any of that?'

Coco smiled demurely. 'Well, if their ass fit on a moped, they weren't fat.'

'What does that tell us?' Demissy considered.

Coco shrugged. 'That they weren't fat. obvs.'

'None of the other witnesses reported any of those facts,' Demissy said wearily.

Coco shrugged. 'They're not me, are they? I'm paid to be observant,' she stated proudly. 'And I'm bloody good at it.'

Demissy flashed her a doubtful look. 'And yet you didn't manage to get to her in time to save her life, it appears.'

'If there was any life to save,' Stella interrupted, sending Coco a dirty look, 'it was down to Captain Brunhild's quick thinking that the poor woman is alive at all,' she reiterated.

'That's all very well,' Demissy snapped. 'What the hell was Emma Fitzgerald doing outside the commissariat, of all places?'

'She was coming to tell us something,' Coco answered.

Demissy pulled back her head. 'You can't know that.'

Coco laughed. 'Then what else can we assume? She was hanging out on the corner of a police station looking for a flic who wanted a good time?'

'Captain,' Demissy warned.

Coco shook her head. 'I saw the bastard running her off the sidewalk into oncoming traffic. I saw the poor woman d...' she stopped, her breath laboured. 'I saw the poor woman thrown in front of a car.'

Demissy nodded. 'I told you, I've read the witness reports,' she responded. 'And as far as I can tell, there was a maniac on the sidewalk and Mlle. Fitzgerald was tragically caught in the way.'

'Then you obviously haven't read my statement,' Coco snapped.

Demissy pulled out her cell phone, holding it close to her face. She coughed and then began reading. 'Captain Charlotte Brunhild stated that the punk bitch slapped the broad into oncoming traffic.'

Coco nodded. 'I rest my case,' she agreed.

Demissy sighed. 'I beg you, Captain, stop making me sigh. It's boring and I have little time for it.'

Coco shrugged. 'What are you worried about? Wrinkles? Crinkles?' She recoiled from the commander's fierce look. 'What about the cameras outside the station? Have you had a chance to look at them?'

'They more or less confirm what you said,' Demissy replied with obvious reluctance. 'Black helmet, black leather jacket, black or blue jeans.'

'And the trainers?' Coco asked.

'I didn't notice anything particular or unusual about them,' Demissy responded.

'And what about a license plate? Did the cameras pick it up?' Coco continued. 'I didn't see one.'

Commander Demissy shook her head. 'Because there didn't appear to be one. I have officers trying to trace what happened to the moped afterwards, though I suspect it will prove to be a fool's errand.' She stepped away. 'Dr. Bertram, please call me the second there is an update.'

Stella nodded. 'Oui, bien sûr.' Coco and Stella watched Demissy stride away. 'Does she always walk as if she's stabbing her stilettos into the ground?' the doctor asked.

Coco laughed. 'Yeah. I suspect she imagines it's me beneath her.'

Stella's tongue darted playfully across her lips. 'We all imagine that, dear Charlotte.'

Coco turned her head, hoping to hide her blushes. *If only I could change my ways,* she thought with sadness before shaking her head and imagining what it would be like, *nah*; she shivered. 'I'd better go,' she groaned.

Stella touched her arm. 'Don't give up hope, as my mother used to say, where there's life there's hope.'

'Hmm,' Coco purred. 'Well, I wanted a break in the case. I'll have to be more careful what I wish for next time, because I may just have gotten one. Merci, Stella. Keep in touch.'

'Toujours, Charlotte, *toujours*.'

MARDI
10H30

Coco sighed wearily as image after image moved past her on the computer screen. A cornucopia of scumbags in rapid succession offended her retinas. She closed her eyes briefly, but she still saw them. The lowlifes of Paris, many of whom she had busted herself. She found she could remember their voices - filled with sneer and grievance, and their smells, B.O mixed with contempt and loathing. She opened her eyes and continued scrolling, stopping over one particular man. She remembered him instantly, and she remembered him well. He smelled different, a sweet musk, and his tone was as smooth as the baby skin on his face. She had watched him in her rear-view mirror as she drove them to the commissariat, and he watched her back. If it was not for the fact she had just arrested him for busting ten high-end cars, their journey was likely to have had a very different sort of ending. She blew a kiss at the screen and continued.

Jihef Abreo. His name and image flashed before her, and she knew instantly it was him. Shoulder length braids and cold, deceitful eyes. His mouth was twisted into a cruel smirk. *Jihef Abreo*. A bust sheet as long as her arm. Drugs, racketeering and running a brothel. Then something caught her eyes. *Kidnapping*. She took a sharp intake of breath. Caroline Severin's pimp-slash-dealer had been arrested for, amongst all his other crimes, kidnapping.

Coco clicked on the "more info" button and waited. Nothing happened. She clicked again. *Access Denied*. 'What the fuck do you mean, access denied?' she hissed. She looked up and noticed Commander Demissy was outside her office talking with Cedric. Coco gestured for them to come into her office.

'What is it, Captain?' Demissy exhaled. 'I'm very busy.'

Coco pointed at her screen. 'Look at this.'

Demissy and Cedric moved behind her. Coco's nose crinkled. 'You stink, Lieutenant Degarmo,' she cried.

Cedric stepped backwards. 'Yeah, well, someone was supposed to come and relieve me first thing so I could go home to shower and change.'

'Yeah, sorry about that,' Coco responded. 'I was rather busy trying to save someone's life.'

'So I heard,' he quipped.

'I am sorry, though. You must be tired,' Coco added sincerely.

He shrugged nonchalantly. 'It doesn't matter. Ebba and I took turns sleeping for a couple of hours because absolutely nothing happened all night.'

'What did you want to show me, Captain?' Demissy interjected impatiently.

Coco pointed at the screen again. 'This creep is the one I saw last night at the squat.'

'The one who you believe knows Caroline Severin?'

'Yeah. That's the charmer,' Coco answered. 'But look what happens when I click on more info.'

They watched as the *access denied* screen appeared again. 'Well, that's odd,' Demissy mused. 'Move out of the way,' she gestured, taking the keyboard and entering her ID number. The message appeared again. Demissy's eyebrows raised. 'Well, that's very interesting.'

'Why would some low-level drug dealer's details be hidden?' Cedric posed.

Coco and Demissy looked at one another. 'I can only think of two reasons,' Coco replied. 'He's either an informant or…'

'Or what?' Cedric interjected.

'Or he's something else altogether,' Coco replied cryptically.

Demissy moved towards the doorway. 'Give me ten minutes, I'll make a few calls.'

Coco and Cedric watched as the commander left. Coco sniggered.

'What's funny?' Cedric asked.

Coco shrugged. 'Oh nothing, just something about the way the commander walks in her stilettos.'

He frowned. 'What about it?'

Coco smiled. 'On nothing, it's just a lesbian thing…'

'Oh, Dieu, don't tell me you've finally slept with all the men in Paris, so you're starting on the chicks?'

She punched his arm. 'Don't be rude and don't call us chicks.' She shook her head. 'Where was I? What was I talking about?'

'You were talking about the lowlife you met last night,' Cedric prompted.

Coco snorted. 'Well, that could be the story of my life,' she snipped, before adding, 'according to you, at least.' She paused. 'His name is, or at least it might be, Jihef Abreo. And look here at his rap sheet.'

Cedric stared at the screen. 'Kidnapping.'

She nodded. 'Exactement. Mais…'

'Mais, quoi?' Cedric questioned.

'Mais, there's something wrong with this picture,' Coco replied. 'In more ways than one.'

'Do you think Emma Fitzgerald was deliberately targeted?' he asked.

Coco considered her answer. 'Well, under the circumstances, we certainly can't rule it out,' she stated finally. 'I mean, I watched the creep on the moped and he veered his way around plenty of other people on the sidewalk, and though it happened so quickly, he most definitely pushed her into oncoming traffic. I watched the CCTV footage myself. It's quite clear.'

Cedric nodded. 'That still doesn't mean it was deliberate. He could have just been pushing some random chick… désolé, femme, out of his way.'

'You're right,' Coco conceded. 'But I don't believe in coincidences. Which brings us to the crucial point. What the hell was Emma Fitzgerald doing outside the commissariat. I saw her and I'm certain she was wrestling with something.'

'Wrestling with something?' Cedric questioned. 'It's possible. I told you last night I got the sense she wanted to say something, or ask something.' He shook his head angrily. 'I knew it, and I should have pressed the point, but with everything going on, I didn't think that…'

Coco raised her hands. 'You couldn't know what was going to happen. None of us could,' she reasoned. 'And besides, whatever was going on with Miss Downton Abbey, she had plenty of opportunities to come forward and spill her guts.' She took a deep breath. 'Nothing about this damn investigation is going to be easy, is it?'

'They never are, not really,' Cedric reasoned.

The telephone on Coco's desk rang. 'Allô?' she answered. 'Ah, he is, merci. Send him up to my office.' She replaced the receiver. 'Emile Severin is here - maybe finally he is going to come clean with me.'

Cedric nodded. 'Do you want me to stay?'

'Non, it's okay,' Coco replied. 'Go home, take a goddamn shower, and meet me back here in an hour or so and then we'll go back to the Severin house. I want to shake Mona Gagnon's cage a little, see what it is she's hiding.'

'Does she know about Emma?'

'Oui. I think so, at least. Demissy told Horst Lavigne, and he said he was going to pass it on,' Coco replied. 'I rather wish she hadn't, because I would have liked to break the news to both of them myself, just to see their reactions.'

'You think they're involved?'

She shrugged. 'I don't know what to think, right now, but I can't ignore the fact I don't trust either of them a bit.' She waved towards the door. 'Go. Shower, masturbate, whatever you need to do.'

He shook his head. 'I hate you.'

Coco smiled. 'Non, you don't. Just remember, if my face is the one you see when you… you know, then well, you are a man of exceptional taste.'

Cedric yanked open the door. 'I'd rather be blind,' he muttered.

MARDI
11H00

Emile Severin sat opposite Coco. He shuffled uncomfortably on the ripped leather seat. He crossed his legs, then uncrossed them, and then crossed them again. Each time, Coco noted, muscular thighs straining against too-tight denim.

'What I'm about to tell you is not something I believe had anything to do with my father's murder,' he began.

Well, you would say that. 'Are you sure?' Coco interrupted.

He stared at her as if he did not understand the question. 'The only thing I'm sure of is that I don't want to be here in front of you,' he stated, before adding with a broad smile, 'no offence.'

Coco smiled sweetly. 'None taken. Believe me, I get that a lot.' She cocked her head. 'Then why are you here, exactly?'

'Because I spoke with Horst Lavigne an hour ago, and my worst fears were confirmed,' he replied.

'You're going to have to level with me, kid,' Coco said, clasping her hands together. 'Because you've gotta know, I have a thousand different thoughts bouncing around in my head trying to work out what the hell was up with your family, but I have to be honest, I'm finding you all hard to read, and that's unusual for me.'

He smiled. 'The Severin family are masters of subterfuge. It was fed to us in our baby bottles. We smile at you with a lie in our mouth and a knife in our hand.' He stopped suddenly, his mouth twisting. 'Bad choice of words, désolé.'

'What happened to you all?' Coco pressed. 'Because I don't understand.'

Emile scoffed. 'And you think I do?' He stood and began pacing the threadbare carpet in Coco's office. 'I lived it, and I <u>really</u>

don't understand it.'

Coco suppressed a sigh. She was used to over dramatics, particularly from those born into wealth, but in this instance, she hoped that was all it was with Emile Severin, because she worried the actual truth may be horrendous. She took a deep breath. 'Did your father sexually abuse you and your sister? Is that it? One of you, or maybe both of you?'

Emile sat down again. 'Our father was a bastard. A complete bastard, but not that kind of bastard. Instead, he was "just" cruel and manipulative.' He paused, manicured nails scratching at his head. 'I'll give you an example. When Caroline was twelve, she got into a fight with another girl at school and she ended up with her two front teeth knocked out. Our father was annoyed. Annoyed, he had to leave his office and go to the school to deal with her. A few nights later he had one of his precious parties at the house, and the kids would be wheeled out by Emma Fitzgerald in all our finery and smile, Caroline was supposed to curtsy, you know the sort of thing, like some fucking warped re-enactment of the Von Trapp family,' he continued, waving his hand dismissively. 'That night we came down as usual, but Caroline had removed her temporary fillings because she said they were uncomfortable. She smiled, and of course, everyone at the party laughed at this cute little girl in her white taffeta dress and tiara but with her two front teeth missing. I'm sure they all thought it was adorable.' He stopped, lowering his head as if the weight of the memory was painful.

When he raised his head again, Coco noticed his eyes were flecked with anger.

'The only person who wasn't laughing was our father,' Emile continued. 'And by the look on his face, I knew what it meant, as young as I was. Mais, by that point in her childhood, I think Caroline had just got to a point where she just didn't care anymore about him, or what he could do to her. She'd always been a bit of a wild child, or "wilful and disobedient" as he liked to call her. Our mother was gone, but when she had been there, I think father kept her away from us as much as he could like he was jealous of the attention taken away from him, or some weird shit like that. We were raised by governesses, and it seemed father chose them based solely upon how cold and rigid they were. I'm sure he told them to be cruel because they most certainly were. In the end, it seemed I could be trained, but Caroline could not.'

Coco stared at him. Her childhood had been far from rosy, but despite how she felt about her parents, their shortcomings were just that - human shortcomings. The mistakes of men and women whose behaviours, needs and desires did not change just because they had become parents. Often it seemed there was no magic gene that kicked in when you were presented with a screaming baby. Love does not always come naturally. Coco had seen that firsthand, time after time. Whatever Richard Severin's public face had been, Coco suspected there was an altogether different beast lurking in his shadows.

'That night, after the party had finished is when it all started for real,' Emile went on, his voice breaking as he spoke. 'The house was quiet when he came up. My bedroom was next to Caroline's, and I'd been waiting for him. The parties always seemed to go on a long time, and even then I knew that meant it would give his anger longer to fester and grow. His steps were light, but I heard every one of them, every creak of the floorboards as he crept up the stairs. And then he was in her room. The first slap was always to the face, but it was light so as not to leave a mark. Afterwards, he would move on to other parts of the body which he could mark, and he certainly did, the ferocity of which dictated only by his temper and how much we resisted.'

Emile swallowed air into his lungs. 'I learnt very quickly not to resist, and certainly not to cry out, and as I was reasonably well behaved, my beatings were few and far between. Caroline, on the other hand, was not only unafraid, she was also challenging. He stopped by my door and I could see in the shadows his hand hovering over the doorknob. But he didn't come in. Instead, he pulled it closed and locked it. That's when I knew what was coming next would not be pleasant.'

Coco reached for her cigarettes. 'Want one?'

Emile nodded, and Coco tossed him the packet and lighter. She inhaled her own. 'I'm not supposed to smoke in here,' she quipped.

Emile gave her a sad smile. 'I get the impression, you do a lot of things you're not supposed to.' He gulped. 'You remind me of Caroline a lot.'

'Is that a good thing?'

He shrugged. 'Oui. I think so. Whatever problems my sister has, she didn't get there on her own.'

'What happened next?' Coco asked.

'He went into her room and I heard the first slap, and she laughed,' Emile continued. 'I thought that was going to make it worse. It usually did. But there was something different that night. When my father spoke, his voice was as cold as ice. *You want to look like a homeless witch, then you don't do it in my house in front of my friends.* Then I heard scraping, and suddenly Caroline was screaming. *You're pulling my hair out!* I jumped up, banging on my door, but he yelled at me to get back in bed and shut my mouth or I'd get the same as Caroline. I was terrified, as always, so I did as I was told. It wasn't long before the dragging stopped and they both were gone.'

Coco drew anxiously on the cigarette. 'Where did they go?'

Emile turned away. 'We had a private courtyard behind the house. I heard the door open and a ruckus so I looked out of the window. *You want to look like a homeless person, then you'd better get used to living like one.* I heard him slam the door, and I heard her cry and scream, and then bitch and complain. That went on for an hour and she stopped, probably because she realised it was no good and that her protests would probably only bring on more punishment.'

He paused. 'I should point out this was his annual Christmas party. This happened on Christmas Eve.'

Coco felt bile rise in her throat. In her mind's eye, she saw the dust jacket photograph of Richard Severin, smiling for the camera. The people's champion, eyes twinkling. 'She stayed out all night?' she asked softly.

'There was a secret way out of the courtyard,' Emile answered. 'We'd found it years earlier, a tiny crawl through under the hedges, large enough only for animals and small kids. Caroline squeezed through. That time, she was gone for four nights and three days. It was only when she was due to go back to school that my father became concerned. I don't know what he did, or how he did it, though I imagine he had some of his lackeys track her down. He certainly knew plenty of shady people. Anyway, they found her and dragged her home, and that was the end of it, for that time at least.'

'Did she tell you where she'd been?' Coco asked.

He shook his head, a cloud appearing on his face. 'We used to talk all the time, but something changed then. She had changed,' he responded. 'We weren't the same. I think she thought I'd let her down, because of course, I had.'

'You were a kid,' Coco pointed out. 'You both were.'

'Not Caroline. She never really was.'

Coco frowned. 'What about your aunt or the other staff? Didn't they see any of this going on?'

Emile laughed. 'Bien sûr, they did. The staff were paid to look the other way, I guess, and tante Mona... well, I never really figured her out, if I'm honest.'

Coco nodded. 'I'm having trouble with that myself. As far as I can tell, there was no love lost between her and your father.'

'That's an understatement,' he snorted.

'Then why did she stay with him all this time?' Coco asked. 'I mean, I get it if it was about protecting you kids, but if she wasn't even doing that…'

He shrugged. 'I suppose I always thought she hung around because she believed my mother would come back, or…'

'She believed your father had something to do with it?' Coco concluded.

'Maybe. We weren't close, so we never talked about it,' Emile stated simply. 'All I really remember about Mona is that she was always standing in doorways like she was watching or listening. She never really paid any attention to me or my sister. I mean, she was just like him in that respect. It seemed she liked to *appear* to care about us, mais I'm not sure she ever did. Of course, I imagine my father enjoyed having her around because it made him look like a good guy. The sainted widower who took in his dead wife's spinster sister was how he spun it.' He stopped, considering something. 'Do you know, I don't ever remember them having a genuine conversation. I mean, they talked, but it was always about household stuff. I don't think there was ever anything real between them.'

'Other than hatred?'

He shrugged again. 'I guess so. I mean, I get why she may have hated him, but I'm not sure why he would have hated her.'

Coco considered. 'Peut être she was a reminder of something, the past, something that happened.'

Emile locked eyes with her, and Coco felt sure she understood the message that passed between them. *I'm not going to answer that question.* She took a deep breath. He was talking, and she did not want to stop him, but the thought that he was only telling her half the story was already niggling away at her. 'When Caroline came back, what happened next?'

Emile tapped his fingers on the side of the desk. He swallowed. 'Father built a brick wall around the courtyard to keep her in. In the end, though, it didn't matter. The older Caroline got, the stronger and more determined she became. Father eventually realised he couldn't punish her in the way he wanted to, so he stopped trying and I guess he stopped caring to even bother. She snuck out, or just plain didn't come home more and more often after that, until it became so routine nobody noticed anymore.' He flashed a reluctant look. 'I suppose in his own way, Richard tried to help her, getting her into rehab, that sort of thing. But it always seemed half-hearted to me, like he was doing his duty, or just that he realised he was fighting a losing battle. Either way, the truth was, he had lit the fuse, which catapulted Caroline out of his house and into her own private hell.'

A silence descended. Coco studied Emile's face. The small lines around his eyes were the only things to spoil a perfect face, and she wondered if that was where he hid all his demons. 'What did you have to tell me about your son, Timo?' she asked gently.

Emile turned back to face her but said nothing.

Coco played with her hair. 'I realise this is difficult,' she said.

'You have no idea,' he snorted.

She nodded. 'I think I do. Timo isn't your son, is he? He's your brother, or rather, half-brother.'

Emile's eyes widened. He was clearly taken aback. 'How on earth do you know that?'

Coco raised her hands in an attempt to pacify him. 'Don't worry, nobody else suspects. It's just a hunch.'

'Damn good hunch,' he grumbled.

She shook her head. 'How the hell did you end up raising your brother as your son?'

'Wouldn't you?' he retorted. 'I couldn't leave Timo to relive mine or Caroline's childhood. That was never an option. Timo was the result of an affair my father had. An affair with someone less than fitting for his perfect image, I guess. So my father did what he did best to hide a scandal. He threw his money around. The mother went off to live the high life in the United States, I think, and he kept Timo. I don't know what he would have done with him, to be honest, other than he had made it clear he would never acknowledge him as his own. I was seventeen when Timo was born, and I was on my own and that had given me a certain amount of strength I never had before. I may have had nothing, but giving up what I had, I realised I had everything.'

Coco pulled back her shoulders. She understood exactly what he meant. She had walked away from a comfortable life whilst a teenager and pregnant because it had seemed to be the only choice to make at that moment. Despite the hard times which followed, she realised she had never regretted that decision.

Emile continued. 'I told my father I would take Timo and claim him as my own, but that I would only do it on two conditions. The first was that he never bothered either of us again or tried to get in touch with us, and two, that he made sure Timo was acknowledged in his will.' He stared at Coco. 'Please don't judge me. I didn't want anything from my father for myself, but I couldn't make that decision for Timo when he was a baby and couldn't make that decision himself.'

'And your father kept his word?'

Emile nodded. 'Bien sûr, he did. He wasn't a fool. He got rid of two of his biggest secrets in one go. It was a win-win for him.'

Coco considered. 'But Timo is in the will?'

'Oui, Horst confirmed it,' Emile replied. He snorted. 'He also confirmed there is a stipulation that Timo only gets his inheritance so long as he never reveals the actual truth of his birth.'

'I'm no avocat,' Coco said. 'Mais, I'm fairly sure that wouldn't hold up in a court. Kids have rights, especially the right to be acknowledged.'

Emile shrugged as if he could not care less. 'I don't think it matters. All I wanted was for Timo to get what he deserves, and I doubt he'll want to shout from the rooftops who his real father was.' He bit his lip. 'I know he comes across as a little abrasive, and believe me, he's hellish to live with sometimes, but underneath it all, he's a pretty decent kid.'

Coco smiled at him, thinking of her children. 'Oh, believe me, I get you. Kids sometimes make you work to see their light, but if you look hard enough, they can't always hide it. You did well by him, I'm sure of that. And not just by getting him away from your father, but by giving him a life away from that house. I can imagine it wasn't very easy.'

He laughed. 'You have no idea. But I have no regrets. I wish I could have taken Laure, but that was out of my hands.' He paused. 'You see why I didn't think this had anything to do with my father's murder?'

Coco stared at him. She was not sure of that at all. 'Is there a chance Timo could have known Richard Severin was his real father?'

Emile's nostrils flared. 'If you're suggesting what I think you are, then I have to tell you, you're way off base. There's no way Timo could have known. Who would have told him? I didn't, and my father certainly wouldn't.'

'Who else knew about it?'

Emile considered. 'Horst Lavigne took care of all the paperwork and the payoffs. Apart from that, there was only me.'

'What about your aunt and Emma Fitzgerald?'

He shrugged. 'I didn't tell them, and as I said, I can't imagine for a second my father would have.'

'And your sister?' Coco asked.

Emile nodded slowly. 'Yeah, she knew. But honestly, I can't imagine how that would make a difference. She's barely seen Timo his whole life, and as I remember it when she overheard me and my father arguing about it, she was high. The likelihood is she probably doesn't even remember anything about it.'

Or she remembered exactly, and had used it as a bargaining chip to extract money from her father, Coco considered. And then there was Emile's assertion that his aunt, Mona Gagnon, was always lingering in the doorway, listening. The same could undoubtedly be said about Emma Fitzgerald. She stared at Emile, and as much as she liked him, she remained convinced there were truths still being hidden.

'How did Timo take the news?' Coco asked.

'Well, he liked the fact he'd just come into a lot of money,' Emile laughed, before his face clouded. 'But he's pissed at me for not telling him the truth. I told him I did it because I thought it was for the best, and that I was saving him from our father.'

Coco nodded. 'And you were. He'll see that in time, I'm sure.'

Emile cupped his hands behind his neck. 'Yeah, probably, but Timo says he had a right to know his father and that I had no right to keep them apart.'

'And did you?'

He shook his head. 'I kept myself away from my father, but I always made it clear to him that the door was open for him to see Timo. He chose not to.'

'Did you tell Timo that?'

'How could I?' Emile retorted. 'All he knows about Richard Severin is that he was some rich, old dude who everyone thought was a saint.'

'Even you?' Coco asked. 'What did you tell Timo about Richard when he was growing up?'

'I never told him the truth,' he replied. 'I couldn't do that to him. I figured the best way to lie to him was by telling a lie that was based on truth. I told him my sexuality was not in keeping with the Richard Severin idea of how a man should act. The best I could do was to try and keep him away from him and make sure he was safe and that when our father was gone, he'd get what he deserved.' He swallowed. 'I thought I was doing the right thing, but seeing how angry Timo was at never knowing his father, now I'm not so sure.'

Coco shook her head. 'You can't second guess yourself,' she

said calmly. 'You did what you thought was best, and judging by what you said, I can't say I disagree with you. Timo will come around, especially when he has some bucks of his own in his bank account.'

'He can't touch it until he's eighteen, so he has two years to torture me,' Emile concluded with a wry smile.

'Did Timo never ask about his mother when he was growing up?'

'Non,' Emile replied. 'I told him she was a girl I met at a party and that it lasted as long as my dabble in heterosexuality and that having a kid didn't fit into her life plan. He never asked about her again. There was nothing true I could tell him about his real mother because I never met her.'

Not so surprising, Coco thought, recalling her own experience. Her eldest children, Barbra and Julien, both had different fathers who were not in their lives. Coco had left her hometown at nineteen years old, leaving Barbra's father behind. They had both been young, and she saw no reason for them both to be chained to each other purely because of a child. It was a decision that still came to haunt Coco during nights when she could not sleep. But it was done and there was no going back. She had met Julien's father shortly after arriving in Paris and when she told him she was pregnant, the thought of raising his own child alongside another man's had proven too much for him. Coco had never seen or heard from him again. Barbra and Julian had grown without their father and as far as Coco could make out, they did not appear to have felt they had missed out on something. Times had changed, she supposed, and single-parent families were not the taboo they once were.

'He'll get over it,' Coco said reassuringly. 'And like you said, if he doesn't, he's rich. By the way, how rich are we talking?'

'Five million euros.'

Coco gasped. 'Wow! And you?'

Emile laughed. 'Rien. Not a cent.'

Cocos's face clouded. 'Oh, désolé.'

He slumped his shoulders. 'I wasn't expecting it, so it's no great loss.'

Coco was not sure she would feel the same. 'Well, you could always write a "Papa Dearest" sort of tell-all book,' she reasoned. 'What about your sister?'

'The same, nothing,' he replied. 'Her daughter will get five million when she reaches eighteen, as well.'

Coco bit her lip. Five million reasons someone might just have had to kidnap her. She stole a look at Emile. She liked him, and she wanted to trust him, but it was clear that he was angry at his father, and no doubt hurt, and to have been left out of his will could have been the final straw. It was understandable, hell; it was *more* than understandable as far as Coco was concerned. There was something she was missing, a piece of the puzzle that she hoped would fall into place.

'And what about your aunt and Emma Fitzgerald?' she asked. 'Are they in the will?'

'I have no idea,' Emile answered. 'You'd have to ask, Horst. He looked after all that. I do not know who my father would leave his money to. I know he gave a lot of it away, but that was only because he still had enough squirrelled away to last him a dozen lifetimes, I suppose.'

Coco nodded. She wanted to believe Emile Severin had nothing to do with his father's murder, but she knew she could not, because although she had nothing to go on, she felt the truth was still bubbling away beneath the surface.

Emile clambered to his feet. 'I'd better get back to Timo. I don't want him to be on his own right now.'

'Bien sûr,' Coco replied.

He stopped by the doorway and turned back to face her. 'I know you must have your suspicions about us all,' he stated.

Coco laughed lightly. 'Hey, suspicion is my middle name. I find it easier not to trust anyone, especially men.'

He smiled. 'Well, I'm with you on that one. The last man I dated turned out to be an undercover reporter trying to get the dirt on my father. He was writing a book about him.'

Coco pushed herself back in her chair. 'A book?'

Emile nodded. 'Yeah. And not the sort of book my father would have approved of, either. He was never good with the truth.'

Coco bit the tip of a pen, sensing she had just discovered something important. 'What was this reporter called?'

'Yannick Vidal,' Emile replied. 'Long blond hair, blue eyes, glorious body. Everything I look for in a guy. It was like he knew exactly what buttons to press.'

She scribbled down the name. 'Do you know how to get in touch with him?' she asked.

'Non,' Emile replied. 'I had a cell phone number for him, but once I told him to get lost, I regretted it after a few too many glasses of wine, so I called him, mais the number was already disconnected.' He sighed. 'I can pick them. The prick even went to the trouble of sleeping with me to get the gossip. The sad thing is, I would have probably told him anyway if only he'd been honest upfront. As you can guess, I wouldn't have been averse to helping ruin my father.' He exhaled. 'Yeah, I can certainly pick the winners.'

Coco flicked her hair over her shoulders. 'That's nothing. The last man I slept with is serving life for murder and child kidnapping and sexual assault.'

Emile held up his hands. 'D'accord, you win!'

Coco watched him leave. 'Yeah, that's me, a real winner,' she mumbled before reaching for her cigarettes.

MARDI
11H30

Coco stared at the ever-increasing amount of files on her desk. Files she knew all demanded every bit of her time and attention, neither of which she had in abundance. She had asked Commander Demissy for help, and it had been greeted with the typical reaction of bureaucracy. *Do more with less, or else.* One of these days, I'll have to take a good long look at my life, Coco thought, knowing it was something she could never really do for fear of what it might mean for her. The fact remained, she did not know what else she could do with her life, and she believed that despite appearances to the contrary, being a flic was something she was reasonably good at it. And being good at something which had the potential to help others made up for a lot of inconsistencies in Coco's life.

Commander Demissy threw open the door into Coco's office with such force it reverberated against the wall.

'You gotta check your attitude before you get in here,' Coco warned, 'because it's only going to get worse when you cross the threshold.'

Demissy's eyes rolled. 'Don't you think I know that? I've spent almost a year working with you, and all I can tell you is this - it feels much longer.'

Coco pointed at the pile of files. 'And yet, I appear to have a pretty damn impressive closure rate, despite the fact that I run a department with only one lieutenant.'

Demissy stared at her. 'Impressive is a stretch.'

'As is the fact you spend most of your day telling me how rotten I am, with no apparent evidence.'

Demissy raised an eyebrow, studying Coco with interest. 'You're feeling brave today, Captain.'

Coco shook her head. 'Not at all. I'm pissed off, tired, and I have raging…'

Demissy raised her hands. 'I beg you, say no more.'

Coco laughed. 'I was going to say raging PMT, but yeah, I got the other rage too, not that I can do anything about that.'

Demissy threw herself into a chair, her nose wrinkling by the sudden gust of stale air released beneath her. She smoothed her hijab. 'I don't know what it is about our relationship that makes you think I have any interest in hearing anything from you other than your professional opinion,' she paused as if for drastic effect, 'and even that is a stretch.'

Coco smiled. 'See, that was almost funny. And I reckon you're coming round to actually liking me.'

'Then you reckon wrong,' Demissy replied, her eyes crossing. 'Mon Dieu, you've even got me talking like you.'

'I am catching,' Coco replied. 'Anyway, as nice as this bonding session is… What about Jihef Abreo?'

'Therein lies a mystery,' Demissy answered. 'Someone big in the drugs division has blocked access to his records. That's all I've ascertained so far. I've put in a call to the commander in charge of that division, but he seems reluctant to return my call.' She paused. 'But while I was waiting, I looked further at Abreo's record, because there was something about it which struck me as odd.'

'Odd?' Coco questioned.

'Oui,' Demissy nodded. 'All his criminal records say is that he was charged with kidnapping a woman called Theresa Marteau. It struck me as odd, and then I realised why. It was because I recognised the name.'

'You did? From where?' Coco asked in surprise.

'Because Theresa Marteau doesn't exist,' Demissy stated with a knowing smile. 'I know because I created her.'

Coco scratched her head. 'I don't get it.'

Demissy smiled proudly. 'Before I got this post, I was given the "challenging" office job of commanding a specialist department in the bowels of the 5e commissariat. Amongst our "challenging" remits, we looked after informants - checking on them, paying them, etc. I imagine they thought I'd get bored and leave or something, but it only gave me the resolution to do my very best. Part of my job was to create false records so that if anyone looked, it would appear that the person they were looking into was a bad guy.'

'Then Jihef Abreo is an informant.'

Demissy stared at her. 'Either that, or he was undercover,' she replied. 'I created false records for a lot of people. Theresa Marteau was used to describe a crime that was committed by someone using or selling drugs - an innocent tourist kidnapped for her money, abused and generally mistreated. The idea was to make the perp look like he was a tough guy.'

'Then a cop, or an informant,' Coco mused. 'That's a pretty big difference, and it would really help if we knew which.'

Demissy nodded. 'Je sais. I'll keep up the pressure. Somebody has to know something, and they can't ignore me forever.' She placed her hand on her hip. 'I can be persistent when I need to be.'

Coco's lips twisted. 'Do you think it could have something to do with Richard Severin's murder?'

Demissy shrugged. 'I don't see how necessarily, but I can certainly use that to force them to tell us what they're up to. What was your impression of him?'

Coco considered her answer. 'He was a twat,' she answered simply. 'And he was antisemitic, but I suppose in the cold light of day, it's hard to tell whether that was his true character or an act.'

'He could have spotted you were a flic and played upon it.'

Coco nodded. 'Yeah, or he could just be a twat. Lots of flics are.'

The door to Coco's office opened and Cedric bustled in.

'Speaking of…' Coco began.

'Lieutenant Degarmo,' Demissy interrupted. 'You could have had more of a rest.'

Cedric shrugged. 'I'm young. I don't need much rest,' he stated, his eyes flicking over Coco.

Coco appraised him. 'You look and smell better.'

'Give me ten minutes next to you and that'll soon change,' he retorted. There was no maliciousness to his tone, only a playfulness.

Coco stuck out her tongue. Demissy sighed. 'You realise we are nowhere with this entire investigation. We are no further forward in understanding what happened to Richard Severin, or where his granddaughter is, or what happened to Emma Fitzgerald. The Minister is breathing down my neck as it is. He wants this closed by morning.'

Coco blew a raspberry. 'Tell Jean Lenoir he can…'

'Expect our full cooperation,' Demissy added with a tight smile. 'I'm sure he will be thrilled to hear that. I think he hopes that this is just a random attack on the métro. I can't say I disagree with him.'

Coco looked down. She almost hoped for that herself, but yet she did not believe it was going to be that simple. 'It's possible, I suppose,' she agreed, 'mais, until we know what happened to the kid, and what Richard Severin knew about it, I don't think we can write this off as some random attack.'

After a few moments, Cedric cleared his throat. 'On my way up, I checked in with the guys in camera operations,' he interrupted. 'They followed the moped into the Panteré banlieue.'

'Bollocks!' Coco exclaimed.

'Bollocks?' Demissy repeated.

Coco chuckled. 'Ha. It sounds funny coming from you.'

Demissy turned to Cedric. 'What does bollocks mean?'

Coco chuckled again, holding her ribs. 'Stop it!' she cried, before repeating the word twice in an affected voice.

Cedric glared at Coco. 'It means… it means… it's an English expression, which means…'

Coco sighed. 'It means that we'll never find the damn moped, that's what it means,' she stated. 'The Panteré banlieue is a housing estate a few arrondissements over. And it's one of the biggest shitholes in Paris. Once you get inside it, it's like Beirut, and there are no cameras because as soon as they're in, someone breaks them. Everything seems to say the cops don't run Panteré, the drug dealers and pimps too.'

'That has to be an exaggeration,' Demissy countered.

'It isn't,' Cedric replied.

'People don't talk about places like Panteré, so that it doesn't worry nice people like…' Coco began, her eyes flicking over the commander, before adding, 'nice people who like to feel as if their lives in their nice clean neighbourhoods are perfectly safe.'

Demissy sighed. 'Your point?'

'My point is that once the moped got inside the banlieue, the chances of us finding it, or who drove it, become nil,' Coco replied. 'Even if we sent in a thousand flics to search for it, we'd never find it. We'd have to go through every flat, every hiding hole, every garage and the chances are it most likely would be on one of the bonfires that burn every day.' She shook her head. 'Nope. We won't find the moped which killed,' she grimaced, '*almost* killed, Emma Fitzgerald.' She stopped, contemplating something. 'Mais, it might just tell us something.'

Cedric leaned forward. 'Quoi?'

Coco reached for a cigarette and, ignoring Demissy's tut, lit it. 'As I said earlier. Whoever it was, he pushed Emma Fitzgerald straight into the road. He didn't do that to anyone else. What that suggests to me is that he deliberately targeted her. And if that's the case, and someone wanted to hire someone to do that, then there are likely plenty of people on the Panteré estate who would willingly do that for a few euros.'

'That's as maybe,' Demissy interjected. 'But it doesn't bring us any further forward or give us an indication as to who, or why someone might have arranged such a thing.'

The three police officers lapsed into silence as if all consumed by their thoughts.

Demissy finally broke the silence. 'And we're no further forward on the kidnapping?'

'After we've gone to the house again, I thought maybe we could go to the cybercafé where the telegram was sent from,' Coco answered.

'Pourquoi?' Demissy countered. 'We've already had officers there, they found nothing.'

'Ebba found nothing either,' Cedric added.

Coco shrugged. 'That's all fine, but they were probably more polite than I am. I'll shake a few people by the neck to see if I get a bit more out of them than, "I saw nothing."' she stated.

'What about this ticket with B4 on it?' Demissy continued wearily.

'Nobody has a clue what that could mean,' Coco sighed. 'Ebba examined it. There are no prints, nothing to show where it came from. It could be a receipt for checking in a coat, or it could be a queue number for a doctor's surgery, or hell, even a place in the queue to order some meat.'

'You mean it's another dead end.'

Coco exhaled. 'It's only a dead end until we figure out where it was to be used, and why Richard Severin had it.'

'What did Emile Severin have to say?' Cedric asked.

'Well, that was interesting,' Coco answered. 'Turns out Richard Severin was a very naughty boy.'

'In what way?' Demissy demanded.

'Timo Severin wasn't his grandson, he was his *actual* son,'

Coco explained.

'Are you sure?'

She nodded. 'Well, according to Emile at least, but I have no reason to believe he was lying because apparently, it's in the will. Five million to Timo, and five million to the grandkid. Nothing to Emile or his sister.' She shrugged. 'I'll have to confirm all that with Horst Lavigne, but either way you look at it, there are five million reasons any one of them might just have offed the old man. Admittedly not the granddaughter, but I think we can pretty much safely assume her kidnapping had something to do with that.'

'I agree,' Demissy added. 'And that's why we need to figure out exactly where everyone was yesterday.' She shook her head irritably. 'One of them has to know something.'

'I'll get it out of them,' Coco replied. 'You see if I don't. Emile claims Timo didn't know the truth, but if he did, he's got a pretty good reason to get rid of the father who never wanted him.'

'The same goes for Caroline Severin,' Cedric reasoned. 'If her father cut her out of his will, she might have decided to use her daughter to get some money out of him. We all know what junkies are like.'

Demissy rose to her feet. 'I would prefer if we were talking about more than supposition.' She glanced at her watch. 'I promised the Minister we would have an update by 17H00 so that he could brief the press in time for the evening news.'

Coco scoffed. 'You're optimistic.'

'Hardly,' Demissy retorted. 'Mais, I want to keep my job, and I suppose you two do as well. So, a quick result is in all of our interests, non?' She moved towards the door.

'There's one other thing,' Coco called after her. 'Emile Severin also told me that some reporter was writing an expose on his father.'

'And?' Demissy questioned.

'Well, I can't imagine Richard Severin was the sort of man

who wanted any kind of negative publicity,' Coco reasoned.

'Peut être,' Demissy responded. 'D'accord, look into it, but don't spend too much time on it. We have other avenues to explore first, some tittle-tattle story about him isn't likely to have had anything to do with his murder, but people being written in and out of wills is far more likely to lead us where we need to look, non?'

'You're probably right,' Coco said reluctantly.

Demissy nodded and left the office. Coco turned to Cedric. 'What do you think?'

He shrugged. 'I think we've got until 17H00 to keep our jobs, that's what I think.'

Coco stood and pulled on her coat. 'That's more time than I usually have,' she said cheerfully.

MARDI
12H30

Mona Gagnon did not turn as Coco and Cedric entered the expansive living room on the second floor of Richard Severin's mansion. Instead, her head was pointed directly towards the telephone in the corner of the room. Coco and Cedric exchanged a look. They had been admitted into Richard Severin's palatial apartment by a small, anxious Asian woman, with a pinched face and scared eyes. She had uttered no words, merely extending a short arm and pointing with a shaking finger in the direction of the living room. Coco had wondered what on earth could have terrified the woman so much, especially considering Richard Severin was dead. She looked around, wondering whether his presence was still lingering in the space he had occupied and ruled for such a long time. Coco faced Mona, and she wondered what it was about the telephone that so consumed her. Was it just because she was worried? There was something about that theory that did not hold true for her. It was something else. Coco was sure of it.

'Mademoiselle Gagnon?' Coco called out.

'Is she dead?' Mona whispered.

Coco was taken aback. 'Is she dead?' she repeated.

'Emma.'

'Ah, désolé, non, Mademoiselle Fitzgerald is still in surgery, I believe. The hospital has promised they'll call as soon as they have news.'

Mona nodded. 'And you haven't found Laure?' she asked, still staring at the telephone.

'I'm afraid not,' Coco replied, suddenly feeling overwhelmed with hopelessness.

'Then what are you doing here?' Mona snapped. 'Have you nothing else better to do?' Her fingers were playing with the pearls around her neck, wrapping around them as if she was attempting to choke herself.

'We have officers doing everything they can to find Laure,' Cedric replied.

Coco took a tentative step across the room. She had not noticed it the last time, but despite the roaring fire in the centre of the room, there was an icy coldness that caused her to pull her coat closer to her body.

Mona dropped her pearls and touched her hair. The tight brown curls were matted, as if she had not brushed it for days. 'Why haven't the kidnappers asked for money? The telegram said they would be in touch, mais…'

Coco wondered about that herself. It was odd. Or was it? 'There could be several reasons,' she offered.

Mona turned to face her abruptly. 'Such as?' she demanded.

Coco shrugged. 'We can't be sure, but they could be waiting for the fuss to die down so that there's not so much police or press presence. We also can't ignore the fact that Richard knew what was happening - that's the only reason I can think of why he told the school Laure was sick.'

'It would also explain why he was in the métro,' Cedric added. 'He could have been following the kidnappers' instructions.'

'We're going to the café where the telegram was sent from,' Coco said. 'I'm hoping that will give us some answers.'

'Do you think they killed Richard?' Mona asked.

Coco shrugged. 'Well, they're certainly high on the list of suspects.'

'What about Caroline? Do you imagine she's involved?'

Coco moved across the room, stopping in front of the full-length windows, her fingers tracing along the heavy netting. 'Again, we can't rule anything out. This could be about her daughter.

That's why anything you can tell us would be helpful. What can you tell me about their relationship?'

Mona moved to a chair in front of the fire, reaching for a blanket, which she placed over her knees. 'There was no relationship. Even if Richard would have allowed it, I don't think motherhood was something which interested Caroline in any way.'

'And what does interest your niece?' Coco asked.

Mona folded her hands in front of her. 'Money. Drugs. Men. That's about all, as far as I can tell.'

'Then this could be about money,' Cedric stated. 'Did you know about the will?'

She shook her head quickly. Too quickly. 'Non, but I can imagine what it contains. Laure will be a very wealthy woman when she reaches maturity.'

If she reaches maturity, Coco thought before angrily dismissing the notion. 'That might explain why Caroline or someone else may have taken her.'

'Peut être,' Mona conceded.

'And Timo?'

Mona twisted her head toward the fire. She said nothing.

'You knew,' Coco pushed.

Mona laughed. 'Of course I knew. Secrets like those are hard to keep in a place like this. Emile did the right thing, the only thing that could be done for Timo's sake.'

'What I don't get,' Coco interrupted with a frown. 'Is why he took Timo but everyone else was happy for Laure to remain here?' She paused. 'Emile told me the sort of father Richard was, and if that is true, I don't get why Laure remained here.'

'I don't know what Emile told you, but I wouldn't be so sure it was entirely the truth.'

Cedric raised an eyebrow. 'You're saying he's lying?'

She shook her head firmly. 'Non, not lying, but maybe exaggerating a little,' she responded. 'He always had a tendency to do that when he was a child. He was always prone to dramatic behaviour. As for Laure remaining in Richard's care, that was an entirely different kind of embarrassment. The issue of Timo was easily contained. Laure was not. You see, we didn't even know Caroline was pregnant. It was only when the hospital, a social worker indeed, called to say that Laure had been born and, like her mother, was addicted to heroin.' She shuddered. 'The poor little thing. Can you imagine? Well, of course, Richard went into full damage control. He swept in, packed Caroline off to some rehab in the middle of America and paid for the best doctors to look after Laure.' She cackled. 'It worked out quite well for Richard in the end. He got a front-page spread in the weekend "Le Monde." The headliner read: *Brave industrialist gives up everything to raise tragic granddaughter.*' Mona pursed her lips tartly. 'Obviously, he only told the story he wanted. And he came out of it looking more like a saint than he did before.'

'And you weren't worried about Laure?' Coco pushed.

'Not at all,' Mona answered. 'In fact, if I had to, I'd go so far as to say Richard was actually quite fond of her.'

'And you?' Cedric interrupted.

Mona cleared her throat. 'As Richard was fond of saying, being as how I was a childless spinster, I had no interest in children or being around them,' she gave by way of an answer. She stared into the fire, the flames illuminating her pale face. 'She was loved,' she stated before correcting herself in a softer voice, 'she *is* loved.'

'What about Emma Fitzgerald?' Coco asked. 'Did she care for her?'

Mona's mouth contorted. 'Emma always considered herself the mistress of this house.'

'Meaning?' Coco interrupted.

Mona cackled. 'Whatever ideas Emma may have had,' she spat, 'I am sure she was disabused of a long time ago.' Her mouth contorted into a cruel smile. 'These days, I would say Richard's tastes ran differently.'

His tastes ran differently. The sentence sounded odd to Coco. 'He had lovers?' she asked.

Mona shrugged. 'I couldn't say,' she snapped, pulling her cardigan around her chest as if she was drawing a close to the subject.

'But Emma was good with Laure?'

'She was,' Mona replied with obvious reluctance. 'I suppose they doted on each other,' she stated, before adding with bite. 'It seems not all spinsters are so anti-children, after all.'

'I get the impression you don't rate Ms. Fitzgerald too highly,' Cedric interjected.

She shrugged again. 'She was staff, and she performed her duties reasonably well.'

'Then you weren't friends?' he pushed.

She continued staring at the flames. 'As I said, she was staff, anything else would be inappropriate. If you're asking whether I liked her, then my answer would have to be no. As far as I could see, she was a bitch and whore.'

Coco's eyes widened. 'That seems rather harsh.'

'To you, peut être,' Mona retorted. 'To me, it is just the truth. I was raised to believe that women, *especially* women of her position in life, should know their place and how to behave amongst civilised people. I suppose you might say that makes me old-fashioned, but it is what it is. Emma Fitzgerald was obviously not taught to know how to behave.'

A bitch and a whore still seemed a particularly harsh way to describe someone, Coco believed, but she suspected Mona was going to say little more on the subject. 'What will you do next?' she asked instead.

Mona turned her head. 'What do you mean?'

'Well, presumably Richard left you comfortable,' she replied. 'And someone will need to look after Laure when she is returned.'

Mona turned away again. 'You are making an awful lot of assumptions there, Captain Brunhild.'

Coco and Cedric exchanged a look. 'What do you mean?' Coco asked.

'If you haven't worked out already, Captain,' Mona said without looking back, 'this is a house filled with secrets. And here, secrets were a form of currency.'

Coco shook her head irritably. 'You're going to have to explain that to me,' she snapped.

'There was no love lost between Richard and me.'

No shit. 'Then why did you stay?'

Mona shrugged. 'I stayed for my sister,' she stated, as if it was the most obvious thing in the world. 'She isn't dead.'

'What makes you say that?' Cedric asked in surprise.

'Because I know.'

'How do you know?' he pursued.

'Because I just know,' she repeated.

Cedric sighed. 'You're going to have to explain what you mean.'

She shrugged. 'I can't. I just know.'

'Then where has she been all this time?' Coco responded. 'Are you suggesting she willingly disappeared and left her children?'

'People leave all the time for a hundred different reasons. And Lauren had a hundred and one,' Mona answered.

Coco moved closer to her. 'I'd settle for one. I have four kids and they drive me crazy, but if I thought for a second they were in danger in their own home, I'd…'

'You'd do what, exactly?' Mona hissed.

I'd kill the bastard who hurt them. 'I wouldn't leave them.'

Mona clapped her hands. 'Then you're a better woman than most.'

Coco snorted. 'It's the first time anyone's accused me of that.' She stopped. 'Seriously, you're going to have to enlighten me.

Either your sister was the type of person who would have faked her own kidnapping, or she wasn't. I'm not getting it. I understand she wanted out of an unhappy marriage. Most women can understand that. I also get that Richard Severin wasn't exactly the prince everyone thought he was. Which meant that if he was controlling, divorce might not have been an option. Leaving her few options, but what I really don't see is, if she left with no money, no ransom, where the hell did she go? And why did she leave her kids?' She stared at Mona. 'I never met your sister, so I'm going to have to rely on you for that. Explain to me where your sister is if she isn't dead.'

Nobody spoke. The only sound was the ticking of an antique clock.

Coco's stomach rumbled. Her cheeks flushed. 'Désolé, I skipped breakfast.'

Mona smiled. 'I could ask Emma to fix you something…' She stopped. 'Ah, non, I couldn't.' She smoothed the blanket on her knees. 'I don't believe my sister is dead purely because I don't feel it, in *here*,' she stabbed her fingers at her heart. 'I have no better explanation than that.'

'Is that why you stayed here?' Coco asked. 'Because you were waiting for her?'

Mona nodded. 'What else could I do? I knew Richard was a dangerous man, and I always believed he had something to do with Lauren's disappearance, but the only thing I could do was to wait and to watch and hope that he made a mistake and dropped his saintly mask.'

'I get that,' Coco reasoned. 'But if you loved your sister as much as you say you do, or did, then why didn't you protect her children for her?'

'I tried.'

Coco shook her head. 'Not according to Emile. Even if he is exaggerating, which I'm not at all sure he is, then this house was not a happy place for either of Lauren's children.'

'And what would you have me do?' Mona cried. 'My presence was all I could offer. We were caught in a dance. A dance of hatred and mutual loathing. Richard couldn't get rid of me, and I couldn't get rid of him. When Caroline wanted to escape, I was the one who gave her a key. When I thought he was being too cruel, I would stand in doorways and make sure he saw me. I looked after my niece and nephew by staying, because if I hadn't, then I believe it would have been much worse for them.'

Coco studied the elderly woman and wondered how truthful she was being. Whatever had happened in the Severin home, it seemed to Coco, Mona could have done more to protect the children. Perhaps she was overthinking it, but something was most certainly off. Mona did not seem to her to be a woman who was easily intimidated, which, as far as Coco was concerned, meant there was another reason for her passiveness. In the end, could it have all come down to revenge?

'What can you tell me about a man called Yannick Vidal?' Coco asked.

The flash of recognition only lasted a second, throwing a shadow over Mona's face. But it was there, and Coco spotted it. 'You finally found a way to get your revenge, didn't you?' she asked.

Mona took a deep breath and then exhaled for what appeared to be a very long time. 'Do you know how many times people have tried to write an exposé on Richard? Literally dozens and each one of them was quashed in one way or another. Horst usually put a stop to them, or if it came to it, Richard would buy the publisher!' She snorted. 'That's how the idle rich deal with embarrassment. They buy their way out of it.'

'So, what's different about Yannick Vidal?' Cedric interjected.

'He isn't attached to anyone,' Mona answered. 'No publisher, no agent. These days, everything is on the internet, or so he told me. No need for hiding, because everything is instant. He said he would publish his findings and that Richard could do nothing about it.'

Coco nodded. 'How did you meet him?'

Mona raised a shaky hand towards the window. 'Every morning at 11H00, I take a short stroll around the park,' she replied. 'I suppose Yannick had been watching the house for some time and noticed that. He approached me. I was surprised that he knew not just my name, but all about me and my life.' She closed her eyes. 'And my darling sister.'

'What did he say to you?'

'He said he had been working on a book about Richard for a long time. A book he had been told to stop writing, but that it had only made him more determined, and in the course of his research he had discovered a whole heap of skeletons.' She smiled. 'It did not surprise me at all. But when he told me he had discovered something about my sister, I knew he was the real deal.'

Coco leaned forward. 'What do you mean?'

'He told he had proof that the ransom was paid.'

Coco frowned. 'What kind of proof?'

'Records. He claimed that the payment was made via a subsidiary business that Richard owned, or was involved in, I'm not too sure about all the details, but it was my understanding that some trickery had taken place which would explain why there was no payment traced from his bank account by the police who were investigating the kidnapping.'

Coco turned to Cedric. He shrugged. Coco could not imagine what it might mean. Had Richard Severin paid the kidnappers? And if so, why had his wife not been returned?

'Why would Richard Severin claim they paid no ransom to his wife's kidnappers if, in fact, he had?' Cedric asked.

Coco extended her hands. 'Because it wasn't a ransom,' she replied, immediately regretting it.

For the first time since they had arrived, Mona Gagnon turned to face them, and Coco could see her eyes glowing. 'It was a payment.' She turned away again. 'I realise it sounds foolish me believing my sister is still alive. But it has kept me going all these years. My hatred for Richard and my love for my sister have been a powerful drug and motivation for me. However, I am not foolish. I saw your face, and your belief my sister would not have left her children in his house unless she had no choice, is one which haunts me when I am at my most vulnerable.'

'Did you see proof from this journalist?' Cedric asked.

She shook her head. 'Non. Not at first, but once he started asking for money to continue his investigation, I said I would only agree if he showed me evidence.'

'And did he?'

She nodded. 'Oui. He showed me a facsimile sent from the company in the exact amount of the supposed ransom demand.'

Coco did not want to say it, but she knew how easily old documents, particularly facsimiles, could be faked.

As if reading her thoughts, Mona continued. 'And it wasn't just that. There were lots of other things. All unrelated, but enough to make sure Richard would be in serious trouble.'

'And a powerful motive for murder,' Coco concluded. 'Mais, not necessarily Richard's, more likely Yannick Vidal's.' She stared at Mona. 'So, you gave him money?'

'Oui,' she replied. 'I have no money of my own, but when Lauren was declared officially dead many years ago, I was given her money. I never spent a cent of it, not until I met Yannick. It seemed appropriate to finally spend some of my sister's money to prove how she… to understand what happened to her.'

'And did you also send him to your nephew?' Coco asked.

Mona considered her answer for a moment. 'I didn't tell him about Timo,' she stated. 'Mais, I told him I thought he should speak to Emile for his story,' Mona continued. 'I think he did, but he never really spoke to me about it. We used to meet once a week or so in the park, and he always seemed to skirt around the questions I asked.' A smile appeared on her face. 'However, occasionally he showed me what he was working on, and… well, let's just say, I was very much looking forward to the book being published if only to see the look on Richard's face.' She wrapped her arms around her chest. 'Now, I am afraid I'm going to be denied even that pleasure.'

Coco stared at her. She was struggling to imagine the sort of life Mona Gagnon had endured. 'And when was the last time you spoke to Yannick Vidal?'

'The day before yesterday,' Mona replied.

The day before the murder. Coco shook her head. She needed to find Yannick Vidal, and she needed to find him quickly. 'You had no other way to contact him?'

'Non, désolé. I was worried Richard would somehow find out and put a stop to it all.' She rose to her feet. 'I think I need to lie down.'

Coco nodded. 'There are officers here, they will stay just in case anyone calls, or anything happens.'

'Merci. Au revoir.'

Coco and Cedric watched as she left.

'What do you think?' Coco asked.

Cedric moved towards the door. 'I think we're no further forward with this damn investigation, and that it's just become even more complicated, that's what I think,' he grumbled.

MARDI
13H30

The man behind the counter of the cybercafé threw a look of panic toward Coco and Cedric. Despite his dark skin, Coco recognised the pallor and fearful eyes of a man who had seen too much in his short life. Whatever he had fought to escape, she surmised he was no doubt working for a pittance in a job he most likely hated and was overqualified for, but had no choice because of his circumstances.

The man moved his shoulders and grunted a communication. 'Ya?'

Coco pushed Cedric aside with her shoulder, sensing he was already getting testy. She personally held no animosity to anyone, whether or not they were illegal, so long as they gave her no trouble. She did not need to speak to the man in front of her to know that all he wanted was a peaceful life and to make enough money to support a family he had likely been displaced from. His eyes told her that. Hunger and fear were as much of a scent as they were an emotion.

'I already talked to the cops,' the man grumbled in broken English.

'I know,' Coco replied. She nudged Cedric irritably upon seeing the smirk on his face. She could not help it, but whenever she spoke English, her accent sounded as if she was auditioning for Downton Abbey. 'But it is very important. A young girl is missing, and most likely in terrible danger.'

Cedric pointed to the cameras in the corners of the room. 'Why don't they work?'

The man shrugged. 'I report to Chef, but...' he spread his

hands in front of him.

'Were you on duty when the telegram was sent?' Coco asked.

He snorted. 'I on duty always,' he replied glumly.

'You told my colleagues the telegram was paid for with cash but that you couldn't remember whether it was a man or a woman who sent it,' Coco continued. 'Or what nationality they might have been.'

'That is correct.'

'How long have you been in France, Monsieur?' Cedric interjected.

A look of fear crossed the man's face. 'One year and one half,' he whispered.

Cedric nodded. 'And you're happy in our great Republic?'

He laughed. 'There are no bombs,' he gave as an answer.

Coco placed her hands on the counter. 'We're not here to cause you any trouble,' she said in the most reassuring tone she could muster. 'But you've really gotta dig deep.' She tipped her head over her shoulder towards Cedric. 'My buddy here is a bit of a knucklehead, and he gets off on causing aggro for people, you know what I'm saying?' She shrugged. 'Me? I just want an easy life, and I have to tell you, I really <u>hate</u> paperwork.' She leaned forward, fixing him with such an intense stare, it caused him to step backwards. 'And listen, I have four kids and I haven't got laid in a while, so believe me, I'm on my last nerve. And to top it all, I've got a commander who rides me like I was a lame horse at a derby.'

'Jesus…' Cedric wailed under his breath.

Coco narrowed her eyes in his direction before continuing. 'All of those things aren't so bad in the grand scheme of things, as I'm sure you know, but as I said, my last nerve is stretched about as far as it goes, and I'd hate for you to bear the brunt of my misery, capeesh?'

The man looked from side to side, clearly bewildered and with little understanding of what she was saying.

'And that's why I know,' she continued, 'that a nice law-fearing citizen such as yourself, has to know that keeping information from a police officer is a pretty stupid thing to do, especially when the said police officer has no interest in that citizen other than nicely asking them for their help in a most heinous crime.' She moved her fingers close to his hand, but it caused him to recoil. 'I know your natural instinct is probably not to talk to the police. But I am different from anyone you've met before. Trust me on that.' Behind her, Cedric snorted. She glared at him over her shoulder. 'Just tell me what you remember and we'll be out of your way and won't bother you again,' she added.

The man lowered his head. 'There were two of them.'

Coco smiled. 'Now we're getting somewhere. Two of them. What can you tell me about them?'

The man glanced around the cafe anxiously. The only other person was a young woman, sat in front of a computer intently watching porn, with loud music blaring from headphones, and she was paying them no attention.

'A man and a woman.'

Coco nodded. 'Have they been here before?'

He nodded quickly. 'Every few days, the woman, at least. She buys cigarettes and cheap wine, I think. I can't really be sure, a lot of people come in and out of here.'

'A woman?' Coco asked keenly. 'Describe her.'

He shrugged. 'The usual. Greasy, dirty brown hair, spotty skin. Tight top, short skirt. White.'

Coco tried to recall the one picture she had seen of Caroline Severin. It was a posed photograph and not a lot of use in this instance, but she surmised he could be describing her after her descent into drugs. 'And the man?'

'Black, with long thick braids of hair,' the man answered. 'The sort of man whose eyes you don't look into.'

Coco looked at Cedric. The man had just described Jihef

Abreo, the criminal veiled in secrecy.

'And what did they say?' Coco asked.

'I'm not sure,' he replied. 'I think she bought a packet of smokes, and she handed me a piece of paper and told me to send the message to the address she'd written.'

'Did you read it?'

The man turned away and said nothing.

Coco decided to try another tactic. 'What about the piece of paper - do you still have it?'

He shook his head, pointing a shaking finger towards a pile of a dozen or more bin bags outside the café. 'Probably in one of those.'

Damn, we'll never find it, Coco thought.

'You said they come to the café often?' Cedric interrupted.

'Yes, the woman mainly. Every day or two, I think.'

'Then she's probably living nearby,' Coco addressed Cedric. 'We need to get plainclothes surveillance down here around the clock.'

'I'm on it,' Cedric replied, stepping quickly outside and café and pulling out his cell phone.

'You're going to have police here?' the man asked, his voice thick with fear.

'Don't worry,' Coco replied reassuringly. 'This isn't about you.'

'It's always about me,' the man whispered. 'And once the boss man finds out I'm the one who has brought the police around, he's going to blame me.'

Coco extracted a card from her bag and handed it to him. 'These are all my numbers. If you have any problems, call me, okay?'

He nodded.

'What's your name?' she asked.

He regarded her with fear. 'Why?'

'Because I want to know,' she replied. 'Not to do you any harm.' She pointed at the card. 'I like to know the names of the men in my life.'

He tried to move his mouth into a smile. 'Tomas.'

Coco laughed. 'Of course it is! Take care, Tomas, and call me.' She moved to the door, laughing to herself.

MARDI
13H45

'Commander Demissy told me you would be here,' Ebba Blom stated tartly. 'I told you, I'd already spoken to the dude who works inside,' she added huffily.

'Well, you obviously don't have my charm,' Coco quipped, 'because he spilt his guts for me.'

Ebba turned her head sharply to Cedric. 'Tell me she didn't sleep with him.'

Cedric covered the mouthpiece on the cell phone. 'Nope. She promised NOT to sleep with him if he told her everything. I've never seen a dude spill his guts so quickly!'

Ebba threw back her head and laughed.

'Hey!' Coco cried. She pointed at Cedric. 'And need I remind you - you've seen the goods so you know what a treat any man would have.'

Cedric's face contorted into a grimace, and he moved away, speaking into the phone.

'Well, what did he have to say?' Ebba asked huffily.

Coco turned towards the grimy cybercafé. It was run down; the windows sprayed with dirt and graffiti. 'Well, he answered questions but only raised more,' she replied mystically. 'Cedric is organising a stakeout. And the more I discover, the more it feels as if Caroline Severin is up to her neck in all of this.'

'Because her father wrote her out of his will?'

'And wrote her daughter into it.' Coco suggested. 'This family dynamic is weird, and I don't pretend to understand it, but it seems to me as if something happened this week which was like kicking a hornet's nest.' She stepped away.

Ebba cleared her throat. 'Captain,' she whispered.

Coco stopped. 'Yeah?'

Ebba lowered her head. 'Oh, it's okay, it doesn't matter.'

Coco moved back towards the diminutive Swedish forensic expert. She cocked her head, fixing Ebba with an interested and long appraisal, causing her to scratch her shaved head. 'You interest me, Ebba,' she said.

Ebba moved across the boardwalk. 'Stop that, you know it freaks me out.'

Coco smiled. 'What's up, buttercup?'

'There's talk,' Ebba said quickly.

Coco felt her heart sink. She had been the brunt of gossip for more years than she cared to remember, and mostly she had managed to rise above it. She had more to worry about than someone gossiping about her behind her back. She had children to raise and food to put in their mouths. 'What talk?' she demanded.

Ebba looked anxiously in Cedric's direction.

'What's up with the gym bunny?' Coco asked. 'Cos he's been more of a bitch than he normally is.'

Ebba took a breath. 'The talk is about Commander Stanic.'

Mordecai Stanic. Coco had hoped the name would disappear from her consciousness. She had tried, but he haunted her. She had loved very few men in her life, but he had certainly been one of them. And that was what made it worse, and the entire reason why she knew she could never trust him again. He had been the father of her two youngest children, but he was so much worse. He was a murderer, and he was a rapist. As usual, when she thought of him, Coco reached to her cell phone, knowing there would be a message from one of the other children he had sired. Coco had promised to help him make his way in life, though she really had no burden to do so, but she had so far not fulfilled her promise. It bothered her, but her days were not her own, and Mordecai had two other children, *her* children, which she was having to raise on her own.

Though, as always, she loved to herself that she would do something about it when she had time.

'Why the fuck are people *still* talking about the *former* Commander of the Commissariat de Police du 7e arrondissement?' Coco hissed.

'Because he wants to get out of prison.'

Coco snorted. 'He's <u>never</u> going to get out of prison,' she snapped. 'And if he does, I'll be standing right outside with a fucking shotgun.' She stopped, offering a sweet smile. 'Peut être,' she mouthed. 'Don't quote me on that…' she trailed off. 'What does this have to do with Monsieur huffy-pants over there?'

Ebba lowered her voice. 'According to what I heard, Commander Stanic claims he has information to trade, but he'll only give it to you, but apparently, you're refusing any contact with him.'

'Damn right I am,' Coco hissed through gritted teeth. 'He's tried writing, calling, hell, even sending over his damn witch of a mother. I won't speak to Mordecai, because I have absolutely nothing to say to him that doesn't involve telling him to tie a noose around his fucking neck. Hell, I even volunteered to kick the fucking chair.' She stared at Cedric, who was still jabbering on his cell phone.

'It appears Commander Demissy asked Cedric to intervene and speak to you, to try and encourage you to speak with him,' Ebba continued. 'Lieutenant Degarmo said he wouldn't ask you, but he would go in your place.'

'The hell he will,' Coco snapped.

'By all accounts, the information he has could bring down a lot of bad guys,' Ebba reasoned.

Coco shook her head. 'I don't give a rats behind about that. This is all about Mordecai thinking he's going to get his foot in the door, and I'm telling you, that will not happen.'

Ebba nodded. 'Don't tell Lieutenant Degarmo I told you.'

'I won't,' Coco replied. 'But I will make sure it doesn't happen.' She flicked her eyes over the forensic expert. 'You're not so bad after all, kid.'

Ebba shrugged nonchalantly, pointing discretely towards Cedric, who had finished his call and was making his way back to them. 'I've arranged twenty-four-hour surveillance,' he called out. 'Commander Demissy was pissed, but when I pointed out that the Minister would expect it, she okayed it. Mais, she made it clear, we only have it for one day, so we either solve the case or lose the surveillance.'

'Commander Demissy is going to be *really* pissed off by the time I'm finished with her,' Coco muttered under her breath.

'Quoi?' Cedric questioned.

'Rien,' Coco answered quickly. She turned to Ebba. 'Why were you looking for us, anyway?'

'I was told to give you an update,' she answered.

Coco moved towards the car and sat on the bonnet. She lit a cigarette. 'So, shoot.'

'I've gone over everyone's alibis,' Ebba began. 'But I'm afraid there's not much there. Mona Gagnon and Emma Fitzgerald effectively alibi one another.'

'And there was no love lost between the two of them,' Cedric interrupted. 'I can't see them lying for each other.'

Coco whistled. 'I wouldn't be so sure. Hatred makes for strange bedfellows, and we only really have Mona's word they hated each other at all. It could all be a ruse. And don't forget, Mona didn't bother to hide how much she hated Richard Severin. What about the others?'

'I accessed Emile Severin's electronic diary,' she lowered her voice before adding sheepishly, 'don't ask how. He had a 09H00 meeting at a youth hostel on the other side of Paris. At 08H15 he emailed from his cell phone informing them he was running late, some problem on the métro, and would get there at about 09H30.'

Coco pursed her lips. 'Can you tell where he was when he sent the email?'

'I checked cell towers,' Ebba replied, 'but it's difficult to pinpoint. If you're asking me if he was anywhere near the métro where his father was offed, then all I can tell you right now is that he was in a five-mile radius.'

Coco raised an eyebrow. 'Then it's possible.'

'It's possible,' Cedric sniffed, 'but practically impossible to prove unless we go through every damn CCTV camera in that five-mile radius.'

'You could ask him where he was, and why he was late,' Ebba offered.

'We could,' Coco agreed. 'But I'd rather not rely on his honesty. What about the kid?'

Ebba shrugged. 'All I know is that he didn't turn up for school, but it seems that's not unusual. Emile Severin has been warned several times by the school that if Timo doesn't buck up his ideas, he won't graduate.'

'He doesn't have much reason to now,' Cedric added.

'We keep coming back to the money,' Coco mused. 'And whether these people knew the truth. Ah well, we're going to see the avocat next. Maybe he'll have some answers. Speaking of the avocat, have you heard of Horst Lavigne?'

Ebba shook her head. 'Nope. Do you suspect him?'

'I suspect everyone,' Coco replied, 'until they prove otherwise. Makes life a bit easier and infinitely more interesting.' She considered. 'But find out what you can on him, because it seems to me that he stood to gain a lot from Severin's death, too. He may have just got bored with waiting, or having to deal with the saint who wasn't a saint at all.'

'I'll see what I can find. Anything else?'

Coco nodded. 'I need you to find anything you can on a man called Yannick Vidal,' she continued. 'I'm not even sure if that's his real name, but I think it might be important to find him.'

'What do you know about him?'

'He's a journalist or a writer of some kind, but that's all I know right now,' Coco replied. She grinned. 'Other than the fact he's drop-dead gorgeous and great in bed. My sorta fella,' she said before pouting, 'apart from the fact he's gay, or at least able to bend that way should he be required to.'

Ebba's eyebrows knotted. 'I don't understand half of the things that come out of your mouth.'

Coco shrugged. 'You and me both, doll.' She clapped her hands. 'D'accord, let's shake a tail feather because we have,' she glanced at her watch, 'less than three hours to save all our jobs.'

MARDI
14H30

Coco found that her second impression of Horst Lavigne was much the same as her first. Irritation in a thousand euro suit with enough smarminess to suffocate anyone who got too close. He gestured for Coco and Cedric to take the seats opposite a large, ornate desk which stretched across the full length of a wall. He sat opposite them, reclining in a chair Coco surmised was designed for him to look down upon whoever was in his office.

'Have you found Laure yet?' he asked, immaculately manicured nails scraping across his perfectly groomed grey beard.

Coco shook her head.

He tutted. 'And Richard's murderer?'

She shook her head again.

He repeated the tut, but this time it was louder and tinged with sarcasm.

'We don't have a lot to go on,' Cedric snapped. 'And it seems to me, everyone is being less than helpful.'

Horst's grey eyes flecked with anger in Cedric's direction. 'What is that supposed to mean?'

Coco leaned forward. 'I think you know exactly what that means. We know you're all lying to us in one way or another. What I'm trying to figure out is why and what it has to do with how Richard Severin ended up stabbed to death on Line 8.'

Horst folded his hands neatly in front of him.

'Why are you so keen on protecting Richard now?' Coco asked. 'I mean, he's dead. What harm can it do?'

Horst snorted. 'You have no idea the harm it could do. Do you know how many people *Severin Industries* employ in France alone? Close to forty-eight thousand, even more worldwide. We also have shareholders. If there was ever a hint of scandal, can you imagine how many lives that could destroy?'

'And that's why you've lied for him all these years?' Cedric pushed.

Horst slammed his fists on the table. 'Bien sûr, it is. Ecouté. I've known Richard since we were kids. He was an asshole then, and he only got worse. The whole self-made millionaire nonsense is a bunch of crap. We sat around his uncle's million euro townhouse and planned it all. We wrote Richard's history, just like we were writing a novel.'

Coco tried to recall the details of the few paragraphs she had read of Severin's autobiography. 'Didn't his parents die in a car crash?'

Horst nodded. 'Oui. And with the fifty-thousand insurance policy they left him, Richard started his first company. Renovating derelict houses and selling them on. The extra money came from his uncle. It's true enough Richard's parents were dead, but the fact was he never knew his father and his mother was a junkie, born into privilege but without the brains to do anything with it. She died in a drug den and was buried without a name.'

Coco looked at Cedric. Horst Lavigne could well be talking about Richard Severin's daughter, not just his mother.

'It suited the dialogue,' Horst continued. 'And when his uncle died, Richard decided it was the perfect time to create his own narrative. The lies began then.' He sighed. 'The actual truth was, he was always a bastard, but the richer he became, the worse he got. And the more acclaim he got, the more he wanted and the more protective he became of losing it.'

'What happened to his wife?' Coco interrupted.

'What do you mean?' Horst snapped. His reaction was instant, and to Coco, she saw it for what it was. It was practised.

'I mean. Was she really kidnapped?' Coco pushed.

'Of course, she was kidnapped,' he shot back, clearly angered. 'What else could it be?'

Coco nodded. 'And what do you think went wrong?'

'The kidnappers bungled it, that's what I think went wrong,' he responded. 'And then they panicked and killed the poor woman.'

'And the ransom was never paid?' Cedric asked.

Horst sighed wearily. 'You know it wasn't.'

I know no such thing, Coco thought. She did not want to reveal her hand too soon in front of the avocat, not at least until she spoke to Yannick Vidal and to evaluate where he had uncovered the information that the ransom had been paid. Instead, she said. 'Well, we know no such thing. Tell me, if Richard was to pay a large amount of money, would that be something you would be aware of?'

Horst frowned. 'The life of the very rich differs greatly from yours and mine,' he replied. 'They don't have bank accounts in the same way as anyone else, par example. Their lives are usually managed by an accountant, or a lawyer, or a business manager. Of course, Richard had credit cards for his day-to-life, but if he wanted to get his hands on a large amount of cash, he would need help, because I know for a fact, he wouldn't have the first clue how to achieve it.'

Coco pursed her lips. 'And that help, it would come from you?'

He nodded. 'Oui. My practice has been looking after his affairs since the beginning.'

'Interesting choice of words,' Coco muttered. 'Then tell me - if he paid the ransom, you would have known about it?'

Horst nodded again. 'I told you, oui. I would have known about it.'

Coco tapped her chin. 'D'accord. We'll come back to that. Next, I would like to know about the will.'

'It would be inappropriate, and legally questionable for me to discuss the will until I have spoken with all the relevant parties,' he replied.

'We already know about some of it,' Coco interjected. 'I guess I'm just after confirmation. Nothing for the kids, and a sizeable chunk for the grandkids. Am I correct?'

Horst nodded slowly, but said nothing.

'I say grandkids…' Coco trailed off.

Horst's head twisted. 'Then you know?'

Coco nodded.

Horst slammed his fists together. 'Emile never could keep his mouth shut…'

'Well, he seems to have managed so far,' she retorted tartly. 'And wasn't that the whole point? Keeping the secret until Richard died and then tying the kid up in some bullshit illegal NDA?'

Horst's mouth twisted. 'While you are correct that the non-disclosure agreement could be challenged, it is unlikely to happen. I would imagine Timo would see sense and take his money. Richard only did it because I told him that under French law, he had to acknowledge his children and that they are all entitled to a portion of his estate.'

'And yet he cut Emile and Richard out of his will,' Cedric stated.

'Who told you that? Emile?' Horst demanded. 'No doubt Richard told him that at various points, but again, it is legally impossible. Emile and Caroline will inherit the bulk of Richard's estate. It's hard to give an exact amount, but I think you could conservatively estimate it to be in excess of five million euros each.'

Coco gasped. She was not sure what she had been expecting, but it was not that. 'Quoi? And Emile and Caroline know about it?'

'I can't answer for them, but if they know anything about the law, they would know they should expect something,' he answered.

Coco frowned. 'Mais, everyone seems to have believed Saint

Richard gave away most of his fortune, so it is possible they expected there was no money to come to them.'

Horst shrugged nonchalantly. 'Such a scenario is certainly workable,' he gave as an answer in a tone that inspired Coco to slap him.

'And was anyone else mentioned in his will?' Cedric asked.

'A few,' Horst replied. 'Mlle. Emma Fitzgerald, par example, will receive one hundred thousand euros,' he stopped, lowering his voice discreetly, 'if she survives, that is.'

Coco nodded. 'And what about Mona Gagnon?'

Horst lowered his head. 'Nothing. And the instructions were if she outlived Richard, she was to vacate his townhouse immediately, and that it was to be sold and the proceeds given to his foundation.'

Coco whistled. 'He really hated her, didn't he?'

Horst did not respond.

'And what about Laure and Timo? What do they get?'

'Five million each also,' Horst considered. 'When they reach majority, that is.'

'And what about custody of Laure?' Coco asked. 'What happens to her?'

'Unfortunately, there are no stipulations in the will regarding the minor grandchild,' Horst answered. 'Which makes it even more important I find her mother as soon as possible.'

'Maybe her mother already has her,' Coco interjected.

He nodded. 'The thought has occurred to me. But don't worry, regardless of all that and whatever happens next, I will make sure I do the best I can for the child.'

Coco regarded him, unsure whether she had any confidence in him. 'And what happens to Severin Industries?'

Horst's face moved into a wide smile. 'Following Richard's death, I have become the major shareholder.'

'Wow!' Coco exclaimed. 'That's quite a windfall, non?'

He smirked. 'Not really. I have been running the company pretty much single-handedly for several years, it was agreed between Richard and me, and the shareholders a long time ago to ensure that there would be a stable handover following his death.' He stopped and chuckled. 'Of course, Richard wasn't exactly keen on it, but he was no fool and realised he had no choice because, to be frank, I know where the skeletons are buried.' He laughed. 'Therefore, it was rather a small price to pay in the grand scheme of things. He paid me for my silence and covering for him all these years. And believe me, he got off lightly.'

'What do you mean by that?' Cedric asked keenly.

'As an avocat, one is bound by client confidentiality,' Horst retorted.

Coco shook her head. 'Unless they have committed a crime,' she blurted bluntly.

'Are we done here?' Horst snapped. 'I have rather a lot to do, and I think I have been as helpful as the law allows. Regarding any further questions in this manner, I must tell you we have to move forward carefully, for legal reasons and for the sake of the company.'

'One more thing, for now at least,' Coco stared at him. 'Where was Richard going on the morning of his death?'

He moved his shoulders quickly. 'How am I to know? Didn't Commander Demissy suggest he may have been on the way to meet the kidnappers?'

'Well, it's certainly possible, but we don't even know for sure that he was aware of it.' She narrowed her eyes. 'Mais, what I'm wondering is - did he have a girlfriend?'

'How am I supposed to know about that?' Horst snapped.

Coco laughed. 'Because I don't think there's a single thing about Richard Severin's life you weren't aware of, like the birth of the illegitimate son, par exemple, and what happened to the mother. I suspect your fingers are knuckle deep in all of those pies.'

Horst stared at her, his face remaining stoic.

Coco tapped her chin. 'If Richard wasn't meeting the kidnappers,' she began, 'there's only one other reason I can think of that a man like him might lower himself to travel with us mere mortals on the métro and it's because he was off doing something he didn't want anyone else to know about.'

'And what might that be?' Horst demanded, a smile hovering on his lips.

'He was going somewhere he didn't want to be spotted going, or where people might see him, or talk about why he was there,' she reasoned. 'Which brings me back to the issue of a girlfriend.'

'I don't know what you want me to say,' Horst said wearily.

'Why do you think Richard Severin was on Line 8?'

Horst continued staring at her as if he was deciding upon something. After a minute, he reached for a thick organiser on the side of his desk and opened it, flicking through several pages until he found what he was looking for. He ripped out a piece of paper and scribbled something on it. 'I believe Line 8 takes you through Opera station,' he said, handing the paper to Coco. She took it, her eyes narrowing to read his small print.

'What's this?' she asked.

'All I can tell you is that once a month I receive an invoice from that address in the name of Ambre Castillon,' he answered matter-of-factly.

'An invoice for what, exactly?'

He shrugged. 'I couldn't say,' he replied not entirely convincingly. 'The amount, a rather large amount, is always the same. Ten thousand euros.'

'Phew!' Coco laughed. 'That's a lot of opera.'

Horst suppressed a smile.

'And what was the invoice for? What did this chick do exactly for ten thousand a month?' Coco asked with a wink.

'The invoice indicated it was for interior design.'

'Ten thousand a month for interior design?' Coco snorted. 'Exactly how much design does one man need?'

'And how long has she been designing for him?' Cedric interrupted.

'The invoices have been coming for several years now,' Horst answered.

'And didn't you think that was odd?'

He nodded. 'I most certainly did, and I questioned Richard about it, particularly since I already pay a company I know for the upkeep of his townhouse…'

Coco smiled. 'And what did old dirty Dicky have to say for himself?'

Horst's jaw flexed with irritation. 'He told me to mind my own business. Which I always have, mais maintenant…'

Coco held up the paper. 'Merci for this. We'll check it out.' She rose to her feet and gestured for Cedric to follow her out of the office. She stopped by the doorway. 'Oh, just one more thing.'

'You said that a moment ago,' he shot back, the veneer of warmth now completely eroded.

She laughed. 'I never was good at counting. Tell me, what do you know of a man called Yannick Vidal?'

The mask had returned. 'I have never heard of him. Should I have?'

Coco studied him. His tone was as practised as the stoic expression on his smooth face, but her instinct told her he knew exactly who Yannick Vidal was. 'He's a journalist, or a writer of some kind. It seems he was writing a book about Richard Severin.'

Horst laughed. 'Do you know how many times someone has tried that over the years? Dozens. And the result is always the same. Richard quashes them all in one way or another. Either I write a cheque, or he buys out the damn publisher. If this man you speak of had planned to write something, it would have been dealt with the same way.'

'What if the story was about to break and he had some real juice to spill on Saint Severin?'

He laughed again. 'Then he'd be the one in a mortuary somewhere, not Richard.'

Coco nodded. 'We don't know where he is. So he might well be in a mortuary somewhere, for all we know. D'accord Monsieur Lavigne, if you think of anything else, call me.' She held up the piece of paper. 'And thanks for this.'

Horst watched them leave, his face pulled into a grim expression. If Coco did not know better, she would have surmised he was worried.

'What do you think?' Cedric whispered.

Coco looked over her shoulder. 'I think he's a lying piece of shit. I think they're all lying pieces of shit.'

'Then what do you want to do about it?'

She grinned. 'Well, for a start - let's go to the Opera, shall we?'

Cedric gave her the once over. 'Maybe the fat lady is really going to sing and this whole damn case will be over.'

Coco looked down. 'Less of the fat, you moron! You know nothing about women. I'm *curvaceous*…'

MARDI
16H00

Ambre Castillon pulled open her front door, her eyes instantly widening with interest. They flicked appraisingly over Coco and then Cedric, perfect blood-red lips sliding into a serene smile. She did not move. Coco tried her best not to appear to be evaluating the other woman, but it was hard for her not to stare. Castillon was striking. Tall and stick thin, dressed in a smart white pantsuit with a plunging neckline, revealing pert breasts without the constraints or need for a brassiere. The hair was white blonde, pushed into a blow-dry which appeared just to have been set. Other than white, the only colour was the matching blood-red lipstick and high heels. The entire ensemble, Coco surmised, likely cost more than she had ever spent on clothes in her entire life. She also suspected Ambre Castillon was older and for once, Coco's natural confidence deserted her. She also knew without a doubt that whatever Castillon was, she was most certainly not an interior designer.

'May I see your identification?' Ambre asked. Her voice was smooth and naturally husky, unlike Coco's own, which was husky from too many cheap cigarettes.

'Sure,' Coco responded, suddenly aware of how common her own voice sounded in comparison. She extracted her identification card and waved it through the air. 'Captain Brunhild and Lieutenant Degarmo,' she said, pointing towards Cedric, whose chest had extended as if he was doing his best to pulsate his muscles. Coco tutted.

'I can't imagine what the police would want with me.'

Coco snorted. 'Can't you?' She raised her voice. 'Can we

come in, or would you prefer we conduct our business in front of your neighbours?'

Ambre stepped inside the room, leading Coco and Cedric down a long, narrow hallway, her heels clicking against the marble tiled floor. They reached the end of the hallway and it opened into a vast living room, with tall windows offering a wide panoramic view. The room was sparsely decorated and furnished in a minimalistic way. *This is not a room someone lives in,* Coco thought. *It is a waiting room.*

'Can I offer you a drink? Champagne, peut être?'

Coco glanced at her watch. She shrugged. 'Yeah, why not?'

Ambre nodded, gliding towards a small bar area in the corner of the all-white room. 'Is Moët all right for you?'

'It would be delightful,' Coco answered, ignoring the glare from Cedric.

Moments later, Ambre returned, handing them both a crystal glass.

Coco took a sip, the bubbles causing her nose to crinkle. 'Aren't you joining us?' she asked.

Ambre shook her head. 'Non, I don't drink, unless…'

'Unless?'

'Unless,' she repeated. She gestured towards a long, narrow sofa. 'Please, take a seat.'

Coco nodded, lowering herself onto the white sofa, doing a silent prayer that she left it as clean as it was now when she stood up again because she still had not had time to have her coat cleaned.

'So, the police…' Ambre began, trailing off and leaving the silence to permeate the air.

'I'll cut to the chase,' Coco began.

'Please do.'

'We're here about Richard Severin.'

Ambre nodded. There was no change to her smooth, pale

face. 'Oui. I read about his murder. Just awful. Tragic.'

'It must have come as a great, *personal* shock to you,' Coco added.

'It should?' Ambre questioned.

Coco stared at her, fixing her with her best, *I know what you are,* look, *so quit messing around.*

'Quite a place, you've got here,' Cedric interjected, breaking the impasse.

Ambre tipped her head in deference. 'Merci. I try.'

'Did you try for Monsieur Severin, also?' Coco asked lightly.

Ambre's pale blue eyes widened, but she did not appear fearful. 'I don't know what you mean,' she stated.

Coco sipped the champagne. 'Oh, I think you do. You know why we are here, so let's save us all a bit of time and dancing around, d'accord?'

Ambre nodded. 'I have acted as a consultant for Monsieur Severin, in the past.'

Coco laughed. 'Is that what they call it in this neck of the woods?' She sighed. 'Look, we're not from vice and have no interest in busting you or throwing a cannonball into your nice, little life. But I'm also not a fool. I know a hooker when I see one. Oh, you may be dressed up all fancy, and have airs and graces, but it's the same thing at the end of the day.' She smiled. 'Apart from the difference in prices, and the way in which money changes hands, of course.'

Ambre turned away.

'I'm not here to make trouble,' Coco stated again, before adding. 'Unless you make me.'

Ambre threw back her head and laughed. 'Do you really think that works as a threat? You do not know how little that threat means to me.'

Coco gulped at the expensive champagne. 'Oh, I have a fair idea. I'm sure your little black book is chock-a-block with names and numbers of men in high and low places. Men who could do me damage.' She shrugged. 'People have tried that threat on me before, and as it stands, and as the song goes, *I'm still here!* She added with a flourish and finished the remains of her drink and waved the empty glass. 'Now, how's about you fill up my glass and then start spilling the beans?'

Ambre appraised Coco as if she had seen nothing or no one like her before. She took the glass and replenished it.

Coco cleared her throat. 'Let's start with yesterday. Was Richard Severin on his way here yesterday morning?'

Ambre sighed. 'What does any of this matter?'

'It matters because we're trying to understand why he was murdered.'

'But the press is saying it was likely a random killing,' Ambre responded, 'and that Richard wasn't targeted.'

'That's certainly a possibility,' Coco answered. 'Mais, that isn't for the press to decide. Something else happened yesterday, something which hasn't been reported by the press, and because of that, we need to understand what the hell was going on. So, I'll ask again. Was Richard Severin on his way here? And if so, don't give me of any that "consulting on interior design?" bullshit.'

Ambre moved her head slowly into a nod.

'What did you think when he didn't turn up?' Cedric asked.

She shrugged. 'It wasn't the first time. Richard was often suddenly called away on business. It mattered little to me, because they always paid me for my *consultations*, whether or not I was called upon to consult,' she added knowingly.

'I bet you were,' Coco interrupted, ignoring a warning look from Cedric. 'Speaking of which - what exactly do you have that's worth ten thousand euros a month.' She pointed downwards. 'I mean, what does it do, whistle tunes on request?'

Ambre smiled. 'Well, one thing my payment ensures is the utmost discretion.'

A beep from Cedric's cell phone caused him to pull it from his pocket. His eyes widened as he read the message.

'Well, it looks as if you haven't always been so discreet,' he said.

Coco looked at Ambre, a smile appearing on her face. 'Girl's got a record, huh?'

'That was a long time ago,' Ambre answered.

'Did Richard know?' Coco asked. 'Because it seems to me that he was all about the discretion, and I'm fairly sure that he wouldn't want people to know he was "hanging out" with a convicted hooker.'

'I can't answer to that,' Ambre snapped. 'Other than I repeat, it was once, and a very long time ago, and I was most certainly a different person then.'

'You were only arrested once?' Coco asked.

'Oui. Twenty-five years ago. Now, tell me I can't be discrete,' Ambre added proudly.

Coco snorted. 'How did Richard find you? I can't imagine he googled you, or found you on some escort site. That's not very discrete at all, now is it?'

'He was introduced to me by a mutual acquaintance,' she replied. 'A woman in my position relies on word of mouth. And men such as Richard Severin rely on being able to ask for what they want and to receive it without fear of being discovered.'

Coco's mouth opened and closed. 'Ah-ha!' she exclaimed, her eyes sparkling. 'He was into something freaky, wasn't he?'

'I never said that,' Ambre shot back quickly.

'You didn't have to. What was it, threesomes? Whips? Chains?'

Ambre laughed. 'If you think those are freaky, Captain Brunhild, then I worry about your sex life.'

'You and me both,' Coco conceded. 'Then what was it? This will go no further. I mean, who would we tell? And besides, as far as I can see, no one would believe anything bad of Saint Severin.'

'I specialise in golden showers,' Ambre stated matter-of-factly.

'Golden showers?' Coco repeated with a frown. 'You do your dudes in the shower, and you get paid ten thousand euros a month for that?' she added with incredulity. 'Hell, I used to do that for free. I used to figure it was a way of killing two birds with one stone. Get the hard-on off my back and save on the water bill.'

Ambre looked at Cedric. 'Are you going to tell her, or am I?'

Cedric leaned in and whispered in Coco's ear.

'Are you crazy? Ten large ones for a pee? Something you have to do, anyway?' She stared out of the window. 'I could do that,' she muttered.

'Your piss is most probably toxic,' Cedric laughed.

Coco turned to him. 'Hey, I pissed on you once, and you didn't pay me bupkis.'

Ambre gawped. 'I'm not sure I want to hear about this.'

Coco shrugged. 'Oh, it's okay. He had his hand in my vagina at the time…'

'I was delivering her baby!' Cedric cried with exasperation. 'Dammit, start with that!'

'So, old Severin liked to do the dirty… *literally*,' Coco concluded.

'It's not as easy as it sounds,' Ambre stated.

'How difficult can it be?' Coco reasoned. 'Do you do it in a bed on rubber sheets?'

'I have a designated wet room.'

'A designated wet room,' Coco repeated in clear amazement. 'What other kinky shit was Richard Severin into?'

'Richard was a very traditional man in most ways,' Ambre replied. 'He was gentle and tender. Most men in his position are. They live a dynamic, cut-throat life, and when they are away, when they feel free, they like to relax and be taken care of.'

'Ah, so he wanted to be mothered,' Coco concluded.

Ambre shrugged.

'Did he talk about his business?'

'Non,' she answered. 'And obviously, nor would I ask.'

Coco nodded, staring at Ambre. She had never known a man who did not like to spill his guts to the woman he was paying by the hour, if only to bitch about his wife or his job.

Ambre looked at her watch. 'I'm afraid I can't help you any more than that, so if that's all, I have an appointment in half an hour.'

Coco nodded and rose to her feet. 'Okay. Merci for your help.' She grinned. There was a large jug of water on the table. She pointed at it. 'You'd better go and pour yourself a large glass if you've got a busy afternoon ahead of you.'

MARDI
16H45

'Captain Brunhild, where are you?'

Coco looked at the display on her cell phone. *Number Withheld*. So, that's how Commander Demissy was making sure Coco took her calls now. 'Bonsoir, Commander,' Coco answered with as much cheerfulness as she could muster.

'Where are you?' Demissy demanded again, her voice rising sharply.

'In the car,' Coco responded more tartly than she intended. The champagne had loosened her tongue, which she realised was probably not a good thing.

'As I told you earlier, I am due to receive a call from the Minister at any moment,' Demissy snapped, 'and he will be expecting an update. Or rather, he will be expecting me to tell him that the case is closed. Am I able to tell him that?'

'Non, but we have found something,' Coco replied with a smile, 'and it may just be enough to get Jean Lenoir off your back for a while.'

'It might?' Demissy asked with undeniable interest.

Coco lit a cigarette. 'We just had a very interesting conversation with Richard Severin's "interior designer,"' she began. 'And, by "interior designer," I, of course, don't mean, "interior designer."'

'Captain Brunhild,' Demissy sighed wearily. 'Get to the point.'

'Well, let's say this particular woman was paid rather a lot to do some rather,' Coco lowered her voice, 'unusual things to Richard Severin.'

'What do you mean, unusual things?' Demissy interrupted. 'Wait. Don't say another word over the phone.' She paused, as if considering. 'How does this help me with the Minister of Justice?'

Coco smiled. 'Because barely three years ago, Jean Lenoir was caught up in his own scandal involving an "interior designer" who wasn't exactly an "interior designer," if you get my meaning. And as far as I can tell, our Minister of Justice barely made it out by the skin of his *admittedly* rather pert, tight ass,' Coco reasoned. 'And therefore, if you explain that we are pursuing several leads in that sort of direction, but must proceed with extreme caution, then good ole Jean Lenoir will not want to rock that particular boat.'

'You may just be right,' Demissy agreed reluctantly. 'Mais, it won't buy us much time with him, I'm sure.'

'I'm sure,' Coco agreed.

'Then what are you planning on doing next?'

Coco fought the urge to say something sarcastic. 'We're going to continue to work diligently,' she said instead.

Demissy sighed again. 'Ebba stopped by. She may have an address for Yannick Vidal. He doesn't seem to have a regular job, but she discovered he signed a lease on an apartment three years ago.'

'The address is three years old?' Coco groaned.

'It's not ideal, I know,' Demissy agreed. 'However, Ebba checked with the letting agent and the rent is up to date, so someone is paying it. Check it out anyway, seeing as you don't have a lot of other leads to follow.'

'Well, if you found out who Jihef Abreo really is,' Coco snapped back, 'then we might have real clues to follow.'

The silence on the line caused Coco's mouth to contort and punch a smirking Cedric's arm.

'You have a point,' Demissy said slowly. 'But nobody is returning my calls.'

'Then tell Jean Lenoir. Let him be the bad guy,' Coco replied.

'And have everyone think the Muslim woman is a snitch?' Demissy reported. 'That would do my career wonders, don't you think?'

Coco shrugged. 'Then call them and leave a message, telling them that if they don't get back to you within the hour that your next phone call will be to Jean Lenoir. They probably will not want to take that risk.'

'Hmm,' Demissy responded, and disconnected the call.

Coco turned to Cedric. 'I think she's warming to me.'

Cedric chuckled, gripping the steering wheel. 'Yeah, sure she is buttercup.'

MARDI
17H00

Coco narrowed her eyes to read the small printed names on the mailboxes in the apartment vestibule. She knew she should probably get glasses, but was not sure whether it was poverty or just plain vanity which was preventing her. 'There had better be a goddamn lift in this building,' she grumbled.

Cedric snorted. 'Why? You wanna see some other kid cut his throat?'

'He's not dead,' Coco whispered. 'He's not dead,' she repeated to herself. *Elliot Bain.* His name still haunted her, as did his smooth olive-skinned face and his rosebud lips. He had tried to kill himself the previous year in front of Coco in the antique lift in their apartment block. His attempted suicide had triggered an investigation into the young man's home and school life. He had survived his injuries, but the damage to his vocal cords had been severe and irreparable. He could not talk and had so far been unresponsive to help. He remained in a psychiatric ward and Coco tried to visit him when she could, which was not very often because she barely had enough time to devote to her own children. However, she knew she would not abandon him, even if she had to buy another roll-up bed to fight for space in her already cramped apartment. Elliot Bain had no family, and Coco was determined that if he made it out of his private hell, she would do whatever she could for him.

'There it is,' Cedric said, pointing at the box with *Y. Vidal.* handwritten on it.

Coco peered inside the box. 'There aren't any letters, so either our guy doesn't get mail, or he's been collecting it.'

'Or he's subletting it to someone,' Cedric proffered. 'This isn't a bad neighbourhood. I'm sure a lot of people let out their apartments to out-of-towner's who are happy to pay silly money for a weekend view of the Eiffel Tower.'

'I suppose,' Coco replied. The door to the vestibule opened, and a man stepped inside, pushing a cycle. Coco smiled at him, moving towards him. She stopped. There was something about the way his eyes widened which caught her by surprise. His hand rose to his face, pushing blond hair into his cycle helmet. 'Hey. Do you live here?'

The man nodded.

'Bon,' Coco replied. 'We're looking for one of our neighbours. A man called Yannick Vidal. Do you know him?'

The young man shook his head quickly. Coco noticed his hand twisting around the handlebars of his cycle. She stepped next to it, pressing her thigh against the wheel, nudging it against the wall. 'Are you sure you don't know him?' she pushed. There was something about his expression which concerned her.

The man licked his lips, and his pupils dilated. *Oh shit,* Coco groaned inwardly. She knew that look and what was coming. 'He's a runner!' she screamed to Cedric.

It only took a second for the man to push his body backwards against the entrance door and push it outwards, and he was flailing into the street.

'Dammit!' Coco cried. 'Let's go!'

They took after him, Cedric pushing past Coco. The man was most likely a decade younger and several kilos lighter than Coco, she reasoned as the soles of her broken boots slapped annoyingly against the cobbles underneath her. Thank Dieu, Cedric's still a lifeless gym bunny, she noted cheerfully.

'Are you okay?' Cedric called over his shoulder.

'Yeah,' Coco answered breathlessly, as she tried to hold down her breasts, which were bouncing against her chest. 'I wish I had a damn sports bra on,' she cried. 'At this rate, I'm going to have two black eyes!'

'Two bruised knees, more like!' Cedric retorted as they turned a corner.

'Less of the cheek, just make sure he doesn't get away!' Coco could still see the young man she assumed was Yannick Vidal sprinting his way between traffic and pedestrians. The streets were busy, which was in their favour because it was slowing him down. 'At least I know I won't be giving birth after this chase,' she gasped.

'At your age, that would be a miracle!' Cedric called back.

Coco stopped for a moment, pressing her ribs and attempting to catch her breath. 'He's heading for the bridge. Try to head him off before he gets onto it, or we might lose him.' She began running again, trying to muster as much strength in her legs as she could. 'I really am going to join a gym after this,' she called into the air, knowing full well she had no intention of doing it.

They turned into the street leading towards the bridge and the young man jumped over a railing, Cedric now only ten seconds behind. Coco noticed that the traffic was at a standstill on the bridge and she realised it might work in their favour. A large police van was at the other end of the bridge, dealing with what appeared to be the fallout of a car accident. Her mind whirled as she tried to decide what to do. She stopped at the bottom of the bridge and cleared her throat. She threw back her head and, with all her strength, screamed at the top of her voice. 'Arrêter! Police!'

The police officers on the bridge stopped what they were doing and looked in her direction. Coco yanked out her ID and thrust it into the air, gesturing wildly at the retreating figure approaching the officers. He stopped dead in his tracks, his head swerving from side to side as if he was trying to assess his next move. Coco saw the realisation and the panic appear on his face when he understood he could not go forward and he could not go back. He stared at the bridge, and with a swift movement, jumped onto the ledge.

'Woh! Woh! Don't move!' Coco shouted.

He pointed at Coco and Cedric. 'Don't come any closer, or I'll jump.'

Coco stopped running, instead inching forward. She looked over the bridge, vertigo overwhelming her. 'You don't want to do that, kid. Do you how much shit is in the Seine? Drowning would be the least of your problems.'

He looked over his shoulder, uncertainty on his face. Coco took the opportunity to move even closer. She and Cedric were now both only a few feet away from him. Cedric gestured for the other officers to back away and secure the area.

'Hey,' Coco began, searching her memory banks for what she had learned on various training courses over the years for dealing with situations such as this. She found nothing. 'Hey, whatever you're thinking, you don't need to do this,' she called out.

'You know nothing about me.'

'I know your name,' she said. 'It's Yannick, isn't it? Yannick Vidal?'

'Why are you after me?' he cried. 'I didn't do what they said I did.'

Coco frowned, unsure what he was talking about. 'Just come down and we can talk about it.'

Yannick pulled his messenger bag across his chest and steadied himself on a railing. His eyes darted around, noticing the crowd of police and spectators who were gathering.

Coco noticed a group of teenagers were already filming with their cell phones. 'Get them out of here,' she instructed Cedric. She took a step closer to Yannick, causing him to stumble.

'Stay back!' he cried.

'Okay, okay,' Coco pacified. 'Just come down kid.'

'I can't go to prison, not for that.'

'What do you mean, "not for that?"' Coco questioned.

'I didn't do what they said I did,' he replied, his voice thick with desperation.

Coco shook her head. 'You're going to have to level with me,' she responded. 'I'm just here to talk to you about Richard Severin. You know he's dead, right?'

'Dead?' He shook his head. 'He can't be.'

Coco studied his face. It was hard to read with the panic and the stressful situation, but she thought his reaction was genuine. 'Oui.'

'How did he die?'

'He was murdered in the métro yesterday morning.' She frowned. 'Where have you been? It's been all over the news.'

'I don't have a TV.' He trailed off. 'He's really dead?'

She nodded.

'And that's why you're here? You think I'm involved?'

Coco shrugged. 'I don't know what to think. We were looking for you because Emile Severin told me you were writing a book about his father, and I suppose I just wanted to see if it had anything to do with what happened.'

'Then there hasn't been a report made about me?'

'I don't think so,' Coco replied. She tutted. 'Look, come down and we can talk about it.'

He shook his head. 'Non. This is a trap.'

Coco tried to ignore the noise of sirens and chatter behind her and focus solely on Yannick. She did not want to spook him. 'What are you afraid of?' she asked.

'Richard Severin found out I was writing a book about him,' Yannick replied. 'And he had his thugs beat me up and searched my laptop. I told him that after what I had on him, he didn't scare me and that I wasn't so stupid as to leave my manuscript lying around. Two nights ago I was out with friends and someone bought me a drink. I guess it was spiked because I woke later that night, naked and in some strange bed. I managed to get home and

Richard Severin was waiting for me. He said I would regret the day I heard his name and tried to bring him down. He told me I had forty-eight hours to give him the manuscript and all my notes and get out of town or else he would make sure I regretted it.'

'What did he mean?'

'He said he had photographs of me, compromising photographs he called them. I knew that wasn't true, because I'd never done anything like that, and then I realised.'

'He'd set you up,' Coco concluded. 'What did he mean by compromising?'

'They said they had photos of me with an underage boy, some rent boy probably, but he said they'd also made sure that there were files on my computer and search histories that would all lead to child pornography.' He grimaced. 'He said, no matter what I deleted, there would be enough proof to get me sent away for a long time. All I had to do was give him the book, leave town and never see his son again.'

'He knew about you and Emile?'

Yannick nodded. 'Yeah. I don't know how. The truth is, I only got close to Emile and Caroline because of the book, but I grew to like Emile, I mean *really* like him, but once his father caught wind of it all, well, he threatened to destroy my life and I knew he could do it. That's why I thought you were after me. There's been no report made about me?'

'I can honestly say I've heard nothing about you, other than you were writing a book about Severin,' Coco stated. 'What about the book? Where is it?'

'It's somewhere safe.'

Coco nodded. 'Were you going to give it to him?'

Yannick did not answer.

'What did you find that scared him that much?' Coco pushed. 'I know he liked the world thinking he was a saint, but it seems pretty extreme to go after you and threaten you like that.'

'It's not just about the business, it was about everything else. The truth about what really happened to his wife, his daughter, the lovechild, the hookers,' Yannick recalled. 'He was eying up a political career, and he knew that he'd never be able to if what I have on him came out.'

'You said you got close to Emile and Caroline. Do you know where Caroline is?'

'Oui.'

'Where is she?' Coco interrupted desperately. 'Does she have her daughter, because her daughter is missing as well.'

Yannick shook his head, clearly confused. 'I need to think. There's something wrong here.'

'Just come down,' Coco pleaded. 'S'il vous plaît.'

Yannick opened his mouth to speak, but he was distracted by a bright flash from the camera of a news reporter. He raised his hand to shield his eyes and stumbled backwards, a scream emerging from his mouth. Coco lurched forward with all her might, throwing her hands in front of her in his direction. She latched onto the messenger bag in his right hand and yanked it to her, but Yannick's body was falling backwards and his hands and arms were flailing behind him. Coco watched helplessly as the young man disappeared into the darkness below, her mouth contorting when moments later she heard the splash of his body as it hit the Seine. She pulled the messenger bag to her. She lifted her leg onto the railing and began hoisting herself upwards.

Moments later Cedric appeared by her side and with a forceful grasp of her arm, yanked her back onto the sidewalk. 'Dammit, you've got four kids, Coco!' he cried. 'You can't go after him.'

'Get the goddamn divers in the water, now!' she screamed into the air, tears rolling down her face.

MARDI
18H30

Coco stared at the cup of café the colour of tar on her desk and tutted. She reached into her drawer and extracted a bottle of whisky and added a healthy glug to the cup. She passed the bottle to Cedric. He glanced slyly to his side.

Commander Demissy shrugged her shoulders. 'You're off duty, I suppose,' she murmured, blue painted lips twisted in contemplation.

Cedric took the bottle and added some of it to his drink.

'Are you sure you're alright, Captain?' Demissy asked Coco. 'You don't look well.'

Coco shrugged off her coat, revealing a torn white t-shirt, causing Demissy's face to wrinkle with distaste. Coco raised her cup. 'I'll be okay when this little beauty hits the spot.' She narrowed her eyes. 'Have the divers found anything?'

Cedric shook his head. 'Non. You know what it's like. His body could turn up in a day, two days, a week, or even longer, and probably somewhere far down-river.'

'Or he could have swum to shore. We weren't so far onto the bridge. He could easily have got out,' she reasoned.

Cedric and Demissy exchanged a doubtful look.

Coco gulped her drink. 'He could. And he was determined, so that would have strengthened him.'

'Tell me exactly what he said,' Demissy demanded.

Coco replayed her conversation with Yannick Vidal as best she could, whilst at the same time evaluating what she could have done or said differently. They had travelled back to the Commissariat in silence, all the time Coco clutching Vidal's messenger bag to her chest. It was only when they had arrived that they looked inside and found a laptop, which they had quickly deposited with Ebba, who was just about to leave for the day. She had reluctantly agreed to stay late, fixing Coco with an angry look.

'Do you believe he didn't know about Richard Severin's murder?' Demissy questioned.

Coco considered her response. 'I don't know. He seemed surprised. He said he had no TV, but he had a laptop. It just seems weird to me that he wouldn't have heard about it.'

'Then why lie?'

'Because he was the murderer,' Cedric interrupted. 'It makes sense. He ran as soon as he saw us and as he said himself, Richard Severin was setting up for some pretty nasty charges.'

'Then why not just walk away?' Coco retorted. 'It was only an exposé, for Dieu's sake. So what if Richard Severin was a dick? He may well have been up to his neck in shit, he may have killed his wife, he may have done a lot of things. Yannick Vidal may have got an award of some kind for his writing, but I can't imagine he would think it worth the price he would have to pay.' She shook her head forcefully. 'Nah. I think he would have just walked away.'

'And yet he didn't,' Demissy stated.

'What do you mean?' Coco retorted.

'Well, according to his story, Richard Severin gave him his ultimatum two nights ago, Dimanche soir,' Demissy continued. 'The next morning, Richard Severin was murdered. Yannick Vidal claims he didn't know Richard Severin was dead. If that's true. Then why didn't he run? Because as far as he knew, if he stuck around, Richard Severin was about to get him in a whole lot of trouble. If Yannick stayed, I can only think of one reason.'

'He knew he didn't have to run,' Cedric concluded. 'Because he'd gotten rid of the problem.'

Coco noticed Demissy smiling. 'You look very pleased with yourself.'

Demissy smiled. 'Well, I think we have an explanation which might just suit everyone.'

Coco's face contorted. 'Very neat.'

'Not everything has to be complicated, Captain Brunhild,' Demissy reasoned.

Coco turned to Cedric. 'And what do you think?'

'I think she's probably right,' he replied. 'Severin was pissed off about the exposé and did his best to put a stop to it, but he went too far with Yannick Vidal and he ended up getting a bit of his own medicine.'

'And how did it happen?' Coco pushed.

He shrugged. 'Vidal slept on Severin's threats, got riled up and went over to his house to confront him, but found him heading for the métro. He followed him and realised he could blend into the crowd and literally get away with murder.'

'It makes some kind of sense,' Demissy agreed.

Coco shook her head. 'Then what about the kidnapping? On the same day? At the same time?' She shook her head more vigorously. 'I just don't buy it. Unless…'

'Unless?' Demissy interrupted.

'Well, it's just that Yannick suggested he was in contact with Caroline Severin,' Coco recalled. 'There could be something there.'

Cedric nodded. 'The junkie daughter and the sleazy journalist combine to bring down the rich father?'

'Something like that, I suppose,' Coco conceded. 'The trouble is we have nothing but supposition to go on. We need to speak to them both urgently.'

'Yannick Vidal is most likely dead,' Demissy stated, 'and if Caroline Severin is involved, once she is found she's going to have a lot of people around her preventing us from getting answers from her.' She glanced at her watch and rose to her feet. 'Well, I think we have enough to go on for now. I'll go and call the Minister. It's a little later than he wanted, but I think he'll be pleased with the result.'

'Are you sure about this?' Coco asked.

Demissy nodded. 'I am.'

Coco and Cedric watched her leave the office.

'You think she's wrong, don't you?' Cedric asked.

Coco thought about her answer for a few moments. 'I like an easy life,' she began.

'Mais?'

'I like to think I've worked for it.'

Cedric frowned. 'What does that even mean?' he demanded.

'We're missing so much of this picture, Cedric,' she replied. 'So much that it bothers me, and more than that, I fucking hate pleasing people like Demissy and Lenoir when I'm not sure about something because if it all goes tits up, they won't remember that I said I wasn't sure, they'll just blame me for making them look foolish.'

Cedric gave her a sad smile. 'What do you want to do?'

Coco noticed Ebba approaching her office with an open laptop. 'I want a miracle!' she cried. 'Say, Ebba, you got me a miracle?'

Ebba dropped the laptop on Coco's desk. 'The dead guy was right. Nothing's ever really hidden, even when it's deleted. It took me five minutes to find the deleted videos, jpegs and search history, all pointing to really sick shit involving kids.'

'None of this proves it was planted,' Cedric reasoned. 'It really could have been Yannick's.'

'They weren't as clever as they think they were,' Ebba interrupted. 'The files were downloaded, and the searches were all done at the same time. If you had files like that on your computer, they would have different dates.'

'Severin and his cronies probably figured no one would look too closely at things like that,' Coco sighed. 'Once someone sees words like "child pornography" then they don't tend to want to defend the person accused.' She paused. 'Then you agree, it suggests Yannick Vidal was framed?'

Ebba shrugged. 'I could argue one way, a lawyer another.'

'Did you find anything else on the laptop?' Cedric asked.

'Like a book about Richard Severin, par example?' Coco added.

'Lots of notes,' Ebba replied, 'in fact, a shitload of notes that it's going to take *someone* days to go through, but nothing that vaguely resembles a book.'

'What about emails?'

'He has a Gmail account, but I don't have the password, obviously,' she replied. 'I can try if you like,' she added, as if saying she hoped she would not.

'I'm not sure what good it would do us anyway,' Coco groaned, stabbing her finger angrily at the laptop. 'There's really nothing useful on it?'

'I don't think so,' Ebba answered. 'I'll keep looking tomorrow if I have time, but right now, I have to go. I've got a date.'

'A date?' Coco asked in surprise.

Ebba glared at her. 'Yeah. I figure one of us in this damn place should at least be getting laid regularly.' She turned away. 'See ya!'

Cedric watched her leave. 'A date,' he repeated. He looked at Coco. 'Do you think she's more Arthur, or Martha?'

Coco smiled. 'She's young. I hope she's Arthur, Martha and whoever the hell he/she/it/they want to be, that's all I care about.'

'Non, it isn't. You're just jealous.'

She stuck out her tongue. 'So are you. Which is ridiculous because you're…'

'I'm what?' Cedric smirked.

'You're presentable,' Coco retorted. 'Stop fishing for compliments, we've still got work to do.'

'What the hell do you think we can do? You heard Demissy. As far as she's concerned, the case is closed. Go home. Be with your kids and give Helga the night off.'

'D'accord…'

She stopped as the telephone on her desk began ringing.

'Don't answer it,' Cedric groaned. 'I want to go to the gym and to the bar and…'

Coco snatched up the receiver. 'Allô, Captain Brunhild. Ah, bonsoir, Stella, amour. Quoi? D'accord. We're on our way.' She dropped the telephone and jumped to her feet. 'Forget being a gym bunny tonight, we've got to get to the hospital.'

'What's happened now?' Cedric asked, as if he clearly did not want her to respond.

'Emma Fitzgerald just died.'

'Merde.'

MARDI 19H30

'Then we have a second murder to investigate,' Coco stated, staring at the sheet which covered Emma Fitzgerald's body. Only her hand was exposed, and it was all Coco could do to stop herself from touching it. She wanted to hold it and say sorry for not being able to save her. When Coco closed her eyes, the image was still vivid. The sort of red dress Coco could only dream of wearing, wrapped around Emma Fitzgerald's mangled body, a high-heeled shoe upturned beside her. Coco looked at the hand, recognising the red-painted fingernails. Coco looked at her own black painted chipped nails and it filled her with overwhelming sadness.

Cedric sank into a chair opposite the hospital bed. 'You don't have to sound so happy about it,' he grumbled.

'Bien sûr, I'm not happy about it,' she retorted. 'I'm pissed off, that's what I am.' She stared at the sheet. 'Somebody deliberately mowed down this woman in front of me and I held her as she struggled for life. I looked into her eyes.' She pointed at her own eyes. 'It's likely these bloodshot eyes were the last thing she saw. And that's fucking tragic.' She took a deep breath. 'Before you say it, I can't think of a single reason why Yannick Vidal would want to murder Emma Fitzgerald.'

Cedric did not answer immediately. He stepped across the room, wrapping his hands around the back of his neck. 'There's a lot we don't know here, Captain,' he said. 'Mais, what I do know is that when money, like the scale of the Severin money, is in play, all deals are off. People become bastards, and they become evil. You know that. You've seen it, too. We've both seen the things people will do for a few bucks, let alone a few million euros. This is about money, and that's all. And because it's about money, nothing about it is going to make sense. People do shitty, out of character things when there's something in it for them, and you can stare into their faces and they'll lie right to you. People like Emile Severin, who have spent a lifetime running from his father, might just wake up one day and say, *fuck it, I'm sick of being broke, and I'm sick of my father holding it over me.* That's when people snap. And when good people snap, they tend to snap with a fucking vengeance.'

Coco smiled at him. 'How did you get so wise?' she asked.

He turned his head. 'I had an excellent teacher.'

The two police officers exchanged a look and then spun away, as if they were embarrassed.

'What do we do next?' Cedric broke the silence. 'Because you know we shouldn't do anything. As far as Commander Demissy and the Minister of Justice are concerned, they have a nice, neat bow to tie up this whole ridiculousness and they're not going to like it if we deviate from that.'

'It feels as if someone is laughing at us, and that really ticks me off.' Coco extracted her cell phone and pressed a few buttons. 'Sonny, it's Coco. I know it's late…'

Sonny chuckled. 'I'll be at the morgue in an hour.'

MARDI
21H00

Dr. Shlomo Bernstein stifled a yawn as he moved across the freshly cleaned floor of the morgue, his covered feet leaving imprints in the moisture as he went. Coco studied the floor, realising if she stepped inside, the holes in her boots would quickly dampen her socks. She stepped gingerly inside, walking around the side of the room where the floor appeared to have dried.

'I'm sorry about this,' she repeated for what felt like the hundredth time.

Sonny shrugged nonchalantly. 'You saved me another boring night alone flicking through Tinder, realising that if anyone cared enough to swipe me, I would never really have the time to have a normal relationship.'

'Amen to that,' Cedric agreed sadly.

Coco tutted, turning her head between the two men she seemed to spend most of her time with. 'What a pair of whingers!' she scolded. 'I have four kids, no money and a job that keeps me out,' she glanced at her watch, 'past my bedtime. If I can find time to exercise the old vajayjay, then you two can find time to exercise your juniors. Capeesh?'

Sonny laughed. He looked at Cedric. 'She has a point.'

Cedric shook his head forcefully. 'She *never* has a point. Haven't you got that yet?'

'Anyhow,' Coco continued, slinking along the wall, still avoiding the wet floor. She pointed at Emma Fitzgerald. 'Shall we get on with this so we can get some sleep tonight?'

Sonny turned to the covered remains. 'I don't know what you think I'm going to find. A dozen or so witnesses, including you, saw exactly how this poor woman died. I'm not sure what else I can tell you.'

'Probably nothing,' Coco conceded. 'Mais, I'd like to be certain. I tend to take it personally when people die at my feet.'

The doctor shrugged again. 'Ah, well, I'm happy for the overtime, Commander Demissy, on the other hand, probably won't.'

'What's new?' Coco sighed.

'Emma Fitzgerald died from a catastrophic head injury,' Sonny announced, flicking off his gloves and throwing them into the medical waste disposal bin. His eyes flicked over the remains. 'The hospital did an admiral job tending to her injuries, most of which would heal. She had broken knees, tibia and several ribs, but they would have gotten better with time, I'm sure. However, the damage to the skull was too severe. They tried to stem the flow of blood, but it was not to be.' He paused. 'I've taken samples and will run toxicology, but I see nothing to suggest anything untoward. She was a reasonably healthy woman in her forties.'

'Nothing unusual?' Coco asked.

Sonny picked up a folder. 'I've gone through her medical records and everything seems to be in order. The only thing which is odd is that there is no mention of her having given birth.'

Coco raised an eyebrow. 'And you're saying she had given birth?'

Sonny nodded, staring again at Emma Fitzgerald. 'Oui. Mais, before you ask, I can't really tell you much more than that, other than I don't believe it was a recent pregnancy.'

Coco scratched her chin. 'Then why isn't it in her medical records? You know what bureaucrats are like - they like to know the ins and outs of a fart and which way it blows.'

Sonny chuckled. 'Well, I don't know about that, mais you

told me she was born in England and spent most of her life there, the reports could just have been mislaid or not updated.'

'And of course, she may have gone private,' Cedric added. 'To keep it secret.' He frowned. 'Is it important?'

Coco stepped forward, her boot sliding on the floor. She grimaced as she felt the lukewarm, clean water seep into her socks. *Ah well, at least they're getting a wash,* she thought. 'Everything is important when we know nothing,' she replied cryptically. 'A baby, eh?' She moved towards the body. 'So, little Miss Prim had a secret.'

'We don't know that,' Cedric responded.

Coco bent over, her eyes moving over Emma Fitzgerald's body. 'And you're sure she had an actual baby, rather than just a miscarriage?' she asked Sonny.

He nodded. 'I observed a series of shotgun pellet-sized pockmarks along the inside of her pelvic bone,' he replied. 'They are usually caused by the tearing of ligaments during childbirth. The bone impressions are actually permanent records of the trauma of childbirth.'

'Trauma's the right word!' Coco exclaimed.

'You're telling me,' Cedric added with a shudder.

'You had the straightforward part,' Coco quipped. 'Men always do.'

Cedric snorted. 'I can just imagine how many pockmarks you've got,' he muttered.

Coco shot him a disparaging look. 'I'll have you know there's nothing wrong with my pelvic bone,' she quipped.

Sonny smiled before continuing. 'As I said, I can't tell you how long ago it was, other than it wasn't recent, nor does it reveal how many children she had, or of what sex.'

Coco flopped into a chair, emitting a loud sigh.

'I don't know what you were expecting,' Cedric said. 'Dr. Bernstein warned you.'

'What about her belongings?' Coco asked. 'She had a handbag and was wearing a long red dress and matching shoes.'

'Ebba already went through them,' Sonny replied. 'There was nothing on the dress, and not much in the bag.'

'Do you have it?'

Sonny nodded and lifted the lid of a cardboard box on his desk, extracting a large clear perspex evidence bag. He tipped the contents onto the desk. Coco studied it. There appeared nothing remarkable or unexpected. 'What've we got. A purse, a makeup bag, some perfume and a book. Hmm.' She unzipped the purse, emptying the contents in front of her. 'A few euros, a métro pass and a bank card. Rien.'

Cedric sighed. 'What were you expecting, a confession note?'

Coco pursed her lips. 'Well, she was on her way to the commissariat, which can only mean she was coming to confess in one way or another. Either she did something, or she knew something.'

'Either way, it does us no good now,' Cedric reasoned.

Coco picked up the bank card and the métro pass. 'We could check these out.'

'Why?' Cedric demanded. 'Don't you think we have enough to do already? I want to have a life outside of work, and I know you do too.' He studied her. 'You do, don't you?'

'Of course I do,' she retorted huffily. 'I just hate loose ends, you know that.'

'Sometimes it's all we have,' Sonny interjected. 'And it's hard to live with, but we have to.'

Coco's cell phone beeped in her pocket. She pulled it out, staring at the screen. 'Ah, it's Ebba. Bonsoir, cher Ebba.'

'Have I told you lately how much I hate you?' Ebba hissed down a noisy line.

Coco strained to hear what the young forensic technician was saying. 'Quoi? What was that? I think you said you were having such a dull time on your date you want me to come down to the pub and liven it up?'

'Over my dead body!' Ebba cried. 'Listen. I just got a call from one of my contacts. You know they've been giving Commander Demissy the run-around about that drug dealer guy?'

Coco nodded. 'Yeah. Jihef Abreo. What about him?'

'I put a call out to some friends…'

'You have friends…' Coco mumbled.

'Hey! You want my help or not?' Ebba yelled.

'Désolé,' Coco said quickly. 'Carry on.'

'Jihef Abreo isn't a real drug dealer,' Ebba said. 'He's a cop. He's been undercover for eight months. He usually works out of the 12th arrondissement.'

Coco gasped. 'Are you sure?'

'No, I'm bullshitting,' Ebba snapped. 'Of course, I'm sure. He's a cop, that's why he has a fake record.'

'I had a feeling it was that,' Coco replied. 'The question is - what the hell is he doing with Caroline Severin?'

'Could he have been investigating her father?' Ebba asked.

Coco considered. 'Well, it might just make sense. Anything else?'

'Both Emile and Timo Severin's cell phones are switched off and have been for a few hours now,' Ebba replied. 'So, I don't know where they are. I have them logged so that when they're turned on, I should get an update, but in the meantime, there's not a lot else I can do.'

'That's odd, isn't it?' Coco thought aloud. 'I mean, in this day and age, it's odd for anyone to have their phones switched off, let alone for a few hours.' She exhaled. 'D'accord. Merci for your time, Ebba. Go back to your date… if it's still ongoing, that is?'

'They're still here, actually,' Ebba replied huffily.

'They?' Coco gasped. 'You sly old fox, you. Two on the go at once! I have to say I'm impressed!'

Ebba tutted. 'They as in that are their pronouns,' she snapped before disconnecting the call.

Coco stared at the cell phone. 'I don't think I'm ever going to understand young people,' she said sadly.

MARDI
23H45

Coco stepped out of the métro station and breathed a sigh of relief to have made it home with no incident, apart from the drunk who had sat next to her, wriggling his tongue vaguely in the direction of her ear. All Coco wanted to do now was to open the door to her tiny apartment, lock it behind her and feel that she was completely safe. It did not matter that her eldest children would likely scowl at her and bitterly complain about one thing or another. It was the complaining that kept them together. Barbra, the daughter who fought so hard to not be like her mother, but had not yet found the courage to leave her, and Julian, the son whose secrets consumed him although she had tried to make sure they did not. And then there were the youngest two. Still babies in their own different ways. They still needed her, and that was all Coco needed to know. To be needed was as good a reward as she could hope for. Each night spent with them in her bed told her that she had done something right in her life.

'Hey,' a deep voice called out from the shadows of the métro station.

Coco stopped dead in her tracks, instantly recognising the deep voice. She spun around, staring into the darkness. 'So, it's the drug dealer slash…'

'Shut your damn mouth,' he hissed.

Coco popped a hip, extracting a cigarette from her bag and lighting it quickly, blowing smoke with determination in his direction, even though she could not see him. She wanted to appear strong, though it was not how she felt at that moment. She turned her head towards her apartment block and realised that despite how much she complained about it; it was home, and it was somewhere she felt safe. She did not want to feel unsafe in her neighbourhood and it annoyed her that this man was doing just that.

'Come out of the shadows you damn creep,' she growled with as much gusto as she could manage, 'or I'll come in there and drag you out by your damn dreadlocks.'

'It's less offensive to just say locks these days, but mine are braids, actually,' he answered tartly.

Coco shrugged. 'As I'm slowly beginning to realise these days, I know bugger all about anything. So, come, you and your "braids," and stop hiding like this is some goddamn awful TV movie.'

Jihef Abreo stepped out of the darkness, shielding his eyes from the harsh lighting of the métro station. 'I've been waiting hours for you to come home,' he grumbled.

'Pfff,' Coco retorted. 'Poor bloody you. I've been at a morgue, not a damn dancing bar full of hot young men. Anyway,' she sniffed, 'you know where I work and how to get in touch with me.'

'You've really made my life difficult,' Jihef replied. He moved closer towards her and Coco was surprised by his appearance. His clothes were dirty and his eyes had more luggage under them than her own.

'You look like shit,' she stated.

Jihef laughed. 'Merci. Part of the job, I guess.'

Coco glanced down at her still filthy coat. 'I'm with you on that.' Her eyes moved over him. 'You need to tell me what the hell you're up to,' she demanded, 'et maintenant. Because I'm on my last nerve, and I'm liable to go loco at any moment.'

He smiled. 'I heard you were weird.'

Coco snorted. 'You have no idea.' She sucked on her cigarette. 'So, c'mon, spill your guts. You're a cop. A drug division cop, but I have a sneaky suspicion you're up to your neck in something else, right?'

Jihef glanced around him. There was no one else around. He moved across the boulevard towards Coco. 'Being undercover sucks,' he said.

'I did it once, and you're right, it sucks,' Coco agreed. 'Then, what's your problem?'

Jihef sank onto the ground, pulling his knees towards his chest. He took a deep breath. Coco glanced around, thinking of sitting next to him on the ground but releasing she would probably never be able to get up again if she tried. Instead, she positioned herself against the wall, dropping her bag between her legs.

'I ran into Caroline Severin a few months ago,' he began. 'I'd been infiltrating one of the biggest drug-smuggling cartels in Paris. She was up to her eyes in debt to them and doing pretty much everything she could to pay them off and get more drugs.'

'Did you know who she was?' Coco asked.

He shook his head. 'Not at first. It's only when I overheard her begging for more heroin and telling them she could get money from her father because he was loaded that I realised who she was. I already knew the name because my girlfriend has been heading up a Taskforce for the last eighteen months - a Taskforce with the sole purpose of taking Richard Severin down.'

Coco raised an eyebrow. 'Really? For what?'

'Money laundering, tax evasion, you name it,' Jihef replied. 'They've been trying to nail Severin for years for one thing or another, but he was slippery and every time they came close or had someone willing to talk, they mysteriously disappeared, never to be heard from again.'

'Do you know Yannick Vidal?'

Jihef tutted. 'Yeah. He claims to have proof Richard Severin was up to his eyes in all sorts, including the murder of his wife, but he refused to cooperate, even when we pressured him. He said once his book was out, he would turn over all his evidence. He claimed he knew for a fact that Severin had cops on his payroll.'

'And did he?' Coco asked.

'Probably,' Jihef replied. 'It would explain why whenever we got close to him, the evidence or the witness were gone before we could do anything with them.'

Coco nodded. 'So, when you met Caroline, you decided to do what, exactly? Use her?'

Jihef's eyes flashed. 'Look, I'm not proud of it, but I was done with the undercover life, and my girlfriend is miserable chasing after someone who seems untouchable.'

'What was the plan?'

'To get Caroline talking.'

'And how did you propose to do that? By giving her drugs?' Coco asked spikily.

'You haven't met Caroline, have you?' Jihef bristled. 'She's one hit away from an OD. She's been on borrowed time for a very long time. She has no interest in anything other than her next hit. And to answer your question, non, I didn't give her drugs. I gave her something else. A way to get back at her father and get a whole heap of money.'

'By kidnapping her own daughter?' Coco cried, her voice rising sharply. 'What kind of cockamamie plan was that?'

'It wasn't my idea, not really,' Jihef shot back. 'Listen. Her father wouldn't give her any more money and money was the one thing she needed, and I needed information. I told her if she gave me something on him, then we would blackmail him and we'd all make some money.'

Coco stepped away, stubbing out her cigarette and lighting another. 'I get that when you're undercover, you have rules to follow, and you have to do things you wouldn't normally do, but helping a drug addict kidnap her young daughter? That's just about as wrong as it can be.'

'I told you, it wasn't my idea. That was all Caroline. She got in touch with someone in her family and they came up with the plan together.'

'Who was helping her?'

'I don't know. She never said. But she told me that this was the only way she'd get money from her father, and of course, I couldn't tell her the real reason I wanted the information, so I had to go along with her,' he continued. 'Once she started trusting me, she started talking anyway, giving me enough to pass on to my girlfriend.'

'Where are Caroline and Laure?' Coco demanded.

'I don't know.'

'The hell you don't!' Coco shouted. 'I know you went along with her to send the ransom demand.'

Jihef nodded. 'Yeah, I did, but that was it. We sent the demand and were supposed to wait, but then we heard he died. Caroline went crazy when she found out. I don't know whether it was grief or sadness, or happiness. Whatever it was, all she could think about was getting higher than she had ever been before, so she took off and I haven't seen her since. She's dead for all I know.'

Coco scratched her head. 'Then where the hell is the kid? Where's Laure?'

'This was never about actually kidnapping the kid,' Jihef responded. 'Caroline didn't want her daughter back. She said she'd never had a mother herself, only a rat-bag of a father, so she'd never learnt how to be a mother. I think the truth was, she just didn't want a kid holding her back, making her responsible. Caroline is pretty messed up, but not when it comes to knowing what she wants, and all she wants is to get high and spend her days watching the world go by. She has no interest in taking part. If you knew her, you'd probably think she was quite happy with her life, apart from the lack of money.'

'Not anymore, she's suddenly become a very rich woman.'

He nodded. 'I figured as much. She always claimed her father had cut her out of her will, but I knew that wasn't true.'

'Do you think she believed it, though?' Coco pushed.

Jihef considered his answer. 'I think she probably did.'

'I don't get it,' Coco continued. 'Someone has Laure.'

Jihef shrugged. 'All I can tell you is that whoever Caroline was in cahoots with, had arranged it all, and told her that Laure was going to stay with some friends who had moved out of Paris and that she would be brought back when the ransom was paid. Everyone knew Richard would never go to the police. He was probably more frightened of them looking into him instead of looking for the kidnappers. Laure would come back to Paris and that would be that. She would have had a lovely time in the country, and it would slowly dawn on her grandfather that he had been duped.'

Coco sucked on the cigarette. 'What did Caroline give you on her father?'

Jihef spread his hands in front of him. 'Not a lot, or so I thought. But she told me about a company owned by her father and his business partner. The company is in the name of her mother, and it's the company they use for all the dodgy dealing. I passed it on to my girlfriend thinking it would amount to nothing, but according to her, it's going to take forensic accountants a long time to sort through it all and make sense of it, but they were all pretty excited about it. If Richard Severin wasn't dead, he would certainly be fucked.'

Coco sighed. 'All the good it will do now. As you said, he's dead. He'll never be punished for whatever the hell he got up to.'

'Mais, it will do some good for all the people he messed over and robbed. They'll get answers. He might not have to face punishment, but people will know the sort of asshole he was,' Jihef explained. 'It's something. And you must know that in our game, sometimes something is better than nothing. Maybe, just maybe, a lot of innocent people who were fucked over by Richard Severin are going to get some kind of closure, not just financial but the fact the truth will come out is going to make a lot of people extremely happy.'

'However, it doesn't help me very much,' Coco replied contemplatively. She turned her head. 'But figuring out who the hell was helping Caroline just might. Where do you think Caroline went?'

'Probably the Panteré estate,' Jihef replied. 'She has a boyfriend of sorts there. He's a low-level dealer, but as far as I can tell, he's decent enough and seems to like her. Don't ask me who he is, or where he is because I don't know, and that banlieue is like a rabbit's warren. You could look for weeks and never find her.'

Coco turned back to face him. 'That's the second time the Panteré banlieue has come up in this investigation.'

Jihef laughed. 'It's hardly surprising. Most of the drug dealing in Paris originates from there.'

'Still…' she trailed off. 'It's odd, and it's interesting, nonetheless.'

'Listen, I have to go,' Jihef said quickly. 'I just wanted to speak to you and ask you to stop looking for me, and stop asking for me, because in my line of work, it can be really dangerous.'

Coco nodded. 'You'll let me know if you think of anything else, or if you hear from Caroline?'

'Oui, bien sûr.' He reached into his pocket and pulled out a piece of paper. 'Here's my number. But I beg you, only use it if you have to, and if you do, always ask for drugs, okay?'

Coco snorted as she took the number. 'Like I could afford drugs. Mais, merci for this.'

She watched Jihef disappear into the night and she stepped away from the station, racing along the boulevard towards her apartment.

'You hang out with some really shady characters.'

Coco jumped, her hands immediately balling into fists. It

took her a moment to realise who was talking. Denis, the friendly neighbourhood homeless man. She flashed him a weary smile. As much as she wanted to spend a moment with him, she was exhausted and just wanted to get out of the night and be with her family. She immediately felt bad for the thought, once again reminded that the likelihood was nobody would have passed a moment with him all day.

'I certainly do,' she said.

'He looked like he was trouble,' Denis replied, concern clear in his voice.

Coco smiled. 'Yeah, but the kind of trouble I can handle. Don't worry, I doubt he'll be back.'

Denis nodded. 'Bon. No offence, but you look even more shit than you did last night.'

She threw back her head and laughed. 'Yeah, I probably do. It's been another very full and decidedly odd day.'

'You caught the bad guy?'

Coco thought about her answer. 'I don't even know the difference anymore.'

'I'm not a bad guy,' Denis whispered.

Coco looked him over. His clothes and his beard, and the dirt on his face told her nothing about him, but his eyes, sparkling in the night light, did. He was not a bad guy; she was sure. But he was also not a man she could entertain any further thoughts of. 'I know you're not,' she sighed. 'Listen, I have to go to bed. I desperately need sleep and I dread what tomorrow brings, so I need wine to gird my loins.'

He nodded. 'I understand,' he said, his voice betraying his disappointment. He watched her leave, and Coco could feel his eyes boring into her.

'Hey, before you go,' he called out. 'I've been thinking about your B4 problem.'

'B4?' Coco asked, momentarily confused. 'Ah, yeah that. No

one seems to have a clue what the hell it could mean.'

'I had a thought about it,' Denis said. 'I've spent the day looking around my old neighbourhoods trying to figure out where I recognised it from…'

'Denis, that's very kind of you,' Coco interrupted, 'but you don't need to do that for me. I have a station full of cops sitting on their lazy asses, and they get paid to do shit like that.'

Denis laughed, raising an almost empty bottle of wine. 'Do you think I have anything better to do with my day?'

Coco smiled and reached into her bag, pulling out her purse.

Denis raised his hand. 'I don't want your money, princess.'

She laughed again. 'Just as well because I think the only things in my purse are mothballs.' She stopped. 'I wished you'd go somewhere warm, though. I hate to think of you out here every night in the cold.'

He shrugged. 'If I get cold, I get up and go for a walk. There's always a brasier under one of the bridges to warm my hands on and someone to have a chat with, share a drink, share a moment.' He smiled at her. 'Don't think of my life as a bad one, because it isn't. This life chose me, and that gave me two choices. Embrace it, or give in and end up dead in a ditch somewhere. I chose life. This life is only what I deserve.'

Coco nodded, but she did not agree with him. Whoever Denis was, he had been someone one day. A man far removed from his current circumstances, she was sure of it, if only because of the eloquent way in which he spoke. 'Hey,' she said, 'why did you think you recognised the B4 paper?'

He shrugged. 'I can't be sure. But I'm fairly positive I've seen it before somewhere. I have a few more places to check, but I'm sure I'll figure it out.'

Coco smiled at him, grateful for his kindness but not sure it would amount to anything. She opened the door to her apartment building and turned back to him. 'Say, if you figure anything out, stop by Commissariat de Police du 7e arrondissement and ask for Coco. If I'm in, what do you say I take you out to lunch, or brunch, or whatever?'

His eyes widened. 'You'd want to do that? With me? In public?'

Coco chuckled, pointing at her coat. 'Are you serious? It should be me asking you if you're happy to be seen out with me in public! À demain, Denis.'

'À demain, princess.'

Coco stepped inside the vestibule, pulling the door closed behind her. In that instant, her eyes locked on the pavement opposite as a figure scurried away from the sudden light thrown from the open door. She frowned, shaking her head, realising it was probably only the imagination of an exhausted and sober woman, both of which she planned to rectify right away.

0000

MERCREDI
08H30

Coco moved slowly down the spiral stairway from the tenth floor, waving at a neighbour in the rickety elevator Coco still found a struggle to deal with. Her children and Helga rode in it regularly, though the shadow of what had happened there did not cover them in the same way it did her, and for that, she was extremely grateful. Her eldest son Julien appeared behind her, touching her arm so as not to startle her.

'How you doing, Maman?' he asked. His voice was light and airy, the complete opposite to her own, but they shared the same eyes. When he looked at her, it felt as if he was looking into her, not at her. She loved him completely, though she did not know how someone so beautiful could have been created by the coupling of Coco and the miscreant who fathered him.

'I'm just dandy,' she replied.

'No offence, but you look like shit.'

'Watch the language, kid!' she scolded gently. 'I mean, where did you learn words like that?'

His eyes widened, and he pointed towards her. 'Err… doh!'

'How dare you! I'm a diamond,' Coco cried, mock offended. 'Where are you off to so early?'

'My classes start at 09H30 these days,' he replied.

Coco nodded. 'Yeah. I should know that.' She realised much of her children's lives seemed to pass by her. Helga took the younger two to school and collected them, gave them their suppers, and put them to bed. Coco knew she should do more, or get a job that freed up her time, but the reality of her situation was stark for her. She did not know what else she could do, and although being a cop was not exactly making her rich, it was supporting them all, just about, but regardless of the inadequacies of their lives together, somehow it seemed to work. 'How's that going? The learning, that is?'

He shrugged. 'I like art, but I'm not sure it's going to get me a job,' he replied, running a hand over his head. He had recently shaved off his mop of curls and it had left him looking like a teenager, rather than the young man he had become.

'Just get good grades. The rest will take care of itself,' Coco replied, wrapping her arm around him. Her heart soared when he did not slouch his shoulders to extract himself from her touch. 'And this isn't the time to be worrying about the future. You're still a kid, enjoy being one.'

Her son looked at her. 'I should be working like Barbra, then at least I'd be giving you some money, rather than just taking it.'

Coco stopped, pulling him even closer. 'Hey kid, we've got food on the table, *mostly*. We've got a place to live. It might be crappy, but it's serviceable, and more importantly, we've got each other - what the hell more could we want?'

Julien's eyes flicked over his mother and her clothes. 'I'd like to be able to buy you a new coat, at least.'

Coco laughed, brushing crumbs from her lapels. 'Well, even if you did, I'd still end up wearing this one. Do you know how much this coat would cost new? Too much, that's what! I love it, and yeah, it's dirty and covered in… covered in things it shouldn't be, but in the end, it's just all stuff and nonsense really, and one day soon, it'll be cleaned and it will look fabulous again, and that's all I need. Tomorrow or the day after, it will be clean, and then probably the day after it will be dirty again. That's life, fils. That's life.'

Julien started walking again, pulling away from her. 'Your pep talks need some work.'

Coco trotted after him, her broken shoes flopping against the stairs. 'You're probably right. Say, how's Matthieu?'

Julien stopped abruptly, causing Coco to crash into him. He started up again. 'He's a pain, that's how he is.'

'Oh,' Coco mouthed. 'You've had a falling out…'

He stopped again, turning back to her. 'I don't know what you think, but…'

She touched his arm again. 'I don't care about anything in this life, other than my kids being happy. Whatever it takes to make you happy, so long as it isn't really freaky or illegal, is fine by me. Capeesh?'

'Not everyone thinks like that,' Julien snapped. 'And it isn't fair.' He moved forward. 'And I'm not talking about this with my damn mother.' He pushed open the entrance door, flooding the vestibule with light. He turned back to her. 'I'm not confirming anything you might think by saying this, but I have to ask you one question.'

Coco grinned so widely she thought her face would burst. 'Anything, cheri.'

'Are men always so fucking difficult and annoying?'

Coco chuckled and ran to her son, wrapping her arm around his shoulders again. They began walking in the direction of the métro station. 'Are men always so fucking difficult and annoying?' she repeated. 'My dear boy, let me tell you a thing or two about men because believe me, I've gotta lot of experience, and a lot of things to say.'

'S'il te plaît, non!' Julien pleaded.

'See you later, Denis!' Coco called over her shoulder, as she always did when passing the homeless man in the alleyway. *Not if I see you first,* the lightning-fast reply would come. But it did not. 'See you later, Denis,' she repeated. Denis still did not reply. 'Wait there a minute, Julien,' Coco said, stepping away from her son. She moved back towards the alley. She could see Denis was in his normal position, bolt upright, wedged between his boxes and bags.

His head was resting on his left shoulder and she realised he was probably just asleep, but something stopped her from turning away. The morning light had not yet quite hit the alleyway, but she could see enough of his face to know that his eyes were half-open, staring distantly in the opposite direction. She inched forward, extending her hand towards his chest, nuzzling him.

'Hey, wake up, Denis.'

He did not move, and she pulled back her hand. Her palm felt warm and sticky and she lifted it towards her face, her mouth contorting in horror as she saw the copper coloured blood on her.

'Fuck me sideways!' she screamed. 'Julien, call the pompiers and tell them to get here quickly!'

MERCREDI
09H30

Dr. Stella Bertram moved swiftly across the hospital emergency ward, grabbing a pair of scissors as she passed the nurses' station. Coco followed a few steps behind, her wet feet slipping on the tiled floors. Stella stopped in front of Denis and moved a nurse out of the way. She deftly began cutting away his clothes.

Coco watched without moving. Her eyes were wide, and she was conscious enough to know that she was probably in shock. An occupational hazard, she thought. She glanced over her shoulder, trying to remember what had happened to Julien, and she vaguely remembered barking for him to get off to college and forget about her.

'Shit! You're covered in blood,' Cedric gasped. He had appeared by her side and she had not even noticed. Coco glanced down at her trusty blue and green checked woollen coat and noticed she was, again, covered in blood.

'Were you hurt?' Stella called over her shoulder, concern clear in her voice.

'Non, it's not my blood, it's Denis's,' Coco replied breathlessly.

'That's his name? Denis?' Stella called.

Coco shrugged. 'I think so. At least that's what he said it was. I don't know if it's his real name, to be honest, but that's what he told me.'

Stella gestured to a nurse. 'Come over here and help me remove these clothes. It looks like he's wearing a lot of layers and they all seem to have matted into one another.'

The nurse flicked on a pair of gloves and moved next to Stella, her nose wrinkling in disgust. 'He's a patient, just like any other,' Stella growled. 'Damn, I can't see where the blood is coming from,' Stella cried. She pulled the last remaining piece of fabric away from his chest. 'Putain! Call the OR and tell them we're on our way up.'

'What's going on?' Coco asked.

'Step back, Charlotte,' Stella instructed as she began moving the bed backwards. 'There's a knife wound to the chest and by the looks of it, he's lost a hell of a lot of blood. I need to get him up to surgery and then we can properly assess the damage.'

Coco nodded, watching as Stella and the nurses pushed Denis away. She noticed the mound of discarded clothing on the ground. 'Can I go through his stuff?'

'Be my guest,' Stella called from the hallway. 'I'll let you know how he gets on.'

Coco bent down, flicked on forensic gloves and began rummaging through Denis' clothes.

'You nearly gave me a heart attack again!' Cedric said softly. 'All the call said was you were on your way to hospital. I thought… I thought…'

Coco touched his arm. She met his gaze and a moment of warmth passed between them.

Cedric pushed her away. 'I thought, what the hell trouble has she gotten us into this time?' he said with bravado.

She punched his arm, her mouth pulling into a smile. 'Admit it, you were worried sick about me.'

Cedric's nose wrinkled. 'What the hell is that smell? Is it you?'

'Bien sûr, it's not me,' she coughed, pointing at the clothes. 'My old pal Denis wasn't exactly high on personal hygiene or cleanliness.'

'How the hell do you know this man?' Cedric asked. His face clouded. 'Tell me he's not your latest boy toy?'

'So what if he is?' she sniffed. 'Don't judge a book by its cover, Lieutenant Degarmo. If you've learned anything from me, it should be that.' She stared at the pile of discarded clothes. 'Non, Denis is just a really sweet man who lives in my neighbourhood.'

'What happened to him?'

She shrugged. 'Some bastard stuck a blade in him, and I want to know why.'

Cedric rolled his eyes. 'You can't. We have more than enough crimes already to investigate. Pass it on to someone else.'

Coco shook her head vehemently. 'Non. This is my case. Denis was…,' she stopped, shaking her head angrily, 'non, IS a sweet guy. He didn't deserve for some fucker to stick a knife in him and I'm going to find out why.'

Cedric looked at the clothes. 'The guy was a tramp. He probably got into a fight over a bottle of booze or drugs, or some other shit.' He grabbed her arm. 'This can't be our problem, Captain.'

'Then who the hell else's problem is it going to be?' Coco pulled away from him. She picked up a jumper and thrust it in Cedric's face, causing him to recoil. 'This is a dirty jumper, and that's all it is. He doesn't have a washing machine, or anyone to do it for him, or the money to pay for it, and that is the only difference between Denis and us.'

'I think there's probably more difference than that…' Cedric interjected.

Coco ignored him and continued rummaging through the clothes, dropping empty cigarette packets and crisp and chocolate wrappers to the ground. 'Ah-ha!' she cried triumphantly, extracting a slim black wallet. She flipped it open and peered inside. There were only three items. She lifted them out. 'A photograph,' she said, narrowing her eyes. The photograph was crinkled and stained, making it difficult to see the image. 'It seems to be Denis,' she whispered. 'A clean and hot Denis,' she added, her mouth indicating it clearly impressed her. Her face crumpled. 'With a pretty blonde and a pair of kids,' she added, handing the photograph to Cedric.

'Nice family,' Cedric said with a nonchalant shrug. He threw the photo onto the bed. 'It wouldn't be the first time someone has thrown that kind of life away because of drink or drugs.'

Coco ignored him and continued. 'And what do we have here?' She held up a card. 'An ID. Shit. He was in the army. Denis Acy.' She stared at the ID. 'Well, it gives us somewhere to start, I suppose.'

'Great,' Cedric grumbled.

'And what's this?' Coco continued unfolding the third item from the wallet. 'Fuck!' she cried.

'What is it?'

She handed him the paper card. It contained just one letter and one number. *D7.*

Cedric frowned. 'What does that mean?'

A myriad of thoughts bounced around Coco's head. 'Oh damn, I have a bad feeling about this.'

Cedric scratched his head. 'I don't understand.'

Coco sank into a chair. 'Me and my big mouth, what is there to understand? I was talking to Denis the other night and mentioned the piece of paper we found on Richard Severin and that I couldn't work out where it came from,' she began. 'And then last night he said he recognised it, but he couldn't work out why, so he was going to figure it out today.'

'It's a piece of paper,' Cedric said wearily. 'It could have come from anywhere, it could be about anything.'

She held up the paper. 'It looks the same.'

'It looks like any random typed letter and number, and just because some random tramp…'

'He has a name,' Coco hissed. 'And it is Denis Acy.'

Cedric nodded. 'Désolé, Denis Acy. Just because Denis Acy's

addled brain might have connected two dots and come up with four, doesn't mean a whole damn lot, does it? And more importantly, it doesn't help our current investigation in any way, does it?'

Coco held the piece of paper to her chest. 'If I find out Denis was hurt because he was trying to help me, then they're going to have me to answer to.'

'You can't know it had anything to do with you,' Cedric reasoned. 'And whoever attacked Denis can't know about your connection to him.'

Coco hurried towards the exit. She stopped suddenly, causing Cedric to crash into her.

'Wait a minute,' she gasped. 'Last night as I was going inside my apartment building, I thought I saw someone watching me from across the street.'

Cedric gave her a doubtful look. 'Why would someone be watching you?'

She shrugged. 'To find out where I live? To find out what I know? Who the hell knows at this point? But what I know is that just before, I was talking to Denis and he told me about his plans to continue looking for "B4." What if the person following me is the same person who murdered Richard Severin? If they overheard us talking, that could have been why… why…' she stabbed angrily at her eyes as if she was pushing away tears. 'If he dies because he was trying to help me… I'll…'

Cedric stopped her and pulled her into his arms. 'He's not going to die, and we're going to clear up this mess once and for all, okay?'

Coco pulled back and looked up at him, the tears causing her mascara to run. 'Do you think?'

He grinned at her. 'When have I ever been wrong?'

MERCREDI
10H30

'Take off your damn coat,' Commander Demissy barked.

Coco regarded her with suspicion, defensively pulling the coat tight around her body.

Demissy sighed. 'Don't worry. I realise how "attached" you are to it. I am merely refusing to look at your blood and whatever-the-hell-else stained jacket a moment longer. The damn thing will walk out of here soon of its own volition.'

'Well, why didn't you just say that in the first place?' Coco grinned, slipping out of her coat. She hesitated to hand it over. 'Wait, this isn't an intervention, is it?'

Demissy turned to Cedric. 'Lieutenant Degarmo - can you take the…' her eyes flicked over the coat, 'offending article and give it to my assistant. She is going to have it dry cleaned and returned to Captain Brunhild forthwith.' She paused. 'If cleaning is at all possible.'

Cedric smiled and left Coco's office.

Demissy lowered herself into a chair, casting her eyes over the office. 'Peut être they could try to work their magic over your office, while they're at it.'

Coco looked around her office. There were several filing cabinets lining the wall, some with drawers open and files poking out. A stained sofa and coffee table overflowing with plastic cups, pizza cartons and other food boxes were the only pieces of furniture other than Coco's desk, which was so overcrowded, Coco could not be sure what colour it was. 'It's not so bad, really,' she stated with a casual shrug of her shoulders.

Demissy cleared her throat. 'Anyway, let's move on, shall we?

Am I correct in thinking you found another dead person this morning?'

'He's not dead,' Coco interjected quickly.

'*Yet*,' Demissy shrugged. 'My point is, it rather seems to have turned into a habit of yours, non? Collecting bodies, that is.'

Coco suppressed a sigh. 'I'm not sure what your point is, Commander Demissy, and I keep coming back to the same point myself - I may have faults, but the truth is, I'm a pretty damn good flic.' She stared at the Commander. 'I understand we never really got off on the right foot, you and I, and there's not a lot I can do about that. We can choose to like or loathe each other, or we can just get on with it. I always choose just to get on with it and I wish to hell you would too.'

Demissy cocked her head, fixing Coco with an interested look.

Coco ignored her and continued. 'Mais, the real point is I believe they deliberately targeted Denis Acy as part of our current investigation.'

'Denis Acy?'

'Oui, Denis Acy,' Coco spoke his name with sadness. 'The man whose blood is on my,' she looked down, her face clouding when she realised her coat was gone, 'whose blood is about to be erased from my coat.'

'What do you mean he was deliberately targeted?' Demissy demanded.

Coco took a deep breath and then lit a cigarette, ignoring Demissy's piercing stare and began explaining her theory to the Commander.

Demissy listened, her head turned to the side. As Coco finished, Demissy did not immediately respond. 'You're basing your theory on a piece of paper with a similar message to the one you found on Richard Severin, and that you suspect there was someone watching or following you?'

Coco laughed. 'Well, when you put it like that, it sounds a little whacky, mais…' she trailed off. 'I believe it to be the truth.' She paused, moving the cigarette between her fingers. 'And there is also the possibility that it wasn't me they were following.'

'You mean Jihef Abreo?'

Coco shrugged. 'It's possible. I don't care whether or not he's a real cop. I think he's got his fingers in some very dirty pies, and he's most likely dragged us all into it.'

Demissy tapped her lips. As usual, they were painted blue and were a stark contrast to her dark skin. 'There is certainly something strikingly odd about it, and it irritates me that he used a drug-addled woman to kick-start an altogether different investigation into her father. It most definitely irritates me, but I suppose it is logical, and despite our misgivings, we have to accept that we would probably do something similar in those circumstances. However, I find myself sharing your belief that it is somehow connected and that Abreo may have just been part of something which triggered what has happened in the last few days.'

'You find yourself sharing my belief,' Coco mouthed, obviously impressed with herself.

'Steady, Captain,' Demissy interjected. 'Don't get carried away.'

Coco smiled a moment before her face clouded. 'I'd be happier if we knew for certain Laure Severin was safe and well.'

Demissy nodded. 'Unfortunately "in the country" isn't exactly very helpful,' she said. 'Peut être if you found Caroline Severin, matters may appear a little clearer.'

'As you know, we stand about as much chance of finding her on the Panteré banlieue as I do… as I do…'

'Getting to a point? Solving a case? Getting a haircut?' Demissy preempted.

Coco chuckled. 'You see, you can be funny when you want to.'

Demissy fixed her with an icy stare. 'Who said I was being funny?' she retorted, her voice deadpan. 'As for the surveillance at the cybercafé, I have called it off.'

'What did you do that for?' Coco begged. 'What if Caroline Severin turns up there again?'

Demissy smoothed her skirt. 'My budget does not stretch to paying for twenty-four-hour surveillance on something which amounts to folly. Find Caroline Severin, but do so without making me pay for two officers to sit in a car for no good reason.'

Coco's mouth twisted. 'There is another connection with the Panteré banlieue,' she continued. 'Emma Fitzgerald's murderer was last seen disappearing into the rat hole.'

Demissy shrugged. 'There may be no connection. No matter what you think you saw, it could have just been an accident. A stupid, dangerous accident that resulted in someone's death, but an accident nonetheless. There is absolutely no evidence to suggest otherwise.'

'Then why was she outside the commissariat?'

'We may never know.' Demissy stood up. 'What are your plans now?'

'I'm going to get a mandate - I'd like to go through Yannick Vidal's apartment, and then I'm going to try to track down Emile and Timo Severin,' Coco replied. 'No one seems to know where they are, and the more I learn about that damn family, the more I'm sure I've been lead down the garden path the entire time. And I'm fed up with it. Time to start cracking some skulls.'

Demissy gave her a disapproving look. 'Keep me updated.'

MERCREDI
11H15

Coco pushed open the door to Yannick Vidal's apartment, a mound of post falling away from the door. She stepped inside, Cedric close behind her. 'It's a bit of a mess in here,' Coco commented. 'Aren't the homes of gay men supposed to be spotless because the dust never has time to settle? That's why I was always hopeful I'd have a gay son who was more interested in flicking a duster than I am.' She turned her head. The room was a mess, with overturned furniture and papers strewn all around. The kitchen surface was littered with what appeared to be the upturned contents of a bin.

Coco poked her way through it. 'Someone certainly did a good job on this place,' she stated.

'What do you hope to find here?' Cedric asked.

Coco shrugged. 'Beat's the shit out of me.' She moved around the room slowly. The drapes were pulled, the blinds behind them closed. 'He's been hiding out here, hasn't he?'

'Seems that way,' Cedric answered. 'But as you said earlier, why didn't he just take off?'

'That's the question,' Coco mused. 'I mean, he could have easily left Paris. He didn't need to be here to do the big expose on Richard Severin. We all have the interweb these days, non?'

Cedric shook his head. 'You never cease to amaze me. It's called the internet, grandma.'

She stuck out her tongue. 'There's something wrong with this picture,' she stated. 'Something we're not seeing.'

'There's something wrong with you, more like,' Cedric retorted.

Coco began pacing the room, tapping her chin as she did. 'Oui. I am using my little grey cells, and there's definitely something wrong here.'

Cedric followed her gaze. 'I just don't see it. It's a messy apartment.' He pointed to Coco. 'You should talk. What's that expression - pot/kettle? There's nothing wrong with this place. Yours is worse. Mine is worse. Who has the time or the energy to clean? And you heard the poor kid. He was beaten up, and he thought his life was in danger. You saw how he ran when he saw us. He was terrified. I doubt good housekeeping was high on his agenda.'

'Hmm, you're probably right,' Coco agreed reluctantly. 'Let's just turn the place over, just in case there's anything Yannick left or Severin's goons missed.'

'Do you really think Yannick Vidal would have left something here after what happened to him?'

'Who knows?' Coco answered. 'All we know is that he was still here up until yesterday. What if...' she paused, considering her next words. 'What if he knew he didn't have to worry about Richard Severin any longer?'

'You still think he was the one who murdered Severin?'

'Or he knows who did.' Her jaw tightened. She turned away. 'Do you think he's dead?'

'Dunno,' he replied. 'They haven't found his body, not that it means he's still alive.'

Coco shook her head. 'Non. He's alive, I'm sure of it. I feel it in my water.' She laughed. 'Do you think I could get paid for that like the hooker?'

Cedric ignored her and went about exploring the apartment. He pulled open a desk drawer, using a pen to leaf through the papers. 'What the hell language is this?' he questioned.

Coco peered over his shoulder. 'It's shorthand.'

'What the hell is shorthand?'

Coco slapped her head. 'Oy vey! How young are you?' She grabbed the paper and held it close to her face. 'My mother thought I should learn shorthand so that I could become a nice, decent secretary.'

'And what went wrong?' Cedric asked.

'I got pregnant by the local beefcake,' Coco retorted. 'Rather put paid to mother dearest's little plan of marrying me off to a nice Jewish businessman.'

Cedric laughed. 'Can you read it?'

Coco frowned. 'I'm a little rusty, but I can make out some of it.' She pointed to the middle of the page. 'That word there is murdered.'

'Are you sure?'

'Sure I'm sure,' Coco answered. 'It's the first word I learned because it was exactly what I wanted to do to my stick-up-her-ass shorthand teacher. Do you know, she had the bare-faced cheek to say I'd make nothing of myself and that the only job I'd be good at was one on my back. How ridiculous is that?'

Cedric raised an eyebrow, his eyes flicking over Coco, but he said nothing.

Coco ignored him and continued. 'We need to get someone who actually knows what they're doing to go over these.'

'Why?' Cedric questioned. 'You know this place was already searched. If it meant anything, surely they would have taken them, or Yannick Vidal would have destroyed them.'

'Not necessarily,' Coco retorted. 'The robbers could have taken one look at the notes like you did, and think that they were looking at gobbledegook, and Yannick may not have destroyed them because they were just notes for his book.'

'Then what good would they be to us?'

She shrugged. 'Who knows? It may just point us in the direction of what Yannick found and why it scared Richard Severin so much.' She gathered the papers together and dropped them into her bag. 'Let's keep looking,' she said, walking into the adjacent bedroom. Like the living room, it was a mess. The duvet was half on the floor, pillows dented, still with the imprint of a head. 'Well, will you look at this?' Coco said, walking to the bedside table and picking up a photo frame.

'That's Yannick Vidal and Emile Severin, isn't it?'

'It sure the hell is,' Coco replied. 'Which is odd, non?'

Cedric frowned. 'Why would it be odd? Emile Severin told you he'd hooked up with Vidal.'

'Emile also told me that Yannick was only using him to get info on his father,' Coco responded. 'If that was true, then why the hell would Yannick Vidal have a picture of the two of them all cosied up on his bedside table?'

She stepped into the bathroom, lifting and replacing various toiletries. 'This stuff costs more than I spend in a year,' she grumbled, turning huffily back into the bedroom. 'Well, let's get out…' She stopped, her attention drawn by something in the corner of her eye. She looked up, realising that one of the ceiling tiles was out of place as if it had been pushed up and not replaced properly. 'Here, give me a leg up,' she called out to Cedric. 'Cup your hands and boost me up.'

Cedric looked at Coco's boots, the tongue dangling from the front of one of them. 'If you think you're putting those into my hands, you're sadly mistaken.'

Coco tutted loudly and looked around the room. Spotting a stool, she dragged it across the room, and placed it under the tile, and jumped up. 'Hold my ass, so I don't fall backwards,' she instructed.

Cedric laughed. 'My previous statement about your feet goes double for your ass.'

She tutted again and reached upwards, using the tips of her fingers to push up the tile, filling the room with the darkness of the loft. She pushed herself up on her tiptoes, slapping her hands around the darkness as she tried to feel her way around. 'There's nothing here,' she complained.

'Bien sûr, there isn't,' Cedric muttered.

'Ah, wait. What's this?' Coco jumped down, landing with a thud on the carpet, a thick envelope in her hand. She emptied the contents on the bed.

'Alors, what do we have here?' She spread the contents of the envelope across the bed, revealing a stack of a dozen or more large photographs.

'They look like surveillance photographs,' Cedric stated.

'They sure do,' Coco confirmed, extending her finger. 'Look - here's Richard Severin, and here is dropping off the kid at school. And that's Emma Fitzgerald leaving the apartment, and that's Mona and...' She stopped, her attention taken by one photograph. 'That's Timo Severin, and he's staring right at the camera as if he knows he's being photographed.'

Cedric nodded. 'Yeah, and he's got that same smirk on his face that you just want to smack off it.'

'Never mind the smirk. Look at who he's in the photograph with,' Coco continued. The photograph appeared to have been taken on a boulevard opposite an outdoor cafe. Timo Severin's body was facing two other people, but his head was turned in the camera's direction, his slender face pulled into a smile. Coco shook her head. 'He's at a cafe with Mona Gagnon and Horst Lavigne.'

'So what?' Cedric questioned.

Coco dropped the photograph and stepped away. 'Well, ain't that a strange thing?'

Cedric shrugged. 'I don't understand why.'

'Because why would a sixteen-year-old kid be meeting up with those two old fogeys?'

'Well, because one is his aunt, and the other his lawyer,' Cedric reasoned.

Coco shook his head. 'We've been led to believe there was no interaction between any of them,' she responded. 'There's only one reason I can think of that Timo Severin would be meeting with Horst Lavigne.'

'He knew about the will, and who he really was,' Cedric concluded.

'Exactement!' Coco exclaimed. 'Which gives him a hell of a lot of motive for getting rid of his grandfather-slash-father. I mean, regardless of the money, it's gotta grind a kid's teeth to know that his real father wanted nothing to do with him and palmed him off on the gay son he also hated.' She scratched his head. 'Which begs the question - was Emile in on it? And what the hell does it have to do with Mona Gagnon?'

'She wanted to get to know him?' Cedric offered.

Coco shook her head. 'I doubt it. She wanted nothing to do with Emile and Caroline and they were actually related to her by blood. Why would she be interested in a kid she had no connection with? Unless…'

'Unless?'

'Unless she was stirring the pot,' Coco continued. 'She's made it pretty obvious what she thought of Richard Severin, and this is a pretty good way to do it.'

Cedric looked at the photograph again. 'Why do you think the kids looking at the camera like that?'

She shrugged. 'Because he was working with Yannick Vidal. For all we know, Vidal could have told Timo the truth and kick-started the whole thing. Damn, we really need to find Timo and Emile.'

Cedric considered. 'Why don't we start by leaning on Mona Gagnon to get her to spill the beans about what the hell she's been up to, and the avocat too. The pair of them get on my nerves.'

Coco nodded. 'Yeah. Let's get the papers and photographs back to the station first. I want to make sure we know exactly what's in these papers before we speak to anyone else.'

'And then we go and crack some skulls?' Cedric asked keenly.

Coco balled her fists and smiled. 'And then we go and crack some skulls.'

MERCREDI
12H00

Coco pushed the files from her desk and spread the photographs in front of her. There appeared to be over forty of them. She crept back and forth, studying them intently in an attempt to understand what they meant. Cedric joined her, Ebba close behind.

'What do you make of them?' Cedric asked.

Coco did not answer immediately. The photographs seemed to be from five separate events. Coco moved them into order. 'Well, this set is the lunch/dinner date between Timo Severin, Mona Gagnon and Horst Lavigne. An appointment that seems to have been set up by Timo and Yannick Vidal. But why? I think we have to assume that Yannick discovered exactly who Timo's father was, and told him.'

Ebba frowned. 'Then why set up the meeting and photograph it?'

Coco considered. 'To discover what Mona and Horst knew about it? And most likely to see what was in it for him?' She sighed. 'Well, we won't know for sure until we find him. Now, the second set of photographs is even more interesting. Yannick Vidal seems to have been following Richard Severin on his morning journey - taking Laure to school and then to the métro station.'

Cedric picked up one of the photographs. 'There's no date on them.'

'That's a different suit to the one he died in,' Coco added. 'So, we can safely assume these weren't taken two days ago. It also tells us that it wasn't Severin's first time on the métro. Probably on his way to see Mademoiselle pissy pants.'

'*Who?*' Ebba asked with alarm.

Cedric shook his head. 'Don't ask, or she'll tell you and then you'll wish you hadn't.'

Coco continued. 'The third set is of Emma Fitzgerald. Now, why on earth would he be following the housekeeper? I mean, all she's doing in them is going to the shops. Hmm. The fourth set is altogether more interesting.' She held one of the photos. 'Bonjour Caroline Severin.' Her eyes flicked over the photograph. Caroline Severin looked exactly how Coco had imagined she would. Painfully thin, with prominently veined arms. Her face was deathly pale, filled with greasy spots and heavy, deep eye bags, and her greasy, mousy coloured hair hung limply around her face. 'The poor woman,' Coco whispered.

'Self-inflicted,' Ebba snapped with more harshness than she seemed to intend.

'Maybe, but she didn't light the fuse herself,' Coco reasoned. 'This photograph is of the cybercafé where the ransom demand was sent from and presumably how Yannick Vidal became involved with Caroline in the first place. And finally, we have a set of photographs all depicting Horst Lavigne.' Her eyes flicked over them. 'Mind you, there doesn't seem to be much to them, just an avocat going about his business, to various meetings and lunch appointments.'

'Do you recognise anyone else in the photos with him?' Cedric asked.

She shook her head. 'I don't think so. They could mean nothing, but the fact Yannick kept them rather suggests otherwise, non?' Nobody answered her. 'Ah, well. Let's find someone who knows shorthand and then we can go and find Emile and Timo Severin.'

'I know shorthand,' Ebba offered demurely.

Coco raised an eyebrow. 'You do?' she asked with evident surprise

Ebba lowered her head as if she was embarrassed and shrugged nonchalantly. 'Why not? I have an IQ of over 150, so I get bored easily. I read manuals because I only sleep four hours a night and get frustrated - not so much fun for whoever is lying next to me if I'm counting sheep and shuffling all night.'

Coco handed her a mound of papers. 'Knock yourself out, honey. Call me if you find anything important or interesting.'

MERCREDI
12H45

Coco pulled the car to a halt and jumped out. The afternoon had brought a bite with it, and she was still without her jacket. She pulled back her head, scanning Emile Severin's small, modest home. *You'll be able to afford better soon,* she thought. *Unless you're in jail.* Cedric moved from the car.

'Do you really think he's in on it?' he asked.

She shrugged. 'The question is - did he know the truth about the will? I have a sneaky suspicion he did. I mean, just look at what he does for a living. It's literally his job to let people know their rights, so for that reason, I can't imagine he wasn't aware of his own. As for the rest.' She spread her hands in front of her. 'Who can say?'

They moved across the sidewalk, and Coco rapped her knuckles against the front door. She cocked her ear next to it, attempting to hear if there was any activity inside, but there was nothing but silence.

'They've gone away,' a voice called from behind them.

Coco turned. An elderly woman was standing on her doorstep, two doors down from Emile Severin's. She was smoking a cigarette and appraising Coco and Cedric with watery, tired eyes.

'Gone away where?' Coco enquired.

The woman cackled. 'What do I look like to you, a nosey old woman?'

That's exactly what you look like, and I bet you don't miss a thing that goes on. 'Not at all,' Coco replied sweetly, extracting her ID card and flashing it in front of the old woman. 'I need to speak to them, that's all.'

Her eyes widened. 'The flics again!' she exclaimed. 'This used to be a pleasant neighbourhood before the foreigners moved in and rabble like those two.'

'Rabble?' Cedric asked.

She nodded. 'Emile's alright, I suppose,' she conceded, wrapping her arms across her chest. 'For one of *them*. But the boy, oh the mouth on him! If it's not foul language, he's shouting rude and disgusting things, morning, noon and night. Nothing but trouble, and comings and goings all times of day and night.' Her lips twisted. 'In my day, he'd be put over your knee and given a damn good thrashing.'

'Peut être,' Coco agreed. She had never smacked her children, because her own father had beaten her, and it had done little for her other than make her even more wilful. 'You said they'd gone away?'

The old woman's eyes flicked over Coco, her eyebrow rising upon seeing her dishevelled appearance. 'Are you really a police officer?'

'For my sins,' Coco replied. 'So, they went away?' she repeated.

She nodded. 'Oui. Last night, the three of them.'

'Three of them?' Coco asked sharply.

'Oui. Monsieur Emile, the boy, and the other one.' She added *the other one*, in a clearly disparaging way.

'Who was the other one?' Coco pushed.

'It's not for me to say,' the old woman continued. 'Mais, he's a little…' she shrugged, 'flighty, you might say.'

Coco's eyebrows knotted. 'Flighty?' She paused. 'Ah, you mean, he's gay?'

The woman nodded but said nothing. Coco and Cedric exchanged a look.

'What did this other man look like?' Cedric asked.

She shrugged. 'Pretty like a girl. Blond hair, too long for a man, and eyes bluer than Sinatra's.'

Yannick Vidal. 'Are you sure?'

'Oui. I'm old, not senile,' she retorted huffily.

'Do you know his name?'

She laughed. 'Calls himself a writer. A writer! How can he be a writer if I've never heard of him?'

Coco took a step forward. 'Was he called Yannick? Yannick Vidal?'

'That's it. Even the way he said it was annoying. Like he was stating a point, not a name.'

'And he was here last night?' Coco pressed. 'And they left together? At what time?'

The old woman shrugged. 'Well, my programme had just finished, so I came outside for a smoke before bed. It was 22H00, more or less.'

Coco raised an eyebrow in Cedric's direction. If it was true, then it meant that Yannick Vidal was alive and well and had managed to swim his way to safety. 'See if you can find a picture of him on the internet,' Coco instructed Cedric.

He pulled out his cell phone and began typing. 'He has a website,' he said, scrolling through the phone. 'Ah, here it is.' He presented the cell phone to the old woman.

She narrowed her eyes and then nodded. 'Oui. That's him.'

'And it was definitely last night, not the night before?' Coco asked.

The old woman glared at Coco. 'I told you already. I'm just old, not gaga.'

Coco flashed her a smile. 'Merci for your time and your help.'

The old woman retreated back inside her house without saying another word.

Cedric turned to Coco. 'Then it looks like he made it out of the Seine.'

Coco nodded. 'It appears that way, doesn't it?' she replied

pensively. 'Which rather begs the question - why was his next move to do a bunk with Emile and Timo Severin?'

'Because they're all in it up to their necks,' Cedric reasoned.

'It certainly seems that way.' She pointed to the car. 'D'accord. Let's go and see what Mona Gagnon has to say for herself,' she said. 'And hopefully, someone will finally give us some straight answers.'

MERCREDI
13H00

The first thing Coco noticed about Mona Gagnon was that she seemed brighter than the last time they had crossed paths. Almost as if a heavy weight had been lifted from her shoulders, which Coco supposed it had. When she had awoken in the middle of the night and had trouble getting back to sleep, in no small part because of the snoring which came in stages from Helga, Cedric and Esther, Coco's thoughts had travelled to the problem of the Severin family.

By daybreak, she had moved no further forward in her evaluation of them. She wondered whether it was because of her own family dynamics. She had long ago come to realise that she could love her family without actually having to like them. It was one of the main reasons she had raised her children alone. Their fathers, while decent and honourable enough men, had not been meant for either Coco, children, or a domestic life. Most days Coco wondered whether she was herself. It was not a life she would have necessarily chosen for herself, but it was a life she had come to love, despite its many pitfalls.

One conclusion she had come to was that people with money, the Severin family kind of money, which far exceeded any money she knew she would ever see in her lifetime, marched to a very different beat to mere mortals such as Coco. She realised that just because she did not understand them, or their motives, it mattered little in the end. Because all she had ever seen, ever understood, was that when it came down to it, everyone from the very richest to the very poorest, were often swayed by the same base instinct, and more often than not, it came down to sex.

Richard Severin had been a man she imagined having lived one of the greatest kinds of life, filled with excess and access to anything he wanted, but it had also become clear he was also a man who was terrified of his truth being discovered. Coco imagined that despite it all, it was most likely a burden. Coco had nothing, barely a euro to her name, but her life was her own and she feared no one, nor their opinion of her, not really, not so long as she made sure her armour was intact when she left her apartment in the morning.

Mona turned around quickly, her eyes widening in a way which told Coco she was fearful of her. She had not been before, and Coco could not help but wonder what might have changed.

'Do you have news?' Mona asked, her voice darting as much as her eyes.

Coco looked at Cedric, exchanging a wry smile. 'News,' Coco repeated. 'Do we have news, Lieutenant Degarmo?' she asked, her voice laced with sarcasm.

'If you have a point, I suggest you get to it,' a man's voice called from behind the sofa.

Coco jumped. 'Jesus wept!' she cried. 'Tell a girl you're there, rather than hiding.'

Horst Lavigne looked around him. 'I'm sitting on a sofa, Captain Brunhild, not hiding in a dark corner.' He stood. 'I sensed your tone was rather mocking, rather than displaying the kindness a person should be able to expect from a police officer, especially under such trying and emotional circumstances.'

Coco began pacing. 'Actually, I'm glad you're here. You just saved the city some petrol, because we were coming to you next. Say, why are you here?'

He frowned. 'I'm an avocat,' he stated simply.

'You're here as an avocat for Mademoiselle Gagnon?' Cedric asked.

Horst smiled at Mona. 'I'm always here as avocat.'

'For Mademoiselle Gagnon?' Cedric pushed. 'Since when?'

He continued smiling. 'Since always, in one way or another,' he responded cryptically.

Coco moved her attention between the two of them and it surprised her because if she did not know better, Horst Lavigne appeared to be flirting with Mona, and as far as Coco could tell by the demure way Mona was batting her eyelashes, she was responding in kind. Coco pointed to a seat. 'Can I sit?'

Mona nodded, extending her hand. 'Make yourself comfortable.'

'And then perhaps you will tell us why you are here?' Horst added.

Cedric sat next to Coco. 'We're here for answers,' he stated forcefully. 'Or else, if we don't get them, we'll arrest you both and take you down to the commissariat. See how quick you talk after you've been in a cell for a night.'

Horst chuckled. 'I'd like to see you try, Lieutenant, because in those circumstances the only talking I will be doing is to insist the both of you are removed from your posts.' He paused, as if for dramatic effect. 'And if you think I'm not capable of that, then I can assure you I am.'

Coco sighed. 'Do you know how tired I am of people, i.e. men in power suits, threatening me for doing my job? I'll tell you. Pretty fucking tired.'

'Captain, s'il vous plaît, mind your language.'

Coco shrugged her shoulders huffily. 'Stop fucking lying to me, and I just might.'

'Why do you think we're lying?' Mona interrupted.

'Yannick Vidal,' Coco spoke his name.

'That *man* is dead,' Horst stated, the word man clearly judgmental.

Coco shook her head. 'Non, he isn't.'

'He isn't?' Mona replied, her voice rising sharply. She moved across the room, resting her hand on Horst's arm. He moved it away as if it were a fly.

'I watched the news, Captain Brunhild,' Horst said. 'And it was quite clear that tabloid reporter jumped to his death because he was guilty of…'

'Of?' Coco interjected.

'Isn't it obvious?' he snapped. 'He was guilty of murder.'

'The murder of Richard Severin?' Coco asked.

He nodded. 'Bien sûr. Even if he made it out of that damn filthy river, he would have just crawled out of it into the nearest sewer.'

Coco laughed. 'Don't hold back, Monsieur Avocat, tell us what you really think!'

Mona lowered herself into a chair in the corner of the room. 'Then, he's not dead?'

'Non,' Coco snapped. 'And like everyone else in this family, he seems to be on the run.'

'What are you talking about?' Horst demanded.

Coco had wondered whether she should show her hand concerning the disappearance of Emile and Timo Severin, but had only come to the conclusion that time was of the essence. And more importantly, now that she had them both in front of her, she wanted to see how well they continued to lie to her face.

'When was the last time either of you saw or spoke with Emile or Timo?' she demanded.

Mona and Horst exchanged an anxious look, but neither answered.

Coco repeated her question.

'I have been in regular contact with Emile, in my capacity as family avocat,' Horst finally answered.

'I tried calling…' Mona trailed off. 'Mais, Emile was never good at taking my calls at the best of times,' she added.

'And Timo?' Cedric interjected.

Horst looked between the two police officers. 'I wish you'd

save us all some time and get to the point.'

'And I wish I was taller and slender with a big bank balance, but we can't all get what we wish for,' Coco quipped.

Horst shot her a confused look.

'But speaking of saving time,' Coco continued, 'it would be nice if you saved us a whole lot of time and energy and stop lying to us.' She raised her hands. 'Before you think of lying, don't. We have evidence.'

'Evidence?' he questioned. His voice had quickly lost some of its confidence.

She nodded. 'Photographic evidence.'

Horst lowered his head. 'That damn journalist,' he hissed. He glared at Mona. 'I told you it was all a set-up.'

Coco scratched her head. 'You're going to have to level with us, and you're going to have to do it soon, or else...' she trailed off, leaving the words hanging heavily in the air. 'Or else I'll assume you're up to your necks in murder, and arrest you both.'

Horst sighed. 'Timo came to see me a month ago at my office,' he began. 'The truth was, I didn't recognise him - I hadn't seen him since he was a baby.'

'And what did he want?' Coco asked. 'Money? The truth?'

Horst's forehead creased. 'Both,' he answered with an angry snort. 'He knew the truth.'

'How? From Yannick Vidal?'

He nodded.

Coco turned to Mona. 'You were dealing with Vidal. Did you tell him the truth about Timo?'

'Non,' she answered quickly. 'I was... I was feeding him information,' she added. 'Business information, that's all.'

Coco turned back to Horst. 'Which I'm guessing she got from you. Mais, pourquoi? What was in it for you?'

Horst clasped his hands together, entwining his fingers. His jaw flexed, a muscle under his left eye twitching angrily. 'Richard and I had a deal. A deal agreed on many years ago. He would retire and I would gain full control of *Severin Industries*. It turns out it was all a con to keep me close and loyal. All the time doing his dirty work, just so he could keep his damn hands clean, but really, all I was doing was tying myself to him, making my hands dirtier than his.' He shrugged. 'I'll be honest. I didn't mind, to begin with, because it worked both ways. I had more than enough evidence to destroy Richard if I wanted to. And I'm not just talking about his precious reputation. There was enough to make sure he spent some real time in prison.'

'And then he reneged on your deal?' Cedric asked.

'Oui,' Horst replied. 'He made a big deal to the press about stepping down to "spend time with his family."' He snorted. 'Spending time with his family! Don't make me laugh. Only two people could stand to be in the same room as him, and that was because he paid them to.'

Coco nodded. 'You mean Emma Fitzgerald and Ambre Castillon?'

'Whores, the both of them!' Mona spat from the corner of the room.

Horst ignored her outburst and continued. 'Richard came to me and told me he would be staying on. He tried to dress it up that he would only be the company figurehead and that I would be in complete charge, but I knew that wasn't true because he made sure he kept controlling interest. I would be the figurehead and he would be the one pulling the strings.' He laughed. 'After all these years, I should have known he never intended to hand over the reins to me, that all he was doing was buying my loyalty and getting rid of his problems. In the end, it didn't matter what dirt I had on him, because it was useless to me.'

Coco considered. 'You couldn't destroy Richard without destroying yourself,' she stated.

He clapped his hands. 'Exactement! Which of course, as far

as you are concerned I'm sure, gives me a perfect motive for his murder.'

'It certainly does,' Coco agreed. 'But don't worry, you're not alone. Most of the people in the family have a pretty perfect motive for offing Papa Severin as far as I can tell.' She cleared her throat. 'So, you were feeding info to Mona to give to Yannick Vidal? For what purpose? As you said, you had a lot on him, but by doing so, you got your own hands dirty.'

Horst flashed her with a wry, perfectly even smile. 'Richard was in business for a long time. He became very rich and very successful, and you don't manage that without stepping on a lot of people. He had many enemies.'

'How did Yannick Vidal make himself known to you?' Cedric posed.

'As I told you earlier,' Mona replied. 'He came up to me one day in the park and told me he was a reporter writing a book about Richard. Of course, I told him to go away, that I didn't speak with reporters, but then he told me he had uncovered something about my sister's kidnapping and that Richard was involved.' She shuddered. 'I've always known Richard was involved. I've always been sure of it, but of course, I had no proof, and Yannick said he did.'

Coco nodded. 'What did you do?'

'Well, firstly I went straight to see Horst,' Mona replied.

'I was intrigued,' Horst added. 'Bien sûr, I knew he was most likely fishing. However, I needed to see the proof.'

'The three of you met?' Coco asked.

Horst nodded. 'Oui.'

'This was the bank payment, the exact same amount as the aborted kidnap drop?' Coco interrupted.

'Oui.'

'How did he get it?'

'I do not know,' Horst responded. 'Bribed someone? He

never told me how he found any of his information. He said it was because he didn't want his informants winding up dead. Knowing Richard as I did, I couldn't entirely disagree.'

Coco turned away as she considered her next question. 'You knew about the money?'

He nodded again. 'Oui. I was instructed to make the payment, and I did.'

'And did you think it was for the ransom?' Coco continued.

'That was what I was told,' Horst confirmed. 'And I had no reason to doubt it.'

Coco stared at him. She was not sure she believed a word that came out of his mouth. He had spent his lifetime covering for Richard Severin, and it appeared he had not cared about what he was doing, so long as it was in his own best interests. 'Did you know the ransom had been paid?' she asked Mona.

Mona shook her head. 'Not until Yannick told me, and Horst confirmed it,' she responded. 'I had always been under the impression that the kidnappers had escaped without collecting the ransom. Richard and the police always said they had murdered her in order to facilitate their escape from justice. I never believed it, not really, and that is why I have spent all these years waiting… waiting for an answer I mostly believed would never come.' She took a deep breath. 'That's why it was so important to me to readily believe Yannick.'

Coco smiled at her. Hope is sometimes all we have. 'And what had Yannick found exactly?' she continued.

'He wouldn't go into the specifics,' Horst answered, 'other than to say the ransom was paid to a local businessman. A businessman who specialised in shady business. Prostitutes, thugs, drugs, you name it.'

'Prostitutes?' Coco interrupted.

'Amongst other things. He wouldn't give us his name. He just said it would all be in the book and that it would be explosive,'

Horst added.

'Then I'm guessing the implication was that Richard Severin's wife was never really kidnapped at all and that Severin paid some lowlife to pretend to do it, and then kill her and dispose of the body,' Coco mused.

'That was the suggestion,' Horst confirmed. 'Again, we're only really talking speculation here. I have little evidence to base it on.'

'Yet, it makes perfect sense,' Mona cried, clutching her necklace.

A minute passed, imposing a deathly silence in the room.

'And Timo? How did Yannick discover he was Richard's son?' Coco asked.

Horst shrugged. 'I told you. I suspect he had help, probably someone on the inside at *Severin Industries*. I do not know who, and believe me, I've tried to find out who the bastard was that helped him. It was actually pretty good investigative work on his behalf. I imagine he found out about the payoff and traced her from that,' he said with reluctance. 'Because very few people outside of the family knew about the birth, and I'm fairly sure none of us would have told him.'

'Caroline might have,' Coco reasoned.

He laughed. 'Caroline didn't know. Richard certainly wouldn't have told him.'

'And nor would Emile, for that matter,' Mona added. 'He took Timo without hesitation, and he was happy to do so. I imagine he saw it as his only chance to have a child of his own.'

'Then who?' Coco pressed. 'If what you say is true about the secrecy, I can't imagine your secret mole at *Severin Industries* knew, which leaves us only one other option.'

'Timo's mother,' Cedric concluded.

'A woman I never knew, or even met,' Horst stated. 'Richard came to me, told me about the pregnancy and that it was too late to do anything about it. He had me make the arrangements. The woman was to go to a retreat in Switzerland for the duration of her pregnancy and then once she delivered, the baby would be brought back to France and the woman paid the sum of ten million euros to disappear. I drew the contract up myself and it was returned to me signed and notarised by her attorney. A grasping British solicitor who kept trying to get more and more money. In the end, I had to be firm and threaten to nix the whole deal. He knew I was bluffing, of course, but in the end he saw sense.'

'And you never heard from her again?'

He shook his head.

'What was she called?'

'Her name was Anna Rowan, I believe,' Horst replied. 'But as I said, I never met nor spoke to her.'

Coco turned to Mona. She shook her head. 'I never met her either, but she was another whore.'

'You're sure?'

Mona laughed. 'Other than my sister, who he chose solely for her breeding, the only sort of women Richard was interested in were women he could control and pay to do his bidding, discreetly, of course.' She smiled knowingly at Coco. 'As you no doubt have surmised by now, discretion was Richard's keyword.'

'And yet he had a lot of secrets, for a man who didn't like to be scrutinised,' Coco reasoned.

Mona snorted with such force it caused her jowls to wobble. 'I doubt we've scratched the surface of the secret he carried. Mais, there's time yet,' she added with a contented smile.

'Alors, back to Timo,' Coco pressed on. 'Emile seemed to suggest that he believed Yannick Vidal only got close to him to get information from him.'

'I don't doubt it,' Mona sniffed. 'And I'm afraid I feel rather responsible for it, because I brought the two of them together. Of course, I knew nothing like *that* was going to happen.'

Revenge was all you were thinking about, Coco thought. *But just how far would you go for it.*

'How did Timo find out?' Cedric asked. 'You said Emile wasn't likely to tell him, so are you suggesting Yannick Vidal went directly to Timo himself. For what purpose?'

'To kick the hornet's nest! All he wanted was as much scandal as he could create,' Horst snapped.

'He shouldn't have told Timo, not like that,' Mona complained. 'Imagine my surprise when the telephone rang and I answered, and he said, Hey, is that tante Mona. This is Timo, the…' she lowered her voice, '*bastard.* I was dumbfounded. I didn't know what to say or do.'

'So, she rang me,' Horst continued. 'We set up a meeting at a discrete cafe I know on the other side of Paris.'

The photographs. Coco frowned. She still did not understand the purpose of the surveillance and for Timo being involved in it. 'Just the three of you?' she pondered.

'Oui,' Horst responded. 'It took me but a moment to see that Timo, despite being raised by Emile, seems to share the traits of Richard. He was rude and direct. He wanted to know about what money he was entitled to and nothing else.'

Coco nodded. 'And what did you tell him?'

'That there was nothing I could do. The will was ironclad. I tried to impress upon him that by law, he was protected and he would come into a substantial inheritance upon…'

'His father's death,' Coco finished. *Another motive.*

'He was impatient,' Horst continued. 'He wanted money, and he wanted it there and then. I told him it was impossible, but that I would speak to his grandfather… his father… and see what I could do, but that unless he wanted to anger Richard, he ought to leave the past buried, for the time being at least.'

'And how did that go?'

Horst smiled wryly. 'Not well. He shouted. He threatened,

but in the end, I think he saw sense. I told him I would get some money for him, so long as he was patient and discreet. As he walked away, he told me he would get what he deserved.'

'And did you take that as a threat?' Cedric asked.

He shrugged. 'I took it as a completely expected response from the illegitimate son of my oldest friend. I knew he was going to be trouble. I intended on making it Richard's problem, mais…'

'I wouldn't let him,' Mona interrupted. 'Because I feared what Richard might do.'

Coco nodded. 'How did Richard find out about the book?'

'He hadn't,' Horst answered quickly.

Coco studied his face. She could not be sure, but it appeared he was telling the truth. However, the fact remained, Richard Severin had discovered the storm which was approaching him. 'Are you sure?' she pressed.

He laughed again. 'I'm pretty sure we would have all known about it if Richard knew a book was about to be published about him.' He shook his head. 'Non. He didn't know.'

And yet he did. Or was Yannick Vidal lying about that? It made no sense for him to, but then little else made sense either. Coco's cell phone vibrated in her pocket. She extracted it and stared at the screen. *This is Ebba. I've translated the shorthand and have news. Come back to the commissariat.* Coco rose to her feet. 'We have to go, but stay close. I may have more questions soon.'

'What about Laure?' Mona called after her. 'Commander Demissy told me you believe she was never kidnapped in the first place, that it was some elaborate scheme by Caroline to extract money from Richard. Is that true?'

Coco stopped by the doorway. There appeared genuine concern in her voice, and it bothered her. If Laure Severin was brought back to Paris, what was she being brought back to? A family so dysfunctional it made Coco's look like the Waltons.

'We're still trying to make sense of it,' Coco answered with a shrug. 'Mais, it appears that Laure is staying with friends in the country. We have police officers tracking her down right now.'

'And then she'll be brought back to Paris?' Horst questioned.

Coco stared at him. 'She'll be brought back somewhere, sure.'

'What's that supposed to mean?' he demanded.

'It means,' she retorted, 'that until I figure out what the hell is going on with this damn family, and what you all have to do with it, I'm going to make sure that little girl is safe, and right now, the only way I can do that is to make sure she isn't around any of you. If she's having a hell of a good time with a pal in the countryside, then that's where she's going to stay until we figure out who the hell is capable of looking after her.'

She took a deep breath. 'Now stay close, because I will be back, and as this conversation began, don't imagine for a second that if I find out you're still lying, either of you, you'll spend the foreseeable in one of my damn cells. Capeesh?' She slammed the door behind her before Horst or Mona had a chance to respond.

MERCREDI
14H00

Coco's eyes scanned the pages of typed notes Ebba had prepared for her. She was desperately hoping for something which would blow the case wide open. Instinctively, however, she knew it was not likely going to be that easy. Cedric was reading over her shoulder. His hot breath was bothering her, but she did not have the strength to chastise him. The notes were interesting, but only really interesting in a tell-all book, not a criminal investigation.

'I'm not seeing a lot here that might help us,' Coco grumbled.

'Maybe not for the murder investigation,' Ebba reasoned, 'but if half of this is true, then it's going to be a pretty big mess for everyone involved.'

'Richard Severin is dead,' Coco snapped. 'So, whatever he did in the past, he will not pay for it now. Damaged reputation or not, it doesn't matter when you're nothing but ashes in a pot.'

Cedric pointed to the bottom of one of the sheets. 'This is interesting. Look at the name.'

Coco followed his finger. 'Found evidence of cash monthly ten thousand euro payment to Emma Fitzgerald. Ten thousand a month for running a damn house!' she exclaimed. A wry smile appeared on her face. 'Do you think she was also doing a little bit of the old *psss psss* for Monsieur pissy pants?'

Cedric suppressed a smile. 'I doubt it,' he responded. 'Richard Severin went out of his way to keep, er, *that* part of his life well hidden. I can't imagine he did it at home with Mona and his granddaughter sniffing around.' He laughed. 'Literally, not sniffing, I hope.'

Coco pursed her lips. 'Peut être, you're right. Then why the hell was she getting paid off?' She pointed at the sheet. 'Look - Yannick Vidal even states he has copies of cheques written by Horst Lavigne in the manuscript box.' She shook her head. 'What the hell is the manuscript box? And more importantly, where the hell is it?'

She pushed herself back in her chair and lit a cigarette.

'I thought you couldn't afford to smoke,' Ebba said, wafting the smoke away from her face.

'I can't afford to do a lot of things,' Coco sniffed. 'My doctor said I have to eat better because my blood pressure and cholesterol are too high, so I've decided to skip lunch and buy a pack of smokes instead.' She grinned. 'And I have to say, I actually fitted into my favourite leather skirt last week, and I've never felt healthier. I might just write my own book. *Coco's guide to healthy living*. It'll be a bestseller.'

Ebba and Cedric exchanged a smile. 'I bet it would,' Ebba agreed, her voice laced with sarcasm.

Coco tapped her fingers on the desk. 'I have a feeling this all comes back to the paper card in Severin's coat. *B4*.'

'What makes you think that?' Cedric asked.

'Because nothing else makes sense,' she replied. 'My friend Denis knew it, and I think it may have just got him...' she looked at the telephone on the corner of her desk. She did not finish the sentence, instead wincing as if it hurt her. She shook her head as if forcing thoughts out of a foggy brain.

Ebba extended her hands. 'I examined the paper. There were no prints, nothing discernible which would indicate where it might have come from. I even checked the major storage depots in Paris and none of them uses anything like that.' She slumped against the wall. 'Hell, most of them don't even use paper, it's all done by an app on a cell phone.'

Coco twisted her head in Ebba's direction. 'What do you do if you don't have one of those fancy cell phones?'

Ebba laughed. 'Then you get in a Tardis and go back to the nineteen sodding eighties.'

Coco shrugged. 'If you'd lived through the eighties, you'd know one thing and one thing only - they were *fabulous*. My point jeune femme is this - B4 means something, and I suspect it's what got Richard Severin murdered.'

'Well, there's nothing in the notes to indicate what it could mean,' Ebba replied.

Coco stood and moved across her office. 'This is a mess, and it appears we're getting nowhere. Hell, if I was Commander Demissy, I think I'd be getting irritated by our lack of progress.'

'What else can we do?' Cedric asked. 'As you said earlier, everyone has been lying to us from the very beginning, and after talking with Mona Gagnon and Horst Lavigne, I'm pretty convinced they're still lying to us.'

Coco nodded and stubbed out the cigarette irritably. 'Me too, mais the damn avocat has a point. He'd have our jobs if we tried to drag him into the commissariat. When this is over though, I swear if I can pin anything on them, I will, and then we'll see how damn cocky he is. Mona bothers me just as much because I suspect she's up to her eyes in it, as well.'

'What's happened with the kid?' Ebba asked.

'The local police and social services have tracked her down,' Cedric responded. 'She was spending some time with her friend's family. Everything seems above board.'

Coco shuddered. 'I dread to think what'll happen to the poor kid,' she added sadly. 'Part of me hopes that Emile Severin is in the clear.'

'Only because you fancy him,' Cedric quipped.

She laughed. 'Yeah, maybe. I do pick 'em, don't I?' Before she could continue, the telephone rang. 'Brunhild,' she answered. 'Oh, hey, Stella. How's my man? Oh, okay. Is that good? Well, keep me posted, and merci for the call. Bissous.' She replaced the receiver. 'Well, Denis is out of surgery and in intensive care,' she said glumly.

Cedric nodded. 'That's good news, non?'

'Yeah,' she agreed with obvious reluctance.

'Well, tell your face,' he snipped.

'It's still touch and go, apparently. The knife nicked his spleen and ruptured it. They've removed it and stabilised him for now. Stella says if he makes it through the night, he's got a fighting chance. I feel responsible,' Coco said softly. 'If he hadn't been helping me…'

'You can't think that way,' Ebba interrupted. 'Whatever life he chose was his business, and what happened most likely had nothing to do with you.'

'Then how do you explain the ticket?' She moved back to her desk and began typing on the keyboard. 'Let's see if he had a record.' Her eyes flicked across the computer screen as it filled. 'Ah, there we are. Hmm. The usual for a homeless man, I guess,' she said. 'Drunk and disorderly, fighting, vagrancy and, wait, that's interesting.'

'What is?' Cedric asked.

Coco tapped some more buttons. 'Two years ago Denis Acy was arrested for domestic assault.' Her eyes darted back and forth as she scanned the report. 'Cops were called after his wife, Camille Acy, reported an assault. Denis was arrested and later released. Camille was treated at a hospital. He was fined and put on probation with a stipulation to keep away from his wife and children.' Coco reached forward and grabbed a piece of paper, quickly scribbling an address on it. 'D'accord. I'm going to see if she's at the same address.'

Cedric frowned. 'Why would you want to do that? They obviously aren't together anymore.'

'Because her husband and father of her children may not make it through it the night,' Coco snapped. 'And no matter what happened between them, she might just want to know, and Denis might appreciate waking up and seeing her face at his bedside.'

'You shouldn't get involved in something you know nothing about, Captain,' Cedric said warily.

She flashed him a sad smile. 'Since when has that stopped me?'

He sighed. 'Do you want me to come with you?'

'Non,' she responded. 'Keep looking for Emile, Timo and Yannick.'

'How?' Cedric retorted.

'The neighbour said they drove away,' she replied. 'Find cameras in the surrounding streets. Hopefully, that will give us a licence plate and Ebba can track it from there.' She headed to the door. 'I'll be back soon.'

MERCREDI
14H45

Coco recognised everything about Camille Acy. Not because they had met before, but because Coco had crossed paths with too many women like her before. They were all the same, more or less. The way they held themselves, a hand always raised to the chin as if instinctively ready to attempt to protect herself. Similarly, her face was devoid of makeup, hair barely styled, and the clothes were drab and ill-fitting. All designed for one purpose, to disappear into the background. *Don't notice me, I beg you.* Camille had opened the door to Coco, her wary expression instantly transferring to one of fear. She had merely gestured for Coco to follow her into the garden without saying a word. Two young boys were playing happily in a sandpit. Coco thought that at least whatever had happened in their home they seemed to be unaffected by it.

'What's he done this time?' Camille asked. Her voice was pitched low, as if she was used to talking in nothing but a whisper.

'What do you mean?' Coco replied.

'The only time flics come is to tell me he's in trouble again.'

'Your husband…'

'Ex-husband,' Camille spat, before adding. 'Well, as good as at least. Denis got very good at hiding and not turning up for court cases, but when he does, we'll be divorced and the restraining order will become permanent.'

'Denis is in hospital,' Coco stated.

Camille sighed. 'Again, this is not the first time someone has shown up at my door and said such a thing.'

Coco moved closer to her and touched her arm. Camille instantly recoiled. 'Désolé,' Coco cried. She locked eyes with the terrified woman. 'Somebody tried to murder him,' Coco said quickly. 'And I'm afraid it's very serious. He may not make it through the night.'

Camille lowered her head. 'What do you expect from me?'

Coco shrugged. 'I just thought…' she stopped, unsure what she thought. She had come to see Camille Acy, most likely because of her own guilt. She wanted to make it neat. She wanted to make it right. But she had not considered how it might distress his wife. *Damn you for being right, Cedric.* 'I just thought you should know,' she concluded.

Camille turned her head. 'He's really going to die?'

'I hope not,' Coco responded. 'Mais, it is serious.' She looked at the happy children as they played. Their giggles were heartwarming and infectious. 'They look like Denis.'

Camille snorted. 'They won't turn out like him, not if I have anything to do with it.'

Coco realised that her impression of Denis had clouded her thoughts. He seemed nice to her, but the way he lived his life should have indicated he was probably not the man she thought he was.

'You speak as if you knew him,' Camille stated. Coco noticed the spark in her eyes. Whatever had happened between Denis and Camille. Whatever he had done to her, there remained a glimmer of the love she had once felt for him. Coco knew that feeling, and like an explosion in her brain, his face and name came back to her. *Mordecai Stanic.* He had touched her in a way few men had, but he had also betrayed her so brutally, she knew she could never forgive him, for the monster he had been and hidden so successfully from her. And yet. And yet. No matter how much she pushed it away, it would return to the surface whenever it felt like it and she would be forced to endure his smell, the memory of his touch, how he had made her feel in the dark of night. And it was in those moments, she hated herself almost as much as she hated him.

'I wouldn't say I know Denis,' Coco answered. 'Rather, you might say he lives in my neighbourhood and I've exchanged a few pleasantries with him. I thought he was a nice man.'

'I thought that too,' Camille muttered bitterly.

'When did the two of you meet?' Coco asked.

'At school,' she whispered her response. 'He was my first love.'

Coco nodded. She still thought daily of her own first love. A man so strong in character and form, he had tarnished all other men who came after him. She had broken his heart because she wanted to before he had a chance to break hers. She had left him because she had thought it was the best for them both and the child he did not know she was carrying. In the intervening years, she had thought of reaching out to him, to try to explain why she had taken so drastic a decision, but each year had stretched further in front of her, making it more and more impossible to right her wrong.

'I was pregnant at seventeen, and as was the pattern of our life, he was away. Always away. Always fighting someone else's battle because it was easier than fighting his own.'

'He was in the army, oui?'

'Oui,' Camille replied. 'And it seemed to me that each time he went away, when he came back he was a little less himself. But it was the last time, two years ago, when he came back from Afghanistan, that was when it all became unbearable. I don't know what he did or saw over there, but it destroyed him. He couldn't stand to be around me, or the boys, and the longer it went on, the more we felt the same. He started disappearing, a day at a time, then a night, and then it became longer and sometimes we wouldn't see him for a week, or even longer. And it was a relief. It was a wonderful relief because when he was home, I would watch the whisky bottle as it disappeared, knowing full well that when he reached the bottom, the man from Afghanistan would return.'

Coco gulped. She wanted desperately to give the woman a hug, but she knew she could not.

'The beatings became more regular,' Camille continued. 'And half the time, I don't even think he knew he was doing it, or that he was doing it to me. Maybe it was someone from the war he saw as he beat me. He wasn't beating me. He was beating someone from the hell he'd been to.' She gasped, wrapping her arms around her chest. 'I put up with it because I remembered who he was before, but I made a promise to myself, just one.'

Coco looked to the boys playing in the sandpit. 'You would protect your children,' she exhaled.

'I don't even know how it started. Maybe one of the boys was being naughty. I can't be sure what the trigger was, but it escalated so quickly, too quickly, and I realised it was getting out of hand. I ran to the room, and I got in between them. I threw my son away and I don't even think Denis realised. He was still fighting his enemy. Luckily,' she breathed, 'he didn't notice I had replaced our son, so instead he beat me until I was unconscious instead.'

Camille closed her eyes. 'When I woke up, I knew I had only one choice if I was to do the right thing for my children. He had to go,' she continued. 'I loved him, but I had him arrested and that was the end of it. I loved Denis, but in the end, one of us had to love our children more, and the fact was, he had to go.' She stared at Coco. 'You must think me a terrible person.'

Coco's eyes widened in horror. 'Bien sûr, I don't. You did exactly what you should have done. I have four kids and believe me, I'd have done the same.' She paused and looked away. 'And the truth is, I've done worse,' she mumbled in a barely audible way. 'Decisions concerning men are troublesome for women. We want to think the best of them and we wait for them to understand their failings, but if they don't, we have to do it for them, and for that, we must never, *ever*, take the blame.'

Camille turned back to Coco. 'You said you liked him. Did

he… did he charm you?'

Coco's eyes narrowed. *Oui*, she wanted to say, but could not. 'I like him,' she said instead. She took a deep breath. 'I like to think I'm a pretty good judge of character. It's important in my job,' she added. 'As I get older, I realise I am, in fact, crap at judging men, but if you're asking me what I believe, then I have to tell you, it wasn't about charm. I mean, as far as I could tell, Denis wasn't even trying to charm me.' She looked down at her raggedy cardigan and tugged at her frizzy hair. 'Which I'm sure you'll agree, is pretty damn unbelievable, mais…' She stared at Camille. 'He wasn't after my body. He just wanted someone to talk to him, to notice him. And I think I was probably the first person who had in a long time.'

Camille glared at her. 'You're saying it's my fault he is how he is?'

Coco shook her head forcefully. 'I'm not saying that at all. He had no right to put his hands on you or your kids. And you did the right thing, the *only* thing you could do. Denis needed help for whatever he'd been through, and often these boys, barely men, come back from war zones barely unrecognisable, and often there's fuck all help available for them to fit back into "normal" society. And that is why it's no wonder men like Denis, who started out okay but are so traumatised by what they've seen, or what they've been asked to do, end up on the streets doing whatever they can to numb their pain. What they do is not just their fault, but more importantly, it's most certainly not yours.'

Camille stepped across the garden, running her hand over her youngest son's head, barely touching it, just close enough for the static to lift stray hairs to her fingers. She looked again at Coco. 'He really might die?' she whispered into the afternoon breeze.

'I can't really say,' Coco answered. 'What I can tell you is that he's being looked after by a doctor I rate highly. He's probably got life-changing injuries if he pulls through, but he is in skilled hands, and although I have nothing tangible to base it on, I think he's got a lot to live for. And who knows, this might just be the thing he needs to find his way back to the person he used to be.'

Camille nodded. 'And who tried to kill him? Another homeless person?'

Coco shook her head. 'I don't believe so. And for what it's worth, I think it was because he was trying to help me, the police, to solve a murder. And I can't tell you how bad that makes me feel, because if he dies, I know I'm going to have trouble forgiving myself if I had anything to do it.'

Camille stared at her. 'You barely knew him. Why do you care?'

Coco shrugged. 'As I said, I knew him enough to believe he was a decent person.' She dropped her head. 'I can't talk about your truth, only my own. So, here's my card. These are all the ways in which you can get a hold of me. If you want to talk, or if you want to go… to go see him, call me and I'll take you. No pressure, no judgement either way.'

Camille lowered her head, her eyes flicking over the card. She then turned to face her children. 'I don't know if I can face seeing him, or even if I'm brave enough to, mais…' she took a deep breath and held it for a few moments, 'mais, if I don't and he dies, how the hell can I explain to them I let their father die alone? They'd never forgive me, I would never forgive myself.'

Coco leaned forward and touched Camille's arm. 'You're brave enough to do whatever you need to do. You're a mother who protected her children from a man who couldn't protect himself, let alone you all. You do what YOU need to do, because that's all that matters, and I'm fairly sure Denis would say the same if he's half the man I imagined he used to be.' She pointed at the children, still happily playing. 'Spend some time with your children. You'll get all the answers you need from them. But remember, whatever you decide - you are their mother, and you are the one who is here, who has always been here, and that's all that will matter to them in the end. Make your decision based on that, and you will feel no guilt because no one with any sense would ever judge you.' She touched Camille's arm. 'Au revoir, Madame Acy.' Coco walked away without looking back, wiping the tears away from her cheeks.

MERCREDI
15H15

Coco slumped into the driver's seat and lit a cigarette. She cranked open the window and blew smoke rings out of it. Her head flopped against the headrest and she took a moment to decompress, realising she had to push the thought of Denis Acy and his wife and children from her mind. She had done everything she could for them, but now she needed to return her focus to her job and the problem at hand. The Severin family troubled her, not just because of the murder, but because it appeared that none of them had managed to live a happy life. She had often wondered what would happen to her if she suddenly came into a lot of money and whether it would make her happy, and she knew with utmost certainty that she would find a way to make it work - and then some.

Her ringing cell phone jolted her back to reality. 'Brunhild,' she snapped.

'Captain Brunhild? This is Tomas.'

'Tomas? Tomas Wall?' Coco cried, suddenly alert, remembering a man with arms and shoulders she could get lost in.

'Er... non,' the shaky voice replied. 'Tomas from the cybercafé, you gave me your card.'

'Oh yeah, yeah,' Coco responded. 'What's up?'

'You told me to call you if anything happened,' he said, lowering his voice. 'The woman you were looking for is here in the café right now.'

Coco leaned forward. 'Caroline Severin?'

'I don't know her name, but yeah, that woman you asked about.'

'Is she alone?'

Tomas paused. 'I think so. I can't see anyone outside waiting for her.'

'And what's she doing?'

'She's looking through her storage locker.'

Her storage locker. 'You have storage lockers?' Coco asked sharply, cursing herself for not checking earlier.

'Yeah,' he answered. 'This isn't the best neighbourhood. People don't tend to like to leave anything valuable in their apartments.'

'And her locker, what number is it?' Coco asked, already dreading the answer.

She could hear him rustling through some papers. 'B4,' he replied finally.

B4. Coco cursed herself for not thinking of it earlier, and yet it made no sense. How had Richard Severin ended up with the receipt for his daughter's storage locker?

'And she lost her receipt,' Tomas continued. 'I'm not supposed to hand out the keys without the receipt, but I figured as I know her and that she paid the outstanding amount that it would be okay.' He stopped, panic invading his voice. 'I did the right thing, didn't I?'

Coco did not reply. 'I'm on my way. Do whatever you can, but try to keep her there until I arrive, d'accord?'

'I'll try.'

Coco threw her cell phone onto the passenger seat and threw the car into gear, the tyres screeching onto the road.

MERCREDI 15H30

The car ground to a halt and Coco jumped from the driver's seat. She spotted Cedric and Ebba on the corner of the street and gestured for them to follow her. She ran into the cybercafé, her eyes darting from left to right. Her heart sank. The café was empty.

'Where the hell is she?'

Tomas gawped helplessly at her. 'I am sorry. I tried to keep her talking, but she wasn't having any of it. I didn't know what to do. I couldn't lock her in, could I?'

'You should have,' Coco snapped before immediately apologising. 'Désolé, I know it's not your fault. I just wish I could catch a damn break in this case.'

Cedric appeared in the doorway. 'She's gone?'

Coco nodded. 'Damn Demissy for calling off the surveillance.'

'She had a point - we can't justify round-the-clock surveillance,' Cedric reasoned.

Tomas cleared his throat. 'I know I couldn't keep her here, but I thought I would watch her when she left to see which direction she went.'

'Et?' Coco demanded.

'She got in a taxi.'

Coco raised an eyebrow. 'A taxi? You didn't by any chance…'

He handed her a piece of paper, trying to hide the fact he was pleased with himself. 'The license number.'

'Oh, Tomas! I could kiss you! In fact, I think I will,' Coco exclaimed, reaching across the counter and planting a kiss on his forehead. He stepped back, clearly dumbfounded. Coco handed the paper to Ebba. 'Can you do your magic?'

Ebba nodded. 'I'll try.' She stepped away and pulled her laptop out of her bag and placed it on a table.

'Can you show me the lockers?' Coco asked Tomas.

He nodded, leading Coco and Cedric to the back of the store, where there was a unit containing rows of small locked boxes.

'Why do you give people pieces of paper as a receipt?' Cedric asked.

'Because they kept losing the keys, and the boss got fed up of having to replace them,' Tomas replied. 'So, they pay for a week, and I give them the receipt and they bring it back to me and I open it up for them. Most of the people here can barely afford the cost of renting, let alone pay a key deposit.' He placed the key in B4 and opened the door.

Coco peered inside. It was empty. 'Putain!' She spun around to Tomas. 'Did you happen to see what she took?'

'I tried, but I can't see back here from the counter. All I can tell you is that she had a large black shopping bag over her shoulder when she left, but I don't know what she put in it if she put anything at all.'

Ebba appeared behind them. 'I called the taxi controller, and he confirmed a driver picked up a woman here and dropped her at the entrance to the Panteré estate.'

'Panteré estate,' Coco repeated. 'Ah, yeah. Jihef Abreo mentioned something about Caroline Severin having a boyfriend from that estate. I guess it makes sense that's where she'd hide out.'

'That's not all,' Ebba continued. 'That's what I was going to tell you earlier. You asked to check on Emile Severin's car and where he went last night. Well, I managed to follow it via the cameras around the city. Guess where he went to?'

Coco gasped. 'The Panteré banlieue?'

'Yup,' Ebba answered with a smile.

'Well, would you believe that?' Coco stated pensively. 'The entire gang's getting back together.'

'We don't know that,' Cedric said warily.

'Why else would they be all heading over there?' Coco proposed. 'Whatever they're up to, we have to get over there right away.'

Cedric shook his head. 'The Panteré banlieue is a no go for cops, you know that.'

Coco wafted her hand dismissively. 'We're not going to break up the little drug gangs. We'll just slip in and have a scout around for our missing millionaires. Easy peasy.'

Cedric gave her a doubtful look. 'At the very least, we should go in with backup.'

'Non,' Coco snapped. 'If we go in mob-handed, then we'll really end up in the shit. Non. As I said, we'll slip in and the gangs will hardly notice us.' She beamed at Tomas. 'Tomas. Thank you again. You are a prince amongst men. I'd have your babies except I can't be arsed to get more stretch marks.' Tomas shook his head, clearly confused. Coco then turned to Ebba and pointed at the lockers. 'Can you dust that for prints and run them through the database? I'd like to see if anyone else had their grubby mitts on the locker.' She pulled Cedric's arm. 'C'mon. Let's go do battle.'

MERCREDI
16H15

'It's like a war zone,' Coco stated, shaking her head in disbelief.

'I warned you,' Cedric grumbled.

'How the hell did this place get so bad?' She stepped through the gates, which lined Panteré banlieue. The estate was on the outskirts of Paris, but it seemed to Coco as if she had stepped into a whole different world. She often complained about her own neighbourhood, and whilst it was not great, she had felt reasonably safe there.

Here, in that moment, safety was not something she felt at all. She tapped the gun on her hip and felt some sort of relief to have it. It was not something she used, and she could count on one hand the number of times she had drawn it. But right now, the cold steel felt soothing against her fingers.

She turned her head slowly. All forms of life were present, it seemed. As far as her eyes could see, there were people lingering, going about whatever business they had, laughing and carrying on in a way that seemed both free and dangerous. Most of the residents appeared to be young men, ambling about, laughing and carrying on. But their games did not appear to be light-hearted. There was almost a malice to them, as if any second a war could break out between friends who only moments earlier were engaged in banter. Coco shifted her gaze, her eyes drifting around the area, and she realised she was probably only a pay cheque or two away from living in such a place herself.

'What the hell you doing here?'

Coco spun around, jolted back to reality. A young man,

seemingly barely into his teens, was sitting sentry at the entrance to the Panteré banlieue and was glaring in their direction, his face twisted into a cruel smirk.

Coco squared up on him. 'What's it to ya?' she asked with as much bravado as she could muster. She did not convince herself, so she was sure she had not convinced him either.

'We don't allow pigs around here,' he spat. His voice was as cold as ice, his eyes dark and menacing.

Coco surmised he was probably still practically a child because of the small splattering of fine hair on his chin. 'You don't allow?' she retorted with a hollow laugh. 'Less of the lip garçon, or else I'll slap the silly out of ya!'

He pulled back his shoulders, his hand tracing his jeans pocket, revealing the outline of a knife. 'I'd like to see you try, grandma.'

Coco sighed. 'How old are you, kid?' she asked.

'Old enough to show you a good time, grandma,' he laughed.

She sighed again. 'I doubt it. Anyway, as delightful as this tête-à-tête is, I don't have time for it. I'm looking for some people who came here recently.'

The young man snorted. 'Piss off, flic. I'm not a grass.' He sucked phlegm into his throat and spat it out, narrowly missing Coco's feet. She looked down at them, fighting the urge to ball up her fists and land the punk one. 'What makes you think I'd do a damn thing to help you?' he continued.

Coco smiled sweetly at him. 'Because if you don't, I can become the biggest pain in your arse, trust me.'

'You should listen to her,' Cedric added with a tight smile. 'She really can.'

'You don't scare me, bitch.'

Coco grabbed his shirt, pulling him close to her. 'You should be scared because if you don't help me, I'm going to make your life a misery. I'll have cops on here day and night, breaking up all the little deals they're making in there.'

'I told you, pigs ain't welcome here.'

She shook her head. 'The cops keep away because it's easier that way, but I don't do easy. You might say I get off on difficult, and if I have to, I will make it my personal mission to bring you all down. Now as for you - how's it going to make you look to everyone when they know all their problems, all the raids, all the arrests were down to you, just because you tried to play the big man?'

His eyes flicked over Coco angrily, but she could see his coolness slipping.

'What the hell do you want, anyway?' he hissed.

She smiled. 'That's better. Listen, we're not interested in your silly little day-to-day shenanigans. This is about a murder, nothing more. So, help me and we won't have a problem, or don't and we most certainly will. About half an hour ago, a young woman got out of a taxi. I need to know where she went.'

'How the hell am I supposed to know?' he snapped. 'I'm not here to keep an eye on the comings and goings of whores and junkies.'

Cedric stepped in front of him. 'Were you here last night?'

'I'm here every day and every night. It's my damn job,' the young man answered, with enough bitterness to make Coco wonder what he might have done to warrant his current occupation.

'Bon,' Cedric nodded. 'There would have been a car with three Caucasian men, two of them about my age, and one yours.'

'The fags you mean?'

'You know them?' Coco asked.

He laughed. 'Of course not, grandma, but I got eyes, and I can spot queers a mile off.'

If he calls me grandma one more time... 'Where did they go?'

'What do I look like, a fucking tour guide?'

Coco extracted her cell phone. 'Well, I guess I'd better get my buddies over here pronto. And you know what flics are like, they just love to talk and talk and talk... I'd hate for word to get out that you were the one who tipped us off. I imagine that would be bad for your health, non?'

The young man glared at her, pointing off into the distance. 'The blond fag gave me a hundred euros if I made sure no one damaged his car. I said sure.'

'Where's the car now?' Cedric asked.

He laughed. 'I gave it to one of my pals. It's probably in a chop shop somewhere getting a spray and new plates. A hundred euros? What did he think, that I have fuck all better to do than look after some random dude's wheels?'

'Where did they go? You must have seen them,' Coco pressed. She tapped her cell phone. 'Or do you want me to make that call?'

The young man yawned and scratched at his groin.

Coco stepped away and then turned back. 'How old are you, kid?'

He smiled. 'I told you, old enough to show you a good time.'

'Thirteen? Fourteen?'

He did not answer, instead he extracted a joint from his coat and lit it. Coco pulled out her card and handed it to him.

'What's this?'

'It's your get out of jail free card if you help me now.'

'What use is that to me?' he snapped. 'As you said, I'm a kid. Pigs can't touch me.'

Coco reached out to stroke his head and stopped. It had been an instinct to do it because she sensed no one had shown him tenderness in a very long time, but she could not be the one to do it. 'Do you really think anyone gives a fuck that you're still a kid?' she demanded instead. 'You're a drug dealer and Dieu knows what else you're up to in this shithole. They'll throw you in jail just like everyone else, and believe me, the lowlife in there will *really* go for a fresh-faced kid like you.' She pointed at the card. 'Help me and in return, keep that card, and if you need me, use it. D'accord?'

He stuffed the card in his pocket. 'Whatever. They went to Block D. I don't know which apartment. Now piss off before I mess you up.'

Coco gestured to Cedric. 'Let's go, Lieutenant.' She looked ahead and began striding purposefully toward Block D.

MERCREDI
16H30

Block D reminded Coco of an apartment block she had once seen in a television programme she had watched on post-war Germany before the fall of the Berlin Wall. There were voices raised in anger and protest, peppered with screams and angry dogs barking ferociously. A fire raged from a large iron drum, a group of youths lining it, warming their hands, their faces lost in the flames. She stopped in front of the block and looked upwards. She counted twelve floors, each with four or five apartments.

'Where the hell do we begin?' Cedric grumbled. 'You want to knock on every door? If someone does actually open it, we'll be lucky if they don't blow us away with a sawn-off shotgun.'

Coco clicked her teeth. 'Don't be melodramatic. It's a council estate, not Afghanistan. I bet there are just as many nice, decent people here as there are toe rags.' She pursed her lips. 'The question is - why are the Severins hiding out here?'

Cedric turned back. He could make out the young man in the distance, watching them still. He shrugged. 'You heard Yannick Vidal. If what he said was true, then some pretty nasty thugs were after him. If you're going to hideout, hiding amongst other lowlifes might just make sense.' He thumbed towards the young man standing sentry. 'And you saw the young security guard. They'd have to get past him first.'

Coco said nothing, instead she continued staring at Block D. All the apartments appeared to be occupied, each with its own small balcony. Her eyes quickly scanned them all, searching for any anomalies. Most of the balconies contained items of clothing drying on airers and many were filled with people, tired, bored faces staring out, smoking cigarettes and drinking beers. Her eyes settled on one particular apartment, about halfway up the block. It was the only one with its door shut and curtains drawn and with no clothes or activity on the balcony. She pointed to it. 'Look up there. There's only one apartment which looks as if there is no one home, or wants to appear as if no one is at home.'

Cedric flashed her a doubtful look. She ignored him and moved quickly towards the block. 'There'd better be a bloody lift,' she grumbled.

MERCREDI
16H35

Coco wrapped her knuckles forcefully on the door, pressing her ear against it, instantly hearing the panicked shuffles of more than one person inside the apartment. It stopped quickly, and the silence returned. She knocked again, louder this time. 'Open the damn door, I can hear you're in there,' she yelled. There was still no response. 'Monsieur Severin. I'm not leaving, so unless you answer this door, I'll have Lieutenant Degarmo break it down, and as I'm sure you noticed, he works out a whole lot, so he can probably easily do it.'

She stepped back upon hearing approaching footsteps, listening intently as whoever was behind the door removed chains and whatever else they had used to block it. Moments later, the door slowly opened, revealing Emile Severin. He stepped sheepishly back into the apartment, Coco and Cedric following quickly behind him. The dark, narrow hallway opened into a sparsely furnished living room, dominated by a thin table and a long sofa. Emile dropped heavily onto one of the dining chairs. Coco stepped into the room, her eyes widening when she saw Yannick Vidal and Timo Severin on the sofa, alongside a woman she recognised but could not immediately place. It took her just a few moments. *Mademoiselle Pissy Pants.* Coco frowned. She could not imagine a single scenario why the four of them would be together.

Coco dropped her bag on the floor and pulled out a cigarette. She lit it and began pacing. 'Well, quite the gathering we have here, don't we?'

Ambre Castillon turned her head, staring towards the darkened windows. She looked exactly as she had when Coco had first met her. Perfectly coffered blonde hair, makeup delicately and expertly applied. She was wearing a simple black dress, which was clearly designed to accentuate her every curve. Coco realised that if she were to wear such a dress, she would just end up looking like a bag of potatoes. Castillon seemed anxious, and Coco assumed it was not just because she was used to a better class of apartment.

'How did you find us?' Yannick Vidal asked.

She squared up to him. 'I see you managed to dry off, Monsieur. That was quite the little stunt you pulled.'

'It was no stunt,' he hissed. 'All I knew is that I couldn't risk you taking me into custody.'

'Because you're guilty?' Cedric interjected.

'Because whatever I've done,' Vidal retorted, 'I knew I wouldn't be safe, wherever I went.'

Coco continued pacing, sucking on her cigarette as she contemplated. 'Where is Caroline?' she demanded of Emile.

He lifted his head slowly. 'She's in the bedroom. She got back, and she was already high. She's sleeping it off, I guess.'

Coco looked around. 'And where are we exactly?'

'This is her place, or her lover's place, at least. I don't know for sure,' he replied. 'My sister's not very good at making sense these days, or any days for that matter,' he added bitterly. 'Mais, she said it's safe, and that's all that really mattered.'

'Safe?' Cedric questioned.

'Apparently her man is a pretty big deal around here,' Emile answered, 'which makes him untouchable. We needed somewhere safe, and,' he extended his arms, 'this is it, it seems.'

Coco looked at Ambre. 'And that goes for all of you, does it?'

Ambre turned her head. Her eyes were bright, but they shone with fear. She turned away again, without uttering a word.

'Oh, it's going to be like that, is it?' Coco muttered. She shrugged. 'Well, it's not so bad, really. I much prefer the sound of my own voice. Don't I, Lieutenant Degarmo?' she asked Cedric.

He nodded. 'She certainly does.'

'So if I have to,' Coco continued. 'I'll do all the talking because frankly, I wouldn't believe a fucking word that came out of any of your mouths at this point.' She looked to the kitchen and glanced at her watch. 'Say, you got any beers? It's about knocking off time for me, sooooo…'

Timo Severin jumped to his feet and went into the kitchen, returning with two bottles of beer. He handed one to Coco and lifted the second to his lips.

'Timo, you're sixteen,' Emile wailed.

Timo laughed. 'And you're my brother, not my damn father. I think you being a great big fucking liar trumps me drinking a beer, doesn't it?' He threw himself back onto the sofa, swigging happily on the bottle.

Coco sipped her own. She sat on the chair opposite Emile. 'Let's talk about your lies. Mind you, I'm not even sure where to begin. Other than to make this point. I believe your life has been a lie from the very beginning in one way or another, hasn't it?'

'I don't know what you mean,' Emile snapped.

Coco stepped closer to the closed door. 'She's in there?'

Emile nodded. 'Don't disturb her, I beg you.'

Coco opened her mouth to respond, but before she could, there was another loud knock on the door. Her lips twisted. 'Well, it looks as if we have another gatecrasher.'

'Don't open it,' Emile pleaded.

'Pourquoi?' she asked. 'Worried about who it might be?' She moved a finger between her and Cedric. 'We're cops, and we're packing.'

'Like that makes a difference,' Yannick Vidal snapped.

'It makes all the difference to me, honey,' Coco said, ambling along the hallway. She yanked open the door, revealing Horst Lavigne and Mona Gagnon standing in the hallway. 'Well, this party just keeps on getting better and better, doesn't it?' She stepped back and extended her arm. 'S'il vous plaît, join us. This shit's just about to get interesting.'

MERCREDI
16H45

Coco watched as Horst Lavigne and Mona Gagnon moved into the living room. Horst strode with the confidence of a man who believed he was always in control, whereas Mona moved slowly, pulling out a dining table chair and moving it as far away from everyone as she could.

'How did you find us?' Coco demanded.

Horst smiled at her. 'I had you followed. *Severin Industries* has an entire roster of ex-cops who are only too willing to assist, for the right price, of course.'

'Of course,' Coco repeated in broken English.

Horst glanced around the room. 'I've spent a very long time searching for you Monsieur Vidal, you're rather a tricky customer.'

Yannick matched his stare. 'And you're going to prison, you bastard.'

Horst threw back his head and laughed. 'Oh, I doubt that. I doubt that very much.'

Mona Gagnon extended her hand across the table towards Emile. 'Is Caroline here?'

Emile did not look at her. He nodded.

'Can I see her?' she whispered, desperation clear in her voice.

'Maybe later,' he mouthed, before repeating, *later*.

Coco clapped her hands together with such force, several people jumped at once. 'Désolé,' she apologised. 'I'm just keen to arrest the bad guys and get back home in time for my bath. You see, I live in a tenement, and the hot water is shared. If I don't want to miss out, I have to get home by,' she looked at her watch, 'well, soonish.' She ignored Cedric's irritated glare. 'Anyho,' she continued, 'let's kick off this afternoon's festivities. Now that we are all here, I think we can safely cut the bullshit and finally get to the point. And to do so, I think we need to go back to the beginning.' She moved across the room and stood in front of Emile Severin. 'Why can't you look your aunt in the face?'

'What are you talking about?' he demanded, his voice faltering.

She reached to him and turned his head, pointing it in Mona's direction. 'Why can't you look at her?' she asked again.

'Because I'm a terrible aunt,' Mona sobbed. 'I've spent the last thirty years obsessed with my sister, blaming everyone, when all I should have been doing was looking after her children. It is what Lauren would have wanted. But I was so damn angry, convinced everyone was lying to me, that I missed my life. It passed me by in a flash because bitterness is a very cruel mistress. She informed my every thought, my every deed, all because I wanted, <u>needed</u>, to know what happened to my sister.'

Emile slammed his fists on the table. 'She died,' he exhaled, as if it was the first breath he had taken in a long time. 'She died,' he repeated.

Mona pulled herself back. 'What do you mean?'

Finally, he turned to face her. 'Haven't you worked it out yet, after all this time? As much as I hated my father and his house, the other reason I couldn't come home was because I couldn't face seeing you and seeing the sadness on your face. A sadness I knew I could make go away.' He lowered his head. 'My mother wasn't kidnapped. Not really,' he said.

Mona looked at her nephew and Horst. 'What are you talking about? There was a ransom demand.'

'There was a cover-up, nothing else,' Emile replied. 'All meant to look real, but it was all just smoke and mirrors.'

Coco sat next to him. 'You're going to have to explain that to us, Emile.'

He took a deep breath. 'When my mother died, I was only three.' He tapped his head. 'My memories of her are so fragmented. I don't know what's real and what isn't. Caroline was older than me. She was eight when our mother died, and I remember Caroline better, probably because I spent more time with her. She was fun, but she was also dangerous.'

'Dangerous?' Cedric interjected.

Emile nodded. 'She learnt it all from *him*.'

'Him?' Coco questioned. 'You mean your father?'

He nodded again.

Mona Gagnon slapped the palms of her hands onto the table. 'I beg you, Emile. Tell me what happened. Finally, let me have that peace of mind, won't you?'

Coco followed his gaze. He was staring at the closed bedroom door. She took in a deep breath. 'I'm no Juge d'instruction,' she began, 'mais, I've been in this game long enough to know that, sometimes, just sometimes, there are reasons and explanations for terrible things that happen. You said your sister was eight when your mother died. What happened?'

'Caroline says she doesn't remember it,' he said distantly. 'And maybe she doesn't, but I do, and I was younger, but maybe that was because I hadn't so many years of dealing with what they had to. Maman et Caroline, that is.' He shook his head. 'And they had to deal with so much. It was only years later that I heard the expression "learned behaviour," but I instantly understood what it meant. It was my family story.'

'Tell me what happened to my sister, I beg you.' Mona cried desperately.

Emile closed his eyes as if he was envisaging the memory right in front of him. He extended a hand, fingers pointing back and forth. Coco inched forward, knowing that whatever came next was important. 'I was playing in my room,' he began. 'I was only three, but I can remember the shouting, the fights because they pretty much happened all the time. My first memory of my father's house is of being scared. It is the only memory I have. Apart from that night.' He rubbed his eyes. 'My parents were fighting. I can't tell you what about, but I remember that whenever they did, Caroline was acting up. Maybe she was doing it to stop Richard from hitting my mother, to distract him or something. Anyway, that night, mother was trying to calm Caroline down, but Caroline just went crazy and she started hitting and punching her. I was watching from the doorway. I didn't scream or speak or move, even. I don't know why, I just couldn't. It was like I was frozen to the spot.'

'The more mother tried to calm Caroline down,' he continued, 'the more violent she became. It was like she was out of control. It was like she was…' he lowered his head, and added, 'father.' He took a deep breath and held it for a long time. 'And then she pushed mother, and she fell backwards toward the stairs. It all seemed to happen in slow motion. I remember the look on Maman's face as she fell, her arms and legs flailing as she tried to grab onto something. The staircase was too wide, so she just kept going because she couldn't reach the banister. She screamed until she didn't. I can still hear the sound of her skull smashing against the marbled floor in the downstairs hallway.'

An anguished cry escaped Mona. She covered her mouth with a handkerchief but said nothing.

'Did your father call for an ambulance?' Coco asked.

Emile shook his head. 'Non. He just kept saying over and over, *she's dead, she's dead*. I don't remember much else, before he locked me in my room. I saw her and I remember thinking that the way she was lying reminded me of what Caroline used to do with her dolls. She would twist their limbs and arms backwards and turn their heads back to front. That's how my mother looked. Like a broken doll.'

Mona spun her head toward Horst Lavigne. 'You knew about

this all the time, didn't you?' She stared at his stoic face. 'What am I talking about? Bien sûr, you did. There wasn't a thing that went on that you weren't involved in.'

Coco stared at Horst. 'Tell us exactly what you did.'

Horst sighed. 'You realise none of this is provable, don't you?'

'Then what the hell you got to lose?' Coco snapped. 'Spill your guts and put Mademoiselle Gagnon out of her misery for once and for all.'

'Horst, I beg, s'il te plaît, tell me,' Mona sobbed. 'I've known you for over thirty years and you've lied to my face for every one of those. It's time to stop that.' She sucked air into her lungs as if she was preparing for something. 'Tell me the damn truth, once and for all!' she roared.

Horst flashed her a sad smile. He nodded slowly before turning back to Coco. 'That night, Richard called me in a mad panic. I'd never heard him like that before, never. He was always so calm and always careful about what he said and how he said it. He told me what happened and what Caroline had done. He told me she had deliberately murdered her mother and if we didn't do something, they would take her away.' Horst sneered. 'And he actually begged me to help him. The only time the bastard ever begged for anything. So I did, and I did it willingly. It wasn't even to help Caroline, to be honest. I did it for myself so that finally I would be on an equal footing with the almighty Richard Severin. I wanted us to be on equal footing. I wanted to be the one who saved him, but also the one who could destroy him if necessary.'

'I hate you with every fibre of my body,' Mona Gagnon hissed.

He stared at her impassively. 'What would you have me do? Regardless of my reasons, I still didn't want Caroline to be put into prison, or a mental institution, because make no mistake, that's what would have happened.'

'It was an accident,' Emile interrupted. 'Don't you get that? And if you had done the right thing, even if Caroline was taken away, she would have gotten help, and more importantly, she would have gotten out of that damn house earlier. And maybe, just maybe, they would have helped her enough, so that she didn't have to spend the next thirty-odd years living a life of hell.'

Horst Lavigne stared at Emile, but did not respond.

'What happened next?' Cedric asked.

'When I got to the house and saw Caroline lying there,' Horst continued, 'it became obvious that there was another reason Richard didn't want the police involved. It was obvious she had sustained other injuries that night, most likely from the fight she had with Richard.'

Coco tapped her chin. She wanted to keep him talking because she wanted to make sure that at least someone would pay for what had happened to Lauren Severin. 'Whose idea was it to fake a kidnapping?'

Horst faced her as if he was weighing up his options. 'Richard's.'

'Mais, you arranged it for him,' Coco shot back, 'because clearly, he wasn't going to get his hands dirty, as you were always the one to do his dirty work. You've already admitted that.'

Horst nodded. 'I made some phone calls. We knew people who would take care of it.'

'And the supposed ransom payment - that was actually the payment for the disposing of her body?' Coco pushed.

He nodded again.

'Where is my sister's body?' Mona whispered, her voice cracking. 'Where did you bury her?'

Horst reached across the table to touch her hand, but she snatched it away. 'Answer me, or so help me, I'll kill you myself,' she spat.

Horst moved to the window, his hand trailing across the

closed curtains. 'Richard didn't want to take the risk her body might be discovered. He said it would be dangerous for us all. Our people bribed someone at a crematorium…'

Mona gasped. Coco looked at her, concerned the old woman was going to pass out, or worse, but she pulled herself erect, her eyes sparkling in a way Coco had not seen before. It was almost as if she had suddenly come alive. She had answers finally. Not the answers she wanted, but answers nonetheless.

'After that,' Horst continued, 'we set everything up to make it look like a botched kidnap and ransom. Richard knew what to do, and he played it to the hilt. I don't think anyone suspected for a second he was involved.'

'I did,' Mona whispered. 'I knew from the beginning it was his doing.'

Horst shrugged. 'Well, as you know, the police, the press, believed in the kidnapping story. Richard also made sure everyone knew he had his own private detectives on the case. Private detectives who found nothing, because that's what we paid them to do - to do nothing.'

'Emile, what happened to Caroline afterwards?' Coco asked.

He lifted his head. 'Nothing. She never spoke about it, and I said nothing, and I know father certainly didn't. In fact, I think that was when the war between them intensified. He sent her off to boarding school the next month, and then to another and another and another. Each time she got expelled, he sent her to a stricter one, but none of them could contain her.'

Coco frowned. 'And you've never spoken of it, even as adults?'

'Non, we haven't,' Emile replied. 'As I said, I don't even know if she remembers what happened. Or maybe she does, and that's why she started taking drugs, to blank it out. Who knows? My sister is barely lucid most of the time, and when she is, you're just grateful for it, so I certainly never wanted to do anything like talking about what happened in case it caused her to relapse.'

Coco turned to Yannick. 'I'm guessing this all came up when you started doing your book, oui?'

He nodded. 'Caroline wanted money. She was fed up with always being broke and having to do whatever she did to get drugs. She was only too willing to help me. I paid her what I could, and everything was going well. She told me about the beatings, but when we got to her mother's kidnapping, it was like hitting a brick wall. I could tell it wasn't just the mention of it that upset her, it was obvious it was something else altogether.'

'Guilt,' Coco concluded.

'Then suddenly it was like the floodgates opened for her,' Yannick added. 'Once she started talking, she couldn't stop. It wasn't easy, because she would disappear for days, weeks at a time, but in the end, she not only gave me so much explosive stuff for the book, she pointed me in the direction of others who could not only verify what she told me but could also give me a lot more. It would have destroyed Richard Severin and everything he'd created for himself.'

'And that's why he wanted it stopped,' Coco interjected. 'Mais, someone stopped him first. And I think I understand who and why now.' She turned around. 'You killed your father, didn't you?'

MERCREDI
17H00

Timo Severin gawped at Coco. He gulped his beer. 'What the hell are you talking about?' he demanded. 'I didn't even know he was my father until recently. Why the hell would I want to kill him?'

'You're wrong, Captain Brunhild,' Emile Severin added. He reached across and stroked Timo's head. It stabbed at Coco's heart because the moment was tender, like a father comforting his son. Emile turned back to Coco. 'You're dead wrong. Timo didn't do this.'

Coco shook her head. 'I don't think I am wrong, but I also don't believe he acted alone, not really. My youngest daughter, Esther, has one of those little toys, I forget what you call them, but it has a little windy up thing on the bottom, and you twist it and twist it and twist it and then let it go on the ground, and the crazy little thing goes tearing off crashing into everything, and then bouncing off and going off again. Pretty boring, but it works wonders if you have a kid who's grouchy. Believe me, I know. I've had four kids and used the same toy with all of them. They turn instantly from a noisy snivelling brat into a happy, giggly clapping child.'

'Your point, Captain?' Horst Lavigne interjected irritably.

'My point, Monsieur Rude,' Coco quipped, 'is that I believe something similar happened in this instance. Someone wound-up young Timo over there, and let him go, knowing full well the path of destruction it could create.'

Horst snorted. 'That sounds like an awful lot of supposition to me, Captain.'

Coco ignored him, instead lighting another cigarette. 'Not really. It's the only thing that makes sense. We already know that both Emile and Timo lied about where they were that morning. They gave each other an alibi.' She pointed to Mona. 'Just as you and Emma Fitzgerald did, but we'll come back to that shortly. It always struck me as odd, because I assumed you were smart enough to know that we would check on alibis. After all, you both had millions of reasons to want your father dead.'

Timo glared at her. 'Then why would we be so stupid as to lie about an alibi? If I really wanted the old man dead, don't you think I would make sure I had an alibi? I'm sixteen, not six, Captain. I'm not stupid.'

She smiled at him. 'I don't think you're stupid,' she responded. 'But as I said, I think you were encouraged to do this by someone else, and for that reason, you weren't being rational and therefore not able to plan what you were going to do. You were angry. You weren't thinking straight.' She sank into a chair again, stubbing out her cigarette. 'This all came to a head the night before Richard's death because I believe someone overheard him talking. One of his thugs had stolen the storage locker receipt from Yannick Vidal's apartment. I presume Richard didn't know where the locker was, but that it would only be a matter of time before he found it, just like we did.' She turned to Yannick. 'What I don't understand is this. What was in the locker, and why did Caroline have it? Was it the manuscript of your book?'

He nodded. 'I'd given her a copy to check over. There's some pretty damning stuff about her too. I wasn't worried about her facing charges for what happened to her mother, but there's a lot of other stuff there, stuff she told me about what she's done, which could result in her being arrested, probably even going to prison. It didn't seem to bother her, but I wanted to be sure. It wasn't the only copy. I've emailed copies to several people and saved it to the cloud under different names, so I wasn't so much worried about losing the original, but I was really worried she might do something stupid with it.'

'Like what?' Coco questioned.

'Like sell it to her father,' Yannick surmised. 'Caroline also told me she had other stuff on her father, documents and photographs she'd stolen or acquired over the years. But she didn't want to give me it, she kept saying she would but never did. I don't know whether she just didn't trust me, or she had some other reason.'

'She was hedging her bets,' Emile interrupted.

'What do you mean?' Cedric asked.

'She was holding back something for herself,' he replied. 'The book would destroy our father professionally, but I doubt she cared about that. It's always been about money for her. The book was a means to an end. She kept the evidence because she knew how much it would be worth to our father.'

'How did you end up with the receipt?' Coco asked Yannick.

'Caroline gave it to me,' he answered. 'I insisted. As I said, I was concerned she would lose it, or worse, sell it to her father. Remember, I was paying her for her help with the book, so I told her to give me the receipt, or else I'd cut her off. Caroline doesn't enjoy being cut off, so she agreed.'

'What did it matter if Richard Severin got a copy of the book if you had your own copies?' Cedric asked. 'And there's something else I don't get,' he added. 'Why wait to publish the book? Why not just leak it online and be done with it?'

Yannick shot a filthy look at Horst Lavigne. 'It didn't matter that I had other copies. The problem was the book wasn't finished and there were several aspects to it which were sensitive.'

'Sensitive?' Coco interjected.

He nodded. 'Yeah. It wasn't just about shaming Richard Severin, there were several other people involved. In a nutshell, I'd found, amongst other things, proof of bribes he'd paid to several high-ranking politicians to push through contracts for public buildings and housing. It really was a can of worms and I couldn't take it to a publisher because I thought they would either chicken out, or worse, tell the people involved what I was up to.'

He took a deep breath. 'I was more worried that if Richard read it before I got it out, he would know where I get some of my information and that it would give him the opportunity to interfere with the people I'd spoke to, like they would suddenly disappear, or something. And until the damn thing's in print, or online, there's always a danger some damn avocat will get it stopped. It's happened before with other attempts to bring Richard Severin down, and I didn't want it to happen to me. If I just dumped everything online, then it would give him and his avocat a chance to just claim it was a lie. I had to get everything ready and in place before I could release anything. I've worked too hard to bring the bastard down for it to come all tumbling down just because he had a chance to erase his past yet again.'

Coco looked around the room. It was filled with so much hatred and it was clearly a family which had been destroyed by its wealth. She still did not understand how Richard Severin had ended up with the storage locker receipt in his coat. 'Tell me what happened the night before Richard Severin's murder,' she demanded.

Yannick cleared his throat. 'After his goons kicked the crap out of me, they searched my apartment. Of course, they didn't find the manuscript, or my notes even, so they held me down and found the receipt in my pocket. I guess they sensed by my reaction that it was something important, so they took it from me. I knew I was in trouble then.'

'What did you do?' Coco asked.

'I had to warn everyone who talked to me. There wasn't time to get in touch with everyone, but I wanted to make sure the people who had the most to lose knew that Richard was on the trail and could get a hold of the manuscript anytime.'

And by doing so, you probably signed his death warrant, Coco mused. She turned to Ambre Castillon. She was perched on the edge of the sofa, her body turned away from the rest of the people in the room. 'Which brings us firstly to Mademoiselle whiplash.'

Ambre's head jerked around, blue eyes flashing dangerously at Coco. 'My name is Ambre,' she snapped.

Coco nodded. 'Oui, je sais, mais, I have to wonder why you're here at this particular party. There's only one reason I can think of, and that it's because you have a vested interest in what happened.'

Ambre turned away huffily. 'I don't know what you're talking about.'

Coco moved across the room, warming to her theory. 'Oh, I think you do. Listen, I've known a lot of sex workers in my time,' she noticed the tensing of Ambre's shoulders. 'Désolé, "interior designers," and they share one common denominator. They love money. The bigger the client, the bigger the pay-off. I don't need to tell you how many important men have been brought down in one way or another by whoever they were schlepping. For some reason, they think paying by the hour buys them a deaf woman for the night, so they let down their guard, and their lips flap open like their dressing gowns.' She smiled at Yannick. 'It makes perfect sense that one of the major sources of information for your manuscript would be Richard's…' she smiled at Ambre, before adding, '*amie.* That's right, isn't it?'

Yannick nodded. 'Ambre has been very helpful.'

Ambre snorted. 'And for her reward, if the book wasn't published, I'd most likely end up in the same furnace as his wife.' She stopped, flashing her eyes in Mona Gagnon's direction, and she mouthed an apology.

Coco began moving back and forth, slowly dragging her boots across the dirty carpet. She stopped in front of Yannick.

'Who else did you warn?'

Yannick looked anxiously around the room. 'Emile and Mademoiselle Gagnon.'

Coco nodded. 'Mademoiselle Gagnon. What did you do when Yannick informed you it was likely Richard was going to get a hold of the manuscript?'

Mona Gagnon toyed with the pearls hanging limply around her neck. She smoothed the chenille fabric of her blouse with a shaking right hand. 'I did nothing,' she mouthed. 'What could I do?' she then demanded. 'I've spent a lifetime of accepting that I could do nothing. Why would that change now?'

Coco smiled. 'Because it did. I think you got the call from Yannick Vidal, and suddenly you saw it all come crashing down around you. You've waited a long time for the truth to be told and for Richard to be punished, and then suddenly, just when it was in striking distance, you realised there was a chance he was going to get away with it again, and you would never get the peace you deserved.'

She laughed. 'And what do you imagine I did about it? I followed him into the métro and killed him? Believe me, Captain Brunhild, I have dreamt of Richard's death for decades, and I have had multiple opportunities to facilitate that, but I didn't, not then, not now.'

Coco exhaled. 'Non, you didn't. Mais, you did something worse. You got someone else to do it for you, non?'

MERCREDI
17H15

Mona Gagnon's head jerked backwards. She ran a hand across her neat brown curls as if she was satisfying herself she looked quite proper. 'I do not know what you are talking about,' she bristled. Her voice was hard and cold. 'Don't you imagine I've conjured a dozen or more scenarios in which the bastard would have died at my own hand?'

Coco nodded. 'I do. However, I don't think this was about his death for you, rather ensuring that the book was published and Richard was publicly embarrassed and shamed and that he would spend the rest of whatever life he had in prison. But that meant you needed the book to be published. You needed his humiliation to satisfy your hunger for revenge.' She took a deep breath. 'Which brings me back to something I said a short while ago. Someone wound up young Timo Severin, whispering half-truths in his ear, and that was you, non, Mademoiselle Gagnon?'

Mona did not respond.

'Your silence doesn't matter. I think it will become quite clear soon,' Coco continued. 'I think you panicked when Yannick Vidal called you, primarily because you worried if Richard stopped the book being published, he would walk away from his crimes yet again, and that you would most likely never discover what happened to your sister.' She moved towards Timo. 'We already know Timo had been told the truth about his parentage, but really, it was only for the purpose of the book. Tell me, Mona, what did you do? Did you call Timo and tell him it was all about to go tits up? That Richard was about to discover what you were all up to and that he was about to put an end to it all?' She stared at Mona.

'Did you lie to him and tell him that if the book wasn't published, that his birth father would make sure the whole truth was buried and that he would end up with nothing?'

'That's exactly what she said,' Timo Severin hissed.

'I thought so,' Coco replied. 'There was a lot going on. I'm guessing Yannick spoke to you, Ambre and told you about the likelihood Richard was going to find the manuscript, so he told you to invite him to see you that morning so that you could see if he had it on him, or if not, at least allow Mona to search the house.'

Ambre nodded, but said nothing.

Coco turned to Mona again. 'Mais, you didn't want to take the chance, did you? I imagine you'd finally had enough. You realised that Richard, with the help of his loyal avocat, Horst, was most likely going to get away with everything, and I think that was more than you could bear. You'd already spoken with Timo. He knew Richard was his father and realised he wasn't interested in a father-son relationship, but that he wanted the money which was owed to him. What did you say? Did you tell him that Richard would never acknowledge him? That he would never admit he'd birthed a son from a prostitute?'

Timo stood. 'The old bitch told me that if he found the book, he would bury it, and once he'd done that, he would find a way to bury me. She said he had the resources and the people in his pocket to alter DNA records to show that I could not have been his son.'

Emile Severin shook his head in disbelief. 'Why didn't you talk to me after you found out?'

Timo glared at him. 'Why would I? You let us live a lie for sixteen years. A lie filled with poverty. When the truth was, we could have been living the life of fucking millionaires, just like him.'

Emile shook his head. 'I did it so that you *didn't* have to live like him, don't you get that? Have I done such a terrible job of being your father that you don't get that at all?'

'You're not my father,' Timo said, his fingers pressing into his thighs. He pointed at Mona. 'The old woman is the only one who told me the truth.'

'Except she didn't,' Coco interjected. 'Whatever happened with the book, Richard Severin was always going to be your father, legally at least. The whole DNA business is nonsense. You would have been declared his legal son, in one way or another. This wasn't about that.' She pointed at Mona. 'She just wanted Richard to pay and she didn't care how he paid, or who she had to use, or what she had to say to make it happen. And in the end, you, his bastard son, were the easiest way to get rid of him. Yannick had already told her of the plan. Ambre Castillon was going to search Richard physically while Mona searched the house when he was out. A perfect plan, only Mona didn't care about that. Her only thought was to make sure that Richard didn't have time to bury the truth, and the only way she could do that was to make sure he didn't get a chance. Once he was dead, the book would come out, the truth would be told.' Her lips twisted at Mona. 'I suppose it wasn't the scenario you wanted. I mean, you wanted him to pay, but more importantly, the thought of him not paying was more than you could bear, wasn't it?'

Mona's lips twisted. 'Richard got away with his crimes for decades, and what made it worse was that he was going to do it again. I looked in the mirror and knew for certain that I couldn't allow that to happen.' She clenched her hands together. 'It was finally time for him to be stopped.'

Coco pointed to Timo. 'So, you sent his sixteen-year-old illegitimate son to confront him. Why was that? Or is it, as I said earlier, you'd just had enough, and you used someone to do the dirty work for you because you couldn't be arsed to do it yourself? Dirty work is dirty. You've lived a life of luxury, even if it was standing in the shadows glaring outwards because you wanted to discover the truth. And then when Yannick told you Richard was hot on the trail of the manuscript, you realised that if he found it, he would quash it and most certainly anyone who had contributed…'

'He was going to get away with it yet again,' Mona interjected. 'And I couldn't let that happen. Not after I waited so long to see him punished.'

'Why the hell did you have to drag Timo into this?' Emile screamed. 'He's a sixteen-year-old kid.'

'I'm fucking sick of everyone going on about how young I am,' Timo snapped. 'Because the fact is, I'm just like the rest of you now. Rich and powerful.'

'Not if you go to prison for decades,' Emile responded.

Timo laughed. 'The flics can't prove a thing. Isn't that right, Horst?'

All eyes turned to Horst Lavigne. 'I always knew you had grubby hands all over this too,' Coco stated.

Horst shrugged nonchalantly. 'I merely pointed out to my client that there was no direct evidence linking him or anyone else to anything that happened. A hundred or more people on the métro could have attacked Richard, and no one is ever going to be able to prove otherwise.'

Coco did not respond, because she knew it was true. But she also knew she would not leave the crummy apartment until she had someone in handcuffs, and at that point, she did not much care who it was. She also understood her only chance was to keep them talking and hopefully give them enough rope to hang themselves.

'Mademoiselle Gagnon,' Coco addressed Mona. 'What did you say when you called Timo?'

'Mona, I counsel you to say nothing,' Horst stated warily.

Mona clicked her teeth irritably. 'What difference does it make now? It's all done and over with. At least the book will come out and Richard's reputation will be destroyed.' She turned to Timo. 'And I suggest you stop taking advice from him too, because he's up to his neck in all Richard's dirt too, and with Richard gone, they're going to be looking for a scapegoat, and,' she smiled, 'I'm happy to say, it's going to be him.'

'Tante Mona is right,' Emile nodded. 'Horst only has his own interests at heart, but so does she. Whatever she did, she didn't do it herself. Don't be a fool, Timo, say nothing.'

Timo glared at Emile. 'You're not my father. You never were. I killed him before he made me spend a miserable, broken life like you and Caroline. And as you all keep pointing out. I'm sixteen. Even if they arrest me, I'll be out before I'm an adult once they see how fucked up our family tree is, and what they made an innocent kid like me do. And when I'm free, I'll be a very rich man, and I'll never look back.'

Coco turned to Mona. 'Tell us what happened.'

MERCREDI
17H30

'When Yannick called me, I knew I had to act quickly if we were to stand a chance of keeping Richard from stopping the book coming out,' Mona began.

'He needed stopping, but we also needed the storage locker receipt back,' Yannick added. 'When I called Mona, we realised we had to hurry, but of course we did not know what he was going to do, and that's when I had a bright idea. There was one way I could think of to derail Richard's morning plans.'

Coco spun on her heels. 'Which brings us to the shallow end. I guess it came as a bit of shock to you that Richard was about to discover one of Monsieur Vidal's major sources was you. And I imagine it terrified you.'

Ambre Castillon smoothed her blonde hair with perfectly manicured nails. 'Men like Richard don't terrify me,' she purred. 'However, the company they keep does. When Yannick called to warn me, my first thought was to run, but then I realised wherever I went, it wouldn't matter because Richard would find me. And then Yannick asked if I would call Richard and invite him over, make some excuse if I had to, but just get him over and find out if he had the receipt on him. It wasn't difficult. I just told Richard that if he didn't come then, I wouldn't be able to see him for our appointment this week.' Perfect blood-red lips spread into a suggestive smile. 'He said he would be there within the hour.'

'And how did you get involved in this?' Coco demanded of Timo.

Timo slapped his thighs. 'You'll make none of this stick, y'know that, don't ya?'

'You're probably right,' Coco conceded. 'But why don't you humour grandma and dish the dirt?'

Timo pointed at Mona. 'When the old lady told me that if Richard stopped the book being published and when he knew we were all involved in it, he'd make sure that I never saw a cent of my inheritance.'

'She lied,' Emile whispered. 'He wouldn't be allowed to.'

'Well, I didn't know that,' Timo shouted. 'She said that he'd hide all his money in fake accounts just so that when he died, there'd be nothing for me. I've heard of that sort of shady shit before. The money had been dangled in front of me, so I wasn't about to let the bastard take away what was rightly mine. So, she told me about his morning regime and I followed him. First to the school and then to the métro.'

'What went wrong?' Cedric pushed.

'I followed him onto the platform,' Timo continued. 'And then, at one point, he looked right at me. I wasn't sure if he recognised me. I mean, it's not like he actually has my photograph on his desk, or has spent any time with me at all. But all the same, the way he looked at me was weird. It was like he was trying to remember where he'd seen me. I didn't think about it, I just went up to him and before I knew what I was doing, the knife was in him.'

'You just happened to have a knife?' Coco questioned.

He shrugged. 'You've seen where I live. Of course, I have a damn knife.'

Coco nodded, realising it might be true, or it could be a convenient excuse for him carrying a knife. The difference was premeditation, and would most likely have serious repercussions for what happened next to him.

'It all happened so quickly. The platform was so full of people, I don't think anyone saw it, and the métro arrived and everyone just rushed forward, taking me and Richard with them.

He was stumbling, muttering something, but it was like he didn't know what had happened,' Timo continued. 'It was easy just to sort of guide him into a chair, but by the time I did that, the doors were closed, so I had to stay on.'

'You were on the train when I found him?' Coco enquired.

He shook his head. 'I decided not to get off the next stop in case that looked suspicious, so I stayed on and got off the one after. I figured no one would even notice me - just another random kid wearing a hoodie and a baseball cap.' He laughed. 'I counted five others on the train at the same time, so good luck proving I was anywhere near it.'

Coco nodded. *But we will, kid, we will.* 'Yet you didn't look for the receipt?'

'There wasn't time,' he answered. 'And if I tried, I thought I'd get caught. It wasn't worth the risk, because I figured with the old man dead, the book would come out, and I'd still get my money.' He clapped his hands together. 'Win-win!'

Coco lit another cigarette. 'Which brings us to something even worse. The murder of Emma Fitzgerald.'

Emile slammed his fists on the table. 'You can't think for a second that Timo had anything to do with that. He didn't even know Emma. I don't think they'd even met. What on earth reason could he have to hurt her?'

Coco noticed the exchange passing between Mona Gagnon and Horst Lavigne, and it told her all she needed to know. She took a deep breath and held it because she did not want to say what she was thinking. But she had no choice. 'When Lieutenant Degarmo spoke to you, Mademoiselle Gagnon, he mentioned that Emma Fitzgerald appeared anxious, as if she had something on her mind. And then, the next day, she was pushed into ongoing traffic outside the Commissariat de Police du 7e arrondissement. I can only imagine that was to stop her telling the police whatever it was that was bothering her.'

She blew smoke across the room. 'At first, I couldn't imagine what it was. I suppose my first instinct was that I didn't quite believe the convenient alibis between you all. First, Emile and Timo alibied each other, even though we quickly discovered that alibi was faked. However, the alibi between you Mona, and Emma also seemed forced, but yet at the same time, I never quite believed you'd followed Richard to the métro and murdered him. If that was the case - then why didn't I believe you? What could you possibly be hiding? At first, I thought the two of you might have been working together to murder the old man.' She shook her head. 'I didn't buy that either, and then there was the conversation I had with Horst.'

Horst coughed. 'What did I say?'

Coco blew smoke at him. 'As usual, you said nothing, but you also said everything. Separating the wheat from the chaff is never particularly easy, mais I have a pretty good bullshit detector,' she stated, before shrugging, 'unfortunately it seems sometimes it's just on satellite delay, but it gets to this,' she tapped her head, 'eventually.'

Horst shook his head with evident irritation. 'As usual, your point, if you are making one, seems to be sadly muted and impenetrable.'

Coco snorted. 'Two things I've never been accused of before, but hell, there's always a first time! My point,' she continued, her tone becoming harder, 'is this. You mentioned something about the birth of Timo Severin, which struck me as odd, but not necessarily important until I attended the autopsy of Emma Fitzgerald. You told me that you never met Timo's mother, but dealt with her, and I quote, "grasping British lawyer." And then there's the fact that Emma Fitzgerald was British, and also, as per her autopsy, had given birth, but yet we could not find what happened to her child.'

Horst cocked his head, fixing her with a withering look.

'And then,' Coco continued. 'You said something else. You

said Richard always kept his friends close, but his enemies even closer. About seventeen years ago, I believe he impregnated a young English dame. I.E. Ms. Emma Fitzgerald. He paid her a lot of money to keep his secret and continued to pay her a lot of money. I don't know why she ended up staying here with him, maybe it was part of her deal, maybe she wanted to make sure the child she'd given up was okay, or it could just have been because she wanted to make sure he got what he deserved from a father who didn't want him and refused to acknowledge him. I suppose we'll never really know her motives now,' she trailed off. 'I imagine she thought that once Richard was gone, you'd both come into a lot of money and could be together.'

Timo climbed to his feet, his fists clenched. 'She was my mother?' he demanded of Mona.

Mona looked away. 'Who knows?' she snapped. 'She was just one of Richard's many whores.'

Coco stepped in between the two of them, blocking Timo's view. 'What did Mona tell you? Was it that Emma had overheard her conversations that morning and was going to the police to report them? Is that what she said? That Emma was going to turn you both in?'

Timo nodded slowly. 'Mona said Emma had overheard the entire plan and was going to tell the police, and that if I wanted my inheritance, I had to stop her.'

Coco glared at Mona. 'You really are a despicable woman, Mademoiselle Gagnon.'

Mona shrugged as if she could not care less. 'Richard was the despicable one. I just made sure he couldn't run from the past forever.'

'You made me kill my mother?' Timo asked again.

She laughed. 'What do you care? She gave you up for money and she never once reached out to you. You're better off without her because the Captain is right - Emma was only sticking around because she knew once Richard died you'd both have a pretty impressive windfall. I guess that would be the point she suddenly decided to be a good mother? Does that impress you? Because believe me, it shouldn't.'

Timo turned to Coco. 'I didn't mean to kill her,' he said. His voice had lost its usual harshness. 'I just thought she'd get hurt and end up in hospital and that would buy us some time. Horst said he would speak to her and make her see sense.'

Coco looked between them all again. She held up her cigarette. 'Do you know, I spend my days deciding between having a cheese baguette for lunch, or skipping it so I can buy an extra pack of smokes. That is my big money decision and I'm pretty content and okay with it. I don't have to decide who I'm going to kill just for a smoke.' She reached across and placed a hand on Timo's shoulder. 'This should never have been about you. I get you wanted money. It's a lot of money and you deserved it, but it shouldn't have come to this, but more importantly, you shouldn't have done what you did for it.'

'Easy for you to say,' he spat.

'Yeah,' she agreed sadly. She stubbed out her cigarette. 'And the homeless man outside my apartment block? Was that you too?'

Timo shrugged.

'His name is Denis Acy,' Coco hissed. 'And he has a wife and two kids. What did he have to do with any of this?' She noticed Timo looking at Mona again. 'So, you told him to do what, trail me? For what possible reason?'

'We didn't want you to find the book,' Mona said. 'Because we knew Horst would stop it. He'd tie it up in litigation, or else he'd pay off someone in the police to make sure it never saw the light of day.'

'I heard you talking to the black guy, and the homeless guy, and it seemed like he was going to show you where to look,' Timo added. 'And I thought, what the hell, who's going to miss another homeless guy?'

Coco tensed her fingers. She wanted to hit out but realised she did not know who she wanted to hit the most. Instead, she pulled open her bag and grabbed a pair of handcuffs. She threw them at Cedric. 'Cuff him and take him away. He really is his father's son.' She looked at Mona and Horst and then moved to Emile. She touched his hair. 'And the really sad thing is, he didn't need to be because at least one of the Severin's had tried to raise him away from the madness.'

Timo jerked his body as Cedric slapped on the handcuffs. He glared at Emile. 'I'm a Severin. I'm not weak. Now arrest me and see how far that gets you. I've got more money than you'll ever see in your entire pitiful lives.'

Coco slapped his back. 'Not yet, kid. You might just find courts frown on kids who murder their father's just so they don't get written out of their wills.' She moved towards Horst. 'Same goes for you, hotshot. Your day is coming too.'

Horst jumped to his feet. 'Do your worst, Captain Brunhild, and see how far it gets you.'

Cedric chuckled. 'Don't say that to her, you fool, she'll only take it as a challenge.'

Coco grinned. 'And I like a challenge. Even more, I enjoy kicking bad guys in the nuts.' She went into the kitchen and returned with another beer. 'There's only one thing left to figure out. Why the hell was Laure Severin pretend kidnapped?'

Mona's nostrils flared. 'Yannick wasn't the only one who called me the night before to warn me about Richard. My stupid niece Caroline rang me as well. She was frantic, in a complete state and not making much sense at all. *For a change*,' she added with venom.

Emile shot his aunt a disparaging look.

'Whatever Richard was up to,' Mona continued, 'it seemed as if he was looking everywhere for the manuscript. Caroline told me she'd seen several men she recognised in her neighbourhood. Men she said she knew worked for her father. They weren't just looking for the book with Yannick, I assume they were also looking for Caroline. She was distraught. She said she had to get away because she knew what they were capable of, but that she didn't have any money. She begged me for some, but of course, I told her I had no money of my own and no way to get any. She said she had to get away, or else she would give her father the book. I couldn't let that happen.'

Coco scratched her head. 'And how the hell did kidnapping her daughter come from that?'

Mona shrugged. 'Why not? It had been done before. And as far as I could tell, it was the only way Richard was likely to part with money. He doted on the annoying little child. I know I had little time. I needed to make sure he didn't find the book himself, or that Caroline sold it to him, so as I sat there reeling from it all, it wasn't just the thought of getting rid of Richard which came to me. It was a way of getting rid of them all.'

'What did Richard Severin know about this?' Coco asked. 'Because I can't imagine he knew of your plan.'

Mona smiled. 'I told him the truth,' she answered, 'or rather, a version of the truth which I knew would infuriate him. I told him Caroline had telephoned and wanted to come over and spend some time with her daughter. Of course, he was furious. He'd spent years making sure the two of them had no contact. I told him we should send Laure out of town until we could deal with Caroline, and he agreed. He arranged for Laure to go into the country with the family of one of her friends, but he said he was going to tell the school she was sick just in case Caroline turned up there. He said she wouldn't have the courage to turn up at the house.'

Coco clapped her hands. 'You're actually pretty good at thinking on your feet, mademoiselle,' she told Mona. 'And then you instructed Caroline to send a telegram making a ransom demand.

But why?'

'I just needed to buy time,' Mona reasoned. 'I needed to make sure Caroline was calm and to get Richard out of the house so that we could get the receipt from him. The kid was out of the way, and Caroline was going to send the telegram. I suppose I assumed everyone would think Richard was on his way to pay a kidnapper and they murdered him.' She stopped, her jaw tightening. 'I was concerned his death would come to Timo, or me, and that's why I needed to make sure there was enough confusion to cast doubt on everything that happened. I assumed the police would believe Laure was kidnapped by her mother and that they murdered her father because of it.'

Coco frowned. 'Then how would you explain Laure's sojourn into the countryside and that she wasn't really kidnapped at all?'

Mona shrugged. 'I wouldn't have to explain anything. This, after all, had nothing to do with me. Richard arranged the trip and Caroline arranged the kidnap - that's all anyone would see. This was about exposing Richard, nothing else.'

Coco nodded. The old woman was right. Her plan, while flawed, was basically sound. She had sprung into action to avert a disaster she could not bear. Coco imagined Mona had realised it was most likely her last chance to seek justice for what had happened to her sister, and that meant she did not care who she had to destroy to satisfy her thirst for revenge. She pointed into the bedroom. 'You were going to throw Caroline under the bus just because you wanted Richard to be exposed?'

'Oui, bien sûr,' Mona retorted. 'No matter what you might think, she wasn't the innocent here. She wasn't bothered about what her father had done, rather what she could get out of him. I thought little of the woman before, but now I know she killed my sister and has shown no remorse for it. I care less for her.'

'She was a child!' Emile wailed.

'I don't care about that,' Mona snapped. She stared at the

closed bedroom door. 'She had thirty years to repent, and even that was too much for her. Her repentance was non-existent and, in the end, she was as bad as him. It is not me who should feel guilty about what has happened…'

Coco grabbed Mona to her feet. 'The hell it is, you old trout. You're going to jail for something, you mark my words. Now c'mon.' She turned to Emile and pointed towards the closed door. 'What do you want to do about your sister?'

Emile turned his head in the direction of the bedroom. 'I've never known what to do about my sister, and now I have even less of an idea.'

Coco shrugged. 'When my kids are in trouble, I've only come up with one way to help them. I crawl into bed with them and wrap my arms around them. Bien sûr, they don't want me to, but that doesn't matter. After sixty seconds, they push their body into mine and they relax and then they sleep. It might not seem like a lot, but by morning, when they wake up and they realise I've been there all night, they understand they've made it through the first night of their misery and that, just maybe, they might make it through the second.' She shrugged. 'I dunno. Seems like it might be worth a try? And more importantly, isn't it about time that this family stepped out of the shadow of the man who's now dead?'

Emile climbed to his feet and moved to the door. He opened it and stepped inside.

Coco smiled, gesturing for Cedric and Timo to follow her and Mona towards the door. 'Now, let's get out of here and hope our car isn't in some damn chop shop,' she grumbled.

MERCREDI
19H00

Coco stepped out of the elevator. As usual, the hospital was a whir of activity. She moved through the hallway, passing a woman sobbing into the hand of a man lying rigid in a cubicle. It stabbed at her heart and though she did not pray often, during a hopeless situation she would pray for the women and the men whose hand she held when they needed it the most. She looked at her own hand and realised she could not remember the last time someone had placed their hand in hers, and she wondered whether they ever would again.

'Charlotte, what are you doing here?'

Coco turned around. Dr. Stella Bertram was standing behind her, eyes suddenly alert but still full of the shadows of a long, trying day. 'I didn't call you,' Stella stated.

Coco shrugged. 'Yeah, I know. I was at the commissariat and I'd about had my fill of checking people into custody, people I'm not even sure will ever make it to court, despite what they've done, and I needed a breather before I go into battle in the interview rooms. Is he… is he?'

'He's made it through the day,' Stella smiled, pointing towards a cubicle. 'Your friend, who, after a good clean, actually scrubs up pretty well, is probably going to survive. It was touch and go, and it will not be an easy convalescence, certainly not one he can do on the streets, but I think with the right intervention, it will be a happy result. He's awake, a little groggy, but awake.'

Coco smiled. 'That's amazing news, Stella. See, I knew that, I knew underneath all the Parisian dirt, he's probably a pretty fine looking fella.'

Stella raised an eyebrow. 'I see,' she said, her tone suddenly brittle. 'Mais, you're not the only one who thinks so. There's a blonde in the cubicle with him. She seems pretty smitten too,' she added tartly.

Coco exhaled. 'Oh, you're kidding! That's great news.' She took a tentative step forward, her hand touching the cubicle curtain. 'Can I?' she whispered.

Stella nodded. Coco pulled back the curtain. Camille Acy was holding her husband's hand. His head was turned towards her, tired eyes locked on her. Coco sucked air into her lungs.

'Forgive me,' Denis Acy said to his wife.

Camille Acy kissed his forehead. 'Come home. Tu me manques.'

Coco turned away. 'He's going to be okay,' she whispered, her voice cracking.

MERCREDI
21H00

Coco flopped onto her seat, emitting a long sigh. There were four reports on her desk. Reports which would take days to figure out. The mess created by the Severin family was going to take a long time to sort out, but for now at least, she had done all she could and she needed to escape the confines of the day. She reached for a plastic cup on the corner of her desk and drank from it, spluttering the content of the cold café onto her shirt.

'I hope you're going to treat it better from now on,' Commander Demissy called from the doorway. 'I can't tell you how many times they had to put it through the machine just to get the filth out of it.'

Coco's eyes widened. Demissy was holding up Coco's old-faithful blue and green checked woollen overcoat. She jumped to her feet and grabbed it, pressing her lips into the fabric. She quickly pulled back. 'Wait. There's something wrong. It smells weird. It smells… it smells…'

Demissy rolled her eyes. 'It smells clean, Captain. A concept I'm sure you're entirely unfamiliar with.'

Coco pouted. Demissy suppressed a smile. 'It's late. You've had a tough few days and I suppose we have a result of sorts. Go home and be with your family. Tomorrow is another day. What else can go wrong?'

Coco slipped into her coat, still unconvinced. 'It's just not the same.' She stared at Demissy. 'You really need to work on your pep talks, Commander,' she grumbled, before adding. 'And don't say things like "what can go wrong." I'm superstitious and saying things like that just tempts fate, as far as I'm concerned. And as we're only halfway through the week, I don't want to take chances it could all go wrong.'

Demissy waved her hand. 'Go home, Captain. À demain.'

Cedric suddenly appeared in the doorway. 'Ah, bon. You're both here. I'm glad I caught you. There's been a murder on Métro line 8.'

Coco shook her head quickly. She pointed at the clock. 'I have children to breastfeed,' she said, pushing past him and disappearing into the darkened bowels of the police station. 'And I'm off duty and I've already solved my murder on Line 8 this week.'

Cedric shrugged. 'I get it. I mean, someone drowns in the métro every day, don't they?'

He smiled as if he knew what was going to happen next.

Coco appeared from the shadows. 'Did you say, *drowned?*'

COCO BRUNHILD WILL
RETURN IN A NEW MYSTERY:

Cercueils en Spirale

Printed in Poland
by Amazon Fulfillment
Poland Sp. z o.o., Wrocław
08 March 2022

d33f0bd0-8719-4a4e-9a72-8da17e77ef5fR01